Angel Eyes

Paris in a Heartbeat: Book One

Ellie Jennings

Inverlea Press, LLC

Cover Design by Books and Moods

Editing by Plumfield Editing

Proofreading by Lilypad Lit

ISBN: 979-8-9900124-1-7 (print)

ISBN: 979-8-9900124-2-4 (ebook)

elliejennings.com

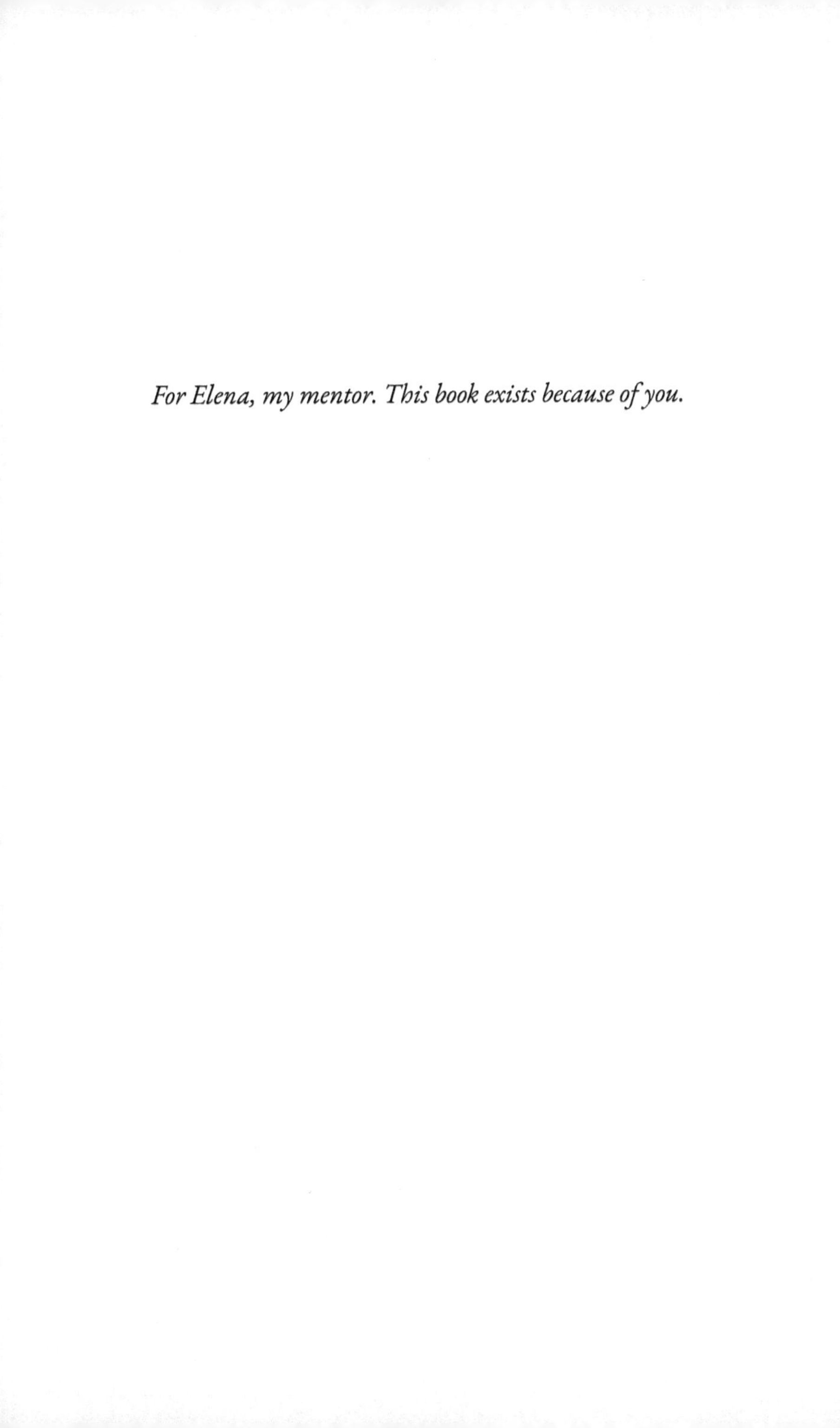

For Elena, my mentor. This book exists because of you.

Playlist

"Sunset Lover" — Petit Biscuit

"Paris in the Rain" — Lauv

"Speak of the Angel" — Jonathan Hutcherson

"Can't Take My Eyes Off of You (I Love You Baby)" — Ms. Lauryn
Hill

"Friends Don't" — Maddie & Tae

"Heaven" — Emilee

"Falling Like The Stars" — James Arthur

"this is how you fall in love" — Jeremy Zucker, Chelsea Cutler

"The Few Things" — JP Saxe, Charlotte Lawrence

"Little Bit More" — Suriel Hess

"The Way I Love You" — yaeow, Neptune

"Only Love" — PVRIS

"My Thoughts on You" — The Band CAMINO

"Never Not" — Lauv

"Ghost" — Justin Bieber

"I'll Be Waiting" — Cian Ducrot

Your eyes. Your eyes hold everything my soul thirsts
for.

— Perry Poetry

One

Juliet

"I'm sorry—he said *what*?"

Ember's shriek ricocheted through my phone, and I yanked it away from my ear, her high pitch nearly taking out my left eardrum. Bailey barked somewhere in the background, and I snorted under my breath.

Good to know I'm not the only one afraid of my sister's angry voice.

"Bailey, shush," Ember said as her Jack Russell terrier abandoned his barking in favor of a low howl. She closed a door, muting the whine of Bailey's protests. "Sorry, he's such a drama queen." She sniffed. "Now, tell me again—what *exactly* did Kyle say?"

"Um ..." I shoved aside a box of kitchen supplies with my bare foot and crossed the living room of my new apartment.

Who knew Parisian buildings didn't have air conditioning?

Unhooking the window latch, I pushed it open and welcomed the breeze sweeping my hair from my forehead. The scent of something freshly baked lingered in the air, and I peered down at the cobbled street littered with pedestrians, the sounds of laughter and rapid French reaching me from three stories above. Sunlight bounced off the blue-green surface of the Seine, and I watched it wind between the Left Bank and the Île Saint-Louis, a smile dancing on my lips.

Despite the hectic days leading up to my arrival, my chest fluttered with excitement now that I was here.

"Oh, my God, Em—there's the cutest café across the street. It's got these adorable red awnings and little cast-iron tables. Here, I'm sending you a picture—"

"Juliet Marie Chandler, stop stalling. Don't make me fly to Paris to pry it out of you. I've got a stash of Girl Scout cookies, and I'm not afraid to use them."

"Samoas or Thin Mints?"

"*Both.*"

I could practically hear the smugness in her tone, and it was all I could do not to make a face at her, never mind that she couldn't see me.

"All right." I released a sigh of resignation. "He said, 'Be serious, Juliet. You aren't capable of doing anything spontaneous.'" I repeated the words in a robotic monotone that mirrored the way I'd felt when Kyle had said it, as though all the life had been sucked out of me with that one curt brushoff.

Ember scoffed. "What a douche nozzle."

I inhaled the warm summer air, propping my chin on one hand, as I monitored a scooter weaving its way down a street lined with shops and restaurants.

"Em, I love you, but you can't call my boyfriend a *douche nozzle*. I'm pretty sure that violates sister code or something." I put the phone on speaker and flipped to my messenger app, trying not to worry over the fact that Kyle had yet to reach out to me, even though it had been at least twelve hours since I'd left New York.

"Okay, how about douche canoe?"

I swallowed, registering that I still had no new messages. "Yeah, same problem."

Part of me understood where Ember was coming from—after all, it *was* a pretty crappy thing to say to your girlfriend of four years. But the other part of me, the logical part, knew I was partially to blame for his outburst given my abrupt announcement that I was taking a leave of absence from our law firm to attend a summer creative writing program at the American University of Paris.

Though, to be fair, I never thought I would get in.

Like almost everything in my life, my decision to apply to the program was prompted by another person—my assistant, Grace. I still remember that day in March when she had slid into my office, silent as an assassin, with her hands behind her back and a lopsided grin pasted on her face.

The minute I clocked her expression, I should've known she was up to something.

"Don't tell me—you won season tickets for the Yankees?" I glanced up from the share purchase agreement I was working on as she closed the door behind her with a soft click.

"No," she singsonged, planting herself in the cushioned chair opposite me.

I tapped my fingers on the walnut surface of my desk, assessing her as she tucked one curl behind her ear, her other hand remaining conspicuously behind her back.

"Is Anthropologie having another sale? Because you know, Gracie, there *is* such a thing as having too many candles."

The familiar ping of an email arriving in my inbox chimed, and my eyes darted to the computer screen. *Tom.* Senior partner and professional pain in the ass. No doubt he was already following up on the agreement I had only just started.

"Nonsense," Grace said with a wave. "Candles are the unsung heroes of décor. It's impossible to have too many. By the way, I love the one you bought me for Support Staff Appreciation Day."

I nodded, forcing a smile even as a trickle of anxiety crept into my chest. I scanned the email, which—yep, there it was—requested an update on the draft agreement beneath a laundry list of other tasks for me to get started on ASAP.

For a deal I'd been assigned to less than twenty-four hours ago.

Awesome.

I buried my face in my hands to mask the misery that had become my constant companion in recent months. Maybe if I hid long enough, Grace and her sunshiny personality would still be able to escape my dungeon of doom unscathed.

"How's your novella coming?"

I perked up despite myself, peeking at her between my fingers. Leave it to Grace to bring up the one topic guaranteed to pull me out of even the foulest of moods.

"Um, I haven't had much time to work on it lately. But—" I continued in a rush as Grace's features collapsed with disappointment. "I have some good ideas brewing." I had even jotted a few of them down in the margins of a legal pad during our team's preliminary diligence call the night before.

Grace leaned forward in her seat. "Can you give me a twenty-second teaser? Cal and I have been *dying* to know what happens next."

I sank back into my chair, the wail of a police siren outside giving me a brief reprieve to collect myself. "Honestly, I still can't believe you showed it to him."

I'd been mortified when I found out Grace's fiancé, who, as fate would have it, was also an attorney in the corporate group at my firm, had read the first few chapters of my romance novella. It had taken an entire box of Sprinkles Cupcakes and repeated assurances from Grace that Cal had actually liked it before I was willing to risk showing my face in the cafeteria, lest I accidentally run into him.

"I'm sorry." She winced. "I should have known better than to read it in front of him. I couldn't stop laughing, and then Cal asked what was so funny and—"

"It's fine. I'm probably just suffering from some form of shock that there are two people in the world who like my writing enough to ask about it."

Well, *three* if I counted Ember, which I never did because she was obligated to love me and all the fanciful ideas in my head.

Grace frowned. "I think you'd be surprised how many people would like it if you were willing to share it with anyone besides your assistant and her secret-romance-aficionado fiancé."

My shoulders stiffened as my email pinged again.

"Seriously, Juliet," she continued as I wondered how much time dropping my computer out of my twentieth-floor window would buy me. "I think you've really got something here."

I blinked up at her. My emotions wavered between utter despair over being assigned to what was shaping up to be one of the most aggressive deals our mergers and acquisitions group had ever handled and mild curiosity about her persistence.

"Grace." My fingers tightened as the ping of death sounded again. "Writing is just something I do for fun. For me." I didn't add it was about the *only* thing I did for myself.

Ever since graduating from Columbia Law and joining Sterling & Bartlit LLP, my life had become a maelstrom. Don't get me wrong—I was proud of all I had accomplished, proud to be a corporate associate at one of New York's premier law firms. After all, if you can make it in Big Law in New York City, you can make it anywhere—or at least that's what people said.

Except I wasn't sure I *was* making it. Some days, it felt like I was barely even surviving.

Between eating meals in my office while poring over binders of due diligence documents, knocking back 5-Hour Energy shots before afternoons of endless conference calls, and keeping our clients' deals moving forward while they checked in from their yachts in the Mediterranean, the days had all started to blend together.

The only time I felt alive, like I still had a living, beating heart somewhere inside the deal-making machinery that had become my body, was when I was wading through fresh ideas and churning out words for my novella.

"Well, maybe it doesn't have to be something you do just for fun." Grace placed a neat stack of papers on the edge of the desk, and I leaned forward to read the top of the front sheet.

Request for Admission, American University of Paris—Summer Creative Writing Institute.

I stared at the page.

"Now," she said, smoothing a wrinkle from her pencil skirt, "before you say no—"

"No." I shook my head, backing away from the application as if it were an explosive set to detonate. "Absolutely not."

"I just want you to consider it. It's only for the summer. Plus, haven't you been saying you want to visit Paris?"

"On *vacation*. I can't just drop everything and go to France."

"Whether you can or can't is entirely up to you," she said matter-of-factly as she rose from her chair, leaving the offending papers behind.

"Grace—"

"It's your life, Juliet." She paused at the door. "You have to decide how to live it."

⇝ ⇜

In the hours following Grace's departure, I had thrown myself headlong into work. I answered Tom's emails (all *seven* of them), sat through a three-hour meeting with the client, during which we discussed the target company's equity structure and litigation history in excruciating detail, and churned out a draft purchase agreement. By the time I clicked Send on the document, my two-day-old blouse was riddled with sweat stains, I was dehydrated, and the only meal I'd had was a granola bar I found at the bottom of my desk drawer.

Life was good.

I collapsed back against my chair, rubbing my eyes. "Siri, what time is it?"

"It's 12:53 a.m.," she responded cheerfully.

Great. Maybe if I rushed home, I might have time to shower and squeeze in a couple hours of sleep before Tom started emailing me again at whatever ungodly hour he woke up.

My gaze landed on the stack of application papers.

I glared at them. The papers glared back.

Before I could think too hard about why I was having a staring contest with an inanimate object, I grabbed the application and flipped through it, reading the requirements for submission.

It's not like I'll actually get in.

I had no formal creative writing education, and I doubted my work would be taken seriously in any case. Maybe if I wrote literary fiction or creative nonfiction or something. Because I was pretty sure a university wouldn't be impressed with a story about a grumpy, small-town ranch hand who falls in love with a disgraced Hollywood socialite.

I grabbed a pen and wrote my name on the line labeled *Applicant*.

Just to get Grace off my back, I had told myself as I scribbled down my contact information.

Two months later, I received an acceptance letter.

➤➤➤ ◄◄◄

Now, watching the sunset behind Notre-Dame Cathedral, I still couldn't believe I had done it. That all those months ago, I decided to forgo a night of much-needed sleep and finish the application in time for the morning mail pickup.

In my twenty-eight years, I had never done anything so unpredictable.

I had always been straitlaced, rule-following Juliet—the Upper East Side debutante turned lawyer who was destined to marry a lawyer, have lawyer babies, and attend high tea and charity events until I died clutching my pearls at the ripe age of eighty-five.

You aren't capable of doing anything spontaneous.

It had hurt to hear those words from Kyle, not simply because they were unkind, but because, deep down, I knew they were true.

All the success I had achieved up until this point had come on the heels of toeing the line and keeping everyone around me happy. My grandparents who had raised me after my parents had died. My overachiever boyfriend from Connecticut who wanted nothing more than to be part of an enviable power couple and make partner before leaving the private sector to run for office. My senior team members who never missed an opportunity to tell me how invaluable I was, all while driving me like a workhorse and piling on demands.

Sure, my life came with perks, including first-class everything and a paycheck with plenty of zeros. But as glamorous as it looked on the outside, I couldn't say it *felt* good on the inside.

So, I had decided to take a leap of faith.

One summer to live out my dream of being a writer. One summer to leave behind all the rules and expectations. One summer to pretend I had a life that I love.

Two

Juliet

In the thirty-six hours since arriving in Paris, I'd learned two things. One, when your boyfriend is pissed at you, don't send him cat memes at two o'clock in the morning. (Spoiler, he won't find them funny.) And two, as tempting as it may be to take a cute selfie while riding your bike across a bridge, this, too, is a bad idea.

The first lesson came late Monday night while I lounged in the kitchen, still wide awake from jet lag and eating my way through half a box of chocolate macarons. The second, the following morning on my way to campus for my first day of class.

Steering my cruiser bike with one hand, I smiled up at the camera as I pedaled across the Pont Marie, trying to capture the clear sky and leafy green trees lining the river's edge behind me.

Almost got it.

I never even saw him coming. The bridge wasn't particularly crowded, just a few passing scooters and people on foot, so I should have noticed another bike. But I didn't.

No sooner had I taken the picture than I lost my balance and veered into the left lane, colliding head-on with someone riding the opposite way. In seconds, we went sprawling to the ground in a tangle of limbs and bicycles, only narrowly avoiding falling into the river.

"*Mon Dieu,*" came a voice from somewhere over my head. "*Êtes-vous blessée?*"

He was already back on his feet and coming over to help me up as I climbed onto my hands and knees, my cheeks flaming with embarrassment.

"I am so incredibly sorry." I took his outstretched hand, silently berating myself for being so careless. Fortunately, he didn't seem injured, though I wasn't sure the same could be said for his bike laying a few feet away, the front wheel now bent at an awkward angle.

How did these things work in Europe? Was I supposed to give him my insurance information? Wait, did my insurance even cover bicycle accidents?

I was so lost in thought about liability coverage that it was several seconds before I looked up. And then I did—straight into the eyes of the most incredible being I had ever seen.

Dark glossy curls formed a halo around a face that could only be described as a collection of godlike features, his long lashes framing irises of deepest blue, as though hewn from sapphire. He was saying something, but I couldn't register a single word.

Am I dying? Is this an angel sent to welcome me to the gates of heaven?

All around us, people were stopping, but still I knelt in front of the Man-God, holding his hand, warm and solid, my gaze locked with his.

A car horn beeped, and I blinked, emerging from my stupor. Apparently, a crowd had gathered during my moment of transcendence and several people now stood around staring at me, their expressions a mixture of amusement and incredulity.

It didn't take long for me to realize why.

In the confusion of nearly tumbling to my death, my skirt had risen above my hips and my underwear, complete with pink hearts, was now on full display.

I yanked my skirt down as I stumbled to my feet, humiliation washing over me.

Why, *why* couldn't I just have a bike accident like a normal person without flashing half of Paris in the process?

I didn't look at the Man-God again as I wrestled my bike from the ground, hopped on as fast as my traitorous skirt would allow, and pedaled away.

Despite my morning catastrophe, I made it to class just as our professor, Julien Benoit, was handing out copies of *A Compilation of Classics*. I shuffled into a seat near the back of the room while he summarized the syllabus before launching into a discussion of Dumas's *The Count of Monte Cristo* and the elements of nine-teenth-century romanticism.

For the next hour, we each took turns reading passages aloud, and I smiled when we came across a particular line that I had dog-eared in my copy back home.

Happiness is like one of those palaces on an enchanted island, its gates guarded by dragons. One must fight to gain it.

Too right you are, Monsieur Dumas.

It was still so surreal to be here discussing one of my favorite classics on a Tuesday instead of back in the office mining through one of Tom's task lists. I glanced around at the group of like-mind-ed individuals, feeling a sense of gratitude. For whatever reason, whether by fate or serendipity, I had been given this opportunity, and I was going to make the most of it, starting with hanging on to Professor Benoit's every word.

Well, almost every word.

Despite my efforts to concentrate, my mind kept drifting to a singular pair of blue eyes, conjuring images of an azure sky, of a deep sea streaked with dappled sunlight ...

"Ms. Chandler?" My head snapped up at the sound of my name, only to find Professor Benoit watching me expectantly. "I'd be curious to hear your thoughts."

"Oh." I blinked several times as I tried to recall the question. "I believe ..."

To my left, a woman with long braids coughed as she shoved her notebook to the edge of the desk, a few words scribbled hastily into the margin.

Theme of the book.

Right.

"I believe," I tried again, straightening in my chair, "the work attempts to reflect the division of the main characters into categories of good and evil. For example, Danglars and Maximilien, with the former being evil and the latter being good."

"And what about Dantès?" Benoit folded his hands behind him as he circled the room. "Is he, in your opinion, good or evil?"

A student with a shock of neon hair interjected before I could answer. "It seems pretty obvious he would fit into the evil category. Given that he becomes completely driven by his desire for vengeance, I don't see how one could conclude otherwise."

Professor Benoit nodded thoughtfully, smoothing down the lapel of his jacket before turning to me again. "And what do you think, Ms. Chandler?"

"Well, I suppose ..." I trailed off, my eyes darting around before landing on the woman again, a faint look of curiosity crossing her features as she twirled a braid around her finger.

"I suppose it depends on how one defines good and evil," I said, returning my attention to the professor. "Society, arguably in both the nineteenth century and present day, is often quick to judge a person's actions as good or evil. But perhaps whether something is right or wrong isn't so easily determined. One could argue that Dantès's actions, which led to the ruination of Mondego and Villefort, were wrong by any basic moral standards, and therefore, he is necessarily evil. But we should also consider whether his actions were justifiable given the original wrong done to him and whether that justification makes his actions right, and therefore, he is good."

My response was met with the blank stares of twenty pairs of eyes, the silence broken only by an obnoxious ticking coming from the wall clock.

Way to make friends, Juliet.

I could have given a simple answer like everyone else, but no—I had to let my nerd flag fly for all to see.

I cleared my throat, throwing an anxious glance at Professor Benoit.

"I see." He turned his back to the room, the faintest trace of a smile on his lips.

***

After class, Benoit motioned me to the front of the classroom, where he sat behind a handsome inlaid lemonwood desk, thumbing through papers.

"This is a beautiful desk, Professor," I said, marveling at the polished wood lined with intricate designs and bronze edging.

"Thank you." He smiled, the corners of his eyes creasing behind wire-rimmed glasses. "It's an antique from the eighteenth century in the Louis XVI style. It took me years to find." I nodded with interest, resisting the impulse to run my fingers over the leather top to see if it felt as smooth as it appeared.

Pushing the papers to one side, he looked up at me, his gray-blue eyes steady. "I was impressed with your input in class today. It is the rare student who can formulate such a thoughtful response."

"Thanks, though I'm not sure I answered your question. About whether Dantès is good or evil."

"Well, that's the point, isn't it?" He leaned back in his chair, pushing a hand through his thick brown hair. "The right answer is not always the one that is factually correct. Rather, it is the one that reasons with an idea that shows our true understanding." After a brief pause, he continued, "I read your application, and I must say I found your writing sample ... compelling."

"Oh?" I tried to picture this buttoned-up professor who shops for antiques finding my work *compelling*, to say nothing of the scene where a sunburned Colton Lee finally works up the courage to ask out the fashionable Harley Rose and they end up making out in the back of his pickup truck.

Compelling, indeed.

"The, ah, topic was rather unorthodox," he said, adjusting his glasses, "at least compared to what we usually see for submissions. But your writing style intrigued me, and you have a good grasp on character and plot structure, all hallmarks of an adept writer. Quite surprising, given your legal background. I imagine this piece was quite different from your usual writing."

"It is, sir." I paused, considering how much to say on the subject. Around my colleagues, I had always been tight-lipped about my preference for creative writing out of fear that such a confession would find a frosty reception. But standing here in front of Benoit, with his tweed blazer and patient expression, I had an inkling he might be more empathetic.

"The thing is, even though I'm a lawyer by training, literature and creative writing have always been my true passions. No matter how hectic my work life is, I always make time to jot down ideas or, if I'm lucky, write a handful of pages." Benoit remained silent, so I pushed on. "I'm glad you liked my writing sample, though, if I'm honest, I never thought it would qualify me for this program. But now that I'm here, I want you to know I intend to apply the same level of dedication to studying the craft as I do to my legal work."

Benoit studied me, appraising me over steepled fingers. Then, without a word, he opened a drawer and extracted a magazine, laying it on top of the desk. The words *La Nouvelle Revue Française* were printed across the cover in large scroll letters.

"Once every season, this magazine publishes short fiction pieces written by promising new writers. It is extremely competitive and sometimes they receive thousands of entries. But—" He tapped his finger on the cover. "I am a close friend of the editor-in-chief, and if I submit a piece to him, he will be sure to read it."

I sank my nails into my palms, not daring to breathe.

"If you are serious, Ms. Chandler, and I suspect you are, then getting published in this magazine would be a great first step for you. So, here is what I propose. Write a new original piece and I will review it. If I think it is good, I will submit it on your behalf. What do you say?"

What do I say?

"Yes, absolutely," I said in a breathless tone. "Thank you for the opportunity, sir."

He nodded once, and I backed toward the door, hoisting my bag up on my shoulder.

"Wait, take this." He pushed the magazine across the desk toward me. "So you can evaluate your competition."

⇒⇒⇒ ⇐⇐⇐

An hour later, I sat nestled in the corner of Café Procope, poring over the pages of *La Nouvelle Revue Française*. It was last year's edition and included a few selections of poetry as well as several short stories, some of which were in English.

These are incredible.

I chewed on a thumbnail, a sliver of self-doubt creeping up my spine.

"Come on, Chandler, get out of your head," I said, tapping a pencil against one eyebrow. "You graduated in the top ten percent of your law class. You got this."

"Do you always talk to yourself?"

Blinking, I looked up from the magazine and there he was.

The Man-God.

And good lord, does he look like an angel among men.

Um, *whoa*. There was no way I should be comparing this guy to angelic beings when I had Kyle waiting for me back in New York. I simply wasn't that kind of girl. No siree Bob.

I shifted in my chair as the Man-God watched me with a bemused expression.

"May I sit?" he said after an extended silence, motioning to the chair across from me. It was only then I realized I had been staring at him without saying a single word.

I bobbed my head, watching as he sat down and made himself comfortable.

"Um, I don't mean to sound rude, but how did you find me?"

His eyes swept over me, his lips curving into a smile as he ran a finger along the line of his jaw. And then, the most extraordinary thing happened. My stomach flip-*flopped*.

Reaching into his pocket, he extracted a small, leatherbound book and set it on the table.

My day planner.

"You dropped this on the bridge earlier." I waited for him to hand it to me, but instead, he flipped open to the first page and recited my name, street address, and phone number aloud. Then, turning to today's date, he continued, "Tuesday, eight-thirty a.m., The Literary Experience with Professor Julien Benoit, Classroom 1A. Ten-thirty a.m.—coffee at Café Procope." He closed the book with a snap. "Thank God I'm not a stalker. If I were, you would have no one to blame but yourself for whatever misfortune befell you."

I huffed. "Okay, so I like to keep a detailed schedule. That's not against the law, is it?"

His smile widened. "Fortunately not, since it led me to you."

Heat crawled along the sides of my neck, and I reached for the menu at the edge of the table, fanning myself generously.

Maybe the café's air conditioner was on the fritz?

"Well, thank you for returning it." I shoved it into my bag. "I'd also like to apologize for earlier. The accident was my fault, and I'm willing to pay for any damage to your bike."

He waved away my offer, folding his arms. "Not at all necessary."

I tried and failed not to notice the way his shirt stretched across his broad, toned shoulders, the thin cotton accentuating his muscular chest. To distract myself, I hastily reached for my coffee mug, nearly upending it.

"Right. So, since you know about me, maybe you can tell me about you. Like your name, for starters." I sipped the lukewarm coffee.

"Gabriel."

I choked, spluttering.

Gabriel, the angel.

"You're joking, right?"

Gabriel the angel stared at me with a hint of amusement. "No, I'm afraid not." Handing me a napkin to wipe my mouth, he said, "Okay, my turn to ask a question."

I gave him a wary look. Then again, I was sitting here with coffee stains down my shirt in front of a guy who'd seen my underwear, so it wasn't like my dignity was on the line.

"Sure, shoot."

"I was just wondering, why are you hiding away in this relic of a café?" I followed his eyes as he surveyed the room with its antique tables and oval-backed chairs, dusty chandeliers, and green-gray walls replete with framed oil paintings. "I am surprised this place even has electricity."

I huffed a laugh. "Excuse me, I'll have you know this café was the preferred haunt of some of the greatest writers in history. Victor Hugo, George Sand, Paul Verlaine, to name a few."

He arched an eyebrow at me. "Are you a walking encyclopedia?"

I shrugged. "No, but as it happens, the world's first encyclopedists were also regulars here."

His face lit up as a laugh burst from him, and—*uh-oh*. I felt it again. That pitching beneath my sternum.

Gah.

"As fascinating as that is, you haven't answered my question. What brings *you* here?"

"I'm a writer." I fiddled with the napkin on my lap. "That's why I've come to Paris for the summer and to this café. I want to surround myself with the presence of those who changed the world with the power of their words. I want to be inspired by what inspired them."

"I see. And do you plan to spend your entire time in Paris writing in corners by candlelight?"

I pressed my lips into a thin line, swallowing a smile. "Actually, I was hoping to visit some art museums too. Even though my weapon of choice is the pen rather than the paintbrush, I've always found illustrative works to be as inspiring as the written word. Literature and art are two sides of the same coin. They sort of belong together."

In an instant, his expression changed from a look of mild amusement to one of ... longing? I blinked, and the look was gone. Maybe I imagined it.

Taking out a pen, he wrote something on a napkin before handing it to me.

"My phone number," he said, rising to stand, "in case you want some company on your journey to find inspiration."

Three

Gabriel

"God, I'm such an idiot."

I slumped on the couch beside the front window of Le Peloton Café, scrolling through my phone. For the better part of an hour, I'd tried to focus on reading emails from prospective art dealers but eventually had given up.

My head just wasn't in it today.

Against my better judgment, I checked my messages for the tenth time in as many minutes. But other than a reminder about an art exhibition I planned to attend later in the week, there were no new items in my inbox.

"Well, of course, you're a bloody idiot. I could have told you that."

I looked up, staring daggers at James behind the front desk of the cycling shop that doubled as a café. He stood folded over a clipboard with the weekly tour schedule.

"Right." I scratched my cheek. "Remind me why I hang out with you again?"

"Because I'm your best mate, and we both know you would be lost without me."

I scoffed and leaned over to prop open the window, letting the fresh air filter in and mix with the scent of coffee, new tires, and recycled oxygen.

"I see someone has an overinflated opinion of himself."

He smiled, pushing a hand through his ginger hair as he scratched out a quick note on the schedule. "Whatever you have to tell yourself, buddy."

As much as we liked to mess around, James was, in fact, my best friend and had been ever since I'd moved to Paris.

I met the British expat and professional cyclist by pure coincidence when I'd stopped in this very café looking for a bite of breakfast one morning. I'd left with a croissant and, rather unexpectedly, plans to return the following Saturday for a bike tour of Paris. At the time, the idea of joining a bunch of tourists bicycling around the city and gawking at sites like the Louvre Museum and the Eiffel Tower had sounded like its own brand of hell. But James's enthusiasm had been infectious, so I caved in the end.

To my surprise, I actually enjoyed the tour. James turned out to be quite the expert on French history and had shown us several sites off the beaten path, including a house built by the famed alchemist Nicolas Flamel. As a Harry Potter fan, I had to admit that was pretty cool.

After the tour, James invited me out for a drink at a nearby brasserie, and we'd been friends ever since. Sometimes, it was hard to believe it had already been three years since we met, but I never doubted that every day since had been that much better for having him around.

Not that I would ever tell him so.

He glanced up, his lips twitching. "Did you really ask her if she plans to spend her time in Paris writing by candlelight?"

"Please shut up." I pinched the bridge of my nose as he snorted a laugh.

"Yeah, not sure I'd expect a call after that."

"Oh yeah? Just for that, I quit."

"Oh no you don't," he said, hanging the clipboard on the wall behind the desk before turning to face me. "You're giving a tour on Saturday morning. We already have a full roster."

I frowned, trying to remember when I'd signed up for a Saturday shift. "James, you know I don't work weekends. I've got stuff to do at the gallery."

"You do now, or have you already forgotten I fixed your bike for free after you nearly destroyed it crashing into that American girl?"

My pulse skittered. "Technically, she crashed into me."

James shook his head. "And you call yourself a gentleman. Blaming a lady for her own misfortune."

Before I could issue a retort, Nora, James's wife and fellow tour guide, appeared from the back of the shop carrying a short stack of flyers. She was in her usual all-black ensemble, her dark hair bobbed, giving her the appearance of the quintessential Parisian woman despite being originally from Manchester.

"You guys still talking about that woman Gabe ran over?" She darted a look between James and me. "What was her name again? Julia?"

"Juliet," I said flatly, "and I did *not* run her over."

It'd been three days since then. Three days since she left me on that bridge, her chestnut hair blowing in the wind as she rode away. Three days since I picked up a book lying on the ground and found a name written inside in neat cursive letters—*Juliet M. Chandler*. Three days of recalling her sitting across from me, her moss-green eyes shining in the dim light of the café.

Three days of reminding myself I swore never to fall for anyone again.

I tossed my phone onto the couch next to me. "Anyway, it doesn't matter if she calls. I was only trying to be nice." James and Nora exchanged a look, which only irritated me further.

"Right," Nora said, eyeing me suspiciously. "Well, I'll just be off then. Gotta hand these out." Dumping the flyers into her messenger bag, she gave James a quick kiss on the cheek before leaving through the door, the bell above it tinkling as she exited.

No sooner had the door closed behind her than James reached under the counter to retrieve two glass bottles from the mini-fridge. "If you're done sulking, want to have a beer?"

I gave him a dubious look. "It's barely three o'clock."

He crossed the room and flopped down beside me. "Five o'clock somewhere, mate. Besides, we don't have any more tours scheduled for this afternoon. Might as well call it an early day." I shook my head but accepted the bottle anyway.

My phone vibrated, but I ignored it this time, turning my attention to the passersby outside. It's not like I was waiting to hear from her, so there was no point in checking it again.

From the corner of my eye, I could see James watching me, a slow grin spreading across his face. I blew out a heavy sigh. "Keep staring at me like an asshole, and I'm leaving you here to drink alone."

"All right, all right. It's just good to see you take an interest in someone, that's all. In all the time I've known you, I've never once heard you mention a woman's name."

I shrugged. "I've been busy preparing for the gallery opening. I don't have time for distractions."

"Mm-hmm. Well, just make sure when you make it to the top, you aren't all alone up there. Success is nothing without someone to share it with."

I paused, the bottle suspended halfway to my lips as the image of a pretty smile flashed in my mind.

Literature and art are two sides of the same coin. They sort of belong together.

I blinked, my brain finally resetting. "Thanks for the advice, but I think I'm good."

He looked like he wanted to argue but seemed to think better of it. "By the way, I forgot to mention some bloke came by looking for you yesterday. Said he's been trying to get in touch with you but wasn't sure he had your correct contact information."

My brows stitched together. "Oh yeah? What did he want?"

"He didn't say exactly. Just said it was important."

"Okay ..." I took a long pull from my beer. "Well, what was his name?"

James blew air into one cheek. "Hmm, now that you mention it, I forgot to ask."

"Wow," I said dryly. "You really know how to gather all the pertinent details. Can you at least tell me what he looked like?"

He snapped his fingers. "Now that I can do. He was tall, blond, and appeared to be in his late twenties. Oh, and he was absolutely loaded. I mean, the guy steps out of a Mercedes and strolls in wearing a three-piece suit and monogrammed cufflinks in the middle of the bloody afternoon. I wasn't sure whether he was here to buy a coffee or the entire building." James scratched his chin. "Peculiar chap. When I asked him if he'd be interested in one of our bike tours, he looked at me like I'd asked him to scrub the floors or something."

"And you say he was looking for me?" I kept a close-knit circle, and I was pretty sure no one I associated with made a habit of sporting monogrammed cufflinks.

James lifted a shoulder. "That's what he said. Asked a lot of personal questions, come to think of it. I told him I couldn't disclose employee details, but he could come back during your shift. But by the time I returned from checking the schedule, he was already gone."

"Well, that's not strange at all." An uneasy feeling settled in my stomach. "What were his initials? On the cufflinks, I mean."

James swirled the beer in his half-empty bottle. "Um, C.A., I think."

C.A.?

"Someone you know?" He eyed me curiously. "Don't tell me you're secretly rich and are just posing as a commoner to get out from under your family's thumb."

The uneasy feeling spread to my esophagus. "What? No, definitely not."

"Hmm, methinks the gentleman doth protest too much." He chuckled, turning to look out the window. "Well, maybe he'll turn up again."

I hummed noncommittally. I had no clue who this guy was or what he wanted with me, but for whatever reason, I wasn't all that eager to find out.

"Yeah," I said into my bottle before taking another sip. "Here's hoping that he won't."

Four

Juliet

"Juliet, right?"

I looked up from my laptop to find the woman from Benoit's class towering over me. Her tall form blocked out the sun as a breeze pushed through the courtyard of the student center where I sat curled up in a wicker chair.

"Um, yeah. Simone, right?"

"Yep." She pushed her hair to one side, the long braids cascading over her smooth brown skin. "I've been meaning to introduce myself but haven't gotten the chance. Nice save in class the other day. I thought for sure you were a goner, but you blew everyone else's answer out of the water. I might have been jealous if I hadn't been so impressed."

"Oh, well, it was thanks to you."

She hummed, watching me with interest. "So, you're from New York?"

I nodded. "Yeah, you?"

"The City of Angels," she said with a wink. "My dad's a film producer." She waved a hand casually as she said this as if it was nothing out of the ordinary. "He's been hounding me about choosing a career, even promising to pay for the program of my choice so long as I 'get serious.'" She used air quotes around the last bit. "Which is basically code for 'cut back on the partying.' I think he was hoping I would follow in his footsteps and go to film school. The joke's on him, I guess. Paris is probably the last place he thought I'd end up."

"Same here," I said, then added, "about ending up in Paris, not about having a famous producer for a dad."

"Yeah, I got that. So, anyway, some of the other students and I were heading out to grab a coffee. Want to join us?"

I glanced over her shoulder to where a group had congregated around a citrus tree at the far end of the courtyard. I recognized the female at the center of the group from class, her bronze skin glinting in the sun as she shifted atop four-inch stilettos. Marlena from Barcelona. She threw her head back and laughed, her red lips parting as a couple of guys crowded her personal space, pinning her with twin looks of fascination.

I wrinkled my nose.

I had always been allergic to popular girls.

My eyes flicked back to Simone, then down to the blank document open on my screen, the cursor blinking ominously. I had yet to make any progress on an original piece for the *NRF* competition, and after three days of false starts, my anxiety was getting the better of me.

"That's thoughtful of you, but I should stay and work on this."

She folded her arms, popping out a hip. "Oh, come on. You look like you could use a break. Just a quick midafternoon coffee and then you can get back to it."

I hesitated, glancing indecisively between Simone's beaming face and the empty page in front of me. I heaved a sigh. Maybe a caffeine boost wouldn't be so bad.

"Sure, why not?"

We arrived at the café fifteen minutes later to find it already packed with patrons, but we still managed to find a couple of unoccupied seats. Simone and I took a table near a window that opened out on to the sidewalk while Marlena and the others claimed a larger one a few feet away. The scent of freshly ground coffee beans wafted through the airy space, and music filtered from in-ceiling speakers, giving the entire place a trendy vibe.

"This place is great, huh?" Simone took a sip from her ceramic espresso cup.

"Yeah, I can see how people would be into it." I took inventory of the modern décor and stainless-steel barista station. "Not really my scene though."

"Oh?" She arched an eyebrow, setting her cup down with a clink. "Don't tell me you're one of those people who prefers vintage hole-in-the-wall coffee shops."

On impulse, I let my eyes drop to the reclaimed wood surface of the table, sketching out a pattern with my fingernail. "Ah, well ..."

"Oh, you so are." She clicked her tongue. "Such a typical New Yorker. I bet you already have a place scoped out here in Paris, don't you?"

"No," I lied.

She gave me a piercing look that told me she saw through the denial, but I let the silence stretch. Simone seemed nice enough, but I wouldn't put money on her ability to keep the information to herself. She might let something slip, and before I knew it, Café Procope would be overrun with university students. The thought alone was enough to make me break out in hives.

No—Café Procope was my private oasis, the one place I could go where no one would find me, and I intended for it to stay that way. There was only one person who knew my secret, one person who, by some twist of fate, now knew more about me than anyone else in Paris.

And I would likely never see him again.

I *wasn't* going to call him. At least, that's the mantra I had repeated for the rest of the afternoon on Tuesday while I finished up my coffee, jotted down a few ideas for a story, and eventually packed up to make the short trek home. But by the time I reached the apartment, my resolve had already weakened. I *could* use a guide around Paris, someone familiar with the city who knew the best art exhibitions and places of interest. Plus, he offered, so it wasn't like I would be imposing.

And, I had added in my head as I paced my living room hours later, *it has nothing to do with the swooping sensation I get every time I think of him.*

Definitely not.

Giving up the fight, I lunged for the couch where I had dumped my purse earlier, rooting around in it for the napkin with his number. And nothing. I turned the bag upside down, even flipped through each of my books in case it'd become lodged between the pages.

No dice. The number was gone.

For the rest of the week, I had tried to convince myself it was for the best. Except, every time I thought of it, my stomach plummeted about a thousand feet before I remembered I had only met him twice and caring this much about a complete stranger was insane. So, I pushed it out of my head and focused on things I could control. Like getting started on my piece for the magazine.

Simone tapped her French-tipped nails on the table. "Earth to Juliet. Where'd you go, girl?"

"Sorry," I said, scratching the tip of my nose. "I'm a bit scatterbrained today. I've got this project I'm working on for Benoit, and I can't figure out where to start."

She hummed. "And the plot thickens. First, you're an all-star in class and now you have a project for Benoit. Seems like you're the one to watch."

A trickle of laughter bubbled out of my throat just as a woman in all black approached our table. "Hi there," she said, removing a pair of aviators and tucking them into her tank top. "You two university students?"

"Yeah." Simone gave the woman a once-over. "How did you know?"

"Educated guess. This place is pretty popular with students, being so close to campus."

"Do you go to the university?" I asked. In truth, she looked more like an intelligence agent than a student with her sleek haircut and dark clothes, to say nothing of the British accent. Only the messenger bag slung over her shoulder suggested otherwise.

"Nope. Name's Nora Russell. My husband and I run a cycling shop on the other side of town." She retrieved a flyer from her bag and shoved it toward me before fishing out one for Simone.

"Paris Bike Tours," I read aloud.

"Interested? We give discounts to students."

I scanned the list of locations included in the tour. It *did* look pretty interesting. Plus, it would be an efficient way to get the lay of the city before tackling it one museum at a time.

"This doesn't look half bad." Simone flipped the flyer over to read the back. "I say we go for it, Juliet. I'm free tomorrow afternoon if you are."

"Yeah, okay," I said with an answering nod. "We'll do the Saturday afternoon tour."

When I looked up again, Nora was staring at me so intently, it was a wonder she hadn't managed to bore a hole in the side of my head.

"Sorry," she said, cocking her head to one side. "Didn't quite catch your name."

I exchanged a quick glance with Simone, whose wide-eyed expression told me she'd also picked up on the odd shift in conversation. "I'm Juliet, and this is Simone."

"You don't say?" Her eyes brightened. "Well, unfortunately, our Saturday afternoon tour is already full. But Saturday morning is wide open."

Simone frowned. "Well, that blows. I'm not much of a morning person, so I'll pass."

I didn't miss the look of annoyance that flitted across Nora's features before she recovered herself. "And what about you, Juliet?"

"Um ..." I darted another glance at Simone, and she lifted one shoulder in a shrug before taking a bite of her raspberry scone.

"Tell you what," Nora said, fishing her sunglasses from the neck of her shirt before donning them again. "If you decide to do the tour tomorrow morning, it's on the house."

"Wait, really?" This woman knew how to drive a hard bargain, but I still wasn't particularly keen on going alone. "That's incredibly nice of you, but I'm not sure if I can make it."

She peered at me over the rim of her sunglasses. "Oh, yeah? Well, that's a shame. Gabriel will be so disappointed."

My mouth fell open with a pop.

She couldn't mean *my* Gabriel. Not that he was mine because he wasn't. In any case, there had to be dozens of Gabriels in Paris, and there was no way she could be referring to the same guy who kept bumping into my thoughts every time I let my guard down.

But why did she mention it, then?

I fidgeted with the napkin in my lap. *Just ask her, Juliet.* But did I even want to know? If I asked her and it turned out to be someone different, I didn't know if I could bear the disappointment. But if I asked, and it turned out to be *him* ...

My stomach fluttered.

"Thanks for your time anyway." She pushed her sunglasses up the bridge of her nose. "You ladies have a pleasant afternoon."

She left as swiftly as she'd appeared, weaving through tables and dropping a handful of flyers by the door before pushing out into the street.

"Well, that was crazy," Simone said. "For a minute there, I could've sworn she knew you."

I chewed on my lip, eyes still fixed on the door. "Yeah, me too."

⟫⟫⟩ ⟨⟪⟪

"A bike tour, Jules? Please tell me you're joking."

The frenzied sounds of New York City filtered through the phone as Ember hailed a taxi, her heels clicking a quick staccato on the pavement just before a car door slammed.

"The Plaza Hotel on Fifth Avenue, please," she said to the driver. "Now, about this bike tour, you can't seriously be thinking of doing it."

I shrugged, the lavender-scented water of the bath lapping around me. "How else am I supposed to get to know the city? Plus, did I mention it's free?"

"I don't care if it's free. Bike tours are for families with kids and retirees on holiday. You're a beautiful single gal in the City of Lights. You should be exploring it on the back of some hot guy's Vespa."

The specter of Gabriel flickered through my mind. As much as I wanted to believe Nora had been referring to my—no, not *my*—Gabriel, I wasn't going to get my hopes up only for them to come crashing down like a punctured balloon.

"Okay, there are two things wrong with that statement. First, bike tours are for everyone. And second, I'm not single, remember?"

"Sorry, wishful thinking. Well, if I can't stop you, then at least promise me you won't do anything embarrassing like wear a fanny pack."

My lips quirked as I reached for a bar of soap. "What's wrong with a fanny pack?" Ember's sigh of exasperation was cut off by the sound of the cab driver leaning on his horn and swearing in a Brooklyn accent. "Why are you headed to the Plaza? I thought you said that place was only for stuffed-shirt investment bankers and women who wear houndstooth."

Her tone brightened. "I'm meeting this guy Declan for cocktails. He's a CFO in town for a board meeting, and we happened to cross paths last night at a rooftop party in Hell's Kitchen."

"I thought you were dating someone named Trent," I said, my brows knitting as I tried to recall my sister's latest guy of the month. "He liked English Premier League soccer, didn't he?"

Ember snorted. "No, that was Levi, and good riddance to him. If I never have to watch another EPL soccer game, it'll be too soon. He was absolutely *obsessed* with it."

"Okay, so who was Trent?"

"Trent was the venture capitalist who lived in Chelsea. Completely OCD, that one. He organized his socks by length and color, Jules. By length *and* color."

I breathed a laugh. "Sounds charming. But seriously, Em, maybe you should take a break from serial dating and find a guy you have a real connection with." My sister went through men faster than *Vogue* magazines, and while I never judged her for it, I was beginning to wonder whether there wasn't something more to her behavior.

"Hard pass," she said, the noise of her surroundings rising as she stepped out of the cab into the bustling thoroughfare that was Fifth Avenue. "I just don't think I'm the settling-down type. The second a man gets comfortable, he's swapping candlelit dinners at Jean-Georges for takeout in the Village."

"Uh-huh." I climbed out of the tub, wrapping myself in a towel. "And you know this how?"

"Call it intuition." She paused. "Speaking of settling down, how are things with Kyle?"

I froze on my way to the linen closet to retrieve my hair dryer. "Um ..." *Crap.* I darted a quick look around the bathroom, as though I might find a way to escape this conversation hidden in the crown molding.

"Please don't tell me that bastard hasn't called you." Her voice echoed like she'd entered a cavernous space, the distinct sounds of a piano playing in the background.

"Oh, sounds like you're in the hotel lobby," I said as panic crawled up my throat. "Maybe we should talk about this later."

"Nice try, Jules. Do I need to go give that dickhead a kick in the ass? Because I've got a new pair of Louboutin heels that need to be broken in."

"No, there'll be no need for any ass-kicking. We've texted a bit, but he's having a hard time adjusting. We had a life plan, you know, and I sort of went off script without consulting him."

"*Consulting* him? My God, are we even related?" She expelled a breath, the tap of her heels on the marble floor mirroring the thrumming of my pulse. "Look, it's none of my business, but I know you. You always put everyone else's needs first. But loving someone doesn't mean swapping your dreams for theirs or putting yourself second so the people around you can feel comfortable. It's okay to choose yourself sometimes, and you don't need anyone's permission to do the thing that's right for you."

I forced a swallow. "Thanks, Em."

I hadn't wanted to admit it, but the tension with Kyle was weighing on me. And, as much as I empathized with how he must be feeling, I couldn't help but notice he didn't seem to care very much about how *I* was feeling. Maybe he had once, in the beginning of our relationship. But now, four years down the line, it was starting to feel like he had lost sight of *me* in the effort to build *us*.

When Kyle and I met, we'd both been first-year associates at our firm. We were eager and ambitious with our entire legal careers in front of us. And after three years of law school, being sworn in as attorneys made us feel like we were on top of the world. Our lives had fit together so seamlessly back then, our goals completely aligned.

But what would happen if our paths diverged? Could our relationship survive it?

Honestly, I wished I knew.

Five

Gabriel

I scanned the roster, then looked up at the group assembled outside of Le Peloton Café. Fifteen people milled around, all waiting to head out on the morning tour, but according to the roster, there should be sixteen.

I blew out a long breath, running my eyes over the list again.

Everyone had checked in except for one person listed at the very bottom. There was no name, just the words *female student* scribbled in Nora's handwriting.

"Is anyone here a student?"

Maybe I had missed the person in the cluster of tourists congregated on the sidewalk.

A scrawny kid with braces shot his hand into the air, bouncing on his toes like he had won a sweepstakes. "I am. Do I get something special?"

"No," I said flatly.

My eyes swept over the rest of the group, but much to my irritation, no one else spoke up. I scrubbed a hand over my face. Why did there always have to be one?

We were already running behind schedule and, as much as I hated to leave without this mysterious student, she was giving me little choice. Fortunately, the rest of the group had been content to wait patiently—no doubt thanks to the mild sunshine and free coffee—but I couldn't keep them waiting much longer.

"Thank you, everyone, for your patience. We'll be heading out shortly. Please dispose of any trash and feel free to use the restrooms." Without waiting for a response, I spun on my heel and headed into the shop.

What was Nora thinking? Standard policy required a name and email address be provided with all reservations for this very reason—when someone didn't show up.

I stalked to the front desk and snatched my phone off the counter, my jaw clenching as I dialed Nora's number. She would likely rip me a new one for calling her this early on a Saturday, but at the moment, I couldn't care less. It was her fault for not including complete information in the first place, so she could just deal with it.

The phone rang once, twice.

"Hello?" A female voice floated across the room.

I glanced up and froze, the phone slipping from my fingers as all the breath punched out of my lungs in a dizzying rush. There she was, standing in the doorway in a pale blue sweater, her brown-gold hair cascading around her shoulders in tumbling waves.

Juliet.

She seemed to recognize me about half a second after I recognized her, and she sucked in a sharp inhale. "It is you," she said, her voice soft like a whisper of velvet.

I'd forgotten how much I liked the sound of it.

I had the presence of mind to hang up the phone but remained rooted to the spot, my eyes roaming over her, not wholly convinced she was even there. I cataloged the almond shape of her eyes and her delicate features dusted with cinnamon-colored freckles before I let my gaze drop to her mouth, her full lips parted on an exhale, her cheeks flushed with color.

God, she was pretty.

Unconsciously, my eyes dipped lower. Her sweater was like the one she'd been wearing when we met, but the bottom half of her outfit was different. Instead of the floral skirt that had since become imprinted on my brain, she was wearing a pair of cutoff denim shorts that hugged her thighs in a way that would drive a blind man to distraction.

"Juliet," I said, sounding sturdier than I felt. "You're ... are you here for the tour?"

As soon as I said it, understanding clicked into place. *The female student.* I had no idea how, but I was certain Nora had something to do with Juliet's appearance. And instead of giving me a heads-up, she deliberately withheld the information from me, the little minx.

Juliet blinked. "Oh, yeah. Sorry I'm late. I got lost on the way."

"Don't worry about it," I said, grinding a fist into my sternum to loosen the tension in my chest. Willing my legs into motion, I rounded the desk only to stop a few feet away from her as a breeze from the window carried her scent toward me. Was that vanilla and lavender?

Shoving my hands in my pockets, I took a decided step backward.

"I was just about to get everyone set up with their safety equipment if you're ready to go."

"Yeah, sure," she said, and I swear my stomach bottomed out when she peeked up at me from beneath her lashes.

Come on. Get your shit together.

There was no reason she should be affecting me this much, and I needed to get myself in check fast. Because whatever this was, this strange electricity that pulsed through my veins every time I got close to her, it spelled nothing but trouble.

And I'd already had enough of that for one lifetime.

In any case, she didn't call, I reminded myself, so I might as well take five on the existential crisis. Steeling myself with that knowledge, I nodded toward the door behind her.

"Shall we?"

Two and a half hours later, I stood at the back entrance of the shop, putting away the last of the equipment and double-checking that all the bikes were securely locked.

The tour went well—better than usual, in fact. I'd been in a good mood, so I spent extra time at each location, expounding on the historical and architectural details of each museum and monument we visited. Whenever anyone showed a particular interest in a place, I made a point to answer all their questions. I offered up my services as an amateur photographer whenever someone wanted a picture. I gave restaurant recommendations, pointed out the best gift shops, and even stopped to let the group watch a street performer on roller skates.

I did anything and everything to keep from focusing all my attention on Juliet.

Occasionally, I'd sneak a glance in her direction and was ridiculously pleased to find her listening attentively. Every time she smiled, I wondered what she was thinking, and I tried to decipher which places she liked from the subtle shifts in her expression. The wrinkling of her nose. The twitching of an eyebrow. At one point, I'd lost my train of thought entirely when she dragged her bottom lip between her teeth.

Good lord.

I stopped watching her after that.

At the end of the tour, Juliet deposited her bike in the place I indicated and then left without saying a single word to me. I tried to ignore the pit in my stomach and distracted myself by talking to the other guests, who all thanked me for the tour and promised to write reviews. But by the time the last person had gone, the pit had grown into a gaping hole. I slammed the door to the bike garage, wondering how many times I would be forced to watch Juliet Chandler walk away from me before she disappeared out of my life for good.

Moving to the front of the shop, I collapsed behind the computer at the front desk, jabbing the password into the keyboard a bit harder than necessary.

It's fine. It's better this way.

If her enduring silence over the past week hadn't been indication enough, her abrupt departure this afternoon without so much as a *thanks, have a nice life* certainly made things clear. Never mind the fact that she'd been living rent free in my mind from the moment I set eyes on her. The point was she *wasn't* interested, and it was high time I got good with it.

Sorting through a few unread emails in our business account, my eyes fell across one from *NoraRRides@PeloCafe.com*. I clicked it open, reading the subject line.

From: NoraRRides@PeloCafe.com
To: Gabe.Beaumont@PeloCafe.com
Subject: Female Student
Date: June 8, 2024, 12:13 PM

Gabe, if you're reading this, I assume you've already received a visit from a certain doe-eyed student who may or may not be confused with a character from Shakespeare. Feel free to thank me anytime. For the record, I will accept payment in the form of ice cream from Berthillion.

Cheers,
Nora

I snorted and typed out a quick response.

From: Gabe.Beaumont@PeloCafe.com
To: NoraRRides@PeloCafe.com
Subject: Re: Female Student
Date: June 8, 2024, 12:46 PM

Nice of you to check in. Yes, I was quite surprised to see her, and I would be more than happy to take you to Berthillion. I'll make sure they add extra walnuts to your sundae.

- G

Leaning back in my seat, I checked the time before scrolling through a couple more emails. I had just finished filling out a purchase order for new bike reflectors when her response arrived.

From: NoraRRides@PeloCafe.com
To: Gabe.Beaumont@PeloCafe.com
Subject: Re: Re: Female Student
Date: June 8, 2024, 12:58 PM

Gabe, I'm allergic to nuts. I thought you knew that.

Cheers,
Nora

I smirked, firing back another message.

From: Gabe.Beaumont@PeloCafe.com
To: NoraRRides@PeloCafe.com
Subject: Re: Re: Re: Female Student
Date: June 8, 2024, 13:01 PM

I do—that's the point.

- G

Her reply appeared less than a minute later.

From: NoraRRides@PeloCafe.com
To: Gabe.Beaumont@PeloCafe.com
Subject: Re: Re: Re: Re: Female Student
Date: June 8, 2024, 13:02 PM

Such gratitude ...

Cheers,
Nora

I blew out a breath of laughter and powered off the machine. In truth, I did owe Nora my gratitude, if only for being a good friend. Sometimes, I wondered what I had done to deserve her and James. The two of them had been my constants since I arrived in Paris as a naive and untested twenty-five-year-old. Paris could be overwhelming for newcomers, and while I hadn't been afraid to fend for myself, I would always appreciate the two of them for taking me into their family and for being my anchor when I had little more than my determination to keep me grounded. I owed them a lot. One day, I would figure out how to repay them.

I crossed the room to switch off the lights and check the security system before grabbing my wallet from the counter and heading for the exit. But no sooner had I pushed the door open than I ran directly into someone standing just outside of it.

"*Merde*, sorry, I—"

The words fell from my lips as I caught sight of Juliet on the sidewalk, equally startled and massaging one elbow. She let out a nervous laugh, the sound of it like tinkling bells.

"Is it me, or are we fated to keep running into each other?"

I scratched the side of my nose, trying to stop the smile that was fighting its way onto my lips. "It would appear so."

She didn't leave after all. What did it mean that she had been waiting here this whole time?

"I really enjoyed the tour. Now I see why you offered to show me around. You definitely know more about the city than your average Parisian."

"Yeah, well ..." I let my sentence drop, unsure what else to say. It's true I had offered to accompany her around because I knew a lot about the art museum scene. But if I was honest, there had been another reason, one I really didn't want to examine.

A beat of silence passed.

"Look, Gabriel, I meant to call—"

"Don't," I said, my tone coming out more forceful than I intended. I inhaled slowly, then tried again. "You don't need to explain."

The only thing more embarrassing than being rejected was having it laid out for you in excruciating detail. If she didn't want to spend any more time with me, it was well within her rights. But I wasn't exactly eager to have it shoved down my throat.

She continued to watch me, her eyes iridescent in the sunlight, and I held on to her gaze, soaking in every shade of green, the flecks of yellow at the center.

"I lost it," she said after a long silence. "Your number, that is."

I stared at her, my shoulders plummeting as I registered what she was telling me. *She lost my number.* She didn't call because *she lost my number.* I kept my face impassive even as my chest exploded with relief.

"So, I was thinking, if your offer still stands, maybe we could check out an art museum sometime?" She reached into her canvas bag and retrieved a folded piece of paper, handing it to me. "Here's my number since, you know, I obviously can't be trusted with yours."

"Thanks," I said, my voice suddenly hoarse.

"Cool," she said, her lips curving into a smile so pretty it came dangerously close to giving me a heart attack. "Well, see you around maybe."

Tucking her bag under her arm, she started down the street, and I watched her go, my heart speeding up the farther away she got.

It wasn't too late to forget this whole thing. I could let her walk away and never call, let the past week fade into a distant memory. Everything could go back to how it was before.

Before *her*.

"Hey." I kicked off the door, striding toward her. She slowed, glancing at me over one shoulder, and I dragged a hand through my hair. "You hungry?"

Six

Gabriel

"Fermé pour renovation." Juliet hooked a thumb into the waistband of her shorts as she peered at the sign hanging in the restaurant window. "And that means ..."

"Closed for renovations."

I fished my phone out of my jeans pocket, the muscles in my jaw working as I suppressed a groan. Just my luck that my favorite restaurant would be closed on the one day I wanted to bring someone here.

I was a regular at this spot in the Saint Germain des Prés district, having developed a taste for its classic French cuisine with an innovative twist shortly after moving to Paris. The food was phenomenal, but the best part was it was often overlooked by tourists because of being tucked away on a narrow side street, thus making it the perfect spot to enjoy a meal in peace. It was the first place that came to mind after Juliet agreed to grab lunch with me, but now I wished I'd thought of a backup. The last thing I wanted was to take her to just any old bistro.

I wanted to take her somewhere memorable.

Juliet shaded her eyes with her hand, the sunlight catching in her hair, and I swiped a bead of sweat from my brow, scanning the search results for restaurants in the area.

Nothing looked appealing.

"Is it too late to make a reservation somewhere else?"

I looked up to find Juliet's face arranged in a hopeful expression. I grimaced. No doubt my expression was one of regret at having blown this outing with her so spectacularly.

"Unfortunately, most places will be closing soon until they open again for dinner, so ..."

I was about to suggest we take a rain check when she shrugged, smiling at me as if she wasn't at all bothered by this information. "That's okay, we can just go back to my place."

My mouth hinged open before I could stop it, and I snapped it shut again as the beginnings of a blush dotted Juliet's cheeks.

"Oh, my God. Talk about an embarrassing case of word vomit. I didn't mean to imply—that is, I only *meant* we could go to my place and I could cook us something. Only if you want to, of course. No pressure."

I watched her fidget for several seconds, suppressing a grin before finally taking pity on her. "All right, I'll agree on one condition."

Her brows lifted. "Oh? Um, okay ..."

"Give me another chance to bring you here." I bobbed my head toward the restaurant, and her gaze followed mine to the darkened windows, our eyes meeting in the reflection.

She watched me for a long moment and I thought she might say no. But then her lips tilted into a smile. "Deal."

⟫⟫ ⟪⟪

Juliet's apartment was the picture of Parisian style with high ceilings, herringbone floors, and tall double windows overlooking the street. I stepped into the foyer as she closed the door behind me, my eyes sweeping over the place she called home.

The kitchen was outfitted with sleek appliances and granite countertops and opened on to the main living space, which was furnished with a mixture of classic and contemporary furniture.

"Make yourself at home," she said, toeing off her shoes and throwing me a quick smile. She disappeared down a hallway, and I shoved my hands in my pockets, turning and making a slow circuit of the room.

The living room had floor-to-ceiling paneling with carved molding, and across from a pair of cream-colored sofas was a marble fireplace, its iron grate clean with a pile of firewood sitting nearby, untouched. I ran a hand over the dust-free mantel. In all likelihood, Juliet wouldn't use the fireplace if she only planned to stay for the summer.

Something in my chest stirred at the thought of Juliet's impending departure. Before I could examine why my heart wanted to trade places with my stomach at the idea of her leaving, she returned wearing a crew neck T-shirt, her hair tied up in a ponytail.

"I hope you like chicken and roasted vegetables." She glided into the kitchen and opened the refrigerator, pulling out handfuls of carrots and potatoes. "Unless you're a vegetarian, in which case, it'll just be roasted veggies."

"Chicken and vegetables sound perfect."

She moved around the kitchen with practiced precision, and I slid onto a bar stool, watching her. "Is there anything I can do?"

She ducked out of sight, her momentary disappearance followed by the clanging of pots and pans. She popped back up from behind the counter, holding a baking sheet in one hand, a cast-iron skillet in the other.

"Yes, there is." She extracted her phone from a back pocket before holding it out to me. "Want to pick some music? I've got a few different playlists, but if you don't see anything you like ..."

I shook my head before she could finish her sentence. No way was I passing up on a chance to see what kind of music she liked.

"I'm sure I'll find something."

I picked a playlist at random and scrolled through the list of songs, some familiar and some not. I was pleased to find that instead of a mix of Top 40 hits, her taste seemed more eclectic with a mixture of indie folk, alternative rock, and even some jazz.

I paused, my finger hovering over one song in particular.

"You like Petit Biscuit?" I blinked at her in surprise.

She looked up from the carrots she was chopping. "Um, yeah. Why?"

I batted away a grin. "Nothing. I just didn't expect to find a French DJ in your playlist. I love his songs."

"I like to think great music is universal." Leaning over the kitchen island, she selected "Sunset Lover," the dulcet tones drifting across the room from a Bluetooth speaker. Something solid lodged itself in my throat as I listened to the opening notes of one of my favorite songs.

Juliet moved to draw her hand back, but as she did, her fingers brushed against mine. I looked up on instinct, the hair on the back of my neck rising when our eyes collided. An unreadable emotion flitted across her expression, and she swallowed, her delicate throat moving with the action.

"So," she said, resuming her chopping with fervor, "are you originally from Paris?"

Small talk. We were moving on from whatever the hell moment that was to small talk.

"No." I scrubbed my knuckles over the side of my face. "I'm from a town called Villefranche-sur-Mer along the southern coast. I moved to Paris a few years back."

She hummed, depositing the carrots into a bowl, and I tracked her movements, noting a slight tremor in her hands as she began dicing the potatoes. Did I make her nervous? I was tempted to take the knife from her before she hurt herself. Except that would involve me touching her again, which I absolutely should *not* do.

"Did your family come with you to Paris?"

A record scratched in my mind.

My family. It was a normal question, practically a mandatory inclusion in any getting-to-know-you conversation. Unfortunately, my family was my least favorite topic.

"No." My tone was brusque, and her eyes shot up, no doubt because I sounded like a complete ogre. "My, uh, father and cousin still live there." *I think.* I hadn't spoken to either of them in years, so I couldn't say for sure. "What about you?" I pushed on before I was forced to sidestep more awkward questions. "Where are you from?"

She frowned but replied without missing a beat. "New York. I moved there when I was eight to live with my grandparents after my parents died in a car accident. Before that, my sister and I lived in a town on the coast of Maine since our dad was a commercial fisherman."

"Oh. I'm sorry to hear about your parents." I knew the feeling of that kind of loss all too well, having lost my mother when I was a teenager.

Juliet's expression softened. "Thanks. It was a long time ago. My grandparents took great care of my sister and me, making sure we were in the best schools and were well provided for. I think, in a way, caring for us helped them cope with the loss of my mother."

I nodded, processing this information and filing it away with everything else I'd learned about Juliet over the past week. *A writer from New York who likes art and Petit Biscuit. Born in a coastal town like me. Raised by grandparents and has one sister.*

"So, do you have a girlfriend?" A second after the words left her mouth, her face bloomed with color. I watched her as she made every effort not to look at me, arranging the chicken in the pan with all the precision of a brain surgeon.

"Are you asking because you want to know if I'm single?" I pressed my lips together to smother a chuckle as the shade of her cheeks graduated from a rosy hue to full-blown crimson.

"No, nothing like that," she said, nearly upending the skillet. "I don't even know why I asked. My filter must be broken today." She rapped one knuckle against her forehead, and I lost the battle as a laugh fell from my lips.

I wondered if she had any idea how adorable she was.

A long stretch of silence passed until I realized she was still waiting for an answer. I folded my arms over my chest, keeping my tone even. "No, I don't do relationships."

And here we go.

We had finally reached the part in the proceedings where most women would give me a disappointed look and try to gauge how serious I was. Not that I'd made any effort to become romantically involved with anyone since coming to Paris, but I had chatted with women at bars and art openings, women who made no secret of the fact that they found me attractive. Every one of them had been convinced they could change my mind on the matter.

So far, no one had succeeded.

Although, I thought as I dragged a hand over my jaw, *I wouldn't hate to see Juliet try.*

She blinked at me, her shoulders relaxing. "Oh, well, that's good."

My mouth fell open. "*Pardon*?" Did she just say *that's good*?

Before I could get to the bottom of whether I was hallucinating, a ringtone blared from the phone I forgot I was holding. The screen lit up with a picture of a girl who looked suspiciously like Juliet, the name *Ember* scrolling across the top.

"Um, someone named Ember?"

"Crap, it's my sister." She lifted her hands, covered in chicken seasoning. "Can you grab that while I wash up?" Without waiting for an answer, she swiveled toward the sink, flicking the faucet on with an elbow. I frowned, hesitating for another beat before answering.

Ember appeared on the screen a second later, followed closely by a chorus of car horns and bits of conversations from passersby as she walked down a grungy-looking sidewalk.

"Hey, Jules," she said without looking at the screen, taking a sip from a gargantuan coffee cup as she maneuvered through pedestrians.

I watched in stunned silence. This girl looked so much like Juliet that it was jarring. Her eyes were the same shade of green, but unlike her sister's, they were ringed with dark eyeliner, as if she were getting an early start on a night out or never went to bed.

Something told me it was the latter.

And her hair—her hair was definitely different. Instead of the soft chestnut waves I associated with Juliet, Ember's hair was a river of gold flying carefree over her shoulder. Her *bare* shoulder. My brows pulled together as I leaned closer to the screen. Was she wearing a black mini-dress? I was fairly certain it wasn't even noon yet in New York.

I stared at her, feeling awkward, but also fascinated. It was incredible seeing another person who shared Juliet's likeness in almost every way and yet was so *other*.

A man sporting a colorful collection of tattoos pushed past her, clipping her shoulder roughly. Without missing a beat, she whirled and shouted, "Watch it, needle dick."

Yeah, definitely *other*.

Juliet rounded the kitchen island, wiping her wet hands on her shorts and reaching for the phone. But before I could hand it off to her, Ember's gaze landed on me, her eyes widening.

"Who the fu—"

"Hey, Em." Juliet plucked the phone from my fingertips, throwing me an apologetic look. "Um, this is my tour guide, Gabriel. We were just having a late lunch and—"

"Your tour guide? Hell's bells, Jules, what kind of tour was this? I had no idea bike tours came with that kind of man candy."

Juliet winced as I smothered a grin behind my fist. "Um, I'm just gonna take this in my room. Be right back." She darted down the hall, almost losing her balance as her socks slid against the hardwood floor. As soon as the door clicked shut, I shook my head, expelling a laugh.

This day was turning out to be nothing short of unbelievable. I'd gone from not having a prayer of seeing Juliet again to being in her apartment, getting eyed up by her sister.

I supposed crazier things have happened.

I moved into the kitchen and stopped in front of the skillet, inhaling the aroma of herbs and spices as my stomach growled appreciatively. After I lowered the fire, I busied myself with finding plates and cutlery to set the table.

It was strange how comfortable I was with Juliet, preparing to share a meal and getting to know her. A week ago, we'd been complete strangers. And what were we now?

The word *friends* rattled around in my brain.

Yeah, that sounded right. Friends I could do. Friendship would satisfy this strange desire I had to spend time with her without compromising the promise I'd made to myself. I'd already been on the wrong end of love once, and I had no intention of letting it happen again.

Although it didn't seem like I would need to worry much on that score.

I carried the plates to the table, my mind turning over the conversation we'd been having before her sister blew in like a tornado and brought it to an end. What did she mean by saying *that's good*? Maybe she didn't believe in relationships either?

Or maybe, I thought, absently pushing aside a stack of papers to make room on the table, *she's one of those women who likes to have multiple relationships at once.*

Something sour churned in my gut at the thought.

No, Juliet wasn't like that. Her sister? Possibly. It took one thirty-second interaction for me to conclude Ember was a force to be reckoned with and you'd be taking your life in your hands if you tried to tame her. But not Juliet.

There was something softer about her, gentler. Not that she wasn't strong because, clearly, she was that too. Coming to Paris to pursue a dream was no small feat. But she also had this air of innocence about her. I'd tried not to put too fine a point on it, but she really *had* put herself at risk by writing all of her personal details in her planner without a thought to the danger of it falling into the wrong hands. A girl like that needed looking after, protecting.

And, God, did I want to be the one to do it.

A door opened at the end of the hall, pulling me from my musings. "Sorry about that. My sister is, um, a bit ... spirited."

"Twins?"

"Almost." She placed her phone on the sideboard and queued up the music again, then proceeded into the kitchen. "Irish twins, actually."

I raised an eyebrow. "As in, you were born in the same year?"

"Yes," she said, giving me a pointed look, "and I'd rather not get into the particulars of how that came about. Needless to say, our parents were very happy together."

"That's a good thing, I would think." I stepped around the table to pull out a chair for her as she returned with the food in serving dishes. She halted mid-step. "Something wrong?"

She shook her head. "No, nothing's wrong. I'm just not used to people being so considerate."

I forced a smile even as something sharp clawed at my chest. "You invited me into your home and cooked a meal for me. I merely pulled out a chair. I still have a way to go before I've given you the consideration you deserve."

Once the food was served and Juliet was seated, I hesitated before taking the seat opposite her, eyeing the empty chair to her right with the stack of papers in front of it.

"You can move those," she said, reading my thoughts, and I wasted no time in collecting the pile and placing them on the side table. As I set them down, my eyes fell across the top page.

Escrow Agreement for T&P Asset Acquisition.

"What's this?" It was none of my business, but I couldn't help wondering what Juliet was doing with what looked like legal documents.

"Oh, um, just a bit of work," she said, pushing the food around on her plate.

"Work?" I joined her at the table, uncorking a bottle of wine and filling two glasses. "I thought you said you were a writer?"

"I am," she said quickly. "Well, that is, I *want* to be. That's why I'm in the writing program at AUP. But I'm a practicing lawyer too."

My eyebrows shot up. "Are you really?"

Well, color me impressed.

She gave me a pained smile, closing her hand around the wine-glass I'd just filled before taking a few healthy swallows. "Yeah. I hate it." Her jaw tightened as she set the glass down and took up her utensils, attacking the chicken on her plate.

I watched her for a long moment before setting my fork down. Clearly, I would need to tread carefully here. "If you don't like it, why do you do it?"

She stuffed a forkful of potato in her mouth without answering, pressing her fingers to her forehead and massaging the space between her eyebrows.

She's frustrated. That much was evident from the way she seemed set on impaling her dinner. Strangely enough, I understood the aggression, that desperate need to let it all out. After all, I'd spent years doing something I didn't want to do just to make my father happy while putting my dreams on hold.

Until I didn't anymore.

"My grandparents," she said, dabbing her mouth with a napkin, "they did everything for me and Ember and asked for so little in return. Just that we keep our grades up and attend the occasional charity event." She turned to look out the window. "My grandfather didn't come from money, but he made his way in the world. He founded his own law firm and built it into a preeminent practice with the help of a few key partners. It was his legacy, and he was so proud of it." I waited for her to continue as she swallowed another bite.

"My mother used to tell me he always hoped she would become an attorney, too, but in the end, that wasn't the life for her. By the time she graduated high school, she'd already met my father while visiting a boarding school friend in Cutler, Maine one summer. That's the town where my dad was from, the town where Ember and I grew up."

"Your grandfather must have been disappointed."

She shrugged a shoulder. "I can't say for sure. I doubt he was particularly thrilled that his only daughter hightailed it to Maine at eighteen to marry a fisherman and sell beaded jewelry out of a storefront." She laughed, the sound of it both warm and hypnotizing. "It was beautiful, the jewelry. She made it herself, actually. Ember and I used to help her sometimes."

"That sounds nice." I ignored the growl in my stomach. No doubt it was wondering why I had yet to touch the perfectly acceptable meal sitting in front of me. Juliet smiled in my direction, and my stomach churned for an entirely different reason.

"It was. We have a lot of good memories." She sighed. "Anyway, it's not like my grandfather pressured me to become a lawyer, but I felt like I owed that to him, to pick up the mantle where my mother hadn't. Especially after his cancer diagnosis during my senior year of college. I convinced myself it was the least I could do after he'd done so much for me and my sister. And for a while, knowing how happy it made him was enough to keep me going."

"And now?"

She shook her head, reaching for her wineglass again. "Now I don't know why I do it. After my grandfather passed, I decided to continue in honor of his memory without stopping to think about what I wanted for myself. And by the time I *did* start thinking about it, I'd become so entrenched in life at the firm, I couldn't see a way out. Thank God for good friends, I guess," she said, toasting the air with her glass. "I wouldn't be here otherwise."

"Forgive me for being blunt, but now that your grandfather is gone, why not leave law behind if that's what you want?"

As if on cue, she darted a look toward the stack of papers. "I don't know. I'm rather good at what I do, so maybe that's part of it. And I'm a *valuable member of the team*." She rolled her eyes. "That's a direct quote from my senior partner, Tom, which he tactfully included at the bottom of his email when he sent those documents over for me to review. I never knew him to be an ass-kisser, but desperate times and all that."

I frowned, not much liking this Tom person. "Doesn't he know you're in Paris?"

She snorted. "I could be trapped in a moon crater, but if there was work to be done, he would find me. I think he might have a coronary if I ever left the firm. Not that I would ..." She trailed off, worrying her bottom lip. "Kyle would never go for it."

"Who's Kyle?"

She knocked back the last of her wine. "My boyfriend."

I dropped my fork with a clatter, my eyes springing to hers. *Boyfriend.* She has a *boyfriend.*

A burning sensation ignited in the back of my throat as a streak of jealousy lanced through me. Closing a hand around my glass, I took a long drink as she continued talking, thankfully unaware of the clash of emotions warring in my chest. And for what? I barely knew this girl, had only met her five days ago. What right did I have to feel jealous?

None, none at all.

She huffed, collapsing back in her chair. "He just doesn't get it, you know? The whole writing thing. He says it's a waste of time. In fact, he's still pretty pissed I came here at all."

In an instant, my confusing jealousy took a backseat to an influx of annoyance. "A waste of time? But it's your passion, right? Surely if he loves you, he would support that."

"Um ..." She scratched an eyebrow, her lips quivering as she forced a smile that didn't reach her eyes. "Yeah, I mean, maybe. I think once I have something to show for my decision, he'll be able to understand it better."

"Right," I said, rearranging the scowl that had no doubt taken up residence on my face.

"I'm sorry. I'm making this awkward. I invited you over for a meal, not a therapy session. None of this stuff is your problem."

The crazy thing was, I *wanted* it to be my problem.

"Don't do that." My hand twitched as she placed hers on the table a hair's breadth away from mine. "Don't apologize for the things you feel."

"Thanks. You're a nice guy, Gabriel." She drew in a breath before blowing it out again. "Anyway, I might have some exciting news to share with him soon. There's this writing competition for a magazine—Professor Benoit seems to think I have what it takes to enter, so I'm going to give it a go."

"That's very impressive." I marveled at the woman in front of me. How anyone, especially her boyfriend, could be anything less than amazed by her was a mystery to me.

"Yeah, well, first I need to put words on the page. At the rate I'm going, the submission deadline will have passed before I can so much as string a coherent sentence together."

"I can help with that." I grinned, letting a hint of mischief bleed into my smile. "I *did* volunteer to accompany you on your quest for inspiration."

Something sparked in her eyes. "Indeed, you did." She sucked her bottom lip into her mouth, making my thoughts scatter. "And when would you want to start this ... quest?"

Now.

"Tomorrow," I rasped. "How does the Louvre Museum sound?"

She nodded thoughtfully. "That sounds good. Only ..." She hesitated. "I have to ask, what do you get out of this? Helping me, I mean."

I smacked away a barrage of inappropriate thoughts, all tackling each other for precedence in my mind. The answer—the *real* answer—was simple.

"I want to see you win, Juliet. Not just this competition, but with your aspirations. I know how hard it can be to leave everything behind and chase a dream when you have no guarantee of success. And if I can improve the chances of you accomplishing your goals, even marginally, then that's all the reward I need."

She gave me a searching look, and I swallowed hard, hoping what I'd said was true.

Because there was no world, no universe in which I would ever allow myself to hope for more.

Seven

Juliet

"Wow, that's incredible."

Ember's face, clad in a rose oil facial mask, filled the screen as I held my phone up so she could take in the scene. It was Sunday afternoon, and I was standing in the sun-streaked courtyard that housed the entrance to the Louvre Museum, waiting alongside hundreds of other people all eager to wander its halls of world-famous art.

Although, the word *museum* was a bit of an understatement.

The Louvre was, in fact, a sixteenth-century palace, spanning a vast complex of wings and pavilions, all made of cut limestone and arranged in a wide U-shape around a courtyard. At its center stood a large crystalline pyramid made of metal and glass that glinted in the sun like a diamond.

Ember tucked a pillow neatly under her chin, stretching out across her bed. "So, what time are you meeting your sex-on-a-stick tour guide?"

"Um, can you please not refer to Gabriel that way?" I said as heat that had nothing to do with the sun warmed the base of my neck.

"Seriously?" She arched an eyebrow. "Tell me you don't find him attractive."

The warmth spread to my ears as I avoided eye contact. "Well, his features are pleasantly ... symmetrical. And he is of admirable height and build compared to the average male. But I'm not sure if I would use the word *attractive*."

Ember chuckled. "Oh, Jules, you are so cute when you lie."

A soft chime signaled a new text message. "He's here." I darted a look around the plaza. "But it's so crowded. I don't see him anywhere."

I spotted a stone pedestal a few feet away, and I hoisted myself on top of it. From this vantage point, I could see over the mass of people, and my pulse skittered when I saw Gabriel's form moving in my direction.

"Okay, I see him. I'm gonna hang up now."

"Have fun," Ember whisper-shouted, "and don't do anything I wouldn't do."

"Well, that's a short list."

"Ouch, the kitten has claws." She blew a kiss toward the screen. "Okay, love you, bye."

I put my phone away as Gabriel approached, his eyes climbing the length of my body.

"Hey," I said with an awkward wave. "I'm sure you're wondering what I'm doing up here, but you see, I'm vertically challenged, and I couldn't find you in the crowd, so ..."

He ran a hand across his mouth, his expression dancing with humor. "Uh-huh. I figured."

"Right. So, I'll just get down, then." I peered at the ground, which suddenly seemed a lot farther away than it had moments before.

With a steadying breath, I shifted my weight forward, summoning the courage to jump. Before I could, Gabriel was in front of me, his hands circling my waist. I clutched his toned arms, my nails digging into his sturdy biceps, as he lowered my body against his in a slow descent that stole all the air from my lungs. When my feet were once again on the ground, I looked up, catching the hard movement in his throat.

"*Là, saine et sauve.*"

I pulled out of his grasp, feeling dazed. "Thanks."

The sound of a violin filtered across the courtyard, its rich and complex tones washing over the silence between us as I searched for something to say. But honestly, what *did* one say after being lifted in the air *Dirty Dancing* style by a strong and admittedly handsome Frenchman?

"So," he said, interrupting my thoughts, "I got you something."

And he comes bearing gifts?

He reached into his pocket and pulled out a small, rectangular card, the words *Paris Museum Pass* printed across the front. "This will gain you access to most museums and other popular sites around the city." He took a step closer, opening the card to reveal a map of monuments. "See, there are quite a few places you can visit close to campus, so I thought this might come in handy if you ever have a free afternoon."

"Thank you. This is incredibly thoughtful. I can pay you back—" The words died in my throat as he closed a hand over mine, his eyes piercing me with a hard look.

"Juliet, let's get something straight from the outset. If I offer to do something for you or if I give you something, it's because I want you to have it. I'm not looking for repayment or return favors. It is a gift freely given. Do you understand?"

I bobbed my head.

"Good."

Ten minutes later, we descended the stairs beneath the pyramid, entering the main atrium of the museum.

"Wow, look how huge this map is." I unfolded it, allowing it to fall open lengthwise.

Gabriel chuckled. "That map is almost as tall as you are."

"Oh, ha ha, you're so hilarious." I skimmed over the four floors of exhibits ranging from Greek and Roman antiquities to artistic panels depicting Islamic poetry.

Gabriel hooked a thumb over his shoulder. "I'll go grab a couple of audio guides. While I'm gone, why don't you decide what you'd like to see first?"

I opened my mouth to protest, but he backed away, throwing me a grin before striding toward the visitors' center. I frowned, raking my eyes over the list of galleries. There was no way we could see all the art on display in a single day. Maybe Gabriel would be open to coming back again sometime?

Don't be desperate, Juliet.

Right. Self-admonishment complete, I turned my attention to the map, redoubling my effort to choose an exhibit.

After a few minutes, Gabriel returned, audio guides in hand. "Find anything interesting?"

"How do you feel about the Italian collection? I've been interested in Leonardo da Vinci's work ever since I took a class on Renaissance art in college."

"That's a good choice." He handed me a Nintendo 3DS that had been repurposed into an audio guide. I stared at it in bewilderment as Gabriel's lips ticked up in one corner. "One must admire French resourcefulness, no?"

I laughed, following him in the direction of the Denon wing.

As we ascended the staircase to the upper floors, I glanced at him from the corner of my eye. "Do you think we should see the French paintings first? We are in Paris, after all. Tribute must be paid, wouldn't you say?"

He slowed, his eyes painting a path over my features. "There is no *should* when it comes to art. Art is about what moves you, what inspires you. I want you to explore your passions, Juliet, whatever they are. My only aim is to satisfy your ... curiosity."

I exhaled, reaching blindly for the railing. *He's only talking about art.* And I was acting like I was sixteen again. No, actually, sixteen-year-old Juliet would be ashamed of me. She had a lot more sense.

I recovered myself by the time we reached the second floor, entering an elegant corridor that was nothing short of palatial. Arching skylights graced the ceiling and columns of beige marble divided the pale walls lined with rows of paintings.

It was breathtaking.

"Gabriel, look at this." I stopped in front of an oil painting, the words *Saint John the Baptist* printed on a placard beneath it. "This is one of my favorite pieces."

"*Vraiment?*" He drew up beside me, considering it. "It certainly is beautiful."

"Isn't it? Art historians believe it was da Vinci's final oil painting." My skin prickled with awareness as I felt Gabriel's eyes on me.

"Interesting. And what about this painting speaks to you?"

I measured my words carefully. I hadn't been lying when I said I developed an interest in da Vinci's work in college. But now, as I looked at the painting, seeing it—*really* seeing it—with my own eyes instead of in the pages of a book, Gabriel's words returned to me.

Art is about what moves you, what inspires you.

"The first time I saw this painting, I was mesmerized by its restrained palette and the way da Vinci used light and shadow rather than color to draw the viewer's eye." I stretched out a hand, tracing a finger over the lines of the image without touching the canvas. "See? The way he handled light brings our attention to the saint, while the rest of the scene he left in darkness."

"And why do you think he did this?"

The heat of Gabriel's body rippled over my skin, causing goosebumps to blossom along my arms. Had he stepped closer, or had I?

"It's hard to say. Historians say it was meant to be symbolic of John receiving God's light, but ..." I swallowed the rest of my sentence. I was no art expert, and my entire knowledge of the subject came from a one-semester course ten years ago.

What did it matter what I thought?

"Go on," he said, his voice softening as though he could sense my hesitation.

"Well, while I understand the mainstream interpretation of the image, I think the focal point isn't meant to be on the man himself, but rather the divine. See how his hands are positioned?" I gestured toward his left hand over his heart, his right pointing upward. "In my view, John wasn't the message—he was the messenger, sent to direct others toward something greater than himself."

Gabriel remained silent for a beat, and I fought to keep my eyes straight ahead even as I itched to see his reaction. Did he think my interpretation was ridiculous?

"You know," he began slowly, "I read somewhere that this painting may have been a derivation of a previous composition, one commissioned by the Florentine government. *The Battle of Anghiari*, it was called. Da Vinci never had the chance to finish it, but sketches show it featured my namesake in much the same position. Hand on heart, pointing upward."

"Your namesake? As in Gabriel the angel?"

His eyes slid to mine, drawing me into a gulf of blue. "*Oui, le seul et unique.* It is curious that your interpretation should be that this painting casts John as a messenger when its predecessor featured a subject whose purpose was to serve in the same capacity."

Oh. So not ridiculous, then.

"Do you think he resented it? Gabriel, I mean. Being sent as an intermediary whenever God intended to intervene in the matters of mankind?"

"No," he said, holding my gaze. "I imagine he was honored to serve. To guide those who only needed a little ... direction."

I swallowed, my pulse fluttering.

What was happening?

"*Juliet.*" Gabriel's voice called out in alarm a second before I heard pounding footsteps rushing up behind me, and I barely had time to react before someone slammed into me. I was immediately thrown off balance, the floor racing up to meet me in a blur.

I could only imagine what Kyle would say when he found out about this, how he would tell me I never should have come to Paris in the first place, how it was my fault for—

Arms. Two of them wrapped around me, breaking my fall and enveloping me in a masculine scent. And someone was yelling. I could feel the vibrations of a deep voice from where my ear was pressed against something warm and hard.

Gabriel's chest.

I couldn't understand what he was saying since he spoke in French, and when I tried to turn to see who the recipient of his ire was, I found his hand cradling my head, long fingers curling protectively around the base of my neck. Another voice joined in the sparring match, and Gabriel's hand pressed between my shoulder blades, his thumb moving in slow, soothing circles.

Was he aware he was doing that?

I drew in a deep breath before letting it go slowly. I'd been seconds away from smacking my head on the floor.

Talk about close …

No, this is close.

Without thinking, I relaxed into him, burying my nose in his chest. *Oh.* He smelled divine. How a man could smell so nice while being so angry was disconcerting. His scent was an earthy mixture of citrus and cedar and something else. Something that reminded me of sun-tanned skin and summer breezes. It was heady and male and lulled me into a protective embrace I never knew I needed. Or wanted.

"Juliet, look at me."

I tilted my head up, my gaze drifting over the elegant cords of muscle lining his throat before landing on the smooth curve of his mouth. I lifted a hand, my fingers inching toward his lips as an overwhelming desire to touch them—to feel them—consumed me.

I blinked.

Wait. What on earth was I doing?

I staggered away from him, heat licking my cheeks. "Oh, my God, I'm sorry."

"Hey, it's okay. I just want to make sure you're all right."

I let out a shrill laugh. "Oh, yes. Of course."

He frowned. "Are you sure you're fine?"

"Yes." *No.* A guilty pang reverberated in my core. I shouldn't have let myself get swept up in the moment like that. He'd just been looking out for me, and I almost crossed a line.

I ran a hand over my mouth, Gabriel's intoxicating scent still clinging to my skin.

I needed air. I needed a moment to regroup and get a grip on reality.

"I should go check in with Kyle."

I spun away from Gabriel, but not before I saw his face fall, crumbling like stone under the weight of what I had said.

And, perhaps, what I hadn't.

Eight

Gabriel

Well, that couldn't have gone worse. What the hell had I been thinking, grabbing her like that? I *hadn't* been thinking, and therein lies the problem.

The whole thing happened so fast—just a couple of asshole teenagers running in the museum. It shouldn't have been such a big deal, except it had become a *huge* fucking deal the minute they hooked a corner, barreling straight toward Juliet.

The moment they crashed into her, time solidified in my mind. I didn't remember moving toward her, only the feeling of all the air leaving my lungs when Juliet's body jerked on impact like a runaway train had hit her.

The rest had been a blur.

Eventually, I realized I was holding her, possibly even suffocating her if the way she wrenched out of my arms was any indication. And then I saw the look on her face. She looked *horrified.* And why wouldn't she be? I had no right to put my hands on her, no right to touch her at all. But something about seeing her in danger made me act purely on instinct, the result of which was her taking off.

To call her boyfriend.

Wonderful.

I dragged a hand up the back of my head, glancing down the corridor. Should I go check on her? She'd gone in the direction of the restrooms, but I hadn't followed because I wanted to give her space. That, and I'd been too stunned by her comment to move. But now that my pulse was returning to normal, the visceral need to make sure she was okay propelled me into action.

Moving down the hall, I paused when my phone vibrated in my pocket. My *phone.* Maybe I should just text her? That way, if she were still upset with me, I could save us both from any further awkwardness.

I pulled it out, swiping up on the home screen, and froze, all the heat draining from my limbs when I saw one new message.

From my father.

What did he want?

I chewed on whether to delete it like I had the other two he'd sent over the past month. We hadn't talked in three years, though that was doubtless due in part to the fact that I changed my number.

But that wasn't the only reason we hadn't spoken. There wasn't much to say after a man disowned his only son.

I flexed my fingers, a buzzing noise sawing in my ears.

Dammit. After all this time, he still had the ability to affect me. Just the sight of his name dredged up a host of painful memories, memories I thought I had long since buried. More than enough time had passed for me to put it all behind me. So why the hell did I still care?

His first message had come weeks ago while I'd been hauling paint across town after a trip to Maison Sennelier. I had just crossed the river, heading north toward Le Marais, the neighborhood that was home to my art gallery and studio, when my phone pulsed with a new message. I'd stopped to check it, thinking it was from James or Nora or, heaven forbid, my nagging art agent, Jean-Claude. But it wasn't from any of them.

Marcel Beaumont.

At first, I couldn't believe what I was seeing. The man I loved and hated. The man who gave me everything, taught me everything. And then took everything.

Is that gallery more important to you than all I have built for you? It's just a fantasy, Gabriel—a means to hold on to her. But she's gone. And she's never coming back.

The memory of my father's words cut as deeply as they had when he'd first said them, and with them came all the familiar emotions—the anger, the hurt, the disbelief. It had taken months after starting over in Paris for me to come to terms with what happened, but eventually, I did. I was finally able to put it behind me, and the last thing I wanted was to drag it all up again.

Some things were better left in the past.

"Excuse me."

My thoughts vanished like smoke, and I glanced down at a petite woman, her round face hidden beneath a layer of too-bright makeup.

"Um, *savez-vous*—err—*où sont les toilettes*?" Her French was heavily accented, her vowels elongated with an awkward emphasis on each syllable. An American, most likely, but at least she was trying.

"I speak English."

A relieved smile crossed her fuchsia lips. "Oh, thank goodness. My French is terrible." I nodded, looking over my shoulder and scanning the area for Juliet. "Would you be able to point me in the direction of the restrooms?"

I looked up at a sign overhead that read *Toilettes* before returning my attention to her in time to catch her twirling a blonde curl around her finger as she fanned her lashes at me.

Oh, for fuck's sake.

I hiked a thumb over my shoulder, looking away. "Just that way."

She let out a tittering laugh that grated on my nerves before stepping into my personal space. Was this woman serious?

I took a step back. "I'm sorry, but I'm not interested."

She smiled, looking thoroughly undeterred. "But I haven't told you what I'm offering yet."

Yeah, I knew *exactly* what she was offering. It was the same thing they all offered with the unflinching certainty that I would cave under the right pressure. The lingering brush of a hand on my knee, a generous glimpse of bare skin ...

God, had women always been this aggressive?

"Gabriel."

I whirled just as a warm hand slid into mine. Juliet appeared beside me, giving my palm a gentle squeeze. "Ready to go?"

"Yes." I didn't care that I sounded relieved—I was just glad to get the hell out of Dodge. The woman gave me a disappointed look as Juliet dragged me away, her hand wrapped firmly around mine. That is, until we were out of earshot.

"So, I guess this makes us even."

"Sorry?" I peered down at my empty hand now hanging where Juliet had dropped it.

Tiny lines framed her mouth as she suppressed a smile. "You looked like you needed rescuing from Goldilocks over there. You're welcome."

"Oh yeah, thanks for that."

She shrugged. "It was the least I could do after you saved me from a trip to the hospital."

Oh, right. I'd almost forgotten about the incident in the wake of being propositioned in broad daylight. I still needed to apologize for the way I manhandled her. "So, listen, I—"

"What do you say to skipping the paintings for now and checking out the Egyptian art?"

I blinked at her, startled. "Wait, you mean, you want to stay? You're not still upset?"

She frowned, tilting her head. "No, not really. I mean, those guys were jerks for running through the museum, and I hope security escorted them out. But otherwise, I'm fine." She gave me a small smile before squinting down at the map open in her hands.

Seriously? She seemed so upset before—why the sudden change in her mood?

An unpleasant thought slithered through my head. Maybe she had talked to her boyfriend, and *he* was the reason she was so at ease.

The muscles in my jaw tightened.

"You know ..." She wrinkled her nose. "I'm not sure how to get down there—"

"I'll take you." I shoved my hand into the crook of my elbow before I could do anything stupid like reach for her again.

On our way to the Near Eastern exhibit, I listened as closely as I could while she recited her knowledge on the history of Egyptian sculpture, but admittedly, my focus was elsewhere.

Namely, on coming up with a solid plan to make sure the rest of Juliet's visit at the museum was damn near perfect and that she had an experience she'd not soon forget.

Nine

Juliet

S orry, I'll have to read it another time. Not all of us are on vacation, kiddo.

I stared down at the text from Kyle, trying to make sense of what I was reading. Not that it was particularly confusing. I was just shocked at how easily he made me feel so insignificant—and in two sentences, no less.

Kiddo? Kyle was barely two years older than me, not to mention we were in the same class year at our firm since he had clerked for a district judge before becoming a full-time associate. And I wasn't on *vacation*. He was just baiting me. Again.

In the few exchanges we'd had over the past week, when he wasn't sending me two-word replies, he was prodding me with double-edged comments like this one as if he were itching for a fight. But

I refused to give him one. Instead, I exercised patience, making an effort to message him updates, pictures—anything to make him feel included in my experience here.

Though, after that last text, it was becoming abundantly clear he didn't want to be.

Glancing around the library, I pushed down my frustration and gathered up the empty snack wrappers from the table where I'd spent the day working. After a long week of attending classes, guest lectures, and writing workshops, Friday had finally arrived, and with it, the opportunity to crank out pages for my competition piece.

The idea for a short story had come to me after my trip to the Louvre on Sunday, and I'd rushed home to dust off my college notes on the Renaissance that were still saved on my hard drive.

The rebirth of art. The revival of classical literature. The rediscovery of humanism. All themes I had never contemplated outside of a classroom setting, but now saw as potential fodder for something creative. The tone of the piece would be more serious than what I usually featured in my writing. But I needed to produce something worthy of publication, and I was more than willing to go outside my comfort zone to do it.

I pulled my hair up in a messy ponytail and plopped back down in front of my laptop, tapping a finger against my mouth. After hours of churning out words, I was happy to say I'd completed a first draft. Not that it was a masterpiece, but still, I was proud of it.

Now for the challenging part: The Edit.

I'd never shown Kyle my romance novella. No doubt he would have just made fun of it. But this piece was mature and thoughtful—a story laced with symbolism and critical thinking. It seemed like something he might appreciate. Only he was too busy to read it, just like he had been too busy to answer my call on Sunday.

I racked my brain for who I could send it to for initial impressions. Grace would read it, but it might take her a while to get back to me. Ember would be willing too, but I never trusted my sister to be completely unbiased. I sank further into my chair, staring up at the overcast sky through the ceiling lined with windows.

Maybe I could read it aloud to myself? No. The truth was nothing could beat the perspective of an outside reader.

My stomach dipped as a new thought occurred to me.

Nope, no way.

Gabriel might be interested in reading my draft, but the idea of asking him made my stomach somersault, especially in light of the way I had behaved at the museum. I could only imagine how I had looked, all wide-eyed, staring at him like he was God's gift to women. *Which, okay, maybe he is.* There was no point in continuing to deny that he was divinely handsome.

Clearly, it wasn't doing me any favors.

What if I hadn't come to my senses? What if I had touched him like I wanted to? Would I have stopped there?

I had replayed the scene over and over again in my head while lying in bed on the nights that followed. It quickly became my favorite bedtime story.

And in the fantasy version, I didn't stop.

In the darkness of my bedroom, as I lingered on the precipice of sleep, I traced my fingers along the straight line of his jaw, running my thumb over the dip at the bottom of his chin before moving up to the soft curve of his mouth. Just as my fingertips brushed his lips, those ocean eyes flared with heat, and he grazed his teeth over the pads of my fingers followed by a lingering sweep of his tongue ...

I swallowed.

This was exactly why I shouldn't call him. I was completely unhinged.

I glanced down at my phone on the table.

I mean, I *could* message him. He had been nothing but kind to me. It wasn't *his* fault I had allowed myself to indulge in one too many nighttime fantasies about him. But that ended today. It wasn't fair to Kyle, no matter how much of a jerk he was being at present. And frankly, it wasn't fair to Gabriel either. He had made it clear he wasn't interested in anything outside of a platonic friendship, and I respected that.

Plus, I am a professional woman, dammit. I could carry on a no-nonsense friendship with a man. After all, I worked with men all the time at the firm. Granted, most of them were married or had a complexion that hadn't seen the sun in a decade, but still.

As I reached for my phone, my eyes snagged on a new message. *Gabriel.* I opened it, ignoring the slight tremble in my fingers.

Hey Juliet, hope you are well. I stopped by Café Procope to bring you a coffee, thinking you might be working. Guess I missed you.

Crap. When had he sent this? I exhaled when I saw it was from only a few minutes ago. Thank God. Biting down on a smile, I shot him a reply.

You brought me coffee on a Friday afternoon? You might just be my hero.

He replied a minute later.

I did. Then I realized I was bringing coffee—to a café. In hindsight, I'm glad you weren't there to witness it.

A laugh burst free from my lips, and I clapped a hand over my mouth as several pairs of eyes swung in my direction.

Well, you know what they say—no good deed goes unpunished. But if you feel like trying again, I know a girl across town who is working and in desperate need of caffeine.

Three dots appeared.

Just name the place.

Gabriel

I had never been to the American University of Paris's campus before, no less had a reason to explore the Learning Commons building. But I have to say, I was impressed. The building was new, with a contemporary facade and floors of functional space, and it took me only a few minutes to find the library. A cursory look around the high-ceilinged room lined with bookshelves revealed

Juliet at a corner table across from the entrance, her face hidden behind a laptop. My lips tilted into a grin.

What was with this girl and corners?

"I hope you like French press coffee." I placed the portable mug I borrowed from James in front of her as I lowered myself into a seat. I hoped the mug had held up and kept her coffee warm, but there was a fifty-fifty chance the promised "seven hours of insulation" was just bravado on James's part.

Her eyes landed on the mug before settling on me. "What's with the thermos?"

"Uh, most cafés in Paris don't have to-go cups. Unlike Americans, most French people enjoy their coffee sitting down rather than in transit."

"So that means you brought this from home?"

"Something like that."

Her eyes brightened, and she reached for her phone. "Excuse me, I just need to text Ember and let her know chivalry isn't dead after all." I chuckled. "So," she continued, setting the phone down after several seconds. "I wanted to ask you something." Her eyes dipped down as a splash of color filled her cheeks. "Would you ..."

I covered my mouth with a fist to stop myself from blurting out *yes* like an insane person.

"Well, I was wondering if you would read the piece I wrote for the magazine." The words left her mouth in a rush, as if she were expecting me to shoot her down. I couldn't imagine why.

"Sure, I'd be happy to read it."

"Really?" The color in her cheeks spread as she looked at me uncertainly.

"Yes, really. Let me see it, Chandler."

In a heartbeat, her face lit up, and she ducked her head behind her computer to hide the smile spreading across her lips. *Those lips.* It was hard to look at them without imagining them involved in a whole range of activities, all of them glorious and none of them the least bit friendly.

I had known I was in trouble where Juliet was concerned after our trip to the Louvre. Though, if I was being honest, I had known long before that. But it wasn't until Sunday that I realized just how strong my attraction to her had become.

For one fleeting moment, I'd thought maybe the attraction wasn't one-sided, that there was something behind the way she looked at me during that too-brief moment when I held her in my arms. But she had absolved me of that delusion when she ran off to call her boyfriend.

So, what was I doing here?

"Okay." She turned her laptop toward me before hiding her face.

"Seriously? Are you going to hide behind your hands while I read your work?"

"Yes. I'm shielding myself in case you don't like it."

On impulse, I took one of her hands in mine, ignoring the sparks racing across my skin from the point of contact. "Don't hide, Juliet. Art is about honesty. You can't be afraid of people's reactions, no matter what they are. As long as you bring your most authentic self to the page, that's all that matters." I set her hand down on the table, drawing mine back with more than a little effort. "Besides, I'm sure I'll like it."

She chewed on her lip in a most distracting way. "How do you know?"

"Because I like you."

Stop. Fucking. Talking.

Without waiting to gauge her reaction, I scanned the open document. It was a lot longer than I'd expected it to be, well over fifty pages. Had she really written this in just a week? I scrolled to the halfway point, deciding to start in the middle.

And ...

"What was that look?"

"Hmm?" I said, my eyes still glued to the page I was reading. "What look?"

"Just a second ago. Your eyes got all big, and you covered your mouth like you wanted to hide your reaction."

"It was nothing." I scratched my eyebrow. "I don't think I should say."

Her eyes narrowed. "Tell me."

"Well, I was just wondering how Colton and Harley managed to, um ... I mean, that tool shed seems pretty cramped, not to mention all the dangerous objects in there. But I guess Harley's pretty flexible so—"

"*What?*" Juliet snatched the computer. "Oh, fuck my life."

Her face metamorphosed through a parade of emotions, all while I fought like hell to keep my face straight. "Is that not what you wanted me to read?"

"No," she whined, burying her face in her hands. "This is my romance novella."

Do. Not. Laugh. "Well, I liked it. It was very … illuminating."

"Yeah, about as illuminating as a tour of my underwear drawer."

I slid a hand over my mouth, losing the battle to a laugh as she peered at me from between her fingers. Her lips curved. "It's not funny."

"Nope, not funny in the slightest." I ran a thumb along my bottom lip. "So, what was that you were saying about a tour of your underwear drawer?"

She swatted me on the shoulder just as the door to the library swung open and a group of students entered, the hum of their conversation like a swarm of bees filling the quiet space. A dark-haired woman at the front of the horde drew up short, blinking at me before shifting her gaze to the left.

"Juliet." The woman crossed the room, her high heels clicking. "Hey, chica, I thought that was you." She planted a hand on her hip, her red fingernails hooking over the hint of bronze skin peeking out from beneath her lacy top.

"Marlena," Juliet said, her smile oddly tight. "To what do I owe the pleasure?"

She laughed, flashing a row of straight teeth. "Come on, we're classmates. I can't stop by to say hi without having a reason?" Her dark eyes drifted to me. "Who's your friend?"

Juliet stiffened noticeably. Or maybe it was only noticeable to me.

"Um, this is Gabriel. Gabriel, this is Marlena from—"

"*Encantada de conocerte*." She extended a hand, leaning forward and giving me an unrestricted view of her cleavage.

I darted another look at Juliet, only to find all the warmth gone from her eyes as they ticked from me to Marlena. "Nice to meet you." I clasped Marlena's hand for half a beat before letting go. "Any friend of Juliet's is a friend of mine."

Marlena's eyebrows lowered a fraction, her smile faltering as she cast a look in Juliet's direction. Juliet, for her part, remained silent, her expression shuttered.

"Right," Marlena said. "So, Juliet, you're coming out with all of us tonight, aren't you?"

Juliet's eyes snapped up, her mouth falling open. "I'm sorry, what?"

"Out with us tonight, silly." Marlena turned to me. "Some students from our program are going to check out this new club tonight. It's supposed to be super exclusive, but I pulled some strings. You're welcome to come, too, of course."

I bit down on my cheek, a rejection dancing on my tongue. I didn't like bullies, and if Juliet's discomfort was any sign, she and Marlena were anything but friends.

But ... maybe I could use the situation to my advantage.

"I'd love to." My eyes ticked to Juliet's, catching her look of surprise. "Only if you'll be there." Some of the familiar glow that reminded me of sunset returned to her cheeks.

"Well, I suppose I could come out for a bit—"

"Great. I'll text you the details." Marlena gave me a departing wink. "See you tonight."

Ten

Juliet

"Coming."

I fumbled into my black leather ballerina flats, not bothering to secure the ankle straps as I rushed toward the front door. After returning from the library, I had spent the better part of three hours showering, shaving, and tearing apart my closet, trying to find something decent to wear for tonight's outing.

It was safe to say it had been a *long* time since I'd gone out clubbing.

Eventually, I had called Simone for a second opinion and was relieved to discover she was coming out too, having received a last-minute invitation from Carter, another classmate who I suspected might have a thing for her. Whatever the reason, I was glad she would be there. After Marlena's stunt earlier, I had a feeling I would need reinforcements.

After a half-hour conversation, Simone had insisted there was no way she could "properly assess my look" without seeing it in person, so we agreed she would swing by my apartment to finish getting ready together before meeting up with the rest of the group.

Pausing by the hallway mirror, I smoothed my hair back, tucking a loose strand into the bun at the nape of my neck.

I was wearing my favorite silk blouse from Bergdorf's and a pair of high-rise skinny jeans that Ember always said looked flattering on me—or, to use her words, made my ass look great. To complete the look, I had donned the diamond studs my grandmother had gifted me on my twenty-first birthday as well as a thin, gold bracelet that had belonged to my mother.

Not too shabby, all things considered.

I scurried to the door and flung it open to find Simone standing on the threshold in a neon-green skater dress with matching heels, her long braids piled up in a high ponytail. I blinked, noting the garment bag she had draped over one arm, a small duffel slung over the other. It was a wonder she'd been able to manage the stairs while hefting such a load.

"Hey, babe." She air-kissed both my cheeks before stepping past me into the living room. She let out a low whistle. "Wow, nice place."

"Thanks." I gestured toward the bags. "What's all that?"

She crossed the living room in three long-legged strides, dumping them onto the sofa. "Oh, I just brought some extra things in case I changed my mind about this outfit."

I plucked my lower lip. "I think you look pretty fantastic already."

"Thanks," she said, rummaging through her bag. "I just have to finish my makeup and then I should be ready to go." She glanced up, her brows drawing together as she skimmed me from head to toe. "What are you wearing?"

I tried not to wince. "Well, I didn't expect to be going to any clubs while in Paris so—" I broke off as a look of abject horror crossed her face.

"Oh no, girlfriend, you can't go like that. Marlena will have a field day." I had already brought Simone up to speed on all things Gabriel while recounting the details of Marlena's ambush earlier. "She's clearly on a mission to steal your man. You can't show up looking like you're going to a parent-teacher conference and give her an advantage."

"He's not *my* man," I said, ignoring the barb about my outfit. "I have a boyfriend." She waved her hand, dismissing my comment as she rifled through her garment bag, pulling out dresses that looked like no more than shiny bits of fabric.

"Lucky for you, we appear to be about the same size." She held up two dresses in front of her before discarding both. Pausing, she cast another look in my direction, eyeing my clothes critically. "You can take *those* off any time. We've got a lot of work to do."

Twenty minutes later, I stood in the center of my bedroom in a gold cowl-neck slip dress, the silky material hugging my frame and tapering just below my hips. It certainly left little to the imagination. I tugged on the hem to cover more of my thighs.

"Stop that." Simone swatted my hand away. "You look absolutely smoking. Now, shoes." I opened my mouth to protest, but she cut me off. "And don't you dare mention those ballet flats I found you in."

I folded my arms. "I'll have you know those are Tom Ford."

"And I'll have *you* know those are strictly for attending class and museum tours." She pulled out a strappy pair of Jimmy Choo heels. "Oh yes, these will do nicely."

I slipped them on as she moved to my side. "Well, you're already gorgeous, so we won't need much makeup. Maybe a touch of lip gloss and some gold bronzer to accentuate your cheekbones." She tilted her head, studying me for another beat. "Let's swap the studs for some gold hoops. Keep the bracelet, though. Oh, and one other thing—this bun has *got* to go." She reached for me, but I shimmied out of her grasp.

"What's wrong with my hair?" I raised a hand protectively. "I think it looks nice."

"Juliet, you can't be serious." When I didn't let go of my defensive posture, she released an exasperated breath. "Okay, listen to me. I don't know if anything is going on between you and this guy or if you even *want* there to be anything going on." I murmured something about Kyle, which she ignored again. "But what I *do* know is Marlena will not go easy on you. She carries herself like a woman who knows what she wants and, right now, she wants Gabriel."

I swallowed an uncomfortable knot in my throat.

"She won't hold back tonight," she continued, her tone softer, "and neither should you." After a beat, I nodded, and she grinned, pulling the pins from my hair. "Got a curling iron?"

As it turned out, Simone didn't just have excellent taste in clothes—she was also a magician with hair. In a matter of minutes, she turned my wavy locks into a cascade of shiny, loose curls.

Pinning up the front half and leaving the rest to hang down my back, she glanced at me over my shoulder. "So, what do you think?"

"I love it. You're like my fairy godmother."

Her eyes found mine in the mirror, sparkling with triumph. "You can thank me later. For now, let's go save your prince from Marlena's fiery wiles."

Eleven

Juliet

Ulterior motives aside, Marlena had been right about one thing. This *was* the place to be.

The thrum of music reached us as the elevator slid open, revealing a corridor with black marble floors. We made our way through a set of double doors inlaid with metallic carvings, entering a room packed with bodies. I glanced around, taking in the lavish décor.

Crystal chandeliers hung from high ceilings painted with frescos, and glass shelves holding expensive champagne lined the walls. Behind a bar with tufted leather bar stools was a wall of infinity mirrors, and across from that was a series of archways that led to a space bathed in dim lighting, a steady beat emanating from inside.

"Come on." Simone clasped my hand in the dark, pulling me toward the arches. "Carter said they're at a booth near the dance floor."

"Hang on." I fumbled with my clutch, extracting my phone as it pulsed with a new message.

Just arrived. Will be up shortly. – G

I clamped my lips together as a flurry of wings stirred awake in my stomach. *Don't*, I admonished, even as my body hummed with anticipation. This was just a fun night out with friends, and Gabriel was one of them. Nothing to get so worked up about.

"You go ahead. I'm going to find the restrooms."

Simone nodded before disappearing through the crowd as I headed in the opposite direction.

I found the ladies' room down a hallway lined with baroque wallpaper, and I pushed inside, grateful to find it empty. Setting my purse on the sink, I fussed with my hair, which, thanks to Simone's ministrations, was still in place, as was the gold eyeshadow, mascara, and nude lip gloss.

Admittedly, it looked pretty.

My phone vibrated again, and I fished it out, my pulse tripping over itself and revealing far too much. While my brain might have a clear understanding of the dynamic between me and Gabriel, my body wasn't getting the memo.

Was he looking for me? It had been at least a few minutes since he'd sent the first message—had he made it upstairs? I glanced down.

Kyle.

I stared at his name flashing across the screen. Seriously, could the man have worse timing? I spun around, ducking under the stalls to make sure the bathroom was empty before answering.

"Hey," he grunted, the steady tap of a keyboard clicking in the background.

Hey?

"What the hell, Kyle? I've called you like a hundred times. Where on earth have you been?"

"I've been busy. We're in the middle of trial prep, and I've been working crazy hours. I assumed if it were something important, you would have let Ember know."

"So, let me get this straight—you didn't return my calls because you thought what I had to say wasn't important? You've got to be kidding. You're my *boyfriend*. Whether or not it's important, I should be able to call you without you blowing me off."

The sound of the keyboard stopped. "Juliet, don't act like a child. I realize I may have neglected you a bit over the last few days, but—"

"Few days? Try weeks."

"Days, weeks—whatever. I'm sure I don't need to remind you that you're the one who took off to another country. Sorry if I don't have time to coddle you from four thousand miles away."

"Coddle me?" I set the phone down on the edge of the sink, placing it on speaker. "Okay, seriously, what is your problem? I get that this whole Paris thing was sudden and maybe you feel like I'm interrupting your plans—"

"Torpedoing them would be a more accurate description. Honestly, what the hell are you thinking? You are single-handedly risking everything we've worked for these past years."

A hard lump rose in my throat, my ears pounding with a rush of blood.

"You should be *here*," he barreled on, "not off wasting time writing poetry or whatever the fuck it is you're doing. Did you even think about the ramifications to your career? You should be focused on impressing Tom if you want to be considered for equity partner in a few years."

I paused at the sound of footsteps in the hallway, but the door remained closed.

"And what if that's not what I want?"

"Don't be ridiculous. Of course it's what you want. It's what we've always wanted."

I shook my head. "No, Kyle, it's what *you've* always wanted. I'm still figuring it out. All I know is, before I came here, I was really unhappy. And I tried to keep my head down and forge ahead, but coming here woke up a part of me I didn't realize had been lying dormant. I know it will be an adjustment, but I want to take writing more seriously. I might even have a shot at publication and who knows where that could lead."

"Oh, give me a break, Juliet. That's a hobby, not a career. Are you seriously going to throw away everything you've worked for so you can spend your life making up stories?"

"It's what I love, Kyle. It's who I am."

I was holding my breath. Maybe the whole world was holding its breath.

Please say you support me. Please tell me you understand.

"Un-fucking-believable. Who are you right now? I don't know if this is some kind of premature midlife crisis, but you need to get your head on straight before you lose your opportunity." He paused. "Before you lose *me*."

My entire body went rigid. *Before you lose me.* Did he really say that? I braced myself against a wall, swallowing lungfuls of air, but I still couldn't get enough oxygen. And my face—why was my face wet? Grabbing a handful of paper towels, I glanced in the mirror to find my cheeks streaked with tears. I hadn't even realized I'd been crying.

"Shit, I shouldn't have said—"

"No, I'm glad you did. It needed to be said. To tell you the truth, I think you love the *idea* of me, Kyle. The version of me that's cooperative and pliable and spends seventy hours a week at work without complaining. But the real me? You don't know her at all. And you sure as hell could never love her."

A protracted silence echoed through the phone as the distant sound of music vibrated against the door. I waited for him to say something, to tell me I was wrong. Because, surely, I had to be. I stared at my reflection, the past four years flashing before my eyes. Four years of birthdays, family get-togethers, weddings, holidays. Nights spent working late and sharing cartons of Chinese food across a conference table. Sundays grabbing brunch near Central

Park with our friends. It all had to count for something. It just had to.

"Kyle?" My voice was a broken thing, and I hated the sound of it.

The thing about the ending of a relationship is it rarely happens all at once. It's easy to believe the narrative of Hollywood, that breakups can be summed up in a two-minute scene where an unsuspecting guy or girl gets dumped at a restaurant or in the on-call room of a hospital, and they never saw it coming. But in real life, breakups happen a little at a time. One misunderstanding left unaddressed turns into an ocean of unsaid things. Two people realizing they aren't as compatible as they once thought but are too afraid to let go. Three weeks of silence uncovering years of truths that hovered just beneath the surface of fake smiles and tepid complacency. And, sometimes, by the time all the little cracks and fissures are exposed, it's too late to stop the whole thing from coming apart and shattering into a thousand pieces.

I exhaled a shaky breath. "It's over, Kyle. We're done."

"Jules—"

"I'll call Ember in the morning and have her arrange packing my things from the apartment. She has a spare key, so—"

"The fuck you will." The sound of a door slamming shocked me into silence. "Enough of this. You do not get to abandon your responsibilities to go chase some bullshit fantasy. And you certainly do not get to walk out on me. I've tried to be patient with you, but

I see that was a mistake. I want you back in New York. Playtime is over."

I gripped the sides of the sink to stop my hands from shaking. "No, I'm not leaving."

"Juliet, I swear, you had better get your ass on a plane or—"

"Or what, Kyle? I'm not your property."

"I am not fucking around with you." He was shouting now, his voice ricocheting off the bathroom walls. "Do *not* test me. You think just because you've spent a few weeks having your ego pumped by some limp-dick professor you can challenge me? Well, I hate to break it to you, sweetheart, but you're not that special. And this—New York, your career—*this* is your reality. Now, I want you on the next flight home, or so help me—"

The door to the bathroom flew open, banging against the wall, and I nearly jumped out of my skin when I saw Gabriel thundering across the room like an angel of death, his face a mask of fury. Without looking at me, he snatched the phone off the counter.

"Hey, asshole, want to threaten someone your own size?"

"What—who the hell are you?"

"The guy who's going to put you in the fucking ground if I ever hear you speak to her that way again." Gabriel disconnected the call, tossing the phone down.

A moment passed, possibly two, and then he closed the distance between us, cradling my face in his hands and tilting my head up to meet his gaze. His cobalt eyes were a sea of emotions, anger warring with concern as he traced his thumbs over my damp cheeks. The tenderness of the gesture shook something loose inside me. As long as I could remember, I'd always had to be the strong one. For Ember, for my grandparents, for the people who relied on me at work. But just now, looking at him, I didn't have to be.

My face crumpled as the tears that had dried up fell again, and he pulled me into his arms.

"Hey, it's all right," he whispered against my hair. "I've got you."

He extracted the paper towels bunched in my hand and gently wiped my face, taking care not to ruin my likely already ruined makeup.

"What are you doing here?"

He grinned. "I was invited, remember?"

I released a watery laugh. "No, I mean, what are you doing *here*, in the ladies' room?"

"Oh, that. I found your friends at their table. The tall one in the green dress told me you had gone to the restroom, so I came to find you." Finished with the paper towels, he tossed them into the wastepaper basket. "There you are. Right as rain, *ma chérie*."

I tentatively touched my flushed cheeks before fumbling through my purse for my compact powder. Hazarding a glance in the mirror, I blew out a sigh of relief when I saw my face wasn't a total wreck. Thank goodness for waterproof mascara.

As I set about reapplying my concealer, I glimpsed Gabriel in the mirror and froze. His eyelids had fallen to half-mast, his expression unreadable as his gaze dragged slowly over me. Finally, his eyes lifted again, locking on mine.

"You look …"

I turned to him, taking in his tailored blazer, gray T-shirt, and dark wash jeans, his usual mess of dark curls slicked back, exposing the strong cut of his jaw. I wet my lips, and goosebumps spread over my flesh when he tracked the motion with his eyes. Hesitantly, he brushed a lock of hair away from my face, his hand lingering, gently tracing the shell of my ear. I sucked in a shallow breath, my eyes fluttering closed as a shiver worked its way up my spine.

"We should go," he said, his voice rough, "before your friends wonder what's become of you."

I nodded absently, wondering the same thing.

⤛⤜

Gabriel held my hand as he shouldered through the crowd, charting a path toward the archways at the other end of the foyer. Stepping through one archway, we entered a large, open area bathed in muted purple lighting, the scent of alcohol and warm bodies filling the air. I scanned the cushioned VIP booths lining the wall and caught sight of a splash of neon green at the booth nearest the dance floor. Simone waved at our approach.

"Hey, babe, I thought I'd lost you. Thank goodness Gabriel went to find you." Her eyes dropped to our interlaced fingers before she shot me a wide-eyed stare, her face splitting into a grin. Evading the question in her eyes, I looked around at the group assembled at the table.

Beside Simone sat Carter, his arm slung over her shoulders as he chatted with someone I didn't recognize. At the other end of the booth was Emile, his hulking form taking up at least two seats with the width of his manspread; next to him was Karin, a slender brunette from Sweden; and Dean, the only other New Yorker in our program. At the center of them all was Marlena, sitting in a little black barely there number, laughing and holding a glass of champagne.

The second she clocked our arrival, she smiled, throwing her arms open in greeting.

"Juliet, you made it." I watched as she zeroed in on our linked hands. "Gabriel, come and sit here." She patted the space beside her. "Dean was telling me the most incredible story about the Paris cabaret scene, and I am dying to get a local's opinion." Her dark eyes ticked to me. "You don't mind if I borrow him for a minute, do you, Juliet?"

I pasted on a smile, my body tensing. "No, of course not." Gabriel shot me a surprised look, and I shrugged. "You should go and mingle." Marlena nodded, beckoning him with a feline grin, and I had to bite my tongue hard to stop myself from taking back my words.

Gabriel frowned. "Are you sure?"

Truthfully, I was about the furthest thing from sure, but I didn't want to look like I was intimidated in front of Marlena. It would only give her more ammunition.

"Don't worry," Simone said to Gabriel, interrupting my pro-longed silence. "I promise to take good care of her until you get back." She moved over to make room for me, and Gabriel hesitated another beat before nodding and releasing my hand.

I plopped down on the cushioned seat next to Simone.

"Everything all right? You were gone a long time."

I shook my head, recounting the details of my blow-up with Kyle.

"What a selfish bastard." She grabbed a bottle of champagne and poured two glasses, handing one to me. "Here's to leaving be-hind everything holding you back from the life you deserve."

"Here's to making new memories." I downed the champagne, my eyes flicking to Gabriel's darkened form. Unfortunately, the look didn't go unnoticed, and Simone flashed me a wicked grin. I rolled my eyes, smiling despite myself.

Around my fifth glass, Simone, Carter, and I started up a con-versation about the sites we wanted to visit in Paris.

"We should go see the catacombs together," Carter said to Si-mone, slurring as his gaze dipped to her thighs. "Who knows what interesting things we might discover."

"Are you asking purely out of academic interest?" she said, her lips curving upward.

"Nope, not at all," he said with a drunken wink, and I snorted a laugh a second before Simone elbowed me in the ribs. Carter blinked at me, seeming to remember my presence. "What about you, Juliet? What places are you interested in?"

"Art museums, mostly. Although Paris is bursting with artistic works in a variety of places, from cathedrals to palaces. It's hard to know where to start."

"Luckily for her," Simone chimed in, "she has a knowledgeable tour guide who I'm sure would love to show her what's what about art ... and many other things."

"Simone, honestly," I said, my neck sparking with heat.

"Oh, please. He hasn't been able to keep his eyes off you this entire time."

Giving in to impulse, I looked in Gabriel's direction and found him leaning forward, resting his elbows against his knees as Marlena prattled on beside him. As if sensing me, his eyes rose, glinting like sapphires as he locked me in the intensity of his gaze. My pulse skipped when his mouth hooked up in a slow grin. The beginnings of a smile traced across my lips, but before it was fully formed, Marlena leaned over to whisper something in Gabriel's ear. I froze, a trickle of ice sliding through my veins.

"What the hell?" I heard Simone say, but I couldn't tear my eyes away from the sight of Marlena in Gabriel's personal space, her hand lingering on his knee. "Um, Juliet?" Simone swiveled in my direction. "Are you just going to sit there and let her hit on your man?"

"For the last time, he's not my man. We barely know each other." I swallowed each word like jagged glass. "He's an adult. He can make his own decisions." I reached for the champagne bottle, but Simone batted my hand away.

"Uh-uh. No way are we letting her get away with this. Let's go, party princess." She seized my hand, dragging me upright and toward the dance floor.

"Where are we going?" I hurried after her, stumbling under the influence of one too many glasses of champagne.

"Marlena may think she's won the battle, but you're about to win the war."

Twelve

Juliet

The dance floor sparkled like starlight, its surface shimmering with LED lights beneath a sea of people dancing. I looked over my shoulder, peering through the throng to where Gabriel was seated, but Simone clasped my chin, turning my face toward her.

"Eyes on me, babe. Trust me on this."

I blinked in confusion. "But—"

"Forget about what's going on over there. Just let the music take you." I watched as she moved, her hips rocking in sync with the beat. I brushed a hand over the base of my throat, a weak laugh trickling past my lips.

"Um, Simone? I hate to tell you this, but I'm not the best dancer." If her master plan depended on my ability to cut a rug, we were doomed.

"Nonsense. *Everyone* can dance. It's just a matter of whether you're willing to let yourself. Here, close your eyes." I hesitated before complying. "Dancing is a sensory experience—sight, touch, sound. Just listen to the music." I exhaled, focusing on the vibrations around me. The sultry sound of a voice rising over undulating notes, the steady thrum of the tempo, the electric pulse ...

"Now, however the music makes you feel, lean into that. Let it take over your body." Her hands coasted over my hips, moving them to the rhythm.

My eyes flew open. "Simone, I—"

"Trust me," she said again, stepping back and leaving me like a kid without training wheels.

I pressed my eyelids shut as I focused on the music again. After a few moments, I realized I didn't feel as self-conscious when my eyes were closed, and some of the anxiety loosened in my chest as I swayed, feeling the beat drumming in my body.

"Yeah, babe, now you've got it."

I breathed a laugh, relaxing as Simone twirled me around, the strobe lights flashing in the darkness and reflecting off her pretty brown skin. I watched as she moved effortlessly, and I mimicked her movements, rocking my hips and swinging my hair.

Carter appeared at her side as the lights dipped low, bathing the room in a red hue. She winked at me as he pulled her back against his chest, his hands gliding over her slender frame. I tossed her a smile, squeezing her hand before retreating a few steps to give them space.

Lifting my arms overhead, I danced on, my fear giving way as I lost myself in the rhythm, my body moving freely as my inhibitions melted away. I couldn't remember the last time I'd let loose like this or had this much fun. It was exhilarating.

"Hey, sexy, want to dance?"

A sweaty hand fastened around my wrist, and I whirled to find a guy with greasy hair leering at me, his open collar revealing a tangle of chest hair. Before I could protest, he dragged me against him, his warm palms slithering over my arms.

"Hey," I shouted, shoving him as he banded an arm around my waist, his free hand coasting down my back before landing on my ass.

"Be easy, love. We're just having a good time." He yanked me closer, encasing me in a cloud of cheap cologne. My stomach turned. "Listen," he said, the scent of whiskey filling my nose, "do you want to get out of here? I know a place we can go nearby—"

A firm hand clamped down on his shoulder, jerking him roughly away from me.

"Mind if I cut in?"

Like an apparition, Gabriel appeared at my side, the surface of his expression calm even as his eyes burned with hostility.

My sketchy dance partner's mouth hinged open. "Hey, who do you think—"

Gabriel cut across him. "Walk away. Now."

The guy clearly had no desire to comply. He stood his ground as he sized Gabriel up, no doubt weighing his odds should the situation descend into a physical altercation.

Gabriel glowered at him. "I won't ask politely a second time."

The guy threw me another glance, then scoffed and pushed his way through the crowd.

"Are you all right?" Gabriel turned to me, brushing my cheek lightly with his knuckles.

"I'm fine. That guy was just ..." I shivered in disgust, batting away the lingering scent of his foul cologne. I peered up at Gabriel. "Did you come over here just to save me again?"

"What? No, I saw you with Simone, and I was working up the nerve to come and ask you to dance. I was headed this way when I saw that creep put his hands on you." A muscle feathered in his jaw, a hint of his irritation resurfacing.

"Where's Marlena?" I hated myself for asking, but the champagne had loosened my tongue.

A look of confusion darted across his features before slowly giving way to understanding. One corner of his mouth lifted. "I have no idea."

The music changed to a slower tempo, and he held out a hand to me in silent question. I hesitated before placing my palm in his, my heartbeat scattering as his eyes flickered with heat. He drew me against him, his familiar scent rolling over me, the warm and earthy notes mixing with something subtler. Something uniquely Gabriel.

He slid my hands over the hard planes of his body, looping them around his neck before his own ventured to my waist. I watched him from beneath my lashes, letting my eyes trail over the sloping line of his straight nose, the sharp angles of his cheekbones, the sensuous curve of his mouth. His hands shifted lower, and my breath hitched as his fingertips drew a line of pure energy over my hips.

"Is this okay?"

"Yes."

The rising notes beat a seductive throb in my chest, and my eyes fell to Gabriel's throat, the strong cut of his jaw. The urge to trace the shape of it, to feel the bite of stubble beneath the pads of my fingers, hit me in a wave, toppling my restraint. I reached up, cupping his face, and he drew in a sharp inhale when I teased my fingers into his hair, his curls soft to the touch. I lifted my gaze to his, his eyes pure black except for a thin strip of blue.

"Juliet..." His voice was husky, setting my nerve endings on fire, and a sudden recklessness took possession of me. I rolled my hips against him, and he let out a low groan. Digging his fingers into my waist, he pulled me flush with his body, and my core turned molten when I felt the evidence of his desire against my hipbone. He dragged a hand up to my face, painting promises against my flesh. And when his thumb coasted over my bottom lip, I sucked the digit into my mouth, my body purring as his eyes darkened with a predatory look.

"You have no idea what you're doing to me," he rasped.

"Why don't you tell me?"

"Keep it up and you'll find out."

I lifted my thigh, resting it against his hip like the vixen I had become over the course of a single dance.

He closed a hand over it, his breath hitching. "Tell me what you want," he whispered against my ear, grazing his teeth over my earlobe. "Because I'm about two seconds away from carrying you to the darkest corner I can find and doing some very indecent things to you." My heart thrashed against my rib cage, my adrenaline spiking.

Tell me what you want.

Everything. I wanted everything. With him.

"Take me home, Gabriel."

Thirteen

Gabriel

As soon as the taxi came to a stop in front of Juliet's building, I shoved the door open, tossing the driver a handful of euros before making quick work of lifting her into my arms.

Inside, I took the stairs two at a time, climbing toward her apartment as she clung to me, her sweet vanilla and lavender scent caressing my senses. I pressed my nose to her hair, and my knees nearly buckled as all the blood in my body raced southward. Reaching her front door, I set her down gently, the gold of her dress shimmering in the hall light.

That fucking dress. I had known it would be my undoing the second I saw her in it.

She fumbled for her keys, her hands shaking, and I gripped the doorpost, fighting the urge to help her. When she finally extracted them from her purse, they slipped between her fingers, falling to the floor with a deafening clatter. She looked up at me, her bottom lip disappearing between her teeth as her eyes shone with desire and a hint of … fear?

My jaw ticked.

"I'm sorry. I'm a bit nervous." She leaned down to retrieve the keys, but I reached out, stopping her. She stared up at me, her eyes wild, her chest heaving, and I inhaled slowly, leaning forward to rest my forehead against hers.

"Juliet, listen to me. We don't have to do anything. I didn't come out tonight with any expectations." Well, I *had*, but it had just been to spend time with her. I never imagined things would escalate so quickly. I swallowed hard. "I can leave right now. Nothing has to happen."

She brushed a thumb over my cheek, and I exhaled, some of the tension draining from my muscles as I let my eyes drift shut. If she wanted me to leave, I would without question. But I couldn't risk looking at her in that dress again.

It might give me a fucking stroke.

"I want you to stay," she breathed, raking her fingers through my hair, and a low moan pushed past my lips as her nails scraped over my scalp.

Opening my eyes, I found her green-gold gaze, and I cupped her jaw in my palm, tugging on her bottom lip with a thumb as her eyes misted over with a heated look. My cock pulsed.

Easy, boy.

"All right, I'll stay." I scooped the keys off the floor. "But I meant what I said. We can take it slow." I turned the key in the lock, sending up a silent prayer that I would be able to keep my word.

As soon as I entered Juliet's apartment, I was met with an explosion of color in the form of dresses flung over every available surface. The kitchen counter, the coffee table, her desk lamp.

In the living room, I spotted a scrap of red lace hanging over the arm of a wingback chair, and I clenched my teeth. Thank God she hadn't worn that tonight. If she had, I would have been forced to gouge out the eyes of any man who dared to look at her for half a beat too long.

"Sorry, the place is a bit of a mess." Juliet scurried around the room, snatching up the discarded clothing. "Simone came over to help me get ready, and it was a marathon deciding what I should wear."

I grunted, a streak of jealousy spearing through me at the idea of anyone helping her get dressed. I had no right to be possessive, but the thought of it made my pulse climb all the same.

If I was being honest, it had been the sight of Simone dancing with Juliet that had stirred me into action earlier. Marlena had looked thunderstruck when I excused myself, and under different circumstances, I might have tried to let her down easy. But seeing Simone with Juliet, twirling her around and making her laugh, had me ready to turn over the table in my desperation to get to her.

"It's fine." I plucked up the red garment. "This yours?" No sooner did she glance up to see what I was holding than her cheeks filled with color.

"Yeah, Simone gave it to me, though I can't imagine where I'd wear something like that."

I had several ideas of where she could wear it and all of them involved me being the only spectator.

She flitted over to me, relieving me of the item in question before darting down the hallway. I tossed my jacket over the back of a chair and sat down across from the fireplace, expelling a breath as I adjusted myself in my jeans.

Get it together, man.

I'd given Juliet my word about taking things slow, and I meant to keep it.

How quickly my resolve was tested.

Not a full minute later, she reappeared in the living room in an oversized T-shirt, the words *Camp Law School* printed across the top, and a pair of fuzzy socks.

But her legs were completely bare.

"Would you like a drink?" she asked as I tried to unstick my tongue from the roof of my mouth at the sight of her sun-kissed thighs. "I just bought a bottle of Cabernet Sauvignon." She padded over to the kitchen, returning with two glasses and handing one to me. Settling onto the other end of the sofa, she eyed me over the rim of her glass. "Did you have fun tonight?"

"Mm-hmm," I said, watching as she tucked her smooth legs beneath her.

God, please let her have something on beneath that shirt. As much as I prided myself on having a fair amount of self-control, I was sure as fuck at my limit.

"Good. I was worried I might have put a damper on the evening with that awful display in the bathroom."

I frowned. "That wasn't your fault, Juliet. Your boyfriend is a real piece of work."

She lowered her eyes. "*Ex*-boyfriend."

Something notched in my throat at the reminder that she was newly single and available for the taking. "Well, your *ex* is a jerk and doesn't deserve you." I took a sip of wine.

"What about you?" she said, watching me beneath hooded eyes. "Do *you* deserve me?"

I choked, eyes watering as I fought for air. "What?"

She set her glass down and crawled across the sofa toward me. My airway closed up completely when she slid onto my lap, straddling me. I fisted my hands at my sides, fighting the urge to touch her, to feel her warm skin beneath my palms. But I knew better. My restraint was dangling by a thread, and if I put my hands on her, all bets would be off.

"Juliet, you're making it damn near impossible for me to behave like a gentleman right now."

"Who says I want you to behave like a gentleman?"

My eyes shuttered as her lips coasted over my ear, and her hands disappeared beneath my shirt, her touch as soft as crushed velvet. I pushed out a heavy breath, my vision swimming as she raked her fingers down my abdomen, arching against me and grinding her perfect ass on my lap.

On instinct, my hands flew to her hips, her skin smooth beneath my rough fingertips as I traced them down the back of her thighs. "You're about to make a liar out of me, you know that?"

My hips rose to meet the apex of her legs as she rocked down on me, and my grip tightened as my lips moved to the slender column of her throat. She sucked in a breath, her breasts grazing my chest through our clothes and setting off a countdown in my head.

Five seconds. That was all the time I had left before I dragged her beneath me on this sofa.

"Juliet, look at me." She raised her eyes to mine, and I swallowed roughly. My dick would be petitioning for a new owner by morning, but I had to know she wasn't doing this for the wrong reasons. She had just broken up with that asshole and then drowned herself at the bottom of a champagne bottle. The last thing I wanted was to take advantage of her. And even if she wanted this, she needed to make that decision with a clear head.

"We don't need to rush into anything, okay?"

She stared at me for a beat, then pressed her eyelids closed, letting her head drop onto my shoulder. "I'm making a fool of myself, aren't I?"

"*Non, ma belle.*" I cupped the base of her head, sliding her silky strands between my fingers as my lips brushed her temple. "Believe me, I want you more than I want my next breath, but I respect you too much to risk you waking up tomorrow with regrets."

Her shoulders trembled, and for one horrible moment, I thought she was crying. Then I heard her snort softly. Closing my eyes, I smiled up at the ceiling.

"Why, Ms. Chandler, are you laughing at me?"

She lifted her head, pressing a hand to her mouth. "I'm sorry, it's just, sometimes I wonder if you're my guardian angel or something."

"I'm just looking out for your best interests, beautiful." She nodded, her shoulders relaxing as she rested her head on my shoulder again.

"Thank you, Gabriel."

I held her for a long time, drawing lazy circles on her back until the sounds of her breathing became deeper, more even. Lifting her from the couch, I carried her to the bedroom at the end of the hallway, settling her onto the bed before tucking her under the duvet. She burrowed beneath the covers in her sleep, and I smoothed her hair away from her face, memorizing the sight of her brown-gold curls spilling over the pillow.

Time to go.

I paused in the doorway. It felt like something had changed tonight. My attraction to her was a foregone conclusion at this point, but there was something else too, something stirring beneath the surface. It was almost as if ...

An unsettling feeling gnawed at my insides.

No. It wasn't possible. I hadn't even known her that long, just a couple of weeks. Grabbing my jacket, I pulled it on and made for the door.

Whatever else might be happening between us, I was at least certain of one thing.

There was no way I was falling for Juliet Chandler.

Fourteen

Gabriel

"Morning ..."

I peeled my eyes away from the tour schedule spread out in front of me as Nora strolled through the front door of Le Peloton Café, slinging her bag onto the couch and crossing the room without breaking her stride. She dropped a paper bag onto the counter. "I brought you breakfast."

"Thanks." I paused, my hand already halfway into the bag. "Wait, what's the catch?"

She smirked, plucking a piece of lint from her sleeve. "Oh, Gabe, always so mistrustful."

I eyed her for another beat before grunting and examining the contents of the bag.

In truth, I was starving, not to mention sleep-deprived. I'd barely gotten any rest after leaving Juliet's apartment last night, the memory of her soft skin tormenting me until long after the sun was up. Extracting a sliced baguette, I broke off a corner and slathered it generously with butter and jam before lifting it to my mouth. I paused, catching Nora's eye. "What?"

She waggled her eyebrows. "Late night?"

I regarded her coolly. "You know, until recently, I had no idea you were such a busybody."

She laughed, not bothering to deny the accusation. "Well, until recently, you weren't nearly as interesting." She propped her chin on her fist. "I heard you and Juliet went to a nightclub last night. I take that to mean things are ... progressing?"

I took a large bite, chewing slowly. "Good to know James can keep a secret."

"I'm sorry to be the bearer of bad news, but wife trumps best friend. He tells me everything."

"Does he now?" I lifted a brow, helping myself to a second slice. "What's my blood type, then?" Her cheeks pinkened after a long silence. "Thought so. A couple of gossips, the pair of you. Do you have nothing better to do than pry into other people's private affairs?"

"Private affairs, is it?" She snatched the half-buttered slice from my hand, taking a meaningful bite. "And to think I played a role in ensuring your eternal happiness."

I applied myself to coating another slice with jam, not able to smother a smile.

"As it happens," she continued, brushing crumbs from the corner of her mouth, "I've come to relieve you of the morning shift."

I frowned. "I thought James wanted me doing weekend tours to pay for the bike repairs."

"Oh, you've more than covered that with all the extra shifts you've been picking up. Besides, we know you have your art opening coming up. We're not total savages."

"Could have fooled me." I grinned as she landed a smack on my shoulder.

"Out, Beaumont." She paused, folding a grin between her teeth. "Unless you'd rather stay and share the details of your *private affairs.*"

She snorted in amusement as I collected my phone and wallet in record time, snatching up the bag with the last slice of bread and making a beeline for the exit.

Outside, I squinted in the morning light, contemplating what to do with the rest of the day. Heading down the street in no particular direction, I fired off a quick text to Juliet. My fingers hovered above the keyboard as I pushed down the urge to ask her what she was up to. After last night, I wasn't sure where things stood between us. The best thing to do would be to keep things simple and uncomplicated. Just because I couldn't get her out of my head didn't mean I should find a reason to see her now that my schedule was clear.

My phone pulsed with a new message, her name lighting up the screen.

Good morning to you too. Hope you're having a great day!

I drew up short, nearly swallowing my tongue when she followed her response with a photo of her sitting on her sofa in a loose-fitting T-shirt and pajama shorts, her hair spilling over one bare shoulder as she smiled at the camera above the lip of a coffee mug.

My throat thickened.

It was no good—I needed a distraction. Luckily for me, I had the perfect one.

⤞⤝

The gold lettering shimmered above the doors of the white brick building, reflecting shards of sunlight onto the concrete sidewalk. *Domus Dei.* I had chosen the name myself when I rented the building several months ago. *House of God.* It seemed like an appropriate name for an art gallery. After all, this was my sanctuary, my personal refuge. The place where I came to paint, to create, and to draw inspiration from the greatest creator of all.

Turning the key in the lock, I stepped inside, pausing to take in the stillness as the glass door slid shut behind me, sealing out the hum of the street. Warm light filled the space, slanting in through the skylight windows and sliding across white walls and pale wood floors. My shoulders relaxed at the smell of sun and air, of paint and fresh canvas.

Punching in the code to the security system, I crossed the main gallery to a door leading to a smaller space I'd converted into a studio. This room was less polished with its battered floors, vintage lighting, and exposed brick. But what it lacked in style, it made up for in comfort.

Against one wall was a weathered oak desk, cluttered with an assortment of sketches alongside my laptop, a brass work lamp, and a couple of framed photos. Opposite that was an overstuffed leather couch that I'd spent one too many nights on. The rest of the room was taken up with crates of supplies—bottles of acrylic paint, brushes, graphite pencils, drop cloths, palettes, canvases—along with several easels, propping up paintings in various stages of completion.

I loitered in the doorway, surveying the space.

Perhaps it wasn't much, but it was mine.

Dropping my keys on the desk, my eyes fell across the pictures in their frames. The one closest to the lamp was a candid of James, Nora, and me at a film festival last year. My face was twisted into a smile as James ruffled my hair while Nora looked on, a laugh splashed across her features.

I shook my head, grinning at the memory.

Slowly, my gaze shifted to the only other photo I cared to keep around. A woman sitting in a bay window, her dark tresses framing a heart-shaped face and falling over the sleeves of her sundress. She was gazing up at the camera, her blue eyes sparkling with amusement.

My mother.

When I first rented the building, I debated whether to keep her photo here, thinking it might be a distraction. But her presence was a welcome comfort, keeping me company for hours on end and whispering bits of encouragement only my soul could hear.

I collected a few items and settled onto a stool in front of my latest work-in-progress. The photo aside, I rarely sat down to paint without thinking of my mother. My passion for creativity, my devotion to art—it had been her gift, one that she passed down to me.

Growing up, it had been common knowledge in our house that my mother had given up her dream of becoming an artist to follow my father to the southern coast where he planned to open a restaurant. I never asked whether she regretted her decision, but it was clear she never lost her love for painting. It became a thing that was special to us both, bonding us together.

I could still remember those afternoons we spent on the terrace of our two-story terra-cotta house, sitting in front of a blank canvas and ruminating over the perfect shade of blue for a slash of sky or the right red for a sunset. I didn't know it at the time, but those moments would stay with me long after she was gone.

My mother died the summer I turned seventeen. The doctors said it was pneumonia combined with iron-deficiency anemia that took her, but the cause made little difference to me. The only thing I knew was, from that day forward, my world was forever changed.

In the months that followed, I considered giving up painting, the empty terrace a painful reminder of all I had lost in her. But, for reasons I couldn't explain, I kept showing up every afternoon whether or not I painted anything. Planting myself in her chair, I would envision an idea coming to life in a burst of color, holding on to my mother's love for creativity until, one day, the images in my mind found their way onto the canvas again.

Everything I had done since then, from those early efforts to the half-finished painting sitting in front of me now, was in honor of her memory and represented all she'd hoped for my future. And even though she wasn't here to see my work or the gallery, I had to believe, somehow, she knew her dream for me was coming true.

I yawned, twisting the cap off a tube of Quinacridone Magenta and squeezing a healthy measure onto a palette, mixing it with Ultramarine Blue. Most people don't know this, but the key to creating a vibrant shade of purple is to use magenta, not red. In a pinch, you could use Alizarin Crimson, but the red hue would dull the purple, creating a subdued color.

I had explained this to my father once, sitting in a booth at our family-owned restaurant while he hovered at the maître d' stand, writing out the evening's dinner menus. At the time, I was in my first semester at the local college and was taking a course on color theory. I *loved* that class. Was I aware the average person didn't find the visual effects of specific color combinations nearly as interesting as I did? Yes. Did I attempt to bring it up in every conversation anyway? Also, yes.

My father might have expressed a vague interest in what I was saying between asking me to check in with the kitchen staff and to inspect the table place settings, but if he didn't, I doubt I minded. That was the silent contract between us—I got to pursue my art studies, and he got my evenings six nights a week, working at the restaurant and learning the business. A win-win for everybody.

That is until it all went to shit.

To this day, I wasn't sure why I'd done it. Why, when my father confronted me on that humid summer night, his eyes flashing with anger and disappointment, I hadn't just told him the truth. The *whole* truth. I'd had my reasons, but those reasons didn't add up to much in the end. When it was all said and done, I still turned my back on him and walked away, the words I refused to speak bitter on my tongue.

I tried to convince myself I'd made the right choice in protecting the people I cared about. But in the end, they both betrayed me, and, whatever my motivations, the price of covering it up had been steep.

A knock at the front door drew me from my thoughts, and I paused, discarding my brush in a cup of water and wiping my paint-smeared hands on a rag. After a moment, the knock came again, and I tossed the rag down on a crate, making my way to the main room. I couldn't imagine who would be looking for me here. Only a few people even knew about this place—James and Nora, Jean-Claude, and the Uber Eats guy.

Passing through the door of my studio, I headed for the front door, only to halt mid-step when I saw who was standing on the other side of the glass.

Speak of the devil and he shall appear.

He looked much the same as I remembered. Ash-blond hair, clean-shaven square jaw, a hand tucked into the pocket of designer dress pants, a ridiculous-looking watch on his wrist.

Still an insufferable asshole, I see.

"Cousin," he said when I opened the door, his tone way too cheerful for my liking. "I must say, it's been too long."

I pressed my lips into a thin line. "Not long enough as far as I'm concerned."

His cool gray eyes slid over me as one side of his mouth tipped up, and I flexed my hand, weighing the pros and cons of just knocking him flat on the sidewalk.

"You're looking well." He nodded to my paint-splattered clothes.

"What the hell do you want, Lucien?" And how had he found out about the gallery?

He chuckled. "Still calling me that, are you?"

"It's your name, last time I checked," I said, my patience draining at an alarming rate.

He smoothed a non-existent crease from his shirt. "Come now, you know I've always hated that name. These days I prefer to go by—"

"Great story, but I really don't care." I moved to push the door shut, but he stopped me, pressing a hand against the glass.

"Wait, can I come in?" Perceptive as ever, he cleared his throat, not giving me the chance to tell him to fuck off. "I've been trying to get in touch with you, Gabriel. I even stopped by your place of business earlier this week, but your colorful employer said you weren't in."

My eyes widened before narrowing to slits. "*You* were the one who came to the bike shop?" I took a quick mental inventory of the description James had given me. *Tall. Blonde. Absolutely loaded.* Of course—why hadn't it occurred to me it might be Lucien? I snorted. Probably because I had spent the last three years trying to forget he ever existed.

Lucien nodded. "Yes. I've come because Marcel is looking for you."

Marcel. I'd forgotten Lucien called my father by his first name instead of *Uncle* or by any other acceptable term of endearment. But I supposed his general lack of human emotion tracked with the rest of his soulless personality.

"Yes, I am aware. If there's nothing else ..." I tried to close the door again, but he slipped one of his perfectly polished shoes in the doorway.

"He wants to see you," he said, dropping the friendly pretense. "He's tried calling, even texting—and you know how much he hates that. But you haven't returned any of his messages."

"Yes, well, that's typically what happens when one doesn't wish to speak to a person."

His eyes drifted to the pavement, hands returning to his pockets. "It's been three years, Gabriel," he said, his voice barely audible. "How long do you plan to avoid him?"

I glared at him, my teeth clamping together so hard I worried I would crack a molar. "I'm sorry. Did he think I would be home every year for Christmas after he disinherited me?"

Lucien let out a long sigh, a bored expression etching across his features as he straightened his cuff links. And that just pissed me off.

"And *you*," I snarled. "You have a lot of nerve showing up here. You're nothing but a traitorous snake."

Cold-blooded Lucien. Always slinking through life with his superior air of disinterest, unaffected by the affairs of mere mortals. If I didn't know what a heartless bastard he was, I might feel sorry for him.

His tongue darted across his lips, his face a mask of cool indifference. "I understand why you might feel that way, Gabriel, but there are things you don't know—"

"Let me offer you some free advice, *cousin*. Stay the hell away from me. I do not wish to see you again. And as for my father, he made his choice. Now he can live with it."

The barest hint of emotion flickered in his expression as we stared daggers at each other, the chasm between us growing wider with each passing second. Once, we had been, if not exactly friends, at least friendly toward one another. But all that was over now.

What he had done could never be undone.

After an extended silence, he retreated a step, a smirk pulling at his lips. "She's here, you know. In Paris."

My body went rigid, my jaw locking up as the anger blazing in my chest sputtered out.

Surely, he didn't mean—but, of course, he did. His eyes gleamed with triumph as he turned away, and I glared after him. *Well played, Lucien.* He might not have gotten what he came here for, but he wasn't walking away empty-handed either.

And we both knew it.

He waved a hand over his shoulder. "Just thought you'd like to know."

Fifteen

Juliet

"Dude, are those birds?" Ember drew the phone closer to her face, squinting at the screen.

"Why, yes they are," I said, cooing at one with olive-green plumage tinged with yellow, tapping a finger against the metal cage. I darted a look around the open-air market to confirm no one was looking my way, then grabbed a seed from the bird feeder and angled it toward my new feathered friend. He directed one beady eye at it before hopping along the wooden perch and plucking it from between my fingers. I grinned, gently stroking his soft wing. "I think I'll keep him and name him Hank."

"You're insane. You can't buy a bird in Paris. How would you even get it home?"

Reluctantly, I bid *adieu* to Hank and turned down an aisle lined with flower displays. "Um, you okay, Em? You seem a bit cranky this morning." I examined a shelf of pink azaleas, inhaling their sweet and spicy clove scent as my sister slumped face-first onto her heather-gray couch, burying her head beneath a throw pillow.

She murmured something unintelligible.

"Sorry, I can't understand you when you're smothering yourself." I paused to adjust the tie shoulder straps of my sundress. "Wait, don't tell me—you went to a five-star restaurant and found your date dressed in khakis and boat shoes." She grunted, and I nodded sagely. "If so, your reaction is completely warranted."

She flung the pillow at the screen. "No, although I agree that would be tragic." She rolled onto her back, her hair rising in a cloud of static. "It's the National Debutante Ball. Grandma got me a spot on the planning committee."

I drew up short, nearly stumbling into a potted fern. "Oh, my goodness. Em, that's fantastic. This is the perfect opportunity for you to flex your event planning skills."

Party planning was practically in my sister's blood. In fact, she was so good at it that at fourteen, she started charging the seniors at our high school to plan their house parties.

"No, it's not. Can you imagine me sitting around a tea table with a bunch of women in pearls trying to select a string quartet and, I don't know, shopping for tiaras?"

I snorted. "Debutantes don't wear tiaras. It's not the ball from *Cinderella*."

"It might as well be. I mean, the tradition is so outdated. It's just an excuse for society women to parade their daughters around in wedding gowns and advertise their good breeding."

"Well, actually, it's more about fostering community and supporting charity—"

"It's not me, Jules," she said, shaking her head. "I'd rather plan literally anything else. An amateur fashion show, a product launch. Hell, I'd even settle for a sweet sixteen party."

"Well, you should talk to Grandma. Tell her how you feel."

"And earn myself a lecture on what an honor it is to volunteer with such an *esteemed organization*? No thanks." She let out a heavy sigh. "Anyway, enough about me. What are you up to on this fine Saturday?"

I passed the last of the market stalls and darted across the street to the river, pedaling down a set of patchwork stone steps before dropping my bag and settling onto a patch of grass.

"Just exploring Île de la Cité. It's pretty close to my neighborhood, so I figured I might as well check it out." I thumbed through my camera roll, selecting a few pictures. "Here, I'm sending you some shots of Notre-Dame Cathedral."

"Ooh, isn't that the church *The Hunchback of Notre-Dame* is based on?"

I rolled my eyes at the mention of our favorite childhood movie. "Yes, and before you ask, no, I did not go up into the bell tower. The cathedral is still closed after that fire a few years back, but I got some great photos of the exterior."

"Ah, bummer." She shifted as Bailey climbed onto her lap, his wet nose sniffing the screen. "So, what's got you glowing then? Besides the almost-sighting of Quasimodo." I flinched, and Ember's eyes narrowed like a hound catching a scent. "Whatever it is, spill it."

I yanked on a blade of grass, winding it between my fingers. "Um, I broke up with Kyle."

Her scream detonated through the phone before I even finished getting the words out.

"Sorry," she said, flapping her hands without looking the least bit sorry, "but this is the best news I've gotten all week." She sucked in a breath. "Wait, we are happy about this, right?"

"That depends on who you ask. The Juliet from a month ago would have been torn up about it, but I realize now it was a long time coming. We wanted different things. Maybe even different ... people." Ember's eyes widened, and my mouth lifted in a grin despite my efforts to suppress it. "I also might have invited Gabriel back to my place last night." Another ear-splitting scream rent the air. "Ember, cut it out. People are going to think I'm committing murder in the bushes."

"Sorry," she said again, "but also, way to go, sister. I love this for you."

"You love that I broke up with my boyfriend and then immediately invited a guy over?"

"No, but if that's the way it went down, I'll be the last person to judge you." She tossed her hair over one shoulder. "What I love is you finally did what *you* wanted for a change. For the last few years, you've been all about making Kyle happy without ever stopping to consider yourself. Like the time you skipped out on front-row seats to the Beyoncé concert because Kyle wanted you to join him for dinner with some work colleagues. Or the time he asked you to drive to Philadelphia after you worked a fifteen-hour day because he wanted to go to the Eagles preseason game. Or the time—"

"Thanks, Em. Point taken."

She leaned against the couch cushions, sporting a pleased look. "And as far as you and Gabriel, I saw that coming from a mile away. You two were already caught in each other's orbit the day he came over to your apartment for a *late lunch*. By the way, is that what we're calling the horizontal tango?" She nodded thoughtfully. "Subtle, very subtle. I'll have to try that sometime."

A blush burned my cheeks. "It's not like that. We haven't even hooked up."

Her smile faltered. "But I thought you said you invited him back to your place?"

"I did, but he said he wanted to take things slow. That he wanted me, but he didn't want me to wake up with any regrets."

Her mouth popped open. "Wait, hold on. Does he have feelings for you?"

"What? No, he—"

"Oh, my God, he totally does. It all makes sense now. Taking you to the museum, bringing you coffee at the library, passing up on a perfectly good chance to score because he doesn't want you to have any regrets—it all adds up." Ember sighed, her expression taking on a dreamy quality. "I'm so happy for you. Now, let's get down to the important details. What do you think about a spring wedding? We should still be able to secure an appointment at an atelier and find you a dress within that time frame. Oh, and for the bridesmaids' dresses, can we please avoid pastels? It really washes me out—"

"Okay, seriously, stop." She blinked, startled, and I blew out a breath. "He doesn't do relationships, okay? He told me so himself."

Her expression collapsed, her former excitement flickering out. "Oh, Jules ..."

"I'm fine with it." I looked away, focusing instead on a boat moving up the river. "I mean, I do like him, but I'm okay with being friends. Just because we had a good time last night doesn't mean I have any expectations."

"Uh, I hate to break it to you, but you're a relationship girl, through and through. You're the falling-in-love, his-and-hers bathrobes, perfect-family-of-four type of gal."

"Yeah, well, I'm turning over a new leaf."

Ember's brows pulled together. "Really? Because I don't think—"

"In fact, I'm going to text him right now and see if he wants to hang out." As much as I understood my sister's concern, she was worrying for nothing. It's not like the attraction between Gabriel and me could go anywhere. What would we do after I returned to New York?

But all that was neither here nor there because Gabriel had already made his stance on relationships clear, and I had to respect that.

"There, done."

Within seconds, three dots appeared as Gabriel typed out a reply.

Sounds good. Where do you want to meet?

Ember chewed on the corner of her mouth. "Look, Jules, about what I said, about you being a relationship type of girl, you know there's nothing wrong with that, right?"

I waved a hand. "Of course, I do. But seriously, Gabriel and I are just friends." My lips pressed into a firm line. "And I'm going to make sure he knows it."

I approached the towering edifice that was Sainte-Chapelle, anxiety spilling over into my limbs like water sloshing over the rim of a cup. As soon as I hung up with Ember, I dropped the bravado act and let all the feelings I was holding inside trickle out. She was right, of course, as she so often was. But that didn't mean I *wanted* her to be right.

My fingers tapped a nervous beat against my thigh as I waited for the light at the crosswalk to change, my eyes drifting up over the Gothic structure across the street, its central spire looming ominously over me. I should have picked a different spot to meet, somewhere across town, so I had more time to collect myself. As it was, the walk over had only taken minutes.

Just friends, just friends.

I mouthed the words to myself as I passed the chapel's exterior wall and entered the main courtyard, trying to smother the memory of the last time Gabriel and I had been together. The feel of his eyes on me, his rough hands gripping my waist, his fingers finding their way into my hair …

I exhaled, shaking my hands to expel a fresh wave of nerves.

I was making a big deal out of nothing. My sister could hook up with a guy and forget his name before breakfast, but here I was, freaking out after one fully clothed evening with Gabriel.

Ridiculous.

I set my shoulders and marched beneath a stone archway.

Everything would be fine. I'd see him today and realize all was as it had been before, that nothing had changed—

"Hey."

I swung around to find Gabriel leaning against the archway, his biceps bulging against a soft, gray Henley, an easy smile on his lips.

"Oh, hi." I tried for a laugh that didn't make it out of my windpipe, and I coughed instead, eyes watering.

"You okay?" He kicked off the wall, striding toward me with a look of concern.

"Fine," I croaked, waving him away. "Have you been waiting long?"

"No, I just got here. Thanks for the invite, by the way. I haven't been to Sainte-Chapelle in ages."

He gazed up at it, and I studied his profile, tugging my lip between my teeth as a breeze moved through his hair. It had been so soft between my fingers, softer than I expected. I wished I could touch it again.

"Juliet?" My vision cleared as Gabriel lifted a brow. "Do you want to head inside?"

I blinked stupidly. "Oh, yes, of course. Um, I think it's this way?" I darted past him without waiting for a response, taking care not to brush up against his body in the narrow archway.

Get it together, Juliet. I wouldn't be able to convince him—or myself—we were only friends if I kept acting like this. From here on out, there would be no more lingering looks, no more touching, no more thinking about things I shouldn't.

Should be easy enough.

The interior of Sainte-Chapelle was mesmerizing. Tucking my arms against my chest, I wandered through the nave of the lower chapel, gazing up at the trefoiled arches and the sweeping golden ribs that supported the vaulted ceiling. Tilting my head back, I squinted at the ceiling, cataloging its deep blue surface dotted with tiny pinpricks of gold that reminded me of stars in the night sky.

"They're fleur-de-lis." Gabriel drew up beside me, nodding in the direction of the ceiling. "This chapel was commissioned by King Louis IX, and the fleur-de-lis was the symbol of the French monarchy."

I blinked at him. "How is it you know everything?"

His mouth curved as he lifted a hand, waving a pamphlet. "Why, Ms. Chandler, I would have thought you, of all people, could appreciate the power of reading."

"Wise ass." He chuckled as I returned my attention to the ceiling. "Well, in any case, it is quite beautiful."

"It certainly is."

Feeling the weight of his eyes, I looked over at him again, and my chest nearly collapsed in on itself at the intensity in his gaze.

Reaching for my hand, he locked his fingers around mine, steering me toward a spiral staircase. My pulse rioted.

Don't read into it.

Friends can hold hands, right?

On the second landing, he let go, and I peered around him, taking in the space beyond. Like the lower level, the upper floor consisted of a long chamber separated into four bays beneath a decorated vaulted ceiling. However, the upper chapel was brighter, each wall featuring a series of stained glass windows that filled the entire space with colorful light.

I darted a wide-eyed look around, pressing my fingertips to my lips.

So beautiful.

We circuited the room in companionable silence, examining the various panes of glass, each depicting a different biblical story. A few other people were milling around, but by the time we reached the far end of the sanctuary, a cursory look over my shoulder showed me we were alone.

I peeked up at Gabriel.

I supposed this was as good a time as any to clear the air.

"Gab—"

"Juliet—"

We blinked at each other, a trickle of laughter passing between us. Gabriel rubbed the back of his neck, and I smiled, pushing down a nervous flutter in my belly.

"Um," I tried again, "about last night …"

"What about last night?" he said, his eyes igniting with a heat I felt all the way down to my toes.

Um, *no*. There was no way I could say what I needed to with him looking at me like that.

Turning toward the altar, I studied a row of carved cherubim decorating an archway. "I just wanted to make something clear—specifically, I don't have any expectations."

A long beat of silence passed. "I see. And what exactly do you mean by that?"

I shrugged. "Just that nothing needs to change. We can continue as we were before. As friends."

"Friends," he said flatly.

"Mm-hmm." I smoothed a hand over my dress, feeling more confident.

Now that I'd initiated the conversation, all I had to do was double down, and, with any luck, I could assure Gabriel I wasn't looking for a relationship.

"We can keep visiting museums like we planned," I continued. "Or maybe you could show me some of your favorite places. In fact, I hope you will. I've made a list of interesting sites, but I'm sure to have missed some."

I had no such list, but I made a show of pulling out my phone and studying the catalog of recipes I kept in my notes app. After a few seconds of examining the ingredients for Tuscan Salmon, I looked up to find Gabriel watching me, his expression unreadable.

"Uh-huh." He traced a thumb over his lower lip, and my eyes tracked the motion, no doubt revealing what a horrible liar I was. "So, to be clear, you still want to explore the city together."

"Yes."

He nodded, slipping one hand in his pocket and ruffling the hair at the back of his head with the other.

God, did he have to be so effortlessly handsome? Between features that looked like they'd been carved by God himself and those lean muscles flexing beneath his shirt, it was all I could do to not climb him like a ladder.

And on that note ...

I put several paces between us, stopping in front of a statue of Saint Paul.

Ah yes, nothing like peering into the face of a saint to temper one's libido.

"What about going to restaurants?" I could feel Gabriel behind me, even though I hadn't heard a single sound to signal his approach. "If memory serves, you promised to let me take you to my favorite bistro."

"That would be acceptable."

"And the cinema? There are a few classic French films you might find interesting."

"Absolutely fine." I shook away the shiver on my skin as his shirt brushed against my back.

Friends, friends, friends.

I'd come too far to fumble this at the last moment. Maybe this was a test to see if I was truly unaffected by him. If so, I was failing miserably. I wanted him. Badly. But what if I gave in to this attraction and couldn't control my feelings?

My sister was right—I *was* the falling-in-love type. And, as much as I liked Gabriel, I couldn't risk that with a guy who didn't want a relationship. I turned to him, drawing on the last dregs of my resilience.

"Gabriel, I—" The words died on my tongue. The heat I had seen in his eyes before was gone, a raging inferno now burning in its place. I retreated a step, colliding with the wall as Gabriel consumed the space between us, caging me in with strong arms.

"And what about this?" he said, his intoxicating scent surrounding me.

"That's ...," I rasped as his lips ghosted over my jawline. "So, are we agreed?" My breath hitched as his mouth changed course, trailing down the side of my neck. "No expectations?"

He stilled, and I glanced up, my pulse skipping at his hardened expression.

"Gabriel?"

He didn't respond, only stared as I flattened my hands against the wall.

Did I upset him? Maybe I—

In a heartbeat, Gabriel's lips crashed into mine.

Sixteen

Gabriel

I had no idea what had come over me. Juliet was offering exactly what I wanted—no expectations, no commitment, just her time and company. And I hated it.

As soon as the word *friends* passed her lips, a feral ferocity seized me, making me wild with the need to claim her, to mark her as mine. To kiss her senseless and obliterate the word from her vocabulary.

The moment our lips collided, the heat of her mouth sank into every corner of my body, and I cupped her jaw, angling her head back for better access. Her lips parted on a soft exhale, and I dove in, my tongue dancing beautifully with hers as her fingers tunneled into my hair.

For a fleeting moment, I remembered we were in public, and in a church, no less. But I couldn't find it in myself to care as my mouth slanted over hers again and again in a kiss that was hot and hungry and spiraling out of control.

She released a throaty moan when my hand slid to the nape of her neck, and I hauled her closer, groaning into her mouth when her breasts pressed against me. *Fuck*, were her nipples hard? This needed to end and preferably before we got caught. And yet, the only thing on my mind, the only thing that made any sense to me, was hitching her legs up around my waist and taking her right here against the fucking wall.

"Gabriel." Her voice floated to me through a haze of lust, and I clung to it like a lifeline. "I want you," she whispered against my lips, tracing her fingers down my stomach before curling them in my waistband.

My throat was dry as sandpaper. "Can we go back to your place?"

"We could, but I think my landlord scheduled maintenance for this afternoon. I wouldn't want us to be interrupted."

I pressed my eyes shut, her husky tone heating my blood. I had to figure out something fast. Because I had no desire to add *defiling the house of God* to my list of sins.

Going to my apartment on the other side of the city was always an option, but the idea of taking a thirty-minute Métro ride in my present state sounded like a special brand of hell.

The only other option was ...

"Come on. I know somewhere close by."

The walk to the gallery took only fifteen minutes, but it felt much longer, tempted as I was to pull Juliet into every semi-secluded side street along the way. At least the sense of urgency was mutual; that is, if her white-knuckle grip on my hand meant she wanted me as much as I wanted her. I hoped so because I was just about tapped out on good behavior where she was concerned.

The second we reached the gallery door, I turned the key deftly, shoving inside. In the entryway, I caught her look of surprise as she peered around the space, and I paused, a hint of pleasure sliding into my chest. It was something to behold, watching this beautiful creature marvel at my unfinished vision, but as much as I wanted to indulge her, it would have to wait.

We had more pressing matters to attend to.

Slipping an arm around her waist, I lifted her, walking us toward the back room and grinning at her squeal of laughter when I landed a smack on her ass.

I slammed the door behind us.

"Anything you don't like, you tell me, okay?"

I laid her on the couch, my hands shaking with the need to touch her everywhere at once. She nodded, the pulse point in her neck fluttering as her fingers unfastened the button of my jeans. She shoved them down along with my boxer briefs, pulling me free in one fluid motion, and her eyelids lowered to half-mast as she stared down at my hardened flesh.

Slowly, she closed her hand around it, giving me a tentative stroke, her eyes lifting to mine for reassurance. I dipped my head in a nod, barely able to take a full breath at the euphoria of having Juliet's hand wrapped around my cock. Tightening her grip, she stroked me again, moving from base to tip, and I buried my teeth in my lip when she swiped her thumb over the swollen head.

Goddamn. If she kept this up, she would bring me to my end before we even got started.

"You have to slow down." I brought her fingers to my mouth, pressing a kiss against them. "I won't last long if you keep that up."

A shy smile feathered across her lips, and my heart barreled into my sternum at the warmth in her eyes, the skin beneath her freckles tinting with a rosy hue.

How had I found this gorgeous girl? Beautiful and brave and perfect in every way that mattered.

And not yours. I frowned at the unwelcome intrusion of my subconscious. *Just friends, no expectations.*

Why did the idea of that suddenly make me feel cold all over?

I brought her mouth to mine again, the heat of it chasing away the chill. Our tongues and teeth clashed as we consumed each other, and her fingers found the edge of my shirt, pulling it up over my head as I made quick work of her dress, dragging it off her body.

Breaking the kiss, my eyes raked over her simple beige bra and panties.

She looked down at herself, a blush rising in her cheeks. "I know my underwear isn't very sexy. I could get something better, some lingerie or—"

"You're perfect." I didn't give a fuck about lingerie. I just wanted *her*.

"Are you sure?" She stared up at me, her green eyes gleaming like a sun-drenched meadow, and I trailed a finger up the slender line of her jaw, tracing the shell of her ear.

"Yeah, I'm sure."

If she only knew how the image of her in the underwear she'd worn on the day we met—the ones with the pink hearts—was permanently etched in my mind. How the memory of her on her knees, her skirt riding up and those pretty panties on display, had fueled every single one of my fantasies since. At first, I'd felt guilty, but, dammit, if I didn't have the best orgasms of my life as I gripped myself in the shower thinking about her in them.

I skimmed a hand along her collarbone, and then lower, brushing a thumb over one taut peak before sliding a finger under her bra strap. "I want this off," I said thickly, and a strangled noise worked its way up my throat as she unhooked the front clasp, baring her naked flesh.

I had never seen anything so beautiful in my life.

With a groan, I cupped her gently, dragging my tongue up the hollow between her breasts, leaving a trail of goosebumps over her skin. Rolling one stiff nipple between my thumb and forefinger, I lowered my head to capture the other with my mouth, brushing my tongue over it, my cock growing heavy at the sound of her breathy pants.

Hooking a finger in her panties, I parted her soft folds, finding her soaked. "Juliet, you are so ready." I rested my forehead on hers. "Open up for me, beautiful."

I dragged two fingers through her wetness before pushing them into her sex, and I nearly came when she clenched around them. She was so fucking tight. My lips found the base of her throat, and I pressed gentle kisses there as she whimpered, her hips bucking as she rode my fingers.

She was close, I could tell.

And, fuck, so was I.

"Gabriel," she panted, her nails digging into my back, "I need you inside me."

The air stilled in my lungs as I looked at her, her soft lashes drawn down, resting on flushed cheeks. I hesitated, the question of whether she was sure balancing on my tongue. But then she met my gaze, her eyes coated with unmistakable desire, and I swallowed the words, hitching up her thighs as I lined myself up with her slick entrance.

"Please, Gabriel. *Now.*"

I almost took her in one swift thrust, all hope of taking things slow retreating at the prospect of having her wrapped around me like a vise, knowing she would fit me just right. But before I could claim her, a horrible realization crashed over me, and I swore under my breath.

"What's wrong?"

I pressed my eyes shut. "I don't have a condom."

And why would I? I didn't need them at the *gallery*. Come to think of it, I wasn't sure I even owned any. It had been so long since I had taken a woman to bed. In fact, I hadn't been with anyone since

…

No. I would not think of *her.*

"Oh," Juliet said, and I frowned at the note of disappointment in her tone. Maybe I couldn't give her exactly what she wanted, but there was no way I was leaving her unsatisfied.

I lifted away from her, leaving a trail of kisses from her sternum to her belly button, taking a brief detour to brush my lips over her hipbone.

She sucked in a breath. "Gabriel, wait. You can't do that."

"Why not? Don't you like it?"

"It's not that. At least, not exactly …"

I rose onto my elbows to get a better look at her, noting her brows tangled in a deep furrow, her eyes swirling with uncertainty. Lacing our fingers together, I kissed each of hers in turn.

"Talk to me, Juliet."

She worried her lower lip, then exhaled in resignation. "It's just I've never …" She broke off, her face turning a brilliant shade of crimson, and understanding descended on me in one fell swoop. I blinked at her in disbelief.

"Never?"

How was that possible? Hadn't she dated her ex for years? I added this new piece of information to the list of reasons to kick his ass. Or, on second thought, I should thank him for giving me the pleasure of being the first one to share this with her. A smug smile crossed my lips, the thought satisfying some baser caveman instinct I wasn't aware I possessed.

"I know that's ridiculous," she said, struggling to sit up. "You're probably used to more experienced women."

I flattened a hand against her belly, holding her in place. "First, there's nothing ridiculous about it. I would be honored to try this with you, but only if you're comfortable."

She stopped squirming.

"And second," I continued, pausing to kiss her inner thigh, "you're wrong about me. I'm not used to anything. It's been ... a while since I've been with anyone."

I waited for her to freak out. After all, what normal guy was celibate for years? It wasn't that I hadn't had opportunities, it was just no woman had interested me enough to justify the distraction.

Until now.

"How long has it been?"

"Three years."

It sounded a lot longer out loud.

I searched her expression, looking for a clue as to what she was thinking and bracing myself for the worst. But, to my surprise, her face softened, and I closed my eyes, exhaling in relief.

Without warning, she lifted onto her knees, pushing me down onto the couch.

"Juliet, what are you—" My voice guttered out as she lowered her head and wrapped those perfect lips right around my cock.

Something in my soul shattered at the sensation of her warm, wet mouth taking me in, shallow at first, and then deeper until the tip grazed the back of her throat.

This was it. This was how I would die.

My hips nearly lifted off the couch as she dragged her tongue along the bottom of my shaft, hollowing out her cheeks as she began pumping me with her fist. My balls drew up tight, aching with the need to come. I squeezed the base of my dick, trying to forestall the inevitable while simultaneously fisting a hand in her hair, urging her faster. I wouldn't last, and, as thrilling as the prospect of finishing in her mouth was, there was no way I was letting her do that. I hadn't earned that privilege yet.

I grabbed her wrists and pulled her up until she was straddling me.

"I want you to feel me." I slipped her damp panties to one side, parting her soft folds and sliding her along the thick underside of my dick. Her head fell back, her face contorting as her lips clamped down on a closed-mouth scream. "Is this what you need?"

"God, *yes*." She rocked on my lap, chasing her own pleasure as I gripped her backside, guiding her warm flesh against mine and praying to all that was holy that I didn't beat her to the finish line. I brushed my thumb over her full lips, the sight of her whispering incoherently making me drunk with the need to please her, to give her everything I had and then some.

"Gabriel." Her eyes flew open, a spark of fear flashing in them. "I think I'm going to—"

"I know, dammit, I know it. Come for me, angel. Let me have it." No sooner had I said the words than she shuddered, jerking her hips and choking on a broken cry that sent me right over the edge after her. "Oh fuck, Juliet."

White stars dotted my vision as the warmth of our combined releases spilled across my abdomen. The sound of our labored breaths echoed in my ears as a tangy scent filled the air. She collapsed on top of me, burying her face in my neck, and I folded my arms around her, tangling a hand in her hair as I whispered her name, over and over again like a prayer.

⟫ ⟪

Juliet stirred from her sleep sometime later, opening one bleary eye and peering up at me.

"Hi there." I pressed my lips against her temple.

"Hi," she said, her gaze shifting to the blanket I had draped over us.

The sun was setting now, the final rays of daylight pouring in beneath the shade covering the window, and she nuzzled my chest as I buried my nose in her hair.

God, I could get used to this.

After she had fallen asleep, I had lain awake, just watching her and thinking about things I shouldn't. About spending future afternoons on this couch with her or lying in bed together. About how my sheets would smell like her after she left and how I would miss

167

her until she was in them again. About texting her every morning and every night and every hour in between.

I thought of other things, too, of things that seemed more intimate. Of her sitting at my desk writing while I painted. Of meeting up with her after she finished classes for the day. Of taking a trip to the countryside, adopting a dog, picking dinnerware sets, and a whole host of other things that went far beyond the bounds of friendship.

Speaking of …

"Juliet, tell me something. Do you really want to be just friends?" There was no way she could deny we had a connection when every time we touched it felt like electricity dancing between us. She sat up, pulling the blanket up over her body, her eyes downcast. "Look at me."

Look at me and tell me you don't feel this between us.

Her gaze flicked to mine, and an emotion I couldn't decipher passed behind her eyes. "Yes, I think it would be best, don't you?"

No. I did *not* think it would be best.

"I think," I said, schooling my expression, "I want to do whatever makes you happy." Even if the thought of being just friends with her after this felt like a knife twisting in my gut. Still, if being friends was all that was on the table, then I would give her that.

At this point, I would probably give her anything.

"Can you at least tell me why?"

She looked down at her hands as she toyed with the edge of the blanket. "I have to focus on why I came to Paris in the first place, you know? This creative writing program is a once-in-a-lifetime opportunity, and now I might even have a shot at publication. It's unlikely I'll ever get another chance like this, and I … I can't afford to get distracted."

I stared at her, her words punching the air from my lungs.

Well, I asked, didn't I? And she was right. If anyone understood the importance of not letting anything stand in the way of one's art, it was me.

"Got it. Friends then?"

She nodded without looking at me, reaching for her dress, and I searched for my own clothes, ignoring the pit in my stomach. *Friends*. I snuck another glance in her direction, watching her mussed hair fall across her face, the muted light from the window casting her in a faint glow.

Absolutely stunning.

I didn't know how it happened, but Juliet, with her sweet smiles and sweaters, had become a fixture in my life, filling it with a light I hadn't known was missing. And even though this thing between us could never be permanent, I wasn't ready to let her go yet.

I glanced at her again, and in a twist of cruel irony, she chose that moment to drop the blanket, giving me a glimpse of her lovely tits as she lifted her dress over her head.

I swallowed a groan.

Yeah, I could be her friend—so long as keeping my hands off her didn't kill me first.

Seventeen

Juliet

"He has an art gallery? *Holy—*"

"Could you keep your voice down?" I hissed, resisting the urge to clap a hand over Simone's mouth. It wasn't that Gabriel's gallery was a secret, but ...

I darted a glance around the classroom, spotting Marlena a few seats away. As if she could sense me looking, she glanced up, her eyes narrowing when they connected with mine. Her lips curled in a sneer before she dropped her gaze again, examining her nails.

Okay, that felt kind of good.

Simone followed the direction of my eyes. "You're not still worried about Marlena, are you?"

I shook my head, rooting around in my bag for my course-book.

"Good," she went on, "because I say she got what was coming to her." She brushed a piece of lint from her corseted mesh top. "Anyway, that's awesome about Gabriel's gallery. He's like ten times cooler than I originally thought." She blinked at my side-eye. "What? I'm not saying he wasn't cool before, but tour guide, art gallery owner ..." She flattened her palms, pretending to weigh their value on scales.

I grinned. "Okay, him having an art gallery is marginally cooler."

"That's all I'm saying, babe," she said, sinking back in her chair.

Simone wasn't wrong—it *was* pretty cool. The moment I stepped across the threshold of Gabriel's gallery, I had been completely enthralled. The space was beautiful—elegant and airy and not open to the public yet. I had wanted to ask him more about it, but we'd both been distracted at the time.

And what a fine distraction it was.

"So, when can we see his work?" Simone stage-whispered.

"Oh, um, well—"

"*Bonjour*, good morning." Professor Benoit swept into the room, dropping a disorganized-looking pile of papers onto his desk and fixing his glasses. "I apologize for being late." He pulled a pocket watch from his jacket, pausing to look at it.

Oh, my God—he has a pocket watch.

"Right, then." He raked a hand through his hair, leaving several strands standing on end. "If you will all turn to the passage from *Anna Karenina*, we will begin with—"

"Excuse me, Professor," Dean interrupted. "I believe we were still discussing *Les Misérables*."

Benoit faltered, furrowing his brow. "Er, yes, of course. That's what I meant."

The class proceeded without further incident, not counting a heated debate on Jean Valjean's transformation from a hardened criminal into a paragon of virtue. I tried to follow the discussion as Emile and Karin engaged in a verbal sparring match over the book's theme and whether redemption required righteous acts or could be found through selfless love alone. But, every so often, my eyes strayed to Benoit. I'd never seen him look so out of sorts.

I wondered if something happened.

After class, I took my time packing up while the rest of the students filtered out. When the room was empty, I rose from my seat and approached Benoit's desk where he sat writing in an appointment book.

"Professor?"

He looked up from the page, blinking at me in surprise. "Oh, Ms. Chandler. I didn't realize you were still here." He closed the book, straightening his tie. "Was there something you needed?"

"No, I was wondering if there was something *you* needed. You seemed a bit preoccupied this morning."

His eyes widened a fraction before he sighed, his shoulders sagging. "Is it that obvious?" He removed his glasses, rubbing his eyes. "It's my assistant. Just this morning, I received a note from him saying he's taking an emergency leave to care for an ailing relative in

Bavaria. I'm afraid he's left me in the lurch. He keeps me organized, you see, helping with my lesson plans, schedule, and the like. And with no notice, I am, well ..."

"When does he return?"

"That's the thing—he didn't say. I don't expect him to return until the fall semester at the earliest." He stared down at the mess of papers on his desk. "What am I going to do ..."

"Maybe I could help. I could fill in for him until the end of the summer." Benoit stilled, his eyes springing upward. "Think about it. I'm extremely organized. You have to be in my line of work, especially when you're juggling multiple deals."

He frowned, his mouth opening and closing. "I ... I couldn't pay you. The university would have to hire you for you to be put on the payroll."

"That's okay. I don't need a salary."

Something like hope flickered in his eyes before he dropped his gaze. "I'm sorry, but I cannot in good conscience accept your assistance without giving you anything in exchange."

I nodded. "Well, there is something you could give me. It's about the magazine submission. If you would be willing to review my draft, I'll help you in return."

He studied me for another beat.

"Well, perhaps we could try it on a trial basis."

A few minutes later, I followed Benoit up a winding staircase toward the faculty offices and down a long corridor until we reached a door with the nameplate *Julien A. Benoit* affixed to it. He turned a brass key in the lock, holding the door open for me, and I stepped inside, blinking as my eyes adjusted to the brightness of the sunlit room. My lips tilted into a grin as I took in the space.

It was so Benoit.

The first thing I noticed was the carved cherry wood desk sitting at the opposite end of the room, nestled between two identical arching windows. The desk looked to be at least a few centuries old, so it was safe to assume it belonged to Benoit. A more modern-looking desk of simple oak sat near a wall of bookshelves, and across from that was a sitting area with two overstuffed chairs, a small circular table, and a copper standing lamp.

All in all, the space was quite cozy.

"This would be your desk." Benoit crossed to the oak desk, opening the drawers and examining their contents.

I followed, peering around him. There were no personal effects in the drawers—whoever his previous assistant was had made quick work of cleaning out his space—though I noted a pitiful remnant of office supplies left in the bottom drawer.

Okay, we might need to do some shopping.

"This looks perfect," I said, observing Benoit's deepening frown as he took in the state of things.

He glanced at me, his expression uncertain. "Are you sure about this, Ms. Chandler?"

"Absolutely." I gave him an encouraging smile. "Now, unless you intend to fire me less than twenty minutes after giving me the job, I think I'll get to work."

The rest of the morning passed in a blur. After emailing my draft to Benoit, I jotted down a quick list of everything I needed to purchase. File folders, tabs, highlighters, Post-its, and a corkboard with some pushpins.

I did love a well-organized corkboard.

I opened my laptop and found a local store with a colorful selection of supplies and filled my cart with items. I was eyeing a small potted plant to liven up the sitting area when Benoit approached my desk. I glanced up. His tweed jacket was gone, abandoned over the back of his chair, and he had rolled up his shirt sleeves, looking decidedly more relaxed.

"Here." He handed me a credit card. "Anything you need to buy, you can put on my card. The school will reimburse me."

"Thank you," I said, surreptitiously adding the potted plant to my cart.

"No, thank *you*, Ms. Chandler. I truly appreciate this." He scrubbed his knuckles across his jaw. "I teach four days a week and prepare the lesson plan for each class the week before. I have examples from past semesters you can review." I nodded, scribbling down notes in my planner.

"I've also checked your class schedule, which conveniently aligns with mine, excluding Fridays. So, it would make the most sense if you work only on your on-campus days. That way, you won't have to come in when you don't have class."

I started to tell him I didn't mind coming in an extra day, but he eyed me over the rim of his glasses, giving me a look that brooked no argument.

"Got it," I said and clamped my mouth shut.

"And," he continued, releasing a sigh, "you'll promise to let me know if it all becomes too much. You came here to study literature and writing, not help an old man keep his wits about him."

I blinked at him. *Old man?* I didn't know Benoit's exact age, but I doubted he was a day over forty, and he wasn't hard on the eyes either. He was well over six feet tall and had broad shoulders, a square jaw, and thick brown hair only slightly tinged with silver at the temples. He might have the *stylistic* taste of a man twice his age, but there was certainly nothing old about the man himself.

"It won't be too much, but I promise anyway."

He nodded. "How are your other classes, by the way? Are you enjoying Professor Lagrange's course?"

"I am. I'm learning a ton from workshopping my writing with the other students. I suspect this is Professor Lagrange's first time critiquing a romance writer's work, but so far, his feedback has been diplomatic. It's really helping me learn to view my work more objectively."

"That's good to hear. Lagrange can be a real stickler when he has a mind to be." He crossed to his desk and returned with a stack of stapled papers. "Now, about your piece for the magazine." He dropped the stack in front of me, and I skimmed the first page.

"Um, that's a lot of red."

"It is. You asked for my feedback, did you not?"

"I did." I swallowed. "I take it you won't be submitting this for me."

"Correct, I will not."

My heart sank.

Crap. How had I screwed this up so badly? Of course, the draft needed work, but I never imagined the quality was poor enough to cost me the opportunity altogether.

"I understand, sir. Thank you for giving me a chance."

He adjusted his glasses. "I will not submit *this* draft because I am certain you can do better."

I blinked up at him, a tiny balloon of hope filling my chest.

"May I ask you something? Why do you want to be a writer?"

"Because it's my passion. It's what I want to do—"

He shook his head. "No, that's not it. I'm sure you already do plenty of writing as a lawyer. Yet you set that aside to come here. So, I ask you again—why do you want this?"

"I ... I don't know."

"You do know, but perhaps you are too afraid to admit it." He circled his desk, retrieving a newer edition of *La Nouvelle Revue*, its shiny cover catching the light as he set it in front of me.

"I offered you this opportunity because I believe you have what it takes to have your work featured in these pages. Not because you're the most skillful writer or because you deserve it more than anyone else, but because you have the passion for it. The path of a writer is a long one, and often it is filled with more disappointment than triumph. If you truly want this and plan to go the distance, then you need to be honest about why you're doing it."

I stared at him.

What if I didn't have a profound reason for wanting to be a writer?

He returned to his desk again, rummaging around in a drawer while I tried to collect my thoughts. I didn't know why, but I had this ominous feeling that if I couldn't come up with a satisfactory answer, I was going to blow my chance.

And this time, for real.

"Why did you write this?" He dropped a second set of stapled papers in front of me, right on top of the first. My writing sample. "Correct me if I'm wrong, but no one asked you to write this. And you weren't paid to do it. So why? Why did you spend your time and energy on this?"

"Because I enjoy it ..."

He shook his head. "No, try again." I balled my hands in my lap, an influx of frustration filling my chest. He frowned. "I'm still waiting for an answer, Ms. Chandler."

My nostrils flared. "Because it's the only place I can be my authentic self, okay?" To his credit, Benoit didn't flinch at the sharpness of my tone. I released a shaky exhale. "There's all this pressure at my firm to be a certain type of person, to conform to the standard that nothing matters more than the work we're doing. Not family or friends or even your own happiness. The environment can be so oppressive."

I looked at the excerpt of my novella I had submitted with my application. "I wrote this because this is where I can be the truest version of myself. On the page, there's no requirement to fit into any pre-designed mold. I can just *be*. And when the pressures of real life become too much, my writing is like a shield, protecting my heart and soul. It's where I retreat to survive. It's where I go to live."

His lips twitched. "There it is. I want you to rewrite the piece from that place."

He raised an eyebrow in question, and I nodded, heart thundering in my chest.

"Good. I look forward to seeing what you can really do, Juliet."

Eighteen

Juliet

My phone flickered to life on the table where I sat hunched over my draft, sifting through Benoit's comments and sipping on my second latte of the day.

I glanced over at it.

Grace_Reads_Romance liked your post on Instagram.

I grinned. While I typically adhered to a strict no-social-media rule whenever I was working, I was willing to make an exception for Grace. I sorely missed her. Between her witty banter and light-hearted nature, she always made my life at the firm significantly more tolerable.

I clicked on the notification and the picture I posted of myself thirty minutes ago filled the screen. I was smiling behind my mug of coffee, the fluorescent yellow wall of the student center framing my face and the word CAFÉ hovering above my head in black vinyl letters. I'd captioned the photo: *Shh ... writing in progress.*

I scrolled down to Grace's comment.

Look at you! So joyful. P.S. Did you get my email?? Please send more chapters of your novella! I'm going through withdrawal. Miss you! Xoxo

I typed out a quick reply, promising to send something soon. I'd meant to send her new chapters before now, but time had become a precious commodity as of late. My plate was pretty full between classes and working as Benoit's assistant, to say nothing of the fact that I now had to rewrite my magazine submission.

I stared down at the draft covered in red ink.

As daunting as Benoit's feedback was, he was right. I *was* trying too hard. Instead of writing something genuine, I'd tried to produce a piece that was serious and intellectual, assuming that was what it would take to get noticed. But what if I just wrote from the heart? Instead of crafting a story mired in detail about the rejuvenation of art during the Renaissance, what if I put a spin on it and presented it through a unique lens?

I rolled my neck, pulled the pencil from my hair, and flipped to a fresh page in my notebook.

Modern-day woman time travels to Florence during the height of the Renaissance, I jotted down. Oh, and of course, I would have to include a romance subplot.

My lips quirked.

If Benoit wanted authentic, I would give him authentic.

"Excuse me, but would you mind if I joined you?"

I glanced up to find a man in a navy chalk-stripe suit towering over me, his gray eyes so devoid of color they were almost translucent. A lock of pale blond hair fell over his brow, and he smoothed it back, his lips curving beneath a pair of sharp cheekbones.

Gripping a manila folder in one hand, he lifted a cup of espresso with the other. "Sorry to impose. All the other tables are occupied."

I looked around. Every seat was taken except for a couch near the pool table, though, it was safe to assume a man dressed in a suit as impeccable as his wouldn't want to attempt drinking coffee on a lumpy cushion.

"Um, sure." I gestured to the seat opposite mine.

He lowered himself into it, setting down his cup to adjust a pair of silver cufflinks emblazoned with the initials *C.A.*

I examined him. Tailored suit, possibly Italian linen. Nice watch too. Cartier, maybe? Interesting. What was a guy like him doing here with a bunch of students in T-shirts and grungy jeans?

"Thank you for sharing your table." He placed a hand on his chest, bowing his head like some Regency-era gentleman. "You're too kind."

I narrowed my eyes. "And you're far too charming."

"What's wrong with being charming?"

I shrugged. "You know what they say. The devil is a charming man."

His eyes fell wide, flickering with surprise and a hint of amusement.

"Well, now I see what all the fuss is about," he murmured, as if to himself. "Beautiful and perceptive." He extended a hand to me. "Lucien Alarie, although my intimates call me Cristian."

"Juliet Chandler." I offered him my hand, catching the faint scent of warm tobacco and woodsmoke lingering against his skin. "Are you a student?"

He drew a finger around the rim of his espresso cup. "Not presently."

"Then why are you in the student center?"

"Visiting."

"Visiting," I repeated.

"Yes, darling, that's what I said." He leaned in closer, wrapping me in his smoky scent. "May I let you in on a secret?"

"Do you frequently share secrets with strangers?"

"Only the pretty ones." He gave me a wicked grin, eyes ticking over me. "I'm new to this city. My uncle owns a Michelin-starred restaurant on the Côte d'Azur, and he's decided to expand his business. He's opening an establishment here in Paris, and he has placed me at the head of the operation."

I blinked in surprise.

Well, I suppose that explains the suit.

"That's your secret? That you're opening a restaurant?"

He shook his head. "No. Our impending opening is already common knowledge on the restaurant scene."

"Then—"

"This," he said, placing a hand on the manila folder. "This is the secret." A spark of enthusiasm flashed across his features. "I've been considering applying for a business graduate program for some time, but ever since my uncle gave me the green light to open the Paris restaurant, I've become even more determined to pursue it. And it just so happens this university has an excellent master's program in international business."

"Why international business? Are you planning to expand outside of France?"

"Eventually, if I can get my uncle on board and secure the funding. But first, I have to ace the opening here in Paris. The rest is a battle for another day."

"Wow," I said, glancing down at my notebook. "And to think I was stressing over a short story while you're planning to launch a restaurant empire." I paused a beat. "But why is it a secret?"

He drummed his fingers against the table. "Ms. Chandler, I am not a betting man, but if I were, I would only gamble on that of which I could be sure. If life has taught me anything, it is to never deal in hypotheticals, only in facts." He lifted his glacial eyes, settling them on a point somewhere over my shoulder. "If I were to disclose my plans and then fail to secure admission, my uncle might lose confidence in me. And I can't risk that, not when all I've ever wanted is finally within reach."

I nodded, considering this. "Perhaps, but isn't your uncle just as likely to admire your willingness to further your education? After all, it sounds like he only stands to gain from your ambition. And having a vision and the courage to pursue it is something that should be celebrated, not kept secret. You shouldn't have to hide yourself from the light."

His eyes flicked to mine, his brow creasing in a frown. After a handful of seconds, he shook his head as if to clear it. "You should come."

"Excuse me?"

"To the restaurant on opening night." He reached into the inner pocket of his jacket and extracted a rectangular flyer printed on elegant cardstock, placing it on the table.

I leaned forward, reading the word *Marcel's* written across the top in fine script. "When is it?"

"End of August, second to last Thursday. You should come as my guest. You could even bring someone ... like, maybe a boyfriend."

"Boyfriend?"

A slow smile crept over his face. "My, you are so very good at repeating what I say. Yes, a boyfriend. Don't tell me a woman as lovely as you is unattached."

"Well, there is someone, but we're just friends. I'm not sure bringing him to a place like this would be appropriate under the circumstances."

My eyes drifted down to the flyer again. From the image and description alone, it seemed like opening night at Marcel's would be lovely. Delicious French cuisine, candlelight, soft music. A flurry of butterflies stirred in my stomach as I pictured Gabriel in a suit, a crisp white shirt open at the collar. Would he bring me flowers? He seemed like the type to show up on a girl's doorstep with flowers.

Cristian's silver gaze bored into me. "Your lips say you and your gentleman are just friends. But your eyes—they are saying something else entirely."

I huffed. "I didn't realize you were a psychologist on top of a businessman."

"Sorry, darling, but you're not that difficult to read. So, what's the issue with this non-boyfriend of yours? Is he blind or just too stubborn to realize he's got a good thing?"

"Gabriel's not stubborn," I shot back, surprising myself with the sharpness of my tone. I wasn't sure where the protective streak had come from, but no way was I going to let anyone bad-mouth Gabriel, stranger or otherwise. And why was I even entertaining this conversation in the first place?

I gathered my laptop and notebook from the table, shoving them both into my bag.

"Wait." Cristian closed a hand around my wrist, something like panic darting across his features. "I'm sorry. I shouldn't have said that about your friend. Please don't go."

My gaze fell to where Cristian's fingers were wrapped around my arm, and, as if on cue, he released me.

"You could tell me about him," he said tentatively, "if you want."

My eyes returned to his.

I *did* want to talk to someone about Gabriel. And preferably not Ember or Simone, who were both too biased to give me an objective opinion. All week, the memory of Saturday had consumed all my available headspace. Had I made the right decision in keeping the truth from Gabriel? In no version of reality did I want to be just friends with him. I wanted more.

So much more.

"He doesn't do relationships."

No matter how often I repeated the words, my heart deflated a little more each time.

Cristian scoffed. "Well, *that's* a lie."

"But he said—"

"Listen to me, darling. *All* men do relationships when they find the right person." He finished his espresso and dabbed his mouth with a handkerchief. "Whatever he may have told you, trust me when I say, all of it will go straight out the window if he wants you."

I took in a shallow breath, trying to contain the wellspring of hope filling my chest, while Cristian patted his pockets as though searching for something.

"May I borrow your pen?" He plucked it from the edge of the table without waiting for a response and turned the flyer over, scribbling something at the bottom.

"My advice to you is if you want to be more than friends with"—he paused, a muscle feathering in his jaw—"*Gabriel*, then I suggest you have an honest conversation with him. He might say he doesn't want a relationship, but that doesn't mean he won't change his mind for you." His eyes raked over me. "I'm guessing he will if he hasn't already."

He rose abruptly, swiping the folder from the table.

"Ms. Chandler, it was truly a pleasure." He bowed his head again like he'd done at the start of our strange meeting, and I gaped at him as he retreated a step.

"Wait—"

"I do hope to see you on opening night."

Before I could utter another word, he crossed the room and disappeared through the exit.

Nineteen

Cristian

The minute I cleared the gates of the student center building, I tossed the empty manila folder in the trash and scanned the street for my waiting car. Spotting the black Mercedes on the opposite corner, I headed for it, extracting the phone vibrating in my pocket.

Caleb Martin.

Staunching a groan of irritation, I swiped right to answer.

"If you're calling to tell me our liquor license has been delayed, I suggest you hang up and consider putting your excellent charisma skills to better use down at city hall."

He snorted. "No, we should have the license in hand in advance of the opening. Though, now that you mention it, as operator of the establishment, you'll need to complete a basic training course before they can issue it. You know, the one that covers things like the prevention of alcoholism, the protection of minors—"

"Yes, I know what it is. How long does it take?"

"Ah." He cleared his throat. "Approximately twenty hours over two days."

I pursed my lips. "Fine. Have Amélie schedule it and put it on my calendar." I slid into the backseat as my driver and personal assistant, Maximilien, looked at me in the rearview mirror.

"Where to, *monsieur*?" he said, the scar across his right cheek stretching as he spoke.

"*Le restaurant, merci.*"

Thank you. A phrase I didn't employ with any regularity, but used occasionally with Max.

I had met Max six months earlier when his employer at the time, a British diplomat, visited our establishment in Villefranche-sur-Mer. While sharing a cigarette behind the restaurant, I'd learned his boss was returning to London and thus would no longer need Max's services. Our arrangement fell into place quite neatly after that, and since then, I'd discovered my instincts about Max were spot-on. He was efficient, discreet, only spoke when necessary, and asked minimal questions.

I quite liked him.

"Caleb?"

"Yes, sir?"

"I might be taking a grand leap here, but I assume you're going to tell me the reason for your call before I arrive within the next twenty minutes?"

"Oh, right. The head contractor has arrived to speak with you, as you requested."

"Is there a question in that statement?" I examined my watch, clearing away a smudge with my thumb as the sound of hammers and drills filtered through the phone.

"Well, he's insisting he can't stay. I told him you were on your way, but—"

I released a breath through clenched teeth. "You may inform Monsieur Gauthier that I expect to see him when I arrive, and, should I find him absent, he very well may not like the result."

I could practically hear Caleb's nod. "Okay, you got it, boss."

I disconnected the call and tossed the phone on the leather seat next to me, massaging the bridge of my nose. My entire staff was excellent at their jobs, Caleb included. I wouldn't have hired them otherwise. But, as much as I wanted to trust them to handle matters in my absence, no one's competence was beyond reproach.

Except for mine, of course.

"Sir," Maximilien said, his eyes still fixed on the road ahead, "while I was waiting, I had your dry cleaning picked up and delivered to your apartment. I also ordered a few bottles of that special reserve bourbon you like. They should arrive within the week."

Consider my statement amended—no one's competence was beyond reproach except for mine *and* Maximilien's.

"Thank you."

I frowned.

That was the third time I'd used that word today, a rare occurrence for me. I'd used it twice with Maximilien and once with Juliet Chandler.

Juliet Chandler.

I propped my elbow on the armrest, dragging a finger beneath my bottom lip as I stared out the darkened window, my gaze settling on the Eiffel Tower standing proudly in the distance.

An intriguing woman. Easy on the eyes and seemingly intelligent. I'd enjoyed observing her from across the café, watching her face pinch in concentration as she sat folded over her notebook. She was agreeable, too, though I was indifferent on that score; it was the hidden edge lying beneath all that sweetness that I found interesting. She'd glared at me like she was prepared to carve my eyes out with a teaspoon when I'd called Gabriel stubborn. *Little does she know.* Gabriel Beaumont could be the most stubborn person on the planet.

I bit down on my cheek. *Fucking Gabriel.* It always came back to him in the end.

This entire enterprise, this foray into the Paris restaurant scene—it was all so Marcel could reconcile with his son. And I'd been too eager, too naive to see it.

The pitch for opening a new restaurant in Paris had been my idea, my brainchild that I had cultivated with several months of careful planning and hard work. And when Marcel had given me the green light, I'd thought for one fleeting moment my uncle was finally acknowledging my business acumen—that he finally saw my true worth and was willing to invest in my vision.

How quickly I had been disabused of that notion.

Personal feelings aside, the objective was simple: Bring Gabriel to the restaurant on opening night. My uncle hadn't elaborated on what he planned to do should I succeed in convincing Gabriel to come, but that hardly mattered. Marcel had asked, and I intended to deliver.

However, getting him there might be harder than I anticipated.

After clocking the look on Gabriel's face when I went to his gallery, it had taken me three seconds to conclude that persuading him outright was going to be a non-starter. But that was no matter; I would find another way.

And find another way, I did.

By the time I returned to his gallery later that same day with my number written on a note, so he could contact me should he change his mind, I had already concocted three separate schemes. But the second I looked through the window of the gallery and saw a woman—*Juliet*—wrapped in his arms, I knew I'd found my ace in the hole.

Nothing motivates a man more than a woman he cares for.

And so, I switched tactics, turning my attention to uncovering who she was. It was child's play, really. I sent Maximilien home, electing to wait at a brasserie across the street until she left again, which she did.

Eventually.

I admit, I'd been surprised Gabriel hadn't tried to accompany her home. It was exactly the sort of Prince Charming bullshit I would have expected from him. Instead, he'd stood in the doorway as she disappeared up the street, hands in his pockets, gazing after her like she hung the stars in the sky.

So much the better for me.

I followed her, walking at a distance but close enough so she remained in my line of sight until she entered an apartment building on the Île Saint-Louis. I sidled up to the mailbox, reading the names listed there. There were only four. Two of them were male and one was preceded by the salutation *Madame.* That left one name at the very top next to the slot for the third-floor apartment: *Mlle. Juliet Chandler.*

Thirty well-spent minutes on the internet later, I probably knew more about Juliet than some of her closest friends. Twenty-eight years old from New York City, an associate at a corporate law firm, and currently a creative writing student at AUP.

I'd flipped over to her social media, and what a gold mine of personal details that was.

She frequently participated in blood drives because her blood type was O-negative. She was in a sorority in college and attended a reunion in the Hamptons with her sorority sisters last summer. Apparently, Jell-O shots were involved. She hates roller coasters, loves The Band Camino, and has a tiny freckle above her belly button.

Thank you, bikini picture.

I leaned forward in my seat, pressing a few buttons on the touchscreen display until the sultry sounds of Debussy's "Beau Soir" floated from the car speakers.

Finding her again hadn't been difficult. I simply kept tabs on her social media, and sure enough, she posted a photo that led me directly to her. Scoping out her location and devising an excuse to talk to her? Easy. Disarming her with my unassailable charm? Surprisingly less so.

And wasn't that refreshing.

I rested my head back, my lips hooking into a grin.

What a curiosity Juliet Chandler was. At a distance, she was just another cliché nice girl, but up close, there was a fire burning in her eyes.

And no one enjoyed playing with fire more than I did.

On top of that, she was quick-witted, discerning, and showed a propensity for loyalty—all characteristics I held in high esteem. Under different circumstances, I might have even liked her.

Too bad she was just a pawn.

Twenty

Cristian

The car pulled up to the centuries-old building of Lutetian limestone, a timeless fixture standing alongside the Seine and a representation of everything Marcel's stood for.

Elegance, commitment, and excellence.

From the moment I first set eyes on the property, I knew no other place would do. The previous owners, a couple operating it as an Italian restaurant, had told me they were interested in selling at some point, but perhaps in a year or two.

I politely convinced them to reconsider.

In the end, I had gotten the fading beauty for a steal. The prior owners either hadn't wanted to undertake the expense of renovating the place or lacked the vision necessary to restore the landmark to its former glory. My money was on the latter, but either way, it worked out. A property such as this one needed a truly innovative mind and an abundance of resources to revive it.

And I just so happened to be in possession of both.

Passing through the wrought iron double doors, I stepped into the entryway that was all dark wood paneling and antique furnishings. In decades past, the first floor had served as the dining room, and, to display the restaurant's history, I'd preserved as much of the original interior as possible. That is, except for the lighting. Sentimentality aside, every restaurateur worth his salt knows excellent lighting is the cornerstone of ambiance, and I intended to set the tone from the moment our guests walked through the front doors.

Speaking of lighting …

I strode past a team of electricians huddled over a wiring diagram and proceeded to the elevator. It chimed as I reached it, the vintage doors sliding open to reveal Caleb, his navy eyes widening when they connected with mine.

"Try not to look like a deer in headlights, Caleb. It's unbecoming."

"Right," he said, pushing a hand into his blond curls as I joined him in the elevator, pressing the button for the sixth floor. "Max just messaged me to say you'd arrived, and not a minute too soon. I was afraid I was going to have to tackle Gauthier to keep him from leaving. Fortunately, I was able to get Amélie to distract him in your office for a bit."

I lifted a brow, casting him a sideways look. "While I applaud your ingenuity, I'm afraid I can't have you pimping out my staff." I masked a smile as he barked a laugh.

"Sorry, but have you met your head hostess? She's more likely to pimp *me* out than the other way around. She might be tiny, but she's a force to be reckoned with."

The elevator doors slid open again on to a magnificent view of the city, the silvery patchwork of zinc rooftops spanning out beyond enormous wrap-around windows and blending seamlessly with the overcast sky. Sidestepping a pair of construction workers removing a large swath of old carpet, we moved through the main dining room, passing beneath the floral motif on the latticed painted ceiling before pedaling up a short flight of steps to a second dining area, its recently refinished wood-paneled walls gleaming in the afternoon light.

"Ah, Mr. Alarie, if you can spare a moment, you must come and try this."

I spotted Edward Campbell, the restaurant's sommelier, standing beside a glass display case, holding a bottle of uncorked wine, his rounded belly peeking out from beneath his suit.

"Genius idea to display some of the wine collection in the dining room." He offered me a half-filled glass of white. "This is our most recent acquisition. If you're amenable to the idea, I would like to include it as part of our tasting menu. I think it would pair nicely with a good shellfish or a full-flavored cheese."

"Excuse me, Mr. Campbell," Caleb said, his eyes darting wildly back and forth. "We are due for an appointment with—"

"He can wait another minute." I lifted the glass, holding it up to the light and examining the brilliant golden yellow before bringing it to my nose. "Very fresh. Is that apricot?"

"And peach." He lifted his wobbly chin, his face glowing with pride. "Underpinning an aroma of gunflint and menthol. Go ahead, try it. You'll find it has a refreshing finish—"

"*Monsieur Alarie*, there you are."

I turned in time to see the rotund figure of Remy Gauthier cresting the stairs with an irritated-looking Amélie trailing in his wake.

"It's a fine selection, Mr. Campbell," I said, returning the glass to him. "Let's talk it over with the chef when he arrives tomorrow."

"Very good, sir." He threw a look over my shoulder, a frown pulling at his brows. "If you need me, I'll be in the wine cellar." He beat a hasty retreat, and I pressed my eyes shut for a moment as heavy footfalls closed in behind me. I turned to face the source.

"*Bon après-midi*, Monsieur Gauthier. So good of you to come."

"Yes, and as I'm sure you can appreciate, I am a busy man." He dabbed his forehead with a handkerchief, his face glistening with sweat. "Couldn't we have discussed this over the phone?"

"I'm afraid not. But don't worry, this should only take a minute." I glanced at Amélie as she drew up beside Caleb, hugging her clipboard as she glared at the man in front of me. "My assistant manager has informed me you submitted a request to push back the opening date. Is that correct?"

A trickle of unease slid across his features as his eyes darted to Caleb.

"I did," he said, his voice taking on an oily texture, "but only by a month or so. As I explained to him, it's an issue with the lighting fixtures. The pendant lights have been delivered, but the crystal chandeliers are proving to be a bit more difficult to obtain."

"Is that so? Because we presented you with multiple options at the outset of the project. Am I to understand that you have not been able to secure *any* of them?"

He chuckled nervously, hooking a finger into his tie to loosen it. "Monsieur Alarie, I'm sure a businessman such as yourself can appreciate the supply issues we all must contend with in this post-pandemic world. I might be able to get them in time, but as a precautionary measure—"

"Allow me to make myself perfectly clear." I stepped into his personal space, letting my six-foot-three frame tower over him. "We will not be changing the opening date because the work will be completed within the agreed-upon time frame, as per your contract."

His Adam's apple bobbed as he retreated a step. "Monsieur Alarie, you have to understand, sometimes these things can happen—"

"Not to me, they don't." I leaned forward, dropping my voice to a low hiss. "Especially not when I discovered there was a mistake on the original purchase order signed by one Remy Gauthier." He blanched, his mouth falling open as my lips curled in a sneer. "You came highly recommended by some of the best establishments in

Paris, which is why I paid you a small fortune to ensure the construction was completed by the end of July."

Straightening, I withdrew a pocket knife from my jacket, delight spooling in my chest as the remaining color drained from his face. I flicked the blade open, giving him a lingering look before using it to clean my fingernails.

"I would caution you not to mistake my youth for weakness, Monsieur Gauthier. I should hate for anything unfortunate to happen to your ... reputation."

He spluttered, fisting his hands at his sides. "Are you threatening me?"

"Why would I threaten you? I have the utmost confidence you will do everything in your power to see the work is completed as originally scheduled." I closed the knife with a snap, my eyes narrowing. "Won't you?"

His mouth slackened, his beady eyes darting around as if in search of rescue. But there would be no rescue. Not a single soul on earth could save him from me if he fucked up this opening.

He swallowed audibly. "I'll see that it is done."

"Excellent." I clapped him roughly on the shoulder before casting a look at my employees. Without a word, they followed me from the room and down a long, carpeted hallway, its dark walls lined with brass sconces and framed food critic reviews.

Caleb drew up beside me. "Have I ever told you I want to be you when I grow up?"

"You're twenty-five," I said dryly.

"Well, maturity-wise, he's twelve at best." Amélie hurried along at my other side, matching my pace despite her small stature. "Did he tell you he left me in your office with that awful man?"

"You asked if you could help," Caleb quipped. "You helped. I don't see what the issue is."

"He asked me if I was over eighteen," she shot back.

My mouth tightened as I unlocked my office door. "And to think, all this time, I thought I was running a restaurant. Imagine my surprise to find it doubles as a daycare."

Caleb snickered as he entered the room behind me, followed by a thwacking noise that sounded suspiciously like Amélie's clipboard against the back of his head. I rounded the mahogany desk at the center of the room, eyeing the liquor cabinet in the far corner as I lowered myself into my high-backed leather chair.

No time for a drink, more's the pity.

"Enough fooling around," I said. "Let's get started."

Amélie glanced up from her clipboard. "Will *she* be joining us?"

A muscle in my jaw twitched as I flipped open my leatherbound diary, uncapping a fountain pen. After a long beat of silence, I looked up again. "Do I need to repeat myself?"

Amélie's rose-gold hair shimmered as she shook her head. "First on the agenda is we need to decide what artwork will be displayed in the dining room. Our buyers have sent over a selection of traditional pieces, including a few landscapes of the French countryside, but ..." She hesitated, her eyes flitting to Caleb. He returned her gaze, raising an eyebrow.

I blew out an exasperated sigh. "If you two are done eye-fucking, I'd like to get through this meeting before I die of old age."

Amélie's face flushed. "Sorry, I was just going to say I think we should consider featuring some pieces from local artists instead."

"And why is that?"

She smoothed a hand over the front of her fitted blazer. "When guests come to Marcel's, we want them to have an authentic encounter with our beautiful city, to experience Paris in the best way possible. From the fresh cuisine to the vintage décor to the panoramic views. But Paris is more than the sum of its history and culture. It's also the people who live here. They are the true lifeblood of this city. So, we—"

"*She*," Caleb interjected.

She pursed her lips. "*I* suggested that, rather than going with the current offerings, we pivot and seek out some unique original pieces that truly capture the essence of Paris."

She lifted her chin as I regarded her for a moment.

My lips twitched. "Good work, Amélie. You've clearly put some thought into your proposal. You should apply for the assistant manager position when it becomes available. I heard there may be a vacancy soon." Caleb straightened in his chair, his face twisting in horror. I arched an eyebrow at him. "Next item on the agenda."

Amélie laughed into her wrist as Caleb scowled, muttering under his breath as he powered up his laptop. "Here is the current website. I would say it's just about finished."

I looked at the screen. "The home page looks good, and the design accurately embodies the restaurant's brand." I paused, clicking through to the menu page. "But this needs a bit more work. Technically, all the menu items are here, but—"

"We need professional photos," he said, swiveling the computer screen back toward him. "If we could get a few shots of the restaurant's premier dishes, perhaps the *filets de sole cardinal* or *les ravioles au foie gras*, it would liven up this page. Not to mention food imagery on digital menus can increase sales and generate new interest. I've already prepared a list of photographers for you to consider."

"Very good. Email it to me. Otherwise, the website is coming along nicely. Good work." Glancing up, I caught the tail end of Amélie's eye roll as Caleb sneered at her.

I pressed a finger to my temple.

These two and their childish rivalry would be the death of me.

"Anything else?"

Amélie flipped through her notes. "The new executive chef arrives tomorrow, but you already knew that. He'll want to meet with you to finalize the menu. Other than that—"

"I hope I'm not interrupting anything important."

A shard of ice slid through my veins as my gaze landed on the figure standing in the doorway, her amethyst eyes piercing beneath a fan of dark lashes, her crimson lips curling. I could feel the weight of Caleb and Amélie's twin looks of horror, but I kept my eyes straight ahead.

"Dismissed."

She slipped into the room, tucking an arm across the cinched waist of her black sheath dress as they hustled to collect their belongings, giving her a wide berth as they darted through the open door without so much as a backward glance. I could hardly blame them. I would rather chew glass than spend a single second alone with this bitch.

I kept my face impassive as she circled my chair, her long fingernails scraping over the leather before sliding over my shoulders.

"Little Lucien." The hair on the back of my neck rose as her breath coasted over my cheek, the cloying scent of her damask rose perfume arresting my senses. "You conveniently neglected to tell me you were having a staff meeting today."

"Because I don't need you here."

She chuckled softly, running her fingers over the buttons of my shirt. "That's a shame. We used to be so good together."

"We used to be nothing." I closed a hand over her wrist, wrenching it away from me. "And do not ever presume to touch me."

She tutted, slipping between my knees and sliding up onto the desk, batting a hand through her dark hair. "You're no fun." Her lips hooked up in a smile. "Not like Gabriel used to be."

My nostrils flared. "How dare you talk about him? I rarely consider myself to be a good person, but after what you did, I am practically in the running for sainthood."

"What *we* did. Or did you forget?" She crossed her legs, leaning back on her elbows. "Look at you. Marcel gives you a bit of leash and already you've let it go to your head. But *I'm* his business manager. I'm the one he trusts implicitly."

I sprang to my feet, relishing the way she flinched as I slanted over her.

"Trusts you? How interesting. That must be why he removed your name from the bank accounts." Her eyes flashed, violence flickering in them, and I lowered my face to hers. "Go ahead. Strike me, darling. I'll add it to the file I'm building for the authorities."

She released a laugh, the shrill sound grating against my nerves. "Empty threats will get you nowhere, Lucien. If I go down, you go down with me. Besides, you wouldn't do anything that would call into question Marcel's high esteem for you, would you?" Her gaze lowered to the muscle flexing in my jaw. "I thought not."

She shoved me away, and I straightened my collar, watching her with a mounting sense of loathing as she crossed to the liquor cabinet and filled two tumblers with brandy. She returned a moment later, raising one to me. I stared at her coldly, and she rolled her eyes, setting it down on the desk before lifting the other to her lips.

"So, have you found him yet?"

"Found who?" I pushed the drink to the edge of the desk and rummaged through a drawer for a cigar instead.

She snorted. "As much as I love playing games with you, you seem to be forgetting one crucial element. You can't con a con woman. I know Marcel sent you to find Gabriel. Why?"

I struck a match, folding the cigar between my lips and taking shallow puffs as I held the flame near the blunt end, drawing in the rich tobacco before releasing it in a cloud of smoke.

"Well, if memory serves, I do believe Gabriel is his son. It might have something to do with that."

"Cheeky bastard." She tossed back the rest of her brandy. "So? Have you?"

"Why do you want to know?"

She rotated the glass tumbler, sending refracted light across the desk. "Maybe I miss him."

"Ah, yes. And maybe hell has frozen over."

She placed the empty glass on the desk, her smile saccharine. "Well, you would know. Tell me, have they moved your quarters to the seventh circle yet?"

"Why? Looking to be bunkmates?" I drew in another mouthful of smoke, letting the smooth flavors glide over my tongue. "Now, as much as I have enjoyed this little visit, I'm going to have to ask you to leave. Some of us have work to do."

She shrugged, playing with the gold pendant at her throat. "I'm returning to Villefranche today anyway. But don't miss me too much. I'll be back in time for the opening." With a wink that made me want to crawl out of my skin, she turned on her heel, crossing to the open door.

"Oh, and Elise?"

She paused in the doorway. "Yes, little Lucien?"

The corner of my lips twisted. "Don't ever fucking interrupt my meeting again."

Twenty-One

Gabriel

Last night was a fever dream, a vivid explosion of colors and sensations, a lifetime of memories reduced to a single moment. It was everything—the Bastille Day fireworks crackling behind the Eiffel Tower, releasing dazzling bursts of crimson and gold; the symphonic orchestra playing "La Marseillaise" in the middle of the crowded Champs de Mars; the breeze stirring the grass against our skin; and *her*.

The entire display had paled in comparison to the sight of Juliet sitting beside me on the lawn, her eyes alight with laughter. Loose wisps of hair stuck to her forehead in the humid air, and her cheeks were blooming with that delicious color that had taken possession of my dreams.

In that moment, I forgot we were supposed to just be friends, forgot I wasn't supposed to touch her. My hand found hers in the dark as the final cascade of light faded from the midnight sky, and I interlaced our fingers, whispering a thousand things in that one gesture.

I want you.

I need you.

You.

I expected her to pull away, to tell me I had crossed a line. Instead, she leaned her head on my shoulder, wrapping me in her sweet aroma, that now familiar scent I wanted to capture in a bottle and carry with me everywhere. I tilted my face toward her, a bone-deep ache settling in my chest as I brushed my lips against her hair, wishing with growing desperation that it was her mouth instead.

I was done denying it, done debating with myself over convictions and pointless promises. The truth was simple, and it had been staring me in the face for weeks.

I was in love with Juliet.

I had fallen for her both slowly and all at once, sinking deeper into the vast ocean of her presence with each passing day. Every moment we spent together, strolling through Luxembourg Gardens or climbing the steps of the Basilica de Sacré Coeur, was like a waterfall filling the well of my soul, and it was a depth I would gladly drown in so long as she was with me.

Over the past few weeks, our days exploring had turned into nights on the phone, and more than once, I canceled plans so I wouldn't miss her call. Sometimes, I would hear her laugh in my head while working in the gallery and forget to concentrate. And every time one of our outings came to an end, I would always find a reason to stay with her a while longer.

She could call this friendship, but we both knew it was anything but.

And there was the issue.

We hadn't talked about our relationship status since that first time at the gallery, and as June stretched into July, it was becoming harder to find the right moment to bring it up again. But I had this nagging feeling I needed to say something. Even though I wasn't entirely comfortable with the idea of a relationship yet, I wasn't content masquerading my feelings under the guise of friendship either.

I was caught in a classic case of will I or won't I, to be or not to be. Risk it all and ask Juliet to be my girlfriend, or play it safe and remain friends.

Did it even matter?

Either way, I was officially screwed.

"Did you enjoy the exhibit?"

My eyes blinked open, landing on a cloud drifting overhead. The edge of Juliet's shadow trailed over my torso as she sat on the patch of grass next to me, and I unhooked my hands from behind my head, rolling onto my side.

After spending the past two hours at the Musée d'Orsay, I could say with absolute certainty I hadn't paid attention to a single painting. Instead, I had studied Juliet's profile from the corner of my eye, committing it to memory and imagining a hundred different ways to capture her likeness on canvas.

"Mm-hmm," I mumbled. "What about you?"

"I did. I particularly liked Renoir's *Country Dancing* and *City Dancing*, the paintings of the couples waltzing. I love how they symbolize different ways of living, with the urban couple moving elegantly through a ballroom while the country couple danced in the open air full of *joie de vivre*. It really resonated with me."

"Very insightful." I reached over and extracted a leaf from her hair. "So, where to next? The Musée de l'Orangerie also has a good selection of impressionist paintings if you want to head over there. They have Monet's *Water Lilies* on display."

She hesitated, winding a blade of grass around one finger. "Maybe we could save that for another day?"

"Okay, sure. There's also the Picasso Museum or—"

"Actually, I was wondering if we could go back to your gallery instead." I froze, my mouth parted on an exhale. "To see your art," she continued in a rush, batting a hand back and forth, as though dispelling the memory of the last time she was there. Under me. On top of me. Naked and panting my name.

And now I'm picturing her naked.

Fantastic.

"I only meant I was hoping to see some of your paintings." She looked down at her hands, and I took advantage of her temporary distraction to adjust myself in my jeans.

"Really? You want to see my art?"

She perked up, a nervous smile gracing her lips. "Yes, if that's okay."

I couldn't help it, couldn't stop myself if I tried. Pushing down a swell of emotion, I took her hand and brought it to my lips, pressing a soft kiss against it.

"It would be an honor, Ms. Chandler."

⫷⫸

The door to the gallery snicked shut, closing us in with the silence. A river of sunlight poured in through the windows, catching on Juliet's hair as she passed beneath one of the skylights.

"It's so peaceful in here."

"It is. I probably spend more time here than anywhere else."

She hummed, running her hand over a hammered bronze wall sconce before coming to a stop in front of the door to my studio. "Do you keep your paintings in here?"

"Mostly the ones I'm still working on. I have a few completed ones here, but most of them are in storage." Stepping past her, I entered the room, and she followed, wandering over to the desk.

"Nora, right?" She traced a finger over the photo of us at the film festival.

"Yeah," I said, coming to stand beside her. "And that's James, her husband."

"Who's that in the middle?"

I caught her smile from the corner of my eye, and my lips twitched.

"If you're referring to the devastatingly handsome figure, then that would be yours truly."

She laughed, and the sound was like sunshine, warming every part of my soul. "Hasn't anyone ever told you pride goes before a fall? You should be careful." She nudged me in the ribs before shifting her gaze to the other photo. "Who's this?"

I looked down at the portrait of my mother, the answer on the tip of my tongue. But before I could voice it, Juliet did.

"Your mother." It wasn't a question.

"Yeah."

"She was beautiful." *Was.* My eyes found hers as she communicated wordlessly, *I know.*

Of course, she did. She'd lost her parents too.

"She was an artist like me," I managed, gesturing around my workspace. "This, all of this, was her dream once. Then it became our dream. She encouraged my early artistic efforts, teaching me everything she knew. She always believed I could do the things she never had a chance to do. So, this gallery, my art—it's all because of her."

Without speaking, Juliet slipped a hand into mine, her fingers tightening as we stood in silent vigil over the woman who'd given me life and so much more.

A passion. A purpose.

With a hard swallow, I turned away from the picture. "I keep the finished pieces in crates over here." Moving to the nearest one, I extracted a painting at random, arranging it on an easel before turning to show Juliet. I blinked at the now vacant space where she'd been standing before scanning the room. I spotted her crouching over a painting in the far corner.

"Oh, that one—"

"Is exquisite." She beamed at me over her shoulder. "What's it called?"

I knelt beside her, sliding my thumb down the edge of the canvas. I studied the image of gold wings spanning across the painting, fanning out in a wide arch to form an elegant circle. "It doesn't have a name yet. I'm waiting to see what it becomes first."

She tilted her head. "There's something unique about it, something that draws the eye."

"You think so? I was hoping it would be my statement piece once it's finished." I propped it up, the gold paint glinting as a rogue shaft of sunlight slid beneath the window shade.

"Statement piece?"

"Yeah, my art agent won't let me rest until I have one. He insists I need a standout piece, something to set the tone for the rest of my work. He's called me about it at least three times in the past week."

"Wow, it sounds like he doesn't go easy on you."

"He doesn't. But he's also my biggest champion."

It was nothing short of a miracle, me finding him. After months of searching for an agent, and receiving more rejections than I cared to track, I had crossed paths with the semiretired gallerist by chance while attending an art exhibition in Montmartre. I'd been ready to call it a night but decided to stay for one last drink, only to find myself at the refreshments table at the same moment as Jean-Claude Blanchet. We'd hit it off right away, and after discussing the particulars of his engagement, a timeline for an art opening, and a few other details, he'd agreed to be my agent.

Juliet's phone chimed, pulling me from my thoughts, and I looked over at her as she frowned down at the screen.

"Everything all right?"

"Um, yeah." Her eyes flitted to mine before darting away again. "Just some work stuff." She rose to her feet, a furrow tangling her brow as she scanned the message.

It's not my business, not my place to ask.

"Lawyer work stuff?"

She nodded once, guilt clouding her expression.

She's not my girlfriend, not my responsibility.

I folded my arms, my jaw clenching as she paced the room.

Screw it. She could get mad at me for overstepping if she wanted to, but I wouldn't stand by and let anyone take advantage of her. "I thought you told your boss you wouldn't be available for the rest of the summer?"

Her lips parted in surprise. "I did. Well, I tried to, but ..."

"But he's still sending you work anyway," I finished for her.

"Just small projects, nothing major. I can knock this out in a couple of hours, no problem."

I dragged a hand over my face, taking a second to get my irritation under control. The last thing I wanted to do was cause more harm than good. "I'm sure you can, but it's not about that. It's about not allowing people to overstep your boundaries."

She grinned sheepishly. "I know. I've never been good at telling people no."

"Now's a great time to start." I took a step closer, extending a hand. "Do you trust me?"

She hesitated for a moment, then bobbed her head, handing me the phone. I didn't bother reading the email, getting the gist of her boss's tone from the multiple sentences in all caps.

What an asshole.

I hit Reply and began to type.

"What are you doing?"

"Writing a strongly worded email to your boss to make sure he understands you will not be doing this assignment or any others until your writing program is finished."

"Wait, *what?* You can't send that." Her hand shot out, and I caught it, only just resisting the urge to press a reassuring kiss against her wrist at the sight of her worried expression.

"I'm not going to send it. *You* are."

She gave me a long, searching look, then pressed her lips into a firm line. "Okay."

It took us almost twenty minutes to craft an email. We revised and re-revised the language until we finally settled on something she was comfortable with while still getting the point across.

"And send." She grinned from where she sat curled up on the couch beside me, and I returned her smile, my heart swelling at the look of pride on her face.

"You did good, Juliet."

Her eyes lifted to mine. "I couldn't have done it without you."

Maybe it was just my imagination, but for a second, I could have sworn her leg brushed against mine, just barely, but enough for me to feel it everywhere. Swallowing, I let my hand linger near her knee, grazing a knuckle over her bare skin.

Tell me to stop, angel.

Instead, she moved an inch closer until there was no mistaking the press of her hip against the outside of my thigh. Angling her body toward me, she reached over and slowly traced the collar of my shirt, her eyelids growing heavy as though she were in a trance. Just as her fingers reached the base of my throat, she pulled her hand away. I caught it and pressed it flat against my chest so she could feel the organ thundering inside it.

A soft whimper escaped her lips. "Gabriel ..."

"I know." I knew she just wanted to be friends, knew she had just gotten out of a relationship. Knew I couldn't drag her onto my lap, pull down the straps of her dress, and paint every inch of her skin with my fingertips.

I knew it, and yet ...

My hand moved of its own volition, fisting the fabric at her waist. She clutched my biceps as our faces drew together, our noses grazing as her warm breath feathered over my lips.

"Tell me you still think about it," I demanded against her mouth. "About the last time we were here together in this room, on this couch."

"I still think about it," she said, her brows pinching together. "I think about it all the time."

"Does it get you off?"

She moaned, and my throat thickened when she pressed her thighs together. It was all I could do not to lay her down right now and bury my face between her legs.

"Yes," she breathed. "I think about you spreading me over your lap, your body hard beneath me, sweaty and aching for relief. And ..." She closed her eyes. "When I touch myself at night, I pretend it's you. I imagine you filling me, making me come apart."

"Juliet ..."

My lips dipped to the skin between her neck and shoulder, drinking in her soft pants even as I tried to rein myself in. But there was no help for it—I was fucking *aching* for her. I was going to unzip my jeans, spread her thighs wide, and sink into her soaking heat.

Friendship be damned.

Her fingers slid beneath my shirt and that was all the encouragement I needed to hitch her leg over mine, lifting her onto my lap so she was straddling me. She rocked once, and I let my head fall back, taking in the flush of arousal creeping up her neck.

"Put me out of my misery, angel."

Her eyes fluttered open, falling to mine, and the desire coating them would have been enough to make my knees buckle had I been standing.

"Gabriel—"

The peal of a ringtone detonated in my pocket, shocking my senses like ice water.

"Shit, I'm sorry." I dragged a hand over my forehead. "I got carried away."

"We both did," she said on a swallow. Slowly, she lifted away from me, and I immediately missed her warmth. "Should you get that?" She nodded to the device peeking out of my pocket, and I grunted.

Whoever was calling must have a death wish.

"*Allô?*"

"Well, good afternoon to you too."

Nora.

I drew in a slow inhale, searching for patience. "Have I ever told you that you have the worst timing?"

"Oh? Interrupting something, am I?" I could practically hear her smile, and my eye twitched. "Well, hopefully, this will make up for it. I'm having a dinner party on Saturday, and I'm calling to invite you."

"Nora, that in no way makes up for ..." I let the end of my sentence fall away. Some information went beyond the pale of friendship. "What time is the dinner party?" I finished before she could put two and two together.

"Six o'clock," she said, then added smugly, "and tell Juliet she's welcome too."

Twenty-Two

Juliet

On the night I met Kyle's family, I had been the picture of composure. Girding myself with a classic black A-line dress and a bottle of his mother's favorite Merlot, I had smiled my way through the five-course dinner without batting an eye. I even secured an invitation to play tennis at his parents' country club before dessert was served. It had been simple, easy.

This, on the other hand, was anything but.

"You all right?" Gabriel peered down at me, a vertical line forming between his brows.

"Yes, fine." I adjusted the neckline of my floral wrap dress. "Just a bit nervous."

When Gabriel invited me to meet James and Nora, my over-analytical mind immediately jumped to conclusions. He'd already told me enough about them for me to know they were more like his family than friends, so agreeing to attend this dinner party felt a lot like meeting a boyfriend's relatives for the first time.

Except, Gabriel wasn't my boyfriend.

Unfortunately, that bit of information did little to calm my nerves as we waited outside their apartment, a bottle of Bordeaux clutched in my sweaty palms.

From the day I met Gabriel, I knew he was a kind and considerate person. But after spending more time together, I now understood there was a part of him that was guarded too, like he didn't often let people into his life. Which is why this invitation to meet his friends felt important, like it meant something.

I just didn't know what.

Every time I tried to convince myself I was misinterpreting things, my mind returned to the conversation I'd had a few weeks ago with that guy Cristian at the student center.

All men do relationships when they find the right person.

Was Cristian right? And if he was, what did it mean that Gabriel had said nothing about us being only friends?

His behavior certainly made me *feel* like what we had was more than friendship, but some part of me needed verbal confirmation too, for him to tell me what all of this—him spending time with me, opening up about his mother, inviting me to meet his friends—meant for him. For all I knew, it meant nothing, which only made the fact that I cared so much about making a good impression—cared in a way I never had with Kyle's family—seem that much more ridiculous.

I swallowed hard as a fresh wave of nerves pounded against my temple.

"Juliet." Gabriel's concerned tone slipped past the ringing in my ears. "If you're not feeling well, we can leave. I don't want to force you through a dinner if—"

Nora threw open the door, grinning as she wiped a hand on her apron. "Gabe, right on time." When she saw me, she brightened, tugging me into an embrace. "Juliet, so happy to see you again," she said, squeezing me, and I blinked, smiling weakly over her shoulder. She drew back, patting my cheek. "Looking a bit peaky, aren't we?"

"We were just discussing that," Gabriel cut in. "We might need to take a rain check—"

"Nonsense," she said, waving him off. "Nothing a glass of wine won't fix." She ushered us inside, closing the door with a slippered foot.

"Shoes there." She pointed to a small shelf near the door. "I hope that's all right with you, Juliet. I'm a bit of a germaphobe. Occupational hazard of being a dental hygienist in a past life. Please make yourselves at home. Dinner should be ready in a minute." She disappeared down the hall, and I moved to follow her just as Gabriel closed a hand around my arm.

"Hey, you sure you're okay?" He pressed the back of his hand to my forehead, frowning in concentration. "You do feel a bit warm. Maybe I should take you home."

"Don't be silly. We can't bail on your friends. Besides, I doubt Nora will let us slip away without a fight."

"You let me worry about Nora. Just promise me you'll tell me if anything is wrong, okay?"

Nodding, I took his hand, letting him lead me down the hall and into an open-concept living space. I peered around, taking in the overstuffed sectional and upholstered ottoman arranged around a flat-screen TV. A long-legged man with a crop of red hair—James presumably—was stretched out on one of the sofas, a beer in one hand, the other tapping his knee nervously.

"Oh, come on, ref," he barked at the screen as a group of men ran around a soccer field.

"Manchester having a bad night?" Gabriel said.

"The bleeding ref can't see for shit. Maybe if he took his balls out of his back pocket—"

"Hey," Gabriel said, grimacing. "Maybe tone down the language. There's a lady present."

"Nah." James waved a hand, slumping against the cushions. "Nora's heard it all before."

"Not me." Nora glided in from the kitchen carrying a roasted chicken. "He means Juliet."

James blinked, jerking his head around to face me. "*The* Juliet?"

"Uh ..." I darted a wide-eyed look at Gabriel.

"Don't answer that," he said flatly.

James rounded the sofa, pulling me into a bear hug that rivaled his wife's. "It's a pleasure to finally meet you." He dropped his voice an octave, leaning in. "So, uh, how's our boy doing? Is he racking up any points on the old proverbial scorecard?"

"*Christ.*" Gabriel dragged a hand over his face. "I don't know why I thought it was a good idea to bring her around you two. I guess I should consider myself lucky you don't have any toilet training pictures of me. No doubt you'd have them teed up on a rotating slideshow."

"What are we talking about?" Nora chimed in from across the room, lifting her head from where she was applying garnish to the chicken.

"Oh, nothing," Gabriel muttered. "Just brainstorming how best to humiliate me before the evening is through."

I laughed into my wrist as James clapped Gabriel hard on the shoulder. "All in good time, mate." He winked at me before turning back toward the television.

"Ah, ah, ah. Don't you dare sit back down in front of that match, James Arthur Russell. We're about to eat." Nora removed her apron, swiping a hand over her forehead. "Juliet, would you be a darling and grab the salad from the kitchen? It's on the counter."

"Sure, happy to help."

Slipping through a doorway, I spotted the salad bowl perched next to a copper teakettle and grabbed it. Upon returning to the dining room, I found James seated at the head of the table, piling chicken onto his plate while Nora settled in beside him, uncorking the bottle of Bordeaux. Gabriel, however, remained standing, his attention trained on the doorway as though he was waiting. For me.

My heart stutter-stepped when our gazes connected.

"Here's the salad."

"Excellent," James said, tucking a napkin into his collar. "Let's eat."

"Wait." Nora craned her neck to peer down a hallway. "Where's—"

"Gabriel!"

A flash of auburn hair was the only warning I received before a young woman appeared out of nowhere and launched herself into Gabriel's arms. Surprise spilled over his features, and his eyes briefly found mine over her shoulder before she pulled back, obscuring him from view.

"Lily?" he said, his voice colored with disbelief. "What are you doing here?"

Lily spun toward James. "You didn't tell Gabe I was coming?"

James shrugged, appearing for all the world to be entirely unbothered as he shoveled a forkful of potatoes into his mouth.

Nora swiped at his arm. "James, how could you forget? Lily's arrival was the whole reason I planned this dinner party." She eyed her husband critically. "I'm sorry, Gabe. I thought James would have told you."

For the first time since our arrival, Nora's expression dimmed, and her eyes sprang from Gabriel to me and back again, a tiny divot forming between her eyebrows.

"Well, it's not a big deal," Lily said, still clinging to Gabriel's person. She pressed a kiss to his cheek. "I'm happy to see you." Her whiskey eyes moved to me, and she blinked, her smile slipping a fraction. "Oh, hello. I don't believe we've met before."

Gabriel extricated himself from her and moved to my side, placing a hand on my elbow. "Juliet, this is Lily, James's little sister. Lily, this is Juliet, my ..." He broke off and glanced at me, uncertainty marring his expression.

"His friend," I croaked, the words rising in my throat like serrated knives.

"Oh," she beamed, "so lovely to meet you." She attempted an embrace, but unable to navigate the salad bowl I was still clutching, she settled for pressing her cheek to mine. I tried not to notice her floral scent or the color blooming beneath her creamy skin, but there was no escaping the truth.

She was beautiful.

"Lily, why don't you come sit here?" Nora patted the empty chair beside her.

"But I want to sit next to Gabriel," she whined. "It's been an age since we've seen each other." She hooked her arm through his, dropping her head on his shoulder.

Gabriel winced, throwing me an apologetic look. "Actually, Lily—"

"It's fine," I said with a stiff smile.

Nora opened her mouth to say something, but closed it again, reaching up to pry the salad bowl from my fingers instead.

Once we were all seated, I poured myself an oversized glass of wine, polishing it off in record time as I tried to ignore the way Lily dominated Gabriel's attention.

Not that I was jealous ...

She laughed at something he said and inched her seat closer to his. My stomach clenched.

Okay, maybe I was a tiny bit jealous.

"So, Juliet," Nora said, distracting me from the green-eyed goddess pitching a tent in my head, "how is the writing going? Are you enjoying your classes?"

"Juliet is in the creative writing program at the American University of Paris," Gabriel explained to Lily, and she gave him an appreciative smile.

I sawed my bottom lip between my teeth, a flicker of annoyance sparking in my chest. Did he have to spoon-feed her information about me? Couldn't she just ask me herself or, I don't know, follow the conversation and engage whatever deductive reasoning skills she possessed?

"How ambitious of you," she said, turning to me. "Better late than never, right?"

Nora coughed into her wineglass just as Gabriel dropped his fork with a loud clatter.

I stiffened. "I'm sorry, I don't understand your meaning."

She shrugged, her face the picture of innocence. "I only meant it's great you're going to university. Our mum is a teacher and is always going on about how the key to success is an advanced education. Even if you don't go straight out of secondary school, it's still a big achievement. You should be proud."

A heavy beat of silence passed. Then, James burst into laughter, the raucous sound of it like a volcanic eruption.

"Oh, my God," he said, wiping the corners of his eyes as he peered gleefully at Gabriel. "This is so much better than any prank I could have planned."

Lily's smile faltered. "Have I said something wrong?"

Nora gave her husband a stony look as Gabriel pressed his eyes shut. "Lily, Juliet isn't—"

"Thank you, Lily," I said, cutting across him. "It certainly is better late than never."

Nora's and James's eyes snapped in my direction, surprise etched on their faces, and Gabriel stared at me open-mouthed. I looked away from all of them, studying my plate. Lily's misplaced congratulations was a bit humiliating considering I'd graduated *cum laude* from Columbia University, but I wasn't going to win points with her family by acting snotty about it.

"What about you?" I continued, swallowing a bite of potato along with my pride. "What do you do with your time?"

She smiled in relief, not seeming to notice the others exchanging glances. "Well, I'm in between jobs right now. I was teaching at a ballet school in London for about a year, but they were a small company and had to make some budget cuts. So there went my gig. Anyway, I moved back in with my parents, but after a while, I felt like I was crowding them out."

James's mouth curled into a smirk. "So, she decided to come and crowd us out instead."

"Nonsense," Nora said. "You're welcome to stay with us as long as you want."

"Wouldn't be the first time," James muttered under his breath.

"That's too bad about your job, Lil," Gabriel said as Nora pinched James's arm under the table. "I know how much you love to dance. Have you ever considered applying to teach in Paris?"

She gave him a look of such obvious adoration that I completely missed her response over the sudden rush of blood in my ears. Gabriel grinned at her, and they laughed, an easy intimacy passing between them as she tucked a few cinnamon strands behind her ear.

Hold on. Oh, my God—why hadn't I thought of this before? In all the time I'd spent trying to understand why Gabriel didn't want a relationship, it never occurred to me that maybe he *did*.

Just with someone else.

Now that I'd seen it, I couldn't unsee it. It was so clear *she* was the type of woman Gabriel should be with. Gorgeous and carefree, no demanding job, and his best friend's little sister. On top of it all, she obviously had feelings for him, and she could give him things I never could, like time and attention.

How could I compete with that?

"I—I'm sorry," I said, placing my napkin down, "but I suddenly don't feel well."

"Oh no," Nora said, sweeping a hand across my back in a gesture I was sure she meant to be soothing but only made me feel worse. "Do you want to lie down in the guest room?"

"I think I'd better just take off. Thank you for such a lovely dinner." I rose without meeting anyone's eye, barely resisting the urge to sprint from the table. In the hallway, I heard heavy footfalls behind me.

"Let me take you home," Gabriel said, closing his fingers around my elbow.

"No." I pulled out of his grasp, inwardly begging myself not to cry. I would never outlive the humiliation if I broke down in front of him. "Please stay. I don't want to spoil the evening."

Slipping on my flats, I collected my purse from the entryway table before lunging for the door. I'd almost gotten it open when Gabriel pressed a firm hand against it, holding it shut and spinning me to face him.

"Juliet, what's wrong?" He gripped my chin with his thumb and forefinger. "Talk to me, angel."

A sob rose in my throat at the endearment. I needed to get out of here—away from this man who I couldn't bear to lose, who was never mine to begin with.

After a stretch of silence, his brows lowered. "You promised."

I *had* promised to tell him if anything was wrong, but what was I supposed to say? *Sorry, I'm feeling insecure about the gorgeous redhead pawing you at the dinner table.* Yeah, not likely.

"I'm sure it's just a twenty-four-hour stomach bug," I lied. "You don't need to worry."

"Juliet—" Gabriel dragged a hand through his hair in frustration, pacing the length of the hallway. Returning to me, he placed a hand at the base of my spine and opened the door, leading me down the stairs and out of the building into the warm summer air.

Turning to me, he said, "If you won't let me take you home, will you at least let me call you a cab?"

I nodded numbly, studying the pavement as he waved one down. Depositing me in the backseat, he hesitated, watching me beneath half-lidded eyes.

"Good night, Gabriel."

I caught the hard movement in his throat as he backed away from the window, shoving his hands in his pockets as the cab pulled away from the curb. A dull ache expanded in my chest as I stared at his shrinking reflection in the rearview mirror.

Why did I even come tonight? I should have found an excuse to stay home. If I had, maybe I could have kept pretending I wasn't already in over my head.

As the cab rounded the corner and Gabriel disappeared from view, I folded over my lap and finally allowed my tears to break free.

Twenty-Three

Juliet

"Does this dress make my boobs look small?"

I dragged my gaze away from the flamingo-pink wallpaper of the dressing room, watching as Simone swiveled in front of the floor-length mirror before darting a glance out the window at the darkening sky.

It was Sunday evening, and after spending most of the day in bed bingeing campy shows on Netflix and hugging a half-liter of *caramel au beurre salé* ice cream, I finally let Simone drag me out on a shopping expedition to Galeries Lafayette. I'd nearly gone blind when I stepped across the threshold of the luxury department store, my tired eyes assaulted by lights reflecting off glass display cases and marble finishings.

Hovering in the entrance, my eyes had traveled around the cavernous space, unsure where to land. Ornate crown molding and gilded ironwork balconies drew my attention up, past floor after floor of upscale merchandise, all the way to the art nouveau glass dome that adorned the ceiling. Bursts of floral décor crept up the marble walls and colorful mannequins stood beside displays of designer handbags and shoes. And the cherry on top was the battalion of salespersons, all impeccably dressed, standing sentry at every corner, armed with sample fragrances and welcoming smiles. To say it had been a shock to my ice cream-addled brain was an understatement.

I studied Simone's lithe figure as she preened in front of the mirror. The backless sequined gown was a rich navy blue with a deep V-neck and a fishtail hem. Very sophisticated. Like the kind of sophisticated that suggested the woman wearing it spent her weekends in Monte Carlo, sipping cocktails and playing high-stakes poker.

"It's a lovely dress, but yes, it makes your boobs look rather small." Simone's mouth fell open, and I winced. "Not that there's anything wrong with small boobs."

"Don't be sorry." She draped her braids over one shoulder, gesturing for me to help her unzip the dress. "I'm just surprised at your candor. You're usually polite to a fault, but I have to say, I find this version of you refreshing."

I let out a humorless laugh. "I think you've got the wrong end of the stick about me."

Despite what Simone thought, I wasn't candid. If I were, I wouldn't have lied to Gabriel about wanting to be just friends. I would have told him how I felt from the beginning.

The memory of Lily's radiant smile swam before my vision, and I pressed my eyes shut to block it out. Last night, I had spent hours replaying the events from the dinner party in my head. Gabriel and Lily side by side, smiling and laughing, perfectly at ease with one another. No pregnant pauses or awkward moments like the ones that sometimes existed between me and Gabriel. Theirs was an open affection. It was effortless and uncomplicated.

"Hey, you good?" I glanced up to find Simone staring at me, a look of concern forming behind her brown eyes as she shimmied out of the dress, letting it fall in a pool around her feet.

"Yeah," I said with a tight smile. "I just had a late night."

She brightened. "Ooh, was it the good kind of late night? Like the kind that involved getting naked and sweaty with a certain artist?"

I rolled my eyes, a real smile touching my lips. "You know, believe it or not, we spend most of our time together with our clothes on." The second the words left my mouth, my eyes flew wide as I realized what I'd said. Maybe Simone wouldn't notice—

"Say what now?"

I groaned inwardly. If I could have fabricated a lie plausible enough to remove the manic gleam from her eyes, I would have whipped that baby out like a winning bingo ticket. But after eight hours of mindless television, I had to confess my mental acuity wasn't the sharpest.

"It was only one time and—"

Simone squealed, pulling me into a full-body hug even though she was half-naked.

"Juliet, that's fantastic." She clasped my arms, beaming at me like a proud mama. Turning her back to me, she reached for another dress to try on. "Just remember to invite me to the wedding, okay? And I wouldn't say no to being a bridesmaid either."

"Simone, it's not like that. We're just friends."

She snorted, hoisting up a pale green bodycon dress. "Oh please, I saw the way he was looking at you at the club. Last time I checked, friends don't eye-fuck each other across the table."

I choked on an inhale. "Please never say that again."

"Oh, Juliet, you're so innocent. Always the perfect lady." She sighed, dropping her gaze over her reflection. "That's probably why he's in love with you."

My breath halted. "No, he's not."

"He *is*," she said to my reflection. When I continued to stare at her, she huffed, giving me an exasperated look. "Seriously? It's so obvious. First, he left Marlena high and dry to dance with you. Second," she said, ticking off her points on her fingers, "he brought you to his super-secret-not-yet-open-to-the-public art gallery. Oh, and let's not forget how he asked you out on a date after your bike tour—"

"Hey," I said, pointing at her, "that was *not* a date. The restaurant wasn't even open."

She gave me a bug-eyed look. "*That's* your takeaway?"

I left Simone alone in the dressing room and pulled out my phone, flipping through the messages Gabriel had sent last night.

Saturday 9:38 PM *Are you okay?*

Saturday 10:02 PM *Hey, did you make it home? If you don't feel like talking, that's fine. Just please let me know you're all right.*

Saturday 10:53 PM *Guess you're sleeping. At least I hope so. I'll be up for a while in case you need anything.*

Saturday 11:15 PM *I never should have left you alone.*

A guilty pang reverberated in my chest. I hadn't responded to a single one of his texts or calls all day. It wasn't that I didn't want to talk to him—quite the opposite. But if last night had shown me anything, it was that things between us couldn't continue the way they had been. I needed clarity, a definitive line in the sand. Because I didn't think my heart could survive another six weeks of us pushing the bounds of friendship, only to find out I wasn't the *right person* or that there was something between him and Lily. I would rather know before things went too far.

Before I got hurt.

Catching a glimpse of myself in the mirror, I noticed the top bun I'd thrown my hair into was now on the verge of collapse. I pulled it loose and rooted around in my purse for a brush. After removing the tangles, I tucked my hair behind my ears, looking marginally more presentable. Though, there wasn't much I could do about the dark circles under my eyes or the faded sweatshirt and yoga pants I was wearing.

The door swung open, and Simone emerged from the dressing room carrying two items—a fuchsia cocktail number and the navy evening gown.

"You're getting the blue one?" I said, eyeing the shimmering fabric slung over her arm.

"Not for me, for you."

"Wait, what?" I hurried after her as she hightailed it to the register, smacking the dresses down in front of a saleswoman before spinning to stand between me and the counter, effectively boxing me out.

"Simone, no." I reached around her, but she slapped my hand away.

"You're clearly in need of a pick-me-up. And nothing picks a girl up like a new look." She raised a hand before I could protest again. "Don't try to talk me out of it, Juliet. I am purchasing this dress. So, here's what's going to happen—either I buy it and you wear it somewhere fabulous, or I buy it for myself and strut around town looking like I have Hershey's Kisses for boobs."

The woman behind the counter gaped at us, her eyebrows disappearing into her hairline.

"Simone, you can't keep giving me clothes."

"Why not? I love clothes." She eyed my sweatshirt and sneakers that had seen better days. "Besides, it looks like you could use all the help you can get. I'm giving you a pass today because you're upset about something, but I can't be seen with you in the future if you insist on dressing like you dug your clothes out of the dirty laundry hamper."

"Wow, how quickly your altruism takes a left turn."

She swiped her credit card, handing me a glossy bag marked Galeries Lafayette. "Hey, I never claimed to be a Good Samaritan. I'm doing this purely out of self-interest. You're my only real friend in Paris, and I need you to look the part."

"Your only friend?" I said as we moved toward the elevator. "What about Carter?"

Simone cast me an *Oh, you poor fool* look from the corner of her eye. "We need to work on your definition of friend. I don't call guys I want to mount in the back of a taxi—"

"Cool, got it," I said, throwing her a thumbs-up. "Not friends then."

When the elevator doors slid open onto the main floor, I looked up at the domed glass ceiling. The sky had grown even darker, and my stomach growled, reminding me that ice cream, no matter how delicious, didn't count as sustenance. I started in the direction of the exit but barely made it a few steps before Simone pulled me toward a jewelry display case.

"So, I take it things are going well with Carter?" I asked, threading my fingers under my chin as she examined a row of diamond rings.

She narrowed her eyes at me. "Let me stop you right there, girly pop. As happy as I am for you, love at first sight is so not my vibe. Besides, it'll take a lot more than one date and three successive orgasms for him to impress me."

"Wow. Thanks for the visual."

"Anytime. Ooh, look at this." Her nose practically pressed against the glass as she stared down at a bracelet lying on a creamy leather pillow, glinting with sapphires set into the shapes of sunflowers.

"Juliet, wouldn't that look lovely with your new dress? You should try it on."

"Simone, no—"

"*Excusez-moi, madame.*" She waved over a saleswoman in a black pencil skirt. "*Pouvez-vous s'il vous plaît nous montrer le bracelet?*" The woman smiled at us, removing the bracelet from its case and fastening it around my wrist before I could escape.

"Oh, my God," Simone whispered, pressing her fingertips to her lips. "It's perfect."

I frowned. "Yeah, except I'm not buying it and neither are you." I grabbed her hand before it could inch any closer to her purse, and the saleswoman excused herself as Simone and I engaged in a tug-of-war with her Chanel. "Seriously, what's with the impulsive buying spree?"

Simone planted her hands on her hips. "Well, excuse me for trying to make my friend happy."

"I am happy," I blurted out too quickly.

"Mm-hmm, and a terrible liar too. You don't have to tell me what's going on, but as long as you keep drooping like a wilted flower, I'll have no choice but to keep buying you things."

I sighed. "Look, why don't we just get out of here?" Hooking an arm around her, I steered her to the exit. "If you want to make your friend happy, you can treat her to a cheeseburger."

She snort-laughed as we pushed our way through the first set of double doors. But before we made it out onto the street, I heard the distinct sounds of shouting. I glanced over my shoulder in time to see the saleswoman in the pencil skirt pointing at me and a security guard hurtling in our direction. Closing in on us, he grabbed my arm, spewing rapid French in my face.

I threw Simone a panicked look. "What's he saying?"

She frowned for a moment, then her eyes widened, falling to my wrist.

My wrist.

"He's saying you're under arrest for shoplifting."

⟫⟫⟫ ⟪⟪⟪

If you've ever wondered what the back room of a department store looks like, allow me to satisfy your curiosity—it's awful. Like *three out of ten, would not recommend* awful.

A light bulb flickered in the windowless room where they'd put me with only a few plastic chairs for company. My skin pebbled under the draft of a rattling air conditioner. Leaning my ear against the door, I could hear Simone arguing with someone in French. Fifteen minutes later, another voice joined hers, a deeper one also speaking in French, though I couldn't make out who it belonged to. Finally, after I paced a mile-worth of circles around the cramped space, the door flew open, and Simone stormed in with Carter close on her heels.

"Can I go?" I didn't like the anxiety creeping into my tone, but even I had to acknowledge it might be warranted after spending at least an hour in this asylum-grade room.

"Security is saying they have no choice but to call the police since you technically left the store with the bracelet. I explained it was a mistake, but they wouldn't listen."

"Can we speak with the store manager? If I can explain what happened—"

Simone shook her head. "We already asked for the manager, but apparently he's gone for the day."

My stomach sank.

"Hey." Carter placed a hand on my shoulder. "We should call someone. Someone more familiar with the customs in France than we are."

Simone nodded in agreement. "Can you call Gabriel?"

"No, absolutely not." After the dinner party fiasco, the last thing I wanted to do was call Gabriel from a pseudo-jail cell. There was only so much humiliation a girl could endure.

"How about Professor Benoit?" Carter suggested.

"Um, that might be the only person worse than Gabriel to call. He's our professor, not to mention my boss." I didn't add he was also the person who had given me a chance to prove myself, so letting him down with an incident like this was a non-starter.

Simone groaned. "Then what are we going to do? We're not letting you get carted to some seedy police station. So, unless you can think of someone else, Benoit is our best option."

I chewed on my thumbnail. "Okay, let me think for a second."

I'd never had to rely on my professional network for a personal matter before, but I knew plenty of attorneys in New York who would help me in a pinch. Unfortunately, given the time difference, it was unlikely any of those people could get me out of this predicament without me being arrested first.

"Oh, here." Simone held out my purse. "I stole this from behind the security guard's desk."

"Please don't say the word *stole* when I'm currently being detained for absconding with a mortgage payment worth of sapphires." I reached for it, but it slipped through my fingers.

"Here, let me help." Simone kneeled beside me as we collected my belongings from the carpet, which, to my horror, was suspiciously sticky. Trying not to think about the range of substances that might be coating the floor, I grabbed my keychain just as my eyes fell across a rectangle of fine cardstock.

The flyer for Marcel's.

I picked it up, skimming over the restaurant details before seeing a phone number written across the bottom.

Cristian's number.

My heart leapt. It was a long shot—a *very* long shot considering it was Sunday evening, and I had only met him one time. Still, Door Number Three was looking like my best option. I glanced up at Simone's and Carter's concerned expressions.

"Hey, would you guys give me a second? I need to make a quick phone call."

Twenty-Four

Juliet

"**A**re you secretly a witch?"

My eyes settled on Simone standing on the curb in front of the department store. Night had descended during my brief stint in lockup, and the chilly air nipped at my skin, making me grateful for my sweatshirt despite its lack of style.

I glanced at Cristian standing beneath the muted light of a street lamp, a phone pressed to his ear as he spoke rapidly in French to whoever was on the other end.

I still couldn't believe he'd answered my call. What's more, I couldn't believe he'd come.

"Am I a what?" I said, returning my attention to Simone.

"A witch," she repeated matter-of-factly. "Because I find it hard to believe you ensnared not one, but *two* insanely hot guys without some sort of secret powers." She peered around me, giving Cristian an appreciative look. "Yeah, no way you're just a muggle."

"Um, I think you have the wrong idea. Cristian's—"

"Hot as fuck, I know."

"Are you allowed to say that?" I looked over to where Carter stood, trying to hail a taxi.

"Relax, I'm just window-shopping. I may be happy with my current situation, but a girl's still got eyes."

Well, I couldn't blame her there.

Despite the late hour, Cristian had showed up looking like he'd just stepped off the cover of *GQ* magazine. We watched him casually slide his hand into the pocket of his gray trousers, his tailored jacket shifting in tandem with his broad shoulders, and the light of the street lamp bouncing off the metallized crystal of his watch.

Yeah, if masculine elegance had a name, it would start and end with *Cristian Alarie*.

Simone nudged me sharply in the ribs when he ended his call, and I gave her some serious side-eye as she tossed her braids over one shoulder.

Just window-shopping, my ass.

"My apologies." Cristian deposited his phone into the interior pocket of his jacket. "A minor work emergency. If you ladies are ready, my car should pull up any minute now."

"Oh, no need to go out of your way. We can grab a cab." Simone extended a hand. "I'm Simone, by the way. *Enchantée.*"

"*Enchanté.*" Rather than shaking her proffered hand, he raised it to his lips, pressing a kiss against her knuckles. "The pleasure is mine."

I was too late to stop the snort that exploded from me, although I disguised it as a sneeze at the last second. But seriously, did this guy ever turn off the charm? My guess was probably not, considering the way Simone was preening under his attention like a show pony.

My gaze lingered on him. His features were a mixture of soft and masculine, the strong cut of his jaw framing a pair of full lips beneath high cheekbones. He was handsome in an obvious way, but something about his flawless exterior made me curious about the man beneath the facade.

Carter rejoined our circle, sliding in beside Simone.

"Did you find a taxi?" she asked.

"No, I had to call an Uber. You'd think there'd be a taxi available at this time of night, but it's like a zoo out here."

"Welcome to Paris," Cristian deadpanned.

Carter gave him a once-over before taking an infinitesimal step closer to Simone. "Yeah, right. So, thanks again for helping us out. How do you know Juliet again?"

"Funny you should ask," Simone said, eyes sliding to me. "I was just wondering the same thing."

Well, I guess the jig is up.

After Cristian swooped in to rescue me like my own personal Batman—if Batman wore designer suits instead of a cape—I had neglected to offer my friends any explanation as to how we knew each other. But how was I supposed to explain that the person who just busted me out of department store jail was some random guy I'd met in the student center?

Didn't exactly roll off the tongue.

"I'm an associate in the Paris branch of Juliet's law firm," Cristian said without missing a beat. "Someone in the New York office contacted us after receiving a message from her, and they sent me to sort everything out. Isn't that right, Juliet?"

I blinked, my mouth hinging open as my eyes bounced between Simone and Carter.

"Um, yes, that's it exactly." Carter nodded, seeming to accept this, but Simone's face pinched with suspicion. "Anyway, I appreciate you guys sticking this out with me, but I'm gonna head home." I turned to Cristian. "You said something about a car?"

His mouth twitched. "I did indeed. I guess this is good night then, Simone, Carter."

He steered me to the curb as a black Mercedes pulled up, and I paused when he opened the door, looking back at Simone. No doubt I would get the third degree about this tomorrow.

I stared into the dark cabin of the vehicle. Was I really about to accept a ride from a guy I barely knew? I lifted my gaze to Cristian's, finding his glacial eyes glinting with amusement and maybe a hint of challenge.

Truth or dare, they seemed to say. Turn around and tell my friends the truth, or follow him down the rabbit hole?

Tossing a final glance over my shoulder, I climbed into the car.

"Oh, my God, this is so good, I could die."

Approximately three minutes after leaving the department store, my stomach decided to make itself known again with a hair-raising growl. Before I could mutter an apology, Cristian simply laughed and asked if I wanted to make a pit stop, which is how we found ourselves in fast-food heaven, otherwise known as McDonald's, with me stuffing my face with hot, salty french fries.

"Well, you may get your wish." Cristian eyed my half-empty tray. "Undoubtedly, your arteries are closing as we speak."

I sneered at him, but with the amount of food in my cheeks, I couldn't quite pull it off. I tossed a fry at him instead. "Don't be such a food snob."

"I run a Michelin-starred restaurant. Being a food snob is practically in the job description."

Rolling my eyes, I hid my grin behind a paper napkin. "Fair enough. And thank you, by the way. For coming to my rescue."

"It was my pleasure, Ms. Chandler."

"Why did you though?" I chewed on the straw of my soda. "I mean, you hardly know me. What reason could you have to rush out in the middle of the night to help me?"

"It's hardly the middle of the night." He chuckled, but his expression dimmed when I pressed my lips together. "You don't trust me, do you?"

"Should I? I mean, you just lied to my friends without even batting an eye."

"Would you have preferred I told them the truth? When you called, I knew I might need a cover story, so I did a quick scan of your professional profile. Impressive background, by the way." He reached over and plucked a fry from my tray, popping it into his mouth.

"But that's exactly what I don't get. Why go out of your way in the first place?"

His silver gaze slid toward the window. "Believe it or not, I am a gentleman. And you are an American in a city with which you are unfamiliar. That's why you called me, no? If you and your friends had been able to get out of that unfortunate situation on your own, suffice it to say, I would not be sitting here."

"It still seems strange."

"No stranger than the fact that you called me instead of your non-boyfriend. Gabriel, wasn't it?" I stiffened as Cristian's lips curled. "Yes, very strange indeed."

My hands balled into fists in my lap. "We're not talking about him. We're talking about you. And you're deflecting."

"On the contrary. You want to know my secrets? Fine. But trust goes both ways, sweetheart. I'll tell you mine if you tell me yours."

A flush of heat crawled up my neck. Who did this guy think he was? Sure, I was grateful for his help, but that didn't give him license to act like an asshole.

I pushed to stand. "You know what? I'm out of here." Shoving my chair back, I headed for the exit, maneuvering around some teenagers loitering in the entrance. Outside, I hung a quick left, darting around the building in the direction of an empty side street. Before I even made it halfway down the block, I heard footsteps behind me.

"Juliet, wait."

"Leave me alone, Cristian." I picked up my pace, passing beneath the glow of a street lamp.

"Would you wait a second?" A firm hand closed around my biceps, and I whirled, nearly crashing into him.

"Why, so you can keep taunting me about Gabriel? I told you about him in—" I almost said *in confidence*, but bit off the word because it sounded ridiculous. But I had, hadn't I? Something about Cristian during our first meeting had lulled me into a false sense of security, making me trust him when I had no reason to. Obviously, that had been a mistake.

"No, that's not—" He dropped my arm. "Fine, you were right, I was deflecting. You asked me a question I wasn't comfortable answering. I know I gave you the impression when we met that I'm an open book, but I'm not. I don't make a habit of oversharing."

"Cool, thanks for clearing that up." I turned to leave, but he stepped in my path.

"But maybe this once, I'll make an exception." I tucked my hand into the crook of my elbow, more than a little agitated. "Please," he added softly.

"Fine," I huffed, plopping down on an empty bench. "What do you want to say?"

He followed, lowering onto the seat beside me and resting his elbows against his knees.

"Before, when you asked me why I came to your rescue tonight, what I told you was true. I do consider myself to be a gentleman. But it was also because ..." He paused, furrowing his brow in concentration, as though he was struggling to voice whatever was on the tip of his tongue.

"How about we make a deal? Whatever we say on the bench, stays on the bench. We'll never speak of it again after tonight."

He cast me a wary look, searching for the lie in my words. Finally, he heaved a sigh, dropping his head between his shoulders. "It was just nice to be needed, okay?"

"What do you mean?" I frowned, trying to reconcile the over-confident man I had met weeks ago with the vulnerable guy sitting next to me now. "But you said your uncle—"

"Doesn't need me. Or at least, he doesn't act like it." His eyes lifted, settling on a spot across the street. "You want to know the truth about me? Well, here it is. For half of my life, I've worked tirelessly to prove my worth, to show my uncle my true value."

My throat bobbed. "I don't understand. Why would you need to do that?"

"For reasons I won't get into at the moment, my mother sent me to live with him when I was sixteen. I was a bit of a hellion back then, always getting into fights at school, walking around angry at the world." He dropped his gaze, studying his hands. "I was all but certain my uncle would put me out, but he didn't. Instead, he enrolled me in the local boxing club to give me an outlet for all my pent-up aggression. And he gave me an occupation, something to focus my mind on and keep me out of trouble. From then on, I worked at our family's restaurant every day."

"He sounds like a good man."

Cristian nodded. "He is, and the closest thing I've ever had to a father. My biological father bailed when I was an infant, and my stepfather was a poor substitute. My life was headed down a dark path, but my uncle gave me a chance at a better life. I will be forever grateful to him."

"But Cristian, if he did all that, then surely he must hold you in high regard."

A muscle twitched in his cheek. "You would think so. But the truth is, no matter what I did or how hard I worked, all of his admiration was reserved for his son. It was like Ga—my cousin could do no wrong." He dragged a hand over his forehead. "You know my cousin barely even showed an interest in the family business? But still, my uncle kissed the ground he walked on."

"But he put you in charge of the restaurant in Paris. Surely, that counts for something."

He released a hollow laugh. "Only because my cousin took off years ago. And me? I'm just the cheap replacement who stuck around."

I placed a hand on his shoulder. "Cristian, you're nobody's replacement. It's true the people closest to us can take us for granted and sometimes, in our desperation to be loved, we let them. But that doesn't make you any less valuable or worthy of their esteem."

His silver gaze landed on me like two high beams in the dark. "Tell that to my uncle."

"I'm telling *you*. You have to decide how you will allow others to treat you. If you feel undervalued, then you need to tell your uncle the truth. Don't fall prey to the narrative in your mind without having an honest conversation first."

Cristian scoffed. "That's a bit rich coming from you. Tell me, have you had an *honest conversation* with Gabriel? Or was there some other reason you called me tonight instead of him?"

My breath stalled. "What?"

"You heard me. Did you tell Gabriel the truth about how you feel? Or are you being a hypocrite and telling me to be honest when you have yet to do the same?"

"You don't know what you're talking about," I said, his words spearing through my chest.

His lids lowered as he leaned into my space. "Don't I?"

I pressed a hand to his chest to push him away but was caught off guard by the steady thrum of his heart beneath my palm, the warmth of his skin seeping through his shirt. His eyes flared for a fraction of a second before dipping to my mouth, sending my pulse into a frenzy.

"You know what I think?" he whispered. "I think you and I are alike, both afraid of the same thing."

"And what's that?"

"Rejection. Of the possibility of loving someone who doesn't love you in return. Of opening yourself up only to discover the truth hurts worse than the lie ever did. So, you hide from the light, slinking around in the shadows to keep yourself safe." I swallowed as the tip of his nose brushed mine. "That's why you called me, isn't it? Because you know I live in the darkness. I'm the place where you can hide all your secrets."

"No," I breathed. "You're wrong. I'm nothing like that, nothing like you."

He stilled, anger flashing across his features. "No, you're worse. You're a coward."

His words were like a slap to the face, and I blinked, my eyes stinging as he pulled away, chilly air filling the space he'd occupied moments before. Rising to my feet, I backed away from the bench. "I never should have called you. You're a cold-hearted bastard."

His smile was brittle. "Trust me, sweetheart, I've been called much worse."

I bit the inside of my cheek hard until I tasted blood. I wanted to scream and make him take back every word. Because it wasn't true. I *wasn't* a coward. Was I?

I swallowed thickly.

Even if there was some truth to what he'd said, I wasn't going to give him the satisfaction of admitting it.

Spinning on my heel, I turned and ran like hell.

Twenty-Five

Gabriel

"Hand me the five-millimeter Allen wrench, would you?"

I reached blindly for the tool cart, my fingers sliding over the familiar shape of metal before handing it to James without looking up from my phone. I'd spent the better part of an hour reading articles about stomach viruses, and quite frankly, I was more alarmed about Juliet's potential condition than I had been before I started. The internet was a dangerous place to diagnose an illness, but here I was, trying my luck anyway.

"She probably has viral gastroenteritis. Apparently, it's fairly common, but maybe she'll let me take her to a doctor, just to be sure."

James looked up from where he was kneeling in front of his BMC Fourstroke, changing a tire that had gone flat during our morning ride. He eyed the tool.

"Gabe, this is a fifteen millimeter."

I nodded absently, thumbing through the webpage of a local health clinic. "Hey, do you think I should go to the market for her? According to this article, she should drink plenty of clear liquids and only eat light foods, but she may not have some of this stuff."

Ever since Juliet's abrupt departure from the dinner party on Saturday, I'd been more than a little worried about her. Which was only made worse by the fact that she hadn't been answering my calls. Against my better judgment, I had gone back inside after she left and tried to reengage in the conversation. But it was no use. All I could think about was how I shouldn't have left her alone. In hindsight, I would have much rather dealt with her annoyance at my persistence than sit there with food turning to ash in my mouth while I wondered if she was okay.

A loud clanging noise interrupted my thoughts, and I glanced up to see James on his feet, frowning at me as he wiped his oil-stained hands on a rag, the wrench abandoned on the tool cart.

"What?"

"Did you even hear me?"

"Oh, sorry. What was it you needed? A ten millimeter?" I reached for the cart again, but he pushed it aside with a foot, stepping forward to block my path. I blinked in confusion as he closed the distance between us, coming nearly nose to nose with me.

"Um, is there a reason you're invading my personal space?" James and I were good friends, to be sure, but I was pretty certain we had never been close enough to breathe the same air.

"Oh, my God," he said under his breath. "You, my friend, have got it bad."

I sidestepped him, even as something terrifying and wonderful unfurled in my chest at hearing the thing I'd known for weeks finally spoken aloud. Grabbing the correct size wrench off the cart, I sat down on the stool he'd vacated to finish removing the tire.

"Juliet and I are just friends, that's all."

"Are you really?" James scrubbed a hand over his jaw. "That's interesting. Because you've never brought a woman to dinner at our place before. And you've spent what—three, four days with her over the past week?"

"Your point?" I rolled the flat tire away, finding its replacement lying on the floor near my foot. My phone chose that moment to vibrate, and I dropped the tire, snatching up the device. I swallowed a surge of disappointment when I saw it was only a message from Jean-Claude.

"*That* is my point exactly," he said, eyeing the phone as I tossed it aside.

I applied the wrench to the wheel axle with renewed fervor. "So, what's the story with Lily? Did your parents actually put her out, or is something else going on?"

"Oh no you don't. You're not getting out of this conversation that easily. Are you really going to sit here and spin me some bullshit tale about how you and Juliet are just friends?"

Finished with the tire, I stood up and turned my back to him, busying myself with organizing the tool cart. "It's complicated."

He snorted. "I doubt it. And if it *is* complicated, it's because you're making it that way." He leaned against the wall, scrutinizing me while I cleaned the wrenches before returning each one to its tray. "Is this another tactic of yours to avoid intimacy?"

I scowled at him. "What are you, a psychologist now?"

"No, I'm your *friend*. I know you, mate. We've spent more days together than not over the past few years, so I know what I'm talking about when I say you keep people at a distance. To be honest, I'm starting to think Nora and I must be a fluke."

"That's not true. What about Lily?"

He rolled his eyes. "Members of my family aside, in all the time I've known you, I've never seen you let anyone into your life in any real way. It's like you keep this shield up, making it impossible for people to get close to you. But with Juliet, you're different. You positively glow whenever she's around—" He dodged as I chucked an empty water bottle at him. "No, I'm serious. You light up like a bloody Christmas tree whenever one of us so much as mentions her. She's special, Gabe, and I don't want to see you blow it because you're too stubborn to let her in."

I had to hand it to James—he had me down to a tee.

There had been a time not so long ago when I'd sworn off relationships—not because I was afraid of commitment, but because I never wanted to be vulnerable again. Opening myself up had cost me a lot once, and the only way I knew to keep that from happening again was to seal off my emotions and shut everyone out.

But James was right—things *were* different with Juliet. She made me want to unlock every room in my heart and tell her to make herself at home. It had been a long time since I'd trusted anyone that way, but, by God, I wanted to trust her.

"Look, it was her idea, all right? I specifically asked her if she only wanted to be friends after we—well, anyway, I asked her, and she told me she thought it was for the best. Not that I blame her. She's got a lot riding on her opportunity here, and the last thing I want is to mess it up by distracting her."

"And you're certain that's the reason?" James glanced at me sidelong. "Because I don't buy it. It's more likely her hesitation has got something to do with you. You probably found a way to fuck it up without even realizing it."

"Oh, piss off. I mean, yeah, I might've said I only wanted to be friends back when we were first getting to know each other. But she had a boyfriend then, so I don't see why that's relevant."

"You don't see why that's relevant?" He gave me an incredulous look. "Well, this confirms it. I always knew I was the brains in this relationship, and you just the beauty." He pushed a chair toward me before taking one opposite it. "Have a seat, mate. The tool cart can wait."

I hesitated for half a beat before tossing down the cleaning rag and sinking onto the chair. He leaned forward, bracing his forearms on his knees as he studied me, and I shifted uncomfortably, unsure of what to say.

The truth was, I didn't have a clue about how to move things forward with Juliet. Like a complete idiot, I'd gone and stuck my foot in my mouth the first day we spent together at her place, waxing poetic about how I didn't want a relationship and digging my own goddamn grave in the process. And then, instead of setting the record straight, I'd let the words sit out there for weeks, drying like cement until even the thought of confessing my feelings to her made my tongue stick to the roof of my mouth.

The situation was hopeless.

"Did I ever tell you how I met Nora?"

My brows furrowed. "At a bar? A cycling event? An all-black clothing boutique?"

He snorted a laugh, pointing a finger at me. "I'm telling her you said that. No, believe it or not, I met her at the dentist. Well, actually, the first time I saw her was months before that when she visited the cycling studio where I used to teach spin classes, but we didn't officially meet until she was five minutes away from having her fingers in my mouth. She was a dental hygienist."

"Wow, that's disturbing."

"I know. Not how I pictured meeting my wife either, but, by the stars, she was beautiful." He smiled, his eyes dropping to his hands. "My life was totally different back then. I was just an amateur cyclist with a dream and a kernel of hope that I could make it come true. I always loved being on a bike, ever since I was a kid. It's the closest thing to flying without leaving the ground. Plus, I loved interacting with people, and I'd been holding on to an idea for years of how I could combine the two."

My lips hooked up in one corner. "And here we are."

"Indeed, here we are."

"Why Paris, though?" I realized I had never asked him before.

"Summer before my fourth year at uni, I scratched together enough coin to come and see the final stage of the Tour de France. There I was on the Champs-Élysées, standing in a sea of people, sweating and craning my neck, trying to catch a glimpse of the first cyclists to reach that final stretch. It was hot as sin, but as soon as I saw them rounding that corner, shiny helmets winking in the sunlight, my heart soared. I felt weightless watching them whiz by, the crowd cheering and waving. That's when the idea for this place first hit me. Bicycling in Paris."

I nodded thoughtfully. "And Nora?"

"Right, so four years later, I'm lying in a dentist's chair with the most beautiful woman I'd ever seen gazing down at me. And you know what I did? I looked her straight in the eye and said, *What do you say to marrying me and moving to Paris?*"

I gaped at him. "And that worked? She came just like that?"

"No, she came later," he said, winking suggestively. "But in all seriousness, I had to just put it all on the line, you know? I barely knew her, but for reasons I couldn't explain, I *knew* she was the one.

And yeah, I could have tried for a lighter touch, but sometimes time isn't on your side. Sometimes you just have to take a risk."

I nodded, turning his words over in my mind. "Okay, so what should I do about Juliet?"

"Come now," he said, clapping me on the shoulder. "I can't do all the work for you. Besides, the finer details are up to you. First, figure out what it is you want. And if what you want is to be with Juliet, then tell her. But you can't just spout sonnets—you also have to show her what's possible, what she can expect if she takes a chance on you."

Something that felt dangerously like hope stirred in my stomach as I contemplated what I might do, how I could show Juliet I believed we could be more if given the chance.

I blinked as an idea came to me.

"Hey, do you still have extra tickets to that charity gala?" I was already halfway across the room, grabbing my phone off the tool cart and flipping through my contacts.

"Yeah, why?"

"Good." I strode for the door, the call already ringing in my ear. "Hold four for me."

Twenty-Six

Cristian

My stepfather was a mean son of a bitch. Granted, I hadn't seen him in years, but I doubted he had changed much.

These days, whenever I spoke to my mother, more often than not, I ended up cutting our conversation short before she could bring him up. She was always slipping in details about him—about how he was doing well with his sobriety, how he'd held down a job beyond the probation period, how he was being diligent with his anger management counseling. It turned my stomach to hear her optimism, as if she actually believed he was capable of being a decent human being. I knew better. The only reason he was doing any of those things was because I had threatened to put a bullet in his head if he ever got violent with her again. That pleasant little interlude had taken place years ago.

It seemed like he had gotten the message.

Before then, I hadn't been able to look him in the eye—the man who had done nothing but make my childhood a living hell until my mother sent me to live with Marcel. Sending me away was the best thing she could have done for me, even though I still harbored lingering resentment over the fact she had put me out rather than that asshole. But for whatever reason, she needed him, and I was no one to judge.

We all had our demons.

For most of my childhood, my stepfather had been that for me—a loathsome entity I had to face on a daily basis. The bastard never missed an opportunity to tell me I was worthless or unleash his bottled-up rage on me, as if I was the reason his life was a train wreck. When I got older, I learned to avoid him altogether, slipping out of the house before he stirred from his drunken slumber and staying out until well after dark. I figured if he wanted to beat the shit out of me, he would have to catch me first. Needless to say, he was a terrible parent.

But then there was that one percent of the time, that random day out of a hundred when he was sober enough to do something halfway decent like take me to the park. He never pushed me on the swings or anything, but he would sit on the bench and smoke a cigarette while I played. It was during one of those rare occasions when he taught me the only lesson he had to offer—*Own your shit.* It was beyond hypocritical coming from a man who would rather drown himself at the bottom of a bottle, but that didn't make it any less valuable.

I'll never forget the day he said it to me. We were at the park, and I was being reckless on the swings, pumping my legs as hard as I could, preparing to launch myself into the air and stick the landing like I was an Olympic gold medalist. Except I didn't stick the landing. I lost control of the swing and flew several meters before collapsing on the ground like a ton of bricks.

I had howled like an animal, more out of shock than actual pain. But before the tears even hit my cheeks, my stepfather hoisted me up by my collar, clapping me hard on the back, which I supposed was his version of a hug.

"You don't get to cry, you hear me?" He knelt in front of me, placing his hands on my shoulders as tears burned the back of my eyes. "You made a stupid choice and now you're paying the price. So, you have two options—you can either stay on the ground, or you can get back up and own your shit."

So here I was, standing outside the literature department on AUP's campus, preparing to do that very thing—to own my shit.

I glanced at my watch as students filtered in and out of the building. Had I gotten the time wrong? I was pretty certain Juliet's class should have ended at least half an hour ago, assuming the online course schedule was correct. But I still hadn't caught so much as a glimpse of her.

Speaking of owning my shit, what the hell had I been thinking the other night?

I'd never meant to call her a coward, never meant to say half of the things I said to her. But it was like she circumvented my defenses, making me reveal things I'd never told anyone. And what was that bit about *it was nice to be needed*? God, I wished I hadn't told her that. Not that keeping it to myself would have made it any less true. It *had* felt good getting that call from her, knowing she had chosen me to help her instead of Gabriel.

If only I hadn't lost my temper.

Little did she know, her words about not being anyone's replacement had been a balm on an old wound. But then I lashed out when she started talking about honesty, accusing her of being a hypocrite. In truth, I was just uncomfortable confronting my own insecurities.

Then, to make matters worse, I'd gone and pushed the envelope, thinking I could turn her words around on her and get her to open up about Gabriel. Except, the second I leaned into her space to disarm her, the reverse happened. It was like I had blacked out and suddenly all I knew were wide green eyes and the scent of lavender. Then she went and touched me, and I totally lost the plot. Goddamn right, I thought about kissing her. She was just hovering there, tempting me with those rosy lips, breathing hard and shuddering, and I was only a red-blooded male after all.

So sue me.

I dragged a hand over my face, checking my watch again. *What's done is done.* I needed to focus on damage control now. If I was going to make sure everything went according to plan, I had to mend fences with this girl.

Just as soon as I could find her.

The door swung open, and I searched for a hint of brown-gold hair and freckles. Instead, my gaze latched on to that guy who had been at Galeries with Juliet and Simone. What was his name again? Calvin? Cedric? I was pretty sure it was C-something.

Shoving my hands in my pockets, I sauntered over to him, tipping my head in greeting. His eyes narrowed when he saw me. Evidently, he wasn't my biggest fan. Not that I could blame him after the way his girlfriend had been checking me out the other night.

"Hey," he said. "Cristian, right?"

"Yeah. Good to see you again." He gave me a look that said the feeling wasn't mutual. I pressed on anyway. "Would you happen to know where I might find Juliet?"

He frowned, his brows drawing together. "Don't you have her number?"

"Left my phone at the office, I'm afraid." *I swear, if Caleb Martin calls me before I get what I need from this guy, I'll gut him like a fish.* "By the way, Juliet appreciated you helping her out the other night. She was telling me what a great guy you are and how lucky her friend is to have you."

He gave me a skeptical look, like he was deciding whether he was in the mood to be helpful. Finally, he sighed. "She's upstairs in Professor Benoit's office. But she's working, so—"

"Thanks, man." I clapped him on the shoulder, leaving him to gape after me, his mouth opening and closing like a landed trout.

A quick glance at the directory told me Julien Benoit's office was on the second floor, and I took the stairs two at a time, haphazardly mulling over what I wanted to say to Juliet. Not that it mattered. If Sunday night had proven anything, it was that all of my scruples would go right over a cliff the second Juliet fixed me with that no-nonsense look of hers.

Finding the office at the end of the hallway, I knocked despite the door being ajar.

"Come," called a deep voice, and I paused on the threshold, frowning.

I didn't particularly like the idea of Juliet being up here alone with some old guy, sequestered in his office down a corridor far away from listening ears. What if he was some pervert who got off on having a pretty young assistant all to himself? What if he made a pass at her? More importantly, why did *I* care? I pressed my mouth into a thin line and pushed the door open.

A shaft of sunlight hit me as soon as I entered the room, pouring in through the floor-length windows. I squinted, spotting a man sitting behind an old-fashioned desk.

He peered at me over his glasses, a fountain pen suspended in his hand. "Can I help you?"

I blinked, shaking off my surprise. His desk may have been old, his style of clothing too, but there was nothing old about the man looking back at me. This was Juliet's *professor*? He didn't even look that much older than me, and his manner was alarmingly debonair for an academic in tweed.

"Cristian?" I spun around to find Juliet standing behind me, holding two steaming coffee mugs, her plaited hair hanging over one shoulder. Her lips curved toward the floor as I stared at her for too many seconds, groping for the slipshod speech I had prepared.

What was I supposed to be saying?

After several seconds, during which I seemed to have lost all brain function, she moved past me into the room. After exchanging a few words with her professor, she took me by the arm and dragged me down the hallway like a naughty schoolboy on his way to the headmaster's office.

I let her lead me down the staircase and out a back exit, all while trying to clear my head.

All I needed to do was apologize. *Easy.* But the minute we stepped outside, she turned and pierced me with a look that eloquently read, *Please fuck all the way off.*

"What do you want, Cristian? Come to take another swipe at me?"

Something like hurt flashed in her eyes, and I reached up to loosen my tie, which was suddenly too tight. "I came to say I'm sorry for my behavior the other night. I crossed a line." She regarded me silently, and I pushed on. "I shouldn't have ..." *Taunted you about Gabriel. Called you a hypocrite. Almost kissed you.* "I'm ... I'm just sorry."

Okay, apparently, I sucked at apologizing.

She looked away, her expression brimming with irritation. But that was a good thing. She might be angry, but at least she wasn't indifferent, which meant I had a shot at making things right with her.

For the restaurant scheme, of course.

"Why should I trust you?"

I swallowed, my Adam's apple getting stuck behind my collar. "Maybe you shouldn't."

There was no maybe about it. She absolutely shouldn't trust me. I was dragging her into a family conflict she knew nothing about, all to serve my own selfish aims. And for what? It wasn't as if I didn't have any other options, any other way to get through to Gabriel. I'd only let those plans fall to the wayside because I was confident Juliet was the easiest means to an end. But if I had to, I could go back to the drawing board. I didn't have to stand here fighting with her.

What was it she'd called me? A cold-hearted bastard? Yeah. That was for the best. Better to let her think the worst of me, to let her walk away before I could do any more damage.

After a beat of silence, she laughed bitterly, backing toward the door. "Got it. Have a nice life, Cristian."

"Wait—" Because fuck *that*. I wasn't giving up that easily.

I darted a look around, searching for a way to keep her from leaving. My eyes snagged on something across the courtyard, sunlight reflecting off its metal slats. It was a Hail Mary, but I was out of options.

"Bench rules," I blurted out.

She hovered in the doorway, wrinkling her nose in confusion. "What?"

"Bench rules," I repeated, nodding in the direction of the lone bench sitting near a fountain at the other end of the courtyard. "Whatever is said on the bench, stays on the bench, right? Ask me anything you want. I promise I won't lie to you." I didn't wait for her to agree before striding toward it. Later, I would pick apart why this woman had me chasing her around like a whipped puppy, but for now, the only thing I wanted was to see this through.

I shrugged out of my jacket, sinking onto the heated metal as the mist from the fountain cooled my skin. By the time I had rolled up my shirt sleeves, Juliet was walking toward me, and my shoulders lowered an inch in relief.

She sat down next to me, cradling her elbows. "I need to be back upstairs in ten minutes."

"That's fine. Ask me anything you want."

She chewed on her bottom lip. "The other night, did you ... almost kiss me?"

I coughed, choking on an inhale. "Way to skip the warm-up and go straight for the jugular." She stared at me without blinking, and I shifted uncomfortably, clearing my throat.

Okay, so she was going to make me work for it.

"Yes, I got caught up in the moment, but it won't happen again. I'm not the type of man to pursue a woman who belongs to someone else. My pride would never allow it."

She nodded, her mouth twitching. "Of that, I have little doubt." She rolled her lips. "That stuff about your family. Was that true?"

"Yes, it was."

"And what you said about being needed ..."

"True. All of it was true, Juliet."

I couldn't remember the last time I'd felt this uncomfortable. Opening up and sharing feelings wasn't my brand of whiskey. I swallowed roughly. Maybe I should just call time on this whole truth-telling thing and let her go back to being pissed at me.

"Thank you," she said. "For being honest with me. And you should know, I *did* need you. There was no one else I could call."

I nodded. "How about we take two on our conversation from the other night? There must've been a reason you called me instead of Gabriel."

"You really won't let this go, will you?"

"I wish I could, darling, but I must know. Was it because you missed the pleasure of my company? My unassailable charm?"

She snorted. "Has anyone ever told you you're a walking red flag?"

"Yes, among other things." She clapped a hand over her mouth but was too late to catch the laugh that fell from her lips, and my mouth twitched, an unexpected warmth filling my chest.

"So, what happened with Gabriel? Boyfriend or not, I have a hard time believing he would have refused to come if you called."

She braided her fingers together. "Well ..." Ten minutes later, she finished recounting the details of a dinner party where someone named Lily had thrown herself all over Gabriel. "The worst part is, I would have *liked* her if she hadn't been vying for Gabriel's attention. To make matters worse, it was hard to miss how beautiful she was. I mean, if perfection could be embodied in a single person, it would be her."

I glanced at Juliet from the corner of my eye. "Are you sure it's Gabriel with the deep-rooted affection? You seem pretty taken with her yourself."

She jabbed me in the ribs. "Don't remind me of what an ass you can be now that I've decided to share." She examined her hands for a long moment. "Anyway, that's why I didn't call him. Because if there *is* something between him and Lily, I don't want to get caught in the middle."

"I see. And what exactly did he do to make you think there was something between them?"

She frowned, a tiny wrinkle forming between her brows. "Well, it wasn't anything he did per se, it was just more of an impression I had. There was this familiarity between them, like the kind that comes from having romantic feelings or—"

"From being his best friend's little sister?"

She crossed her arms. "I know what I saw, Cristian."

"No, you know what you *think* you saw. I can't speak for this Lily person, but I'm certain there is no way he prefers her to you."

"How do you know that?"

Because I've seen the way he looks at you.

"I just do. But you don't have to take my word for it. Ask him yourself. You're basing a lot on assumptions. If I might offer you your own advice, you shouldn't fall prey to the narrative in your mind without having an honest conversation first."

"I'm not sure it's that simple."

"It's exactly that simple." I hooked an arm on the bench. "When are you seeing him next?"

"Um, tomorrow evening. He asked if I was available, though he didn't say what we're doing yet. I think it might be a surprise."

Good. All wasn't lost yet.

"You should go and enjoy yourself. I'm sure another woman will be the last thing on his mind after having spent days without your radiant company. Speaking of radiance, I almost forgot." I slipped a hand into the inside pocket of my jacket, pulling out a small leather box and handing it to her. "I brought something for you."

"Is this the bracelet from the department store?"

"It is. How do you think I was able to get you released from custody? I might be charming, but that saleswoman was out for blood. Anyway, it's yours now."

She hesitated. "Cristian, I can't accept this. You should give it to a friend or a girlfriend."

I swallowed an uncomfortable lump in my throat. I had no one else to give it to, but she didn't need to know that.

"My apologies. Of course you wouldn't want it. I should have realized." I reached for the box, but she held on to it, her eyes running a lap around my face.

"I'm sorry. I didn't mean it as a rejection. I only meant it's too nice to give to someone who's practically a stranger. But if you want me to have it, at least allow me to pay for it."

"How about this instead?" I said, ignoring the wrench in my gut that warned me I was about to do something I would regret later. "Go out with Gabriel tomorrow and tell him the truth. No matter what, you'll feel better for having been honest with him. If things work out, you can bring him to my restaurant opening, and we'll call it an even trade."

"That's hardly a fair trade." She looked down at the bracelet, the sapphires winking in the afternoon sunlight. "But all right." The unsettling feeling in my abdomen expanded as her eyes returned to mine, crinkling in the corners as she smiled.

This girl is making me soft.

The only reason I was here was to accomplish a task for Marcel. And with the opening less than a month away, this was no time to become sentimental.

I had to be calculated, strategic.

Never mind the fact that the idea of Juliet getting caught in the crossfire of all this suddenly made me ill at ease.

Twenty-Seven

Gabriel

At eight o'clock sharp, I rapped on the door to Juliet's apartment. Dressed in black tie and sweating bullets, I took a solid breath, clutching the bouquet of roses in my fist so hard that it was a wonder the stems didn't snap.

Were the flowers too much? Should I have gotten pink instead of red?

Fuck, probably.

Needless to say, it had been a long time since I'd been on a date. Not that this was a date. At least, that's not the way I had presented tonight's charity gala at the Hôtel Salomon de Rothschild to Juliet when I'd met up with her earlier, tickets in hand and heart in my throat.

As soon as I'd stepped inside Café Procope, I spotted her at her usual table in the corner, huddled over her laptop and staring intently at the screen. For a moment, I lingered in the doorway, drinking in the sight of her. I could picture her cinnamon-sugar freckles from across the room when she wrinkled her nose, and when her lips hooked up in a smile, a dangerous thought careened through my head.

Mine.

No, not yet. I still had to earn the right to call her that.

So much had changed since my conversation with James, and now I was looking at this whole thing with Juliet in a new light. I hadn't forgotten what she'd said about wanting to be just friends, and before now, I hadn't been willing to fight her on it or give her a reason to believe this thing between us could be something real.

But that was all about to change, starting tonight.

The door opened to reveal Juliet in a midnight-blue evening gown that trailed over her figure, clinging to every elegant curve of her body. My eyes swept up to her face, and my Adam's apple got caught behind my tie when I saw her usually rosy lips were painted blood red.

By all the saints.

How was it this woman was custom made to fit every one of my desires?

"Hi," she breathed.

I wasn't sure if I was imagining the warmth in those pretty green irises, but I would take it, real or imagined.

"Hey."

God, I had missed her. I'd spent every minute since the dinner party worrying about her, and it wasn't until she finally texted me back yesterday that I'd been able to inhale properly again.

She smiled, following my gaze to her dress. "Is it too much?"

I bit down on my knuckles, weighing my desire to impress her tonight against the sudden urge to cancel all our plans, carry her inside, and strip her right out of that dress.

"No," I said, my throat raw. "You look exquisite."

She nodded toward the roses. "Are those for me?"

"What? Oh yeah, they are." I passed them to her, my eyes catching on a sapphire bracelet hanging from her wrist as she took them.

"Thank you. I'll just put these in water." She turned her back to me, and I nearly cursed a blue streak when I saw her dress dipped to the base of her spine, revealing a flawless expanse of bare skin. Looking over one shoulder, she said, "Do you want to come in?"

Fuck no. I didn't trust myself to be alone with her. Because, given half the chance, there was no way we'd leave this apartment before I had explored every inch of her body twice over and a third time for quality assurance.

"I'll just wait in the hallway."

Or out on the sidewalk, possibly handcuffed to a light post.

"All right. I'll be just a minute then." She disappeared inside, and I let go of an exhale. I was going to need a will of steel to get through the evening without attempting to undress her in a coat closet or something. But it would be worth the wait if everything went according to plan.

My phone vibrated, and I fished it out, James's name lighting up the screen. "Hey."

"Hey, buddy. Are you in the queue? Nora and I just got here." I heard an odd grunting noise, followed by a series of heated whispers. "Sorry, for whatever reason, Nora wants me to tell you Lily's coming tonight."

"Oh yeah?" I said absently, my eyes trailing back to the door at the sound of Juliet's returning footsteps. "What for?" Not that she needed a reason to attend a charity event, but if memory served, she had never shown an interest.

"I don't know, she didn't say. But she seemed pretty keen on coming. Anyway, how long till you and the missus get here?" I caught Nora's snort of laughter in the background and made a mental note to puncture her bike tires at the next available opportunity.

"We should be there in about twenty minutes if traffic is good."

"Excellent. We'll wait for you at the table then. And what about your special guests?"

Before I could answer, Juliet stepped into the hallway. "Ready?"

"Is that Juliet?" James said, evidently overhearing. "Tell her we look forward to seeing her again. Since our dinner party was cut short, I never had the chance to regale her with all my favorite stories about you. Like the time you got foxed and fancied a naked swim in the river—"

"Bye, asshole." The sound of James's chuckle cut out as I ended the call.

"Who was that?" She took my hand, and I brought it to my lips, pressing a kiss against it.

"James. He's already waiting for us with Nora and Lily."

A look of surprise that I didn't quite understand flickered across her features, her lips tilting down. "Oh, Lily's coming tonight?"

"Mm-hmm." I glanced up the street as we exited the building, searching for a taxi. "Most likely she just wants to tag along with James. He's a huge supporter of the foundation hosting tonight's event. It's a great cause. This particular charity supports children with disabilities by providing opportunities to increase their mobility. They even hosted a sporting tournament this past spring, sort of like a junior Paralympics."

Juliet hummed without looking at me, her expression oddly blank.

She waited on the sidewalk while I secured a cab, seemingly lost in thought, and I wondered whether I had said something wrong. But before I could worry over it too much, she slid her hand into mine again, and we fell into a comfortable conversation about the charities her family supported in New York. In no time at all, we were pulling up to the gates of the historic mansion.

We headed up the stone pathway to the entrance, and Juliet's expression brightened as she took in the marble foyer and sweeping grand staircase. Closing my fingers around hers, I led her up to the second floor, watching as she marveled at the neoclassical design and vintage fixtures.

Every damn day. That's how often I wanted to wake up to this breathtaking woman, to see her face light up with wonder.

Her lips parted as we moved into the main hall, her gaze bouncing from the polished onyx fireplace nestled between two French doors to the nine-paneled mirror reflecting the light of a gilded candelabra. My eyes followed hers as they climbed up the center of the hall, which opened onto a third floor enclosed by a marble balustrade underneath a glass ceiling.

"Sometimes," she said quietly, "I have this inescapable feeling that some things aren't meant for this world."

My eyes returned to her, roaming from the soft arch of her cheek to her hair that was pulled away from her face, exposing her elegant neck that I desperately wanted to explore with my mouth.

"On that, angel, we agree entirely."

Placing a hand at the base of her spine, I led her through to the adjacent salon, soaking in the heat of her skin beneath my rough fingertips. My hand twitched with the urge to haul her against me. *Just a few more hours*. Then she would be mine.

A waiter passed with a tray of champagne and I grabbed two flutes, handing one to Juliet.

"What should we toast to?"

"To getting everything our hearts desire," I whispered against her ear. My pulse kicked up a notch when I felt her shiver against me.

"And what does your heart desire, Gabriel?" Her lips hovered so close I could almost taste them. One tiny movement and her mouth would be mine. I brushed her cheek with my knuckles, letting my fingers unfold over the angle of her jaw.

"I think you already know."

Did I imagine her pupils dilating? No, that wasn't my imagination. I tilted her chin up as her breath quickened, moving my thumb beneath the curve of her mouth, bringing our lips level.

Mine ...

"Oh, there you are."

A voice dragged us from our intimate bubble, and I grunted in protest as Juliet pulled away from me, taking all the warmth with her.

"Lily," she said under her breath.

"Lily?"

A second later, Lily herself appeared, planting a kiss on Juliet's cheek before turning to me. "We've been waiting for you." She tossed one auburn curl over her shoulder as she beamed up at me, and I forced a hard swallow, trying to restart my smile.

Calm down. She doesn't mean any harm.

But as I watched her loop an arm through Juliet's and drag her away, I wondered whether that was true.

Juliet

We pressed through a sea of people in tuxedos and evening gowns, and my nose twitched as I breathed in a potent mixture of colognes and perfumes.

Goodness, hadn't anyone heard that less is more?

Warding off a sneeze, I craned my neck to look for Gabriel, but a woman draped in a fur stole, a cigarette poised between her plum-colored lips, blocked my view.

"Lily." I strained against her iron grip. "Shouldn't we wait for Gabriel?"

"Oh, don't worry about him. I'm sure he'll find us in no time." She led me past tables covered with white linen tablecloths, glass centerpieces, and intricate floral arrangements.

I followed her reluctantly, taking in the champagne gown clinging to her slender frame, its satin straps crossing over the porcelain skin of her exposed back.

Of course, she looked like a fairy-tale princess tonight. Had Gabriel noticed?

Before I could follow that train of thought all the way to crazy town, we arrived at a table near the center of the room, half of its seats already occupied.

I spotted James and Nora.

"Juliet." Nora rose from her seat, wrapping me in an embrace that nearly cut off my flow of oxygen. "I'm glad you could make it tonight. Gabe has spoken of little else for days."

I blinked, my heart tripping at this new information. *Days?* Gabriel seemed so casual when he invited me to the gala earlier this afternoon. Had he really been planning this for days?

"Juliet." James engulfed me in a hug, and a laugh bubbled out my throat.

Extricating myself, I placed my hands on his shoulders, giving him a once-over. "Wow, you sure do clean up nice."

He threw me a wink. "Don't let Gabe hear you say that."

"Don't let Gabe hear you say what?" On cue, Gabriel's hand hooked around my waist, and my whole body hummed at the simple contact. Instinctively, I turned toward him, and he folded me into the crook of his arm like we'd done this a thousand times before. I caught the rapid exchange of glances around the table but was distracted when his lips brushed over my temple in a featherlight kiss.

"There's someone I'd like you to meet." He drew me toward an older man and a young woman sitting opposite James and Nora, speaking to each other in hushed tones. The man stood at our approach, eyeing me curiously beneath a cloud of white hair.

"Juliet, I would like to introduce you to Jean-Claude Blanchet."

"Oh, your art agent, right?"

Gabriel gave me an affectionate smile. "You have an excellent memory. But I forgot to mention he's also the man responsible for my shot at success."

"*Enchanté.*" Jean-Claude bent over my hand, planting a polite kiss on the back of it. "And nonsense. You, *mon cher*, are responsible for your own success." Jean-Claude turned, gesturing to the woman still seated behind him. "And this delightful lady is my niece, Celine."

She rose, assessing me with shrewd eyes, her chin-length hair framing the sharp line of her jaw. *"Je suis ravie de faire votre connaissance."* When I extended my hand, she grasped it firmly, and I took an instant liking to her.

Gabriel pulled out the chair beside hers for me, and I lowered myself into it as he took the seat to my left. Celine resumed her seat, extracting a cigarette from a thin metal case.

"So, you're Mr. Blanchet's niece?"

The corner of her mouth curled as she blew out a long column of smoke. Leaning in, she lowered her voice conspiratorially. "I'm actually his *great*-niece. But don't tell him I told you. He would never admit to being old enough to have a great-anything." I bit my lip before a smile could surface, dragging two fingers over my mouth in a zipping motion.

"And you?" Several waiters appeared, depositing bowls of soup in front of us. "I hear you are a writer."

"Um, well, aspiring writer."

She raised an eyebrow, regarding me over the rim of her wineglass. "Aspiring? *Ma chère,* you either are a writer or you are not. Do Americans always make things so complicated?"

Sparks of heat trailed up my neck as I stared down at my steaming bowl of bouillabaisse.

She chuckled. "I am only kidding. Though, I suggest you drop the aspiring line in the future. If you want to be in this industry, you cannot be timid about it. There's a writer on every corner in Paris, and you won't be doing yourself any favors by playing coy."

"Right, um—"

"She's submitting a piece to *La Nouvelle Revue Française* pretty soon," Gabriel said over my shoulder. I turned to find his eyes on me, his hand folding around mine under the table. "Isn't that right, Juliet?"

"Yes, that's right."

She eyed me thoughtfully. "*Ç'est vrai*? That's a competitive publication. You must be confident to submit to them." It was meant as a statement, but I could see the question in her eyes. The challenge.

I swallowed, grateful for the reassuring pressure of Gabriel's hand.

In the legal industry, you constantly had to prove yourself. Pass the bar exam. Secure a position in a reputable firm. Show your colleagues you have what it takes to be among their ranks. But this new pursuit of mine was different. I wasn't sure whether it was because of what Celine said or because Gabriel had backed me up, but I felt an unexpected surge of confidence. All my life, I had colored inside the lines, following all the rules out of fear of making a misstep. But I didn't need to do that anymore.

I could write my own damn rules.

"This will be my first time submitting a creative piece to a publication, but I've been writing for years. I'm a practicing attorney in New York and have coauthored several published articles. Writing about things like social issues in M&A transactions differs from what I'm writing now, but I'm confident in my ability to learn and adapt. And even if I don't win this competition, I'll have learned something for trying."

Celine gave me an assessing look.

Had I said too much?

I glanced around the table, my eyes trailing over James and Nora before falling on Lily. I blinked, surprised to find her staring at me with parted lips, her face pale.

"You should send me your piece," Celine said, drawing my attention back to her. Unsnapping the clasp of her clutch, she rummaged around inside it before extracting a card and handing it to me. I examined it.

Celine Blanchet. Co-Editor-in-Chief, *La Femme*.

Holy crap. She was an editor-in-chief?

"Don't worry," she said, apparently mistaking my shock for discomfort. "I won't use anything you've written without your permission. Our magazine might not be as established as *La Nouvelle Revue Française*, but we are carving out our place in the market. Since *La Femme* is a digital-only publication, we can produce content faster than some of the larger print magazines. Undoubtedly, that is why our readership has tripled in the last year alone. We're looking for new contributors, so if you ever have any interest in doing a weekly column or something similar, keep us in mind."

Weekly column? I glanced over at Gabriel who was now chatting with James, his hand still wrapped securely around mine.

Gabriel.

After the dinner party, I'd told myself I wanted clarity on where things stood between us, a definitive line in the sand. But now that line was more blurred than ever. Instead of reestablishing boundaries, I was teetering on the precipice of something huge, something life-changing.

And I was one breath away from toppling over the edge.

"Juliet?" I blinked at the sound of Gabriel's voice. "Are you all right?"

"Yes," I croaked, my heart beating in the back of my throat. "I just need some air."

Pushing my chair back, I hurried toward the exit, pressing a hand to my chest and praying I hadn't just fallen head over heels for Gabriel Beaumont.

Twenty-Eight

Juliet

I ducked into the crisp night, entering a courtyard bathed in low lamplight and surrounded by a line of hedgerows. The moon hung low in the sky, and I set off at a brisk pace toward the far end.

An unexpected sob worked its way up my throat, and I pressed a hand to my mouth, catching it before the sound could escape.

So what if Gabriel had brought me to a stunning mansion to wine and dine with Parisian high society, all while supporting a good cause? So what if he'd just helped me make professional inroads by introducing me to a female editor-in-chief? It didn't change anything—didn't change the fact that he didn't want a relationship.

I fumbled for a tissue, only to remember I left my purse inside. I sniffed instead, pressing the heels of my hands beneath my eyes to staunch the liquid heat threatening to spill over.

Buck up, Chandler.

If I could power through a three-hour call with opposing counsel, I could dry my face and make it through the rest of this dinner. Before I could decide on whether to return to the dining room or let myself have a good cry first, I heard footsteps.

"Juliet."

I sensed him without turning around, his hand gentle on my elbow.

Don't fall prey to the narrative in your mind without having an honest conversation.

Cristian was right. I *was* being a coward, and I was tired of it. Whether or not this was destined to end in heartbreak, I needed to understand once and for all if Gabriel and I were just friends or if we had the potential to be something more.

I turned to him, my eyes colliding with those twin pools of sapphire. "Gabriel, why did you bring me here tonight?"

He searched my face. "Because I know how important your writing is to you. And even though I have no doubt you'll be a success, I want you to know you have options. No matter what happens with the *NRF* competition, I want you to find what you are seeking."

"But why? What does it all mean? For … for us."

His brows softened, his lips parting in the half-light as he consumed the remaining space between us.

"It means," he said, eyes falling to my mouth, "that we have a lot to talk about, angel."

In the space of a breath, he slanted his mouth hard over mine, kissing me like he would die if he didn't, like his only reason for breathing air was to share it with me. I whimpered, parting my lips to taste more of him, and his tongue brushed against mine as his hand slid to the nape of my neck. He drew me closer, the hard planes of his chest pressing against the swell of my breasts, and heat bloomed in every corner of my body when I felt him stiffening against me.

"Juliet," he said, his voice full of gravel. "I promised not to do this again, not until ..." He didn't finish his sentence, his conflicted eyes boring into mine. I stared back beneath heavy lids, my pulse scattering as his fingers painted a path down my spine.

If there was ever a moment for honesty, now would be it. But our lips were already gravitating toward each other again, our breaths tangling.

"Gabriel," I breathed, eyes fluttering.

An answering groan rose in his throat as he looped an arm around my waist, lifting me in one smooth motion and moving us backward until my shoulders brushed against a hedge. Fisting the fabric of my dress, he pushed it up around my hips, settling himself between my legs. And when he rocked his erection against me, a shower of sparks danced across the back of my eyelids.

"Understand this," he said, thrusting harder and making my core clench with need. "The only reason I'm not dragging your panties down your thighs right now is because you deserve more than a quick fuck in a public garden."

I moaned, burying my teeth in his lower lip. I would happily accept anything this man was willing to give me. Let him bend me over a bench and have his way with me? Done. Allow him to carry my panties around in his pocket as a trophy of his conquest? Gladly. God, where was my sense of propriety? Gone apparently, carried off on a summer breeze.

"Come home with me tonight," he rasped, his thumb sliding along the crease of my hip.

A resounding yes danced on my tongue, but before I could voice it, we heard the sound of crunching gravel. Gabriel hastily lowered me to the ground, fixing my dress before adjusting himself. We were barely presentable when a man in a waiter's uniform rounded the hedge and drew up short, the cigarette between his lips going slack when he took in the state of us.

"Oh, *excusez-moi de vous déranger*," he said, his eyes flitting away from us as a flush rose in his cheeks. "*Je n'avais pas réalisé que quelqu'un était ici.*"

"*Ne vous inquiétez pas.*" Gabriel raked a hand through his disheveled hair before taking my hand. "We were just leaving."

Gabriel

The evening couldn't have turned out better. I had Juliet in my arms, the slow rhythm of a jazz band keeping time as we swayed back and forth. After dinner, the chandeliers had been dimmed, creating an intimate atmosphere, and I lost track of the rest of our group as I led Juliet to the dance floor.

I buried my nose in her soft hair, breathing in her sweet scent and imagining those silky strands wrapped around my fist. A low groan rumbled in my chest. *Later.* There would be time for everything later. First, I had to talk to her and make my intentions clear. Because there was no being just friends for us.

It would be all or nothing.

"Are you having a good time?" I asked, brushing my lips over the shell of her ear and relishing the way her eyes fluttered shut. She hummed into my shoulder as I slid my fingers along her spine.

God, she felt so right.

"Gabriel?" Her tone was soft, hesitant. "There's something I want to tell you—"

I jolted as my phone vibrated in my pocket, pulsing repeatedly. Not a text message then—someone was calling. Juliet blinked, jarred by the interruption, and I growled in irritation as I dug the device out, preparing to shut it off. But no sooner had I glanced at the number than all the warmth seeped from my limbs.

What the ...

"Should you get that?"

My eyes shot to Juliet, taking in the little wrinkle between her delicate brows as a cold sweat broke out over my skin. I wet my lips, mopping my forehead.

"Yeah, just one second." Taking her by the elbow, I moved to the edge of the dance floor, my thumb hovering over the screen. A second before I pressed the green button to accept, a voice somewhere inside my head shouted for me not to answer it.

I did anyway.

"*Âllo?*"

"Hello, Gabriel."

Blood turned to ice in my veins, the voice on the other end as familiar and foreign as the fleeting traces of a nightmare.

"Elise?" My voice sounded strange, as though it belonged to someone else.

"Did you miss me, *mon cher amour*?"

With a grimace, I walked away from Juliet, loosening my tie as I went and clutching the phone in a death grip. "How did you get this number?"

She clicked her tongue. "So hostile. Is that how you speak to the love of your life?"

"You are nothing to me," I gritted out, horrified to find my hand was shaking. "Did my father give you this number?"

She scoffed. "Of course not. In spite of everything, his loyalty to you endures."

In spite of everything. As if all that had occurred—all that she and Lucien had done to me—could be summed up in such a simple phrase. Like it meant nothing, even though it had cost me everything.

"What do you want, Elise?"

She paused. "I've missed you—"

"Don't you dare. I don't know what pit of hell you crawled out of, but you can turn right the fuck around because I want nothing to do with you." A heavy silence emanated through the phone as I stood rooted to the spot, the music fading to a low hum as blood rushed in my ears.

After a long beat, she spoke again. "I'll be seeing you soon, Gabriel." She disconnected the call, and my hand dropped, the phone sliding from my grasp as my heart thundered against my rib cage.

What the hell just happened?

The room suddenly felt too small, and I pulled at my collar to release the pressure on my windpipe.

"Gabriel?" A warm hand closed over my clammy one, and I whirled to find Juliet behind me, her face etched with worry. "Goodness, you're cold as ice. What happened?"

"Nothing." I scrubbed a hand over my face, pulling out of her grasp.

I didn't want her to see me like this, to get an up-close look at all the raw and broken pieces of me, the old wounds now freshly exposed.

First Lucien shows up out of the blue and now Elise. What had I done to deserve this? Just when my life was taking on new meaning, the two of them showed up like thieves in the night, intent on taking everything away from me. Again.

And Juliet ... what must I look like to her?

"Something's come up," I forced out, nearly choking on the lie. "I need to take you home."

She sucked in a sharp breath, her eyes glistening in the dim light.

This is hurting her. I'm hurting her. But I needed to get my head on straight and clear up this mess with Elise before I took things any further.

For the entire ride back to her apartment, I held her hand. The silence of the cab was an abrupt change from the music and laughter that had surrounded us minutes before. A beautiful moment that might have become a cherished memory until Elise called and ruined it. I shouldn't be surprised. That had always been her modus operandi—ruining things.

At Juliet's door, I pressed a kiss to her forehead. "I'll call you tomorrow." Without waiting for her reply, I strode for the stairs, pedaling down them as quickly as possible before I could change my mind and go back up. Juliet deserved the best, and I wanted to give her that. But not like this. Not until I shut this shit down with Elise.

I pushed out on to the dark street as the image of Juliet with tears in her eyes swam before my vision.

I'm going to fix this, angel.

I just hoped she could hang on until then.

Twenty-Nine

Cristian

I wiped the sweat from my eyes and reached for the pull-up bar again, hoisting myself up for another set. It was already half past ten, but I was restless and needed to burn off some energy if I had any hope of getting some sleep. On any other night, I might have ventured out to a bar to pick up a woman, but the idea didn't appeal to me tonight. Instead, I'd pulled on sweatpants and headed for the spare bedroom I'd converted into a workout space, determined to drive my body to exhaustion in a more constructive way.

The sharp peal of a ringtone cut through the sound of my heavy breaths, and I lowered myself to the floor, striding toward the weight bench where I'd left my phone. Pushing back the hair clinging to my forehead, I swiped right to answer. "Marcel."

"Lucien, *comment les choses avancent*?" he said without preamble.

"Good evening to you too." I grabbed a towel from the closet as I headed to the bathroom. Was a simple greeting too much to ask for? Possibly. There had been a time when my uncle had been kinder, less business-like in his manner, but that was before.

Before I screwed everything up and let our family be torn apart.

I turned on the shower, dragging my sweat-soaked shirt over my head. "Things are progressing fine. You don't need to worry."

Things were better than fine, actually. We were now ahead of schedule with the construction. The new chef was settling in nicely with the rest of the staff. And just last week, I secured a lucrative supply deal with a winery in Burgundy.

I returned to the bedroom in search of clean clothes, weighing which update to give Marcel first. But he cut my musings short when he said, "So you say, but Gabriel still isn't taking my calls. Have you been in touch with him?"

My foot faltered as my hand slipped from the drawer handle. *Gabriel.* Of course, that's what this unexpected call was about. Silly of me to think he might call to inquire about how preparations for the actual opening were going.

I measured my words carefully. "I have spoken with him, yes."

A beat of silence. "And? What did he say?"

Stay the hell away from me.

"He'll be there," I said, dodging the question. "I promise."

Marcel grunted. "I am relying on you, Lucien. Don't let me down." He disconnected the call before I could make further assurances, which was just as well since I didn't have any to offer.

I kicked off the rest of my clothes and stepped under the spray of hot water, turning over the next steps in my mind. Step one: Pull off the best restaurant opening Paris has ever seen. Step two: Make sure Gabriel is there.

I closed my eyelids and rested my forehead against the dewy tiles of the shower.

Step three: Take a long look in the mirror and figure out why I always come in second place in the eyes of everyone I've ever loved.

⌁

By a quarter to twelve, I gave up on sleep altogether and focused on work instead. Sitting behind my desk with a glass of whiskey in hand, I thumbed through the day's emails, making mental notes about scheduled deliveries, outstanding payments for contractors, and final staff positions that needed filling.

And what does any of it matter? The restaurant could be a raving success, praised by every restaurant reviewer and food critic in the city, but if I didn't get Gabriel to the opening, I would be nothing but a disappointment to Marcel.

I washed down a surge of anger with a generous swallow of whiskey, letting the smoky flavor slide over my tongue as I flipped to my text messages.

After my phone call with Marcel, I'd considered shooting a quick text to Juliet. But after drafting and deleting at least three separate messages, I finally gave it up, feeling ridiculous about reaching out to her in the middle of the night. Not that I wanted to see how she was doing. I just wanted to confirm whether she had taken my advice concerning Gabriel. A lot was hanging in the balance, so I was invested.

In their relationship, not in her.

I threw back the rest of my drink and scrolled to her number.

What's the worst that could happen? If she didn't answer, I would take that as a sign she was otherwise occupied. I rose to my feet and paced the floor as the phone rang once, twice ...

"Hello?"

I froze mid-step, picking up on a slight waver in her tone, followed by a soft hiccup.

Shit, had she been crying?

"Juliet? What's wrong?" She didn't answer, just hiccupped again. "Where are you? Tell me what's going on." I was halfway to my bedroom before I even realized my feet were moving, pulling on a sweatshirt and searching for my keys.

"Nothing's wrong," she said, sniffling and fooling absolutely no one.

"Bullshit." As a person who specialized in deceit, I could always tell when someone was lying. I shoved my wallet in my pocket before striding out the front door. "Tell me where you are."

"I'm ..." She blew her nose. "I'm at home."

"Text me the address." I stepped out onto the sidewalk, a breeze whipping through my damp hair as my phone chimed with an incoming message. I gave it a quick glance and hailed a taxi. "I'll be there in twenty minutes."

As soon as I arrived at Juliet's apartment and found the front door unlocked, I knew it was a bad sign. I pushed it open a crack and stepped inside. The apartment was dark except for a flickering light coming from the far corner, and I moved in that direction, swiping at a bead of sweat on my forehead. Why was it so warm in here? I got my answer a second later when I rounded the corner to the living room and saw the fireplace was lit. Small flames danced in the grate, casting shadows around the room.

"Juliet?"

I scanned the space before my eyes landed on a figure lying on the sofa, an empty wine bottle sitting on the floor. Her head was resting on a pillow, her hair spilling down the planes of her back like Sleeping Beauty. I drew closer, noting the evening gown clinging to her frame, the fabric glinting in the firelight like so many stars.

I paused, taking in the sight of her. I might have promised not to cross the line with her again, but I would have to be a dead man not to notice how beautiful she was.

Her eyes fluttered open as I dropped to a crouch in front of her, resting my elbows on my knees. I pushed down a spike of anger when I saw traces of mascara trailing over her cheeks.

She *had* been crying.

"Hey," she breathed, her green eyes settling on mine. "You came."

"You doubted me?" I feigned a look of hurt, and the tiniest trace of a smile crossed her lips. "Want to tell me what happened?"

She lifted onto one elbow, swiping at her tear-stained cheek. "It's nothing. I'm probably being ridiculous."

"Don't do that." I pinched her chin between my thumb and forefinger. "Don't invalidate your feelings like they don't matter. If you're crying, there's a reason."

She hesitated, her eyes darting back and forth. "I don't want you to think badly of him. It wasn't his fault. I think something happened to upset him."

"And by *him*, you mean ..." I asked, even though I had a good idea of who she was referring to. The corners of her mouth tightened, and I cleared my throat, deciding to try for levity. "Do I need to invoke bench rules, Ms. Chandler?" Her face split into a grin as she released a watery laugh, and a trickle of warmth spread through me. "There she is."

"Um, I hate to be the bearer of bad news, Cristian, but this is a sofa, not a bench."

I swiped a thumb over her cheek. "Use your imagination, sweetheart."

She held my gaze for a long moment, then loosed a breath, her eyes settling somewhere over my shoulder. "We ... Gabriel and I went to a gala tonight and everything was ... amazing."

"Mm-hmm. And then what happened?"

"I don't know. He got a call, and his demeanor changed completely. I didn't hear the conversation, but I could tell from his body language something was wrong."

A stone dropped into the pool of my stomach. "Did he say who it was?"

She frowned, a crease forming between her eyebrows. "It was a woman, I think. Her name was Elena ... no, Eloise—"

"Elise?"

Her eyes snapped to mine. "Yes, that was exactly it. How did you know?"

Nice going, idiot.

"Lucky guess."

She nodded, dropping her gaze and falling silent for so long I wondered whether I should come up with a better excuse for my slip of the tongue. But those thoughts fell to the wayside when she drew in a shuddering breath, her lashes suddenly wet.

"I don't know what to do," she cried, her expression full of anguish, and a hard object lodged itself in my throat as a tear escaped down the side of her face. "Every time I'm certain of his feelings, something happens. Some person appears out of the blue and makes me doubt everything between us or ..." She hiccupped. "Or he pulls back at the last minute."

Another sob broke free of her throat, and it was all I could do not to blow the entire plan to hell by calling Gabriel to give him an earful.

"What do I do, Cristian? He won't let me in. And maybe it's my fault for not telling him the truth, but I ..." She swiped a hand over her cheek. "Should I give up on him?"

Her shoulders trembled as she cried in earnest, and I gathered her into my arms without hesitating, letting her tears soak into my sweatshirt.

Fuck. This had gone too far. *I* had gone too far. Even though I was sure Juliet's feelings for Gabriel were genuine, perhaps she would have been spared this if I hadn't kept pulling her strings like a puppet master. I was as much to blame for her current state as Gabriel and, for the first time, I experienced a new emotion, one I had never felt before.

Shame.

As much as I wanted to please Marcel, I was done using Juliet to do it. And even though it was too late to take back my past falsehoods, I could be honest with her starting now.

"I can't answer that. Only you can decide whether to give him another chance. But ..." I extended an arm toward a tissue box on the coffee table. "What I can tell you is no man is perfect. Gabriel may care for you, but there may be things in his past"—I forced a swallow—"things that might be difficult for him to share. I'm not excusing his behavior tonight, but whatever happened, I promise it had nothing to do with you."

She blinked, her eyes searching. Then she dropped her head again, nodding into my chest.

"All right, it's time we got you to bed." She stumbled as she stood, and my eyes darted suspiciously to the empty wine bottle. "I'm going to carry you, okay?"

Without waiting for an answer, I swept her up in my arms and moved carefully through the dark in search of her bedroom. Finding it at the end of a short hallway, I pushed the door open with a knee and settled her onto the bed before switching on a lamp on the bedside table. My eyes returned to where Juliet sat perched on the bed, looking at me expectantly.

I scratched my ear. "Can you get changed on your own or ..."

She bobbed her head in a manner that told me she was three sheets to the wind, and there was no chance she could undress herself.

Perfect.

I crossed to the armoire, opening drawers and pushing aside articles of clothing until I found a T-shirt and a pair of silk pajama shorts.

"Come on, then." I grasped both of her hands, lifting her to her feet. She pivoted slowly, sweeping her hair over one shoulder and revealing a bare expanse of skin courtesy of her backless dress. My mouth dried out as my eyes slid over her, mapping out every freckle and curve until they finally landed on the soft dip at the base of her spine.

My cock twitched with interest.

No—you shut the fuck up.

"Everything okay?" She swayed dangerously, and I reached out a hand to steady her.

"Mm-hmm," I mumbled, fumbling with the clasp of her dress, which was conveniently situated over the swell of her ass.

Sweet Mary and Joseph. Who had I pissed off in a past life to land myself with this particular brand of torture?

With a bit of effort, I unfastened the dress, and it slid to the floor, pooling around her ankles and leaving her in nothing but a lacy pair of black panties. I snapped my eyes shut.

Gabriel's an idiot for leaving this girl alone.

And I'm an even bigger idiot for being here because she is one hundred percent off-limits.

I started to open my eyes but thought better of it. Best not to test the bounds of my newfound good nature. Instead, I reached for the place where I'd left her clothes until I felt the cotton of her T-shirt brush against my fingertips. Furrowing my brow in concentration, I traced the outline of the fabric, mapping out which way was right side up.

Juliet hiccupped again. "What ... what are you doing back there?"

Dying a slow and painful death.

"Helping you get ready for bed." I grimaced in frustration as I located a gap in the shirt that might have been an armhole.

"Yesss," she said, slurring, "but why are your eyes closed?"

Because you're drunk and I'm horny and this is all going to go south very quickly if I don't get you clothed.

"Less questions," I grunted, lifting the shirt over her head and sliding it over her body as carefully as I could without making contact with her skin.

She blew out a laugh. "Cristian, this shirt is on backward."

My lips twitched. *Sucks to be you then, sweetheart.* Because there was no way I was going to attempt to fix it, least of all with my eyes closed. Who knew what irreversible consequences might result if I blindly groped her?

I cast a hand around for her shorts before kneeling in front of her. "Okay, put your hands on my shoulders." *And for God's sake, do not fall on top of me.* If she did, it would be game over for honorable Cristian.

She planted her hands on my shoulders, stepping into the shorts, and I dragged them up her legs, my heart ramming into my Adam's apple when my thumbs grazed her hips. The second I got the shorts up around her waist, I shot to the other side of the room, propping myself against the wall with a hand and breathing heavily.

Fucking hell. I had undressed models, waitresses, girls looking for a good time on vacation—but *none* of it compared to what I'd just experienced putting Juliet's clothes *on*.

Bringing myself under control, I turned to find Juliet already tucked beneath the covers, her eyelids drooping as she watched me. "You okay?"

I smirked. "Nothing a tranquilizer can't fix."

She snorted a laugh, and my chest hummed with satisfaction. "You're funny, Cristian."

I nodded. "Yeah, well, I should get out of here so you can get some sleep."

"No, please." She rolled onto her side. "Would you stay with me?"

"I can assure you that is a terrible idea." I wasn't about to mince words with her. I already deserved sainthood for the amount of restraint I had shown this evening, but I didn't think for one second my resolve was foolproof.

"Please," she whispered, folding back the coverlet and patting the space beside her. I sawed my lip between my teeth, throwing a desperate look toward the hall, then sighed.

"Just to sleep," I said as much to myself as to her. I pulled my sweatshirt over my head and tossed it on the floor, pointing at the empty pillow. "Do you have another one of those?"

"There should be one in the closet ... but why do you need another pillow?"

"Trust me," I said, crossing the room to retrieve it, "it's for your benefit."

I climbed into the bed and placed the pillow between us, switching the light off as Juliet snuggled against the opposite side of the makeshift barricade. For a while, I listened to the sound of her breaths, my eyes lingering on her in the darkness. She was silent for so long, I thought she had fallen asleep. But then she whispered, "You're a good man, Cristian. Honest and good."

I swallowed, blinking at her silhouette. "No, I'm not, sweetheart. You only think that because you don't know me."

Her hand lingered on the pillow, and I inched mine closer until my fingers brushed hers, my heart thundering behind my ribs. Why this girl had so much faith in me was a mystery, but perhaps an even greater mystery was why I wanted to be a man worthy of such faith.

My hand trailed up to her wrist, pausing to trace the cool metal chain ridged with sapphires.

The bracelet. She was wearing the bracelet I bought her. Pulling in a slow breath, I closed my fingers around it, letting myself feel something I would never allow in the light of day.

Hope.

The dangerous thing about hope was, too often, it led to wishing for things one should not. Like me wishing I had met Juliet under different circumstances. That I was just a guy, and she was just a girl, and this fragile friendship blossoming between us hadn't sprouted from a bed of lies.

And then there was Gabriel. I didn't think for one second she would ever choose a friendship with me over a relationship with him. Still, as I lay beside her watching the rhythmic rise and fall of her chest, I realized a small part of me, a part I would forget existed when the sun rose, wished she had room in her heart for me too.

Thirty

Gabriel

My fingers drummed against the table as I watched the steam rolling up from the espresso I had yet to drink. From behind the shelter of my sunglasses, my eyes flitted to the other outdoor café patrons. It was too sunny today, especially in light of the black mood that had been hanging over me like a cloud since I left Juliet on her doorstep last night with little more than a kiss and a promise I would call.

Speaking of which ...

I glanced at my phone. *13:01*. Was it already that late? I should have called her first thing this morning, like I wanted to. Instead, I had gone straight to the gallery and rummaged through my desk in search of the note I'd found shoved underneath the front door weeks ago. Then, I did the unthinkable and arranged to meet up with the last person I wanted to see.

"*Bon après-midi,* cousin."

I looked up in time to see Lucien sliding into the chair opposite me, and my jaw ticked as I took in his appearance. Because of course he rocked up to this meeting in his standard attire of designer suit, perfectly styled hair, and general air of assholery.

He adjusted his watch before folding his hands on the table, his gaze moving from my aviators to the onyx dog tag resting above my T-shirt. "I must say, Gabriel, your choice of clothing leaves much to be desired."

I pushed my sunglasses into my hair. "Yeah, well, unfortunately, my wardrobe was fresh out of bullshit. Maybe you can lend me something next time."

He chuckled, relaxing back into his chair. "I miss this back-and-forth between us."

"Do you?" I tossed back the shot of espresso, wishing it were whiskey instead. "That's surprising, given the three years of silence."

The humor drained from his expression. "You were the one who shut me out, Gabriel. You were the one who took off without so much as a goodbye."

"Yeah," I said, setting the cup down so forcefully the table rattled, "and you of all people should know why since you're the reason I left. Or did you forget? Maybe you've become so blinded by your own lies you don't even know what the truth is anymore."

A muscle twitched in his cheek. "Still so self-righteous. Did it ever occur to you that there may be more to the story than what you know? If you had just talked to me—"

"You would have what? Fallen on your sword and taken responsibility for your actions?" I huffed a humorless laugh. "Not fucking likely. We both know you're an unapologetically selfish person who makes every decision based on personal interest."

"And I don't pretend to be otherwise," he said without even a hint of remorse. "But we could have figured it out. We may not have been friends, but we were always family."

"That's touching, but I didn't ask you here to reminisce." I swallowed, pushing down the anger in my throat. "Elise called me last night." He blinked, his features still as he regarded me with a blank expression, and my anger burned back up my esophagus. "You already knew."

"I had nothing to do with it, if that's what you're implying."

I shook my head. "After all this time, you still surprise me, Lucien."

"And you're still a stubborn jackass," he said, his usual mask of indifference slipping. "I had no idea she reached out to you until after the fact. What would I have to gain from it anyway?"

"You tell me. I know it's not a coincidence you both showed up in Paris right around the time my father started calling. No doubt you two are up to some scheme." A trickle of satisfaction settled in my chest when his face paled. "Well, whatever game you're playing, you might as well give it up. I meant what I said before. My father made his choice, as did the both of you."

"None of this is a game, Gabriel. If you would just listen—"

"I don't want explanations. I only want one thing from you, and that's for you to tell Elise to leave me alone. For good."

His eyes fell wide, genuine surprise coloring his tone. "That's why you asked me here?"

I gave him a curt nod. "It is."

After a long pause, he said, "I'm not sure what sort of influence you think I hold over Elise, but I can assure you, nothing I say will sway her. The woman is primordial chaos in human form."

"I'm sure you'll think of something." I stood to leave. "If nothing else, you can always resort to your powers of seduction. After all, they seemed to work so well the first time."

"You know what your issue is?" He rose from his chair, blocking my path. "All you ever do is run away from your problems instead of facing them. You act like they don't exist under some misguided notion that if you keep ignoring them, they'll disappear. But they won't, Gabriel. They'll be right there where you left them until you deal with them."

"Get out of my way."

"No." His voice echoed around the seating area, and several people looked in our direction.

"Lower your voice before you cause a scene," I gritted out.

"Then listen to me for once in your life. I'm not discounting what happened three years ago, but I am telling you that you will have to face it at some point. You keep pretending like you're fine when you're not. And I know you won't believe me, but I regret the role I played in it. If I could go back and do things differently—"

"Well, you can't, can you?"

"*Talk* to someone, Gabriel. Don't keep your feelings bottled up inside. Over time, they will fester and you might end up hurting someone you love. Someone who is innocent in all this."

I narrowed my eyes.

What the hell was he getting at?

He leveled me with a pointed look, and, for a second, I could have sworn his expression was sincere. But this was Lucien. He didn't do or say anything unless it was of personal benefit to him. And despite him flinging the word *family* around, I knew the truth of what I was to him, what I had always been to him.

Competition.

"Get Elise off my back." I shoved past him, clipping his shoulder.

"And if I don't?"

I turned to face him again. "If you don't, I might pick up the next time my father calls and tell him the truth. About everything this time."

⟫⟫⟫ ⟪⟪⟪

"How about a picnic in Luxembourg Gardens? Or one of those candlelit dinner cruises?"

I shot a look of annoyance at Nora hovering over my shoulder as I scoured the internet for date ideas. It was an hour past closing time, and despite spending the better part of the afternoon sequestered behind the front desk of the bike shop, I was no closer to coming up with a plan for how to make things up to Juliet.

"No way," James said from where he sat on the couch, his long arms draped over the back of it, his legs spread wide. "He'll need to go bigger than that if he wants to seal the deal."

"Can you not say *seal the deal*?" I kneaded my eyebrows, reigning in my agitation. "I'm not some teenager trying to deflower my date in the back seat of a car."

"You know what you should do?" James snapped his fingers, ignoring my comment. "You should do something to get the adrenaline pumping. You know, like, skydiving or heli-skiing."

"Heli-skiing?" Nora propped a hip on the desk. "How is that better than a dinner cruise?"

"Come off it." James snorted. "The only thing that's guaranteed after hours of being trapped on a riverboat is a good night's sleep. But after the rush of heli-skiing?" He blew out a low whistle, a sly grin sliding over his features. "I bet the sex would be phenomenal."

Nora scoffed. "Nonsense. You can have great sex after a cruise too."

James cocked an eyebrow. "Care to test that theory, Mrs. Russell?"

I cleared my throat noisily. "You know what? I think I can take it from here."

"Are you sure?" Nora said. "Because we could—"

"Quite sure. You guys go ahead. I'll lock up the shop."

We exchanged our goodbyes, and as soon as the door closed behind them, I released an exhale, slumping in my seat.

Last night should have been perfect. I had come so close to making things official with Juliet, so close to telling her how I felt about her. But then Elise showed up like a bad dream, pulling me back into that dark place in my mind where nothing but anger and pain existed.

You might end up hurting someone you love. Someone who is innocent in all this.

I shook away the memory of Lucien's words and pulled out my phone, my thumb hovering over Juliet's number. I would never hurt her. Except, maybe I already had? I groaned, tossing the device down on the desk.

How the hell was I going to fix this?

"Hey."

I swung around to find Lily standing in the doorway leading to the back of the shop.

"Oh, hey. I didn't know you were here." I nodded toward the front door. "You just missed James and Nora. I, uh, kicked them out."

A smile unfurled from one corner of her mouth as she crossed the room. "Well, I can't blame you there. Those two can be a hand-ful." She lifted herself onto the desk, her denim-clad legs dangling over the edge. "So," she said, twirling a strand of auburn hair around her finger, "how was last night? You and Juliet seemed to be having a nice time."

"Yeah, we were. But then, I kind of messed things up so ..."

She hummed without looking at me, and an unexpected wave of guilt hit me as I realized this was the first time we had talked since the dinner party.

"Beer?" I offered, and she nodded as I retrieved two from the fridge. "It's good to see you, by the way. I haven't had the chance to ask, but how long are you in Paris?"

She twisted the top off the bottle. "Haven't had the chance to ask or just haven't asked?"

I scratched my eyebrow. "Well, you got me there." Truth be told, if Lily had shown up a few weeks earlier, I probably would have made more of an effort to spend time with her. She was like a little sister, always tagging along with me and James whenever she visited. But this time, I had hardly paid attention to her at all. "I'm sorry. I've been distracted lately."

"It's all right. I get it." She rolled the glass bottle between her palms. "A lot is changing in your life. Has changed already maybe." Her eyes flickered to me, a question dancing in them I wasn't sure how to answer.

"We'll always be friends, Lil, no matter what."

Her cheeks reddened, and she turned to look out the window at the pinkening sky. After a stretch of silence, she said, "You know, my mum always used to tell me I was a free spirit, flitting through life, landing in this place or that, but never settling anywhere. The only thing I've ever truly stuck with is ballet, and for a long time, I was okay with that. I never wanted to commit to any place or thing I wasn't sure I loved with my whole heart." She glanced at me before looking away again. "But then I met someone, someone who made me want to stick for the first time in my life, who made me believe I could be happy in one place, so long as he was there."

My brows pinched together. "Who? Some guy in the UK?"

Did James know about this mystery guy? No way he did—he couldn't keep a secret if his life depended on it.

Lily let out a soft laugh, shaking her head. "No, Gabriel. Not some guy in the UK."

Her eyes bounced over my shoulder to a photo pinned to the wall of James and me at one of his cycling races the year before. My arm was slung over his shoulders as we smiled at the camera, his hair damp with sweat and my own noticeably shorter.

"Your hair is longer now," Lily said, her words mirroring my thoughts.

I ran a hand through it, the locks curling around my fingers. "Yeah, it's been a while since my last cut." If I wasn't careful, I would end up sporting a man bun like those hipsters who hung around Canal Saint Martin drinking oat milk lattes.

"So, what happened with the guy?" I asked, bumping my knee against hers.

"Oh." She brushed a hand over her collarbones. "I never told him how I felt. I thought I'd have more time. But I think ..." She swallowed, her throat bobbing as her eyes settled on me. "I think it's too late now." I stared at her, a hint of awareness tingling at the back of my neck, like I was missing something important. After another beat, she rose abruptly. "Versailles."

I frowned. "What?"

"You should take Juliet to Versailles." She shoved her hands in her jeans. "Get out of the city and spend some time together without all the interruptions. Plus, it's beautiful out there. I'm sure she'll love it."

I opened my mouth to reply, but she retreated before I could get a word in.

Pausing in the doorway, she threw a glance over her shoulder, her eyes glimmering with moisture.

"Be happy, Gabriel."

Thirty-One

Juliet

The curious thing about being self-absorbed is one never notices it until it's been pointed out. It certainly wasn't a quality I would have attributed to myself. I'd always been kind, thoughtful. Dutiful, committed, gracious. But after talking with Cristian the other night, it occurred to me I might possess another trait, one I had never considered before.

Selfishness.

As soon as I had woken up the morning after the gala, two things became apparent. One, I had a wicked hangover, the likes of which I hadn't seen since winter ski trip during my senior year of college. And two, Cristian was nowhere to be found.

Glancing at my phone, I flipped to the message I sent him later that day once my bedroom had stopped spinning long enough for me to type a sentence.

Thanks for everything.

Days later, he still hadn't responded.

I blinked up at the thick clouds gathering overhead as I waited on the train platform.

The night of the gala, I had been so consumed with my feelings that I'd been ready to call it quits with Gabriel. But then Cristian offered me some much-needed perspective and an uncomfortable bit of clarity. The only thing I'd taken into consideration since meeting Gabriel was *my* wants, *my* fears. But had I ever stopped to consider what Gabriel needed?

I looked around the crowded platform, shivering as the wind whipped my legs.

Gabriel may care for you, but there may be things in his past, things that might be difficult for him to share.

Despite all the time we'd spent together, I still knew little about Gabriel's life before he came to Paris. But if there *was* something in his past, something painful, it would explain his hesitance to open up to me. And as far as him not wanting a relationship, I could see now it had never been about me or anyone else.

It was about him.

Between the two of us, Gabriel had always been the steady one. He'd shown an unwavering confidence in me and my potential as a writer, even when I didn't. He helped me learn to stand up to Tom when I never would have before. He even defended me against Kyle. He'd supported me in a hundred different ways in the short time we'd known each other and had never asked for anything in return. But maybe he needed someone to show up for him too.

"Juliet."

I whirled at the familiar tenor.

Gabriel.

"Oh, hi," I said, suddenly feeling both calm and out of control.

We hovered there as a crush of people moved around us, and he ran a hand up the back of his head, a look of uncertainty forming behind his eyes. I swallowed.

No. I didn't want him to look at me like that. I wanted him to feel like he could trust me even when he wasn't at his best, to know he didn't have to shut me out.

My arms were around him, circling his waist before I was aware of what I was doing, and he stiffened for a half second before relaxing against me, his body folding over mine.

"What's brought this on?" he murmured into my hair.

"Just happy to see you."

"Yeah, same here." He pulled back, the former awkwardness seeming to vanish. "Though I'm not sure today is the best day to venture out to Versailles after all." He peered up at the darkening sky. "Rain check?"

My lips quirked. "Not a chance. You already owe me a rain check to visit your favorite restaurant. You'll have to make good on that promise first before I give you any more."

He chuckled, tucking me under his arm. "Fair enough."

The train whisked into the station, tossing leaves and debris in the wind as it came to a stop with a screech, and we crowded inside along with a few dozen other people.

"There's a seat here," Gabriel said, guiding me to the rear of the car. "You take it."

I shook my head as the train lurched into motion. "I don't want to sit if you'll have to stand the whole way." Last I'd checked, it was a thirty-minute journey.

The corners of his mouth twitched. "Well, you could always sit on my lap."

My gaze snapped up, noting the silent challenge in his eyes. Did my belly flutter at the thought of spending half an hour in Gabriel's lap? Yes. Was I about to back down when he so obviously thought I would? No way.

I lifted a shoulder. "Sure, why not?"

His face fell in open surprise and I smiled, relishing the satisfaction of catching him off guard. Planting a hand on his chest, I gave him a gentle shove down into the seat, and his eyes flared with heat. "Careful, angel."

I slid into his lap, pushing my hips up his thighs until I heard his sharp intake of breath. I peeked over one shoulder. "Why's that?"

"Play with fire and you might get burned." As if in demonstration, he hooked his thumbs in the waistband of my shorts, dragging his thumbs along the crease of my hips. I pressed my lips together, sealing off a moan. If he was trying to get me to wave the white flag, he was doing an expert job of it.

I swirled my hips in retribution and Gabriel groaned against the nape of my neck.

"How about a truce?" I whispered, eyeing a vacant seat. "I can move across the aisle."

"I don't think so." Gabriel shifted beneath me and every soft place on my body turned molten when his hard-on pressed against my ass. "If I'm not getting relief, neither are you."

"Seriously?"

He smirked, folding his hands behind his head. "Starting to regret your life choices?" I rocked on his lap again and let out a squeal when he banded an arm around my waist.

"Behave," he hissed in my ear. "Instead of making my life flash before my eyes, why don't you tell me what you want to see while we're in Versailles?"

"Well, the Palais Royal, for starters." I paused, hesitating.

Gabriel nudged my cheek with his nose. "Come on, Chandler, don't be shy. If I know you, you've already thoroughly researched the entire palace and its history."

"All right, but just remember you asked." I extracted a guidebook from my bag. "I'm interested in touring the private apartments of the royal family, particularly those of King Louis XIV. Did you know he was called the Sun King because he identified with Apollo, the sun god?"

"I did, but tell me about it anyway. I love it when you talk nerdy to me."

Warmth rose in my cheeks, though whether it was at the mention of the word *love* or the way he dragged his unshaven jaw against the crook of my neck while saying it, I couldn't say.

"Well, apparently, the king's bedchamber was strategically placed so it faced east toward the sunrise. Every morning, he had a rising ceremony where a valet would draw back the curtains and address the king with the customary phrase, 'Sire, it's time.'"

Gabriel huffed a chuckle. "Humble guy."

"Right? I think his preference for gold décor really drove the point home." I flipped the page. "Besides that, I'd love to see the Chapel, the Opera Royal—oh, and the famous Hall of Mirrors. And then, there are the gardens, the groves, the fountains, and the orangery, which has over one thousand trees, including palm trees, pomegranate trees, Eugenia—" I let the book fall to my lap. "We might not have time to see it all."

"Yeah, it might be difficult, but I'll do my best to make sure you see everything you want."

Everything I want.

"What do you want? It's not just about me, you know."

He tugged me closer, his arms tightening around my center. "I already have what I want."

"I'm serious," I said, ignoring the way my heartbeat spread throughout my entire body. "I want to know what interests you too."

He drew back, giving me a long look. "Well, the main palace is great and certainly worth visiting. But my favorite place is the Grand Trianon, northwest of the Château. The king built it as sort of a retreat, an escape from the etiquette of courtly life. Thus, it's more private. More intimate."

"Oh." It was suddenly hard to breathe. "Okay, let's do it."

His brows lifted. "Are you sure? I don't want you to feel pressured—"

"I don't. I want to know about the things that matter to you. Will you show me?"

The air felt heavier as the weight of my question hung between us.

"Yeah, angel, I'll show you."

⇢⇢⇝ ⇜⇠⇠

"Okay, we definitely should have come here first."

Stepping onto the portico that connected the courtyard to the gardens, I ran my hand over a column of pink marble, blinking up at the carved ceiling. The Château and surrounding grounds were stunning, unmatched in their opulence and grandeur. But Trianon, with its remote location and floral motif, had a certain serenity that the larger estate lacked. It was more refined, less ostentatious.

"Yeah, I spent hours here the first time I visited Versailles." Gabriel took my hand, leading me down a set of stone steps toward a tree-lined path. "It's a great place to be alone with your thoughts."

Alone with your thoughts? I glanced up at him, the back of my neck tingling with curiosity. "So," he continued, "how is your piece for the magazine progressing? The deadline is coming up, no?"

"Yep. Benoit's doing a final read over the weekend and will let me know his decision on Tuesday." I didn't even want to think about the possibility of him declining to submit it.

"You'll be fine," Gabriel said as if reading my thoughts. "I have faith in you." He squeezed my hand and something warm unfurled in my belly.

"Thanks. You know what's surprising though? When I first agreed to submit to the competition, I did it because I was excited about the chance to be published. But now I've gained something more valuable. I've realized that practicing art—any art—isn't about gaining recognition. It's about becoming, about discovering what's inside you. So, win or lose, I'll always be grateful for this experience."

Gabriel grinned. "A good insight, but I still think you'll win."

"Well, I certainly hope so, especially since not only would my work be published but I would also get to attend the magazine's annual networking event. All the competition winners are invited, and it's a great opportunity to rub shoulders with the crème de la crème of the Paris writing industry. In fact, I think the networking event is the more valuable prize. As my grandfather used to say, it's not what you know, it's who you know."

"Truer words have never been spoken. I wouldn't be debuting my work if it weren't for Jean-Claude."

I nodded as we rounded a bend in the path, a garden folly rising in the distance.

"Speaking of, are things on track for your opening?"

"They are. I've already moved all the completed paintings out of storage to be framed, and the invitations will go out next week."

"Are you expecting a lot of guests?"

We approached the folly, which resembled a temple that would have been better suited to ancient Greece, with its Corinthian capitals and domed roof, than the French countryside.

"A fair number." Gabriel trailed a hand over the carved sculpture at the center of the structure. "Jean-Claude curated the guest list. He's a bit of a snob when it comes to exclusivity." He glanced down at me. "Don't worry, I made sure you and your friends were included."

"Oh, cool," I said, trying for nonchalance, but not pulling it off as my lips curved in a smile. A roll of thunder rumbled overhead, and I peered at the sky. "We should head back."

"Wait, there's something else I wanted to talk to you about." His eyes ventured over my shoulder before returning to mine. "About the gala, I want to apologize for taking off on you. I had some things to sort out. Still, I never meant for things to turn out the way they did."

"I know. I mean, I was upset at first, but I understand you must have had your reasons."

"Whatever my reasons, I'm sorry I let them get in the way."

"In the way?"

He nodded, brushing a thumb over my cheek. "Do you remember what you said at the beginning of the summer about us just being friends and there being no expectations between us?" I bobbed my head, my lungs barely pulling in air. "Well, I agreed at the time because I didn't want to become a distraction or get in the way of your aspirations. And I still don't. But the truth is, I want more with you, Juliet. This thing between us is more than friendship, and I think you know that. And maybe you think betting on me is too much of a risk, but I'm asking for a chance to prove to you it's worth it. That *we're* worth it."

"I don't understand." Blood thundered in my ears, drowning out the very real thunder. "What are you saying?"

"I'm saying be with me, Juliet."

"As in ... a relationship?"

A prolonged silence passed between us before he gave me a stiff nod, the muscles in his jaw clenching.

Did he mean it? Did he actually want a relationship with me? Or ... my stomach shifted uncomfortably. Was he just saying it because he thought it was what *I* wanted?

I swallowed thickly. "No, I can't ..." *Force you into a relationship.* I'd promised myself I would stop being selfish, and no matter how much I wanted this, wanted *him*, I wasn't willing to give in at the expense of his convictions.

His eyes hardened with the rejection of my words. "Oh, okay, I get it."

"Gabriel—" Another streak of lightning scorched across the sky, and my chest caved in as his expression shuttered.

No, no, no. I needed to find a better way to explain myself, to make him understand. I wet my lips, searching for the right words just as a deafening crash split the sky.

Then the heavens opened up.

Thirty-Two

Gabriel

No. The word sliced through the air, piercing my chest with a sharp finality. *She said no.*

My hands felt numb, and I balled them into fists. *Be with me.* Why had I opened my mouth? Juliet had made herself clear, and I was a fool to think I could change her mind.

"Gabriel."

I jolted out of my stupor, blinking down at her as she stared up at me with wide, pleading eyes. She opened her mouth to say something just as the wind sent a torrent of biting, cold rain barreling toward us, soaking our clothes through instantly. She squeezed her eyes shut, a shiver visibly racing over her skin, and my jaw tightened.

"We have to go." I grabbed her hand, pulling her alongside me.

We didn't speak again as we splashed up the path, avoiding rivers of mud and deep puddles on the road that led through miles of farmland back to the entrance of the estate. Eventually, the lights of the train station came into view, and we sprinted toward it, climbing the steps as quickly as our frozen limbs would allow. Inside, we found a mass of people waiting on the platform, some of whom were as drenched as we were, others who were dry but no less irritable.

I scanned the train schedule for the next departure time but couldn't find it anywhere.

"*Pardon*," I said to a woman standing nearby, her face streaked with exhaustion as a screaming red-faced child clung to her, "*Quand part le prochain train pour Paris*?" Her eyes clouded with confusion, so I tried again in English. "Do you know when the next train leaves?"

Her expression cleared before morphing into a scowl, frustration eating up her features. "That's what I'd like to know. Last I heard, there are no more trains departing this evening due to reports of flash flooding. I've just sent my husband to find a conductor."

No more trains? Fan-fucking-tastic.

"What about a taxi or an Uber?"

She shook her head, bouncing the child. "It'll be the same problem as with the train, I expect. They say the tracks are flooded, so I can only imagine the roadways are too." She turned away from me as a man pushing a stroller approached, shaking his head.

I glanced at where Juliet stood with her arms wrapped around her. I had to do something. She might not be complaining, but she had to be freezing. Running a hand over my mouth, I weighed options in my head. But after several minutes, I could only come up with one solution that would solve the immediate need of getting her warm and out of this weather.

I fished my phone out of my pocket, swiping a thumb over the damp screen. I wasn't particularly thrilled with this plan, but I didn't have time to think of a suitable alternative. I did a quick internet search, then hit the call button.

⠶⠶⠶⠶ ⠶⠶⠶⠶

I placed the card against the electronic keypad, waiting for it to flash green before pushing the door open. Reaching into the darkness, I found a switch on the adjacent wall and flipped it on, the recessed lighting of the entryway flickering into existence.

Alone in a hotel room with Juliet was the last place I wanted to be. Not because I was angry with her because I wasn't. But being cloistered in such intimate accommodations might be uncomfortable, if not for her, then at least for me.

Moving farther into the room, I looked around at the blue-gray wallpaper and modern furniture. A plush sofa stood against one wall and beside it was a sleek, utilitarian desk positioned beneath the room's only window. It all looked rather posh, which had been the least of my concerns. All I required was a place that was clean, comfortable, and had two beds—

I stopped, coming to a standstill as my mind caught up with what my eyes were seeing.

One double bed stood in the center of the room, its white sheets and matching duvet folded down as if in greeting. Heat shot up my neck, and I darted a look at Juliet standing behind me. She stared past my shoulder, a look of comprehension dawning on her face.

"I reserved a room with two beds," I said before she could draw the wrong conclusion. "I'll just call down to the front desk and ask for a change." I practically dove for the phone on the bedside table as Juliet moved around, opening drawers and examining their contents before wandering toward the bathroom. She returned a minute later just as I was hanging up the phone.

"Um," I said, scrubbing a hand over my face and fixing my eyes on the framed artwork hanging above the bed, "unfortunately, they don't have any other rooms available." I hazarded a glance at her as she drew back the curtains, peering outside where the storm still raged.

"We could try a different hotel," I offered, but there was no conviction in my voice. Most hotels were already full because of the storm, and we'd been lucky to find this place.

"I honestly don't mind." Dropping the curtain, she came to stand in front of me, and my eyes slinked down her face, snagging on the swell of her bottom lip.

God, I wanted to kiss her. To take her lips slowly and swallow those sweet little moans she made whenever my tongue teased the seam of her mouth. As if reading my thoughts, her lips parted on an exhale, her warm breath falling against me, and I lifted a hand, grazing a thumb over her skin. No, I *definitely* wanted more than a kiss. And from the way she was looking at me, her pupils blown wide, so did she.

But she didn't want to be with me, and as long as that was the case, this visceral need between us couldn't go any further than heated stares and heavy breathing. Because there was no version of me joining my body to hers that wouldn't involve me worshiping her, claiming her, owning her. One time wouldn't be enough. Two times, five times—it didn't matter.

I would *never* get enough of her.

"Gabriel." Her voice dropped to a husky whisper as she raked her fingertips down my abdomen, and my dick hardened so fast, the edges of my vision darkened.

"You should shower," I said hoarsely, the words tripping over themselves on the way out. "You've been in those damp clothes too long." I turned my back to her before she had the chance to notice the physical evidence of how she affected me.

After a handful of seconds, the bathroom door clicked shut, and I slumped onto the sofa, letting my head fall back.

Come on, you're better than this. I wasn't some depraved beast—I was a man with a sense of decency and control. But the second the shower turned on, my mind betrayed me with images of Juliet naked on the other side of the door, and a strangled groan caught in my throat.

Nope, I was definitely a beast. Wild and ravenous for her.

I blinked an eye open, glancing at the door. What would she do if I went in there? I could tell she wanted me from the way she looked at me, the way she touched me. She wouldn't deny me if I stepped into the shower with her, pushed her up against the wet tiles, and—

I shot up from the sofa and swiped the key card off the desk, storming out the door before I could finish the thought.

Juliet

Steady rain pattered against the window above the desk where I sat running fingers through my damp hair. Pulling the fluffy bathrobe tighter around me, I glanced over my shoulder at the closed bathroom door. After a brief disappearance to I didn't know where—though from the faint scent of whiskey, I suspected the hotel bar—Gabriel had returned to the room and made a beeline for the bathroom without saying a word to me. The silence had stung, but it was no less than I deserved after the way I had shot him down earlier.

Was I wrong to reject him? No, I didn't think so. I cared about him too much to let him be pressured into something he wasn't ready for. Even if I had spent half the summer hoping he would change his mind, I couldn't accept his offer—not if it wasn't what he truly wanted.

And what about Elise? I swallowed, forcing a surge of jealousy back down my throat. The more I thought about the way Gabriel had reacted to her phone call the night of the gala, the more I wondered what their connection was. What was she to him? Was she an ex? Did she have something to do with Gabriel's feelings about relationships?

The bathroom door swung open, and I swiveled in my chair. All the air immediately hissed out of me when my eyes collided with the powerful lines of Gabriel's frame, a towel hanging loosely around his waist. His dark hair was pushed back, the wet strands falling in gleaming rivulets down the column of his neck, and my eyes dipped lower, exploring the ridges and valleys of his flesh. The carved expanse of his chest. The plateau of muscle at the base of his stomach. I had seen his naked body once before, but I must not have been truly looking.

I was looking now, though.

"Sorry," he said, interrupting my shameless perusal. "I forgot to grab a robe before showering." He turned to the closet, and I bit my tongue hard as I took in the broad landscape of his back, elegantly carved with lean muscle, muscle I wanted to sink my nails into while he—

"Would you mind turning around?"

I blinked, my mental faculties rebooting and transmitting the message that he was no longer facing the closet, but was staring straight at me. I looked away, releasing a nervous laugh.

Really smooth, Juliet.

"Decent?" I called over my shoulder. He grunted in response, and I turned toward him again, making a solid effort to keep my eyes on his face this time.

He crossed his arms. "You should get some rest. You can take the bed. I'll sleep on the sofa." As though the matter was decided, he took a purposeful step forward.

"I want to talk first," I said, moving into his path. Talking was probably the last thing he wanted to do. Hell, it was the last thing *I* wanted to do. But not talking hadn't gotten us anywhere, and I was tired of it.

He clenched and unclenched his jaw before settling onto the edge of the bed.

"Before, when I said I wouldn't be with you, I didn't get a chance to explain why."

"I know why." His tone was neutral, but his eyes swirled with such intense emotion, it sent my heart spiraling down to the base of my stomach.

"You do?"

He nodded. "You already told me, remember? At the gallery when we ..." His voice tapered off, his throat moving on a hard swallow. "You said you needed to make the most of your time in Paris, and I get that. You're right to put your ambitions first."

"Wait, what? You think I said no because of my writing?"

"Well, yeah ..." His brows furrowed. "That's what you told me, isn't it?"

"Gabriel, I only said that because you told me *you* didn't want a relationship. I'm not the kind of girl who can be with you for the summer and then just return to normal life like nothing happened. And if I had any sense at all, I would have just talked to you about it instead of hiding the truth." *Like Cristian told me to all along.* "But I'm talking to you now, and whatever your reasons for not wanting a commitment, they're yours to have. You don't owe me any explanation. But I can't say yes to more with you when I know a relationship isn't what you want."

"I want *you*." He pushed to his feet, his hands cupping my face. "Don't you get that? If you need a label, Juliet, you've got it. I was an asshole for telling you that in the first place, for letting you believe it all this time. But I won't make the same mistake twice." He tilted my chin up, his eyes settling on mine. "I *want* a relationship, Juliet. With you."

I shook my head. "I'm forcing you into this. I'm making you break your rules—"

"Angel, there is no rule this side of heaven I would not break to make you mine."

"It's not that simple," I said, my throat tight with the pressure of unshed tears. "If I say yes, I'll fall in love with you. So hard. And the thought of falling for you only to lose you terrifies me."

"You think I'm not terrified? Juliet, I've been terrified since the day you crashed into my life and upended my entire world. With just one look, I was a goner. And I tried—I fucking tried not to want you. But I might as well have tried to hold back an avalanche because there was no stopping this. You and I are inevitable."

Liquid heat slid down the sides of my face. "But what about after I leave Paris?"

"Then we'll figure it out." He brushed one thumb over my cheek. "If I have to give up the gallery and start over in New York, I'll do it. I will do whatever it takes to keep you."

"But why? Why would you give up everything you've worked so hard for?"

"Because I *love* you. And there is no prize on earth worth more to me than you. So go ahead and fall in love with me, beautiful. I'll be right here, ready to catch you."

A sob escaped my throat just as our lips collided, our mouths claiming, tongues delving, and I wreathed my arms around his neck as his teeth grazed my bottom lip. There was nothing gentle about this kiss. It was wild and desperate, buoyed by desire, laden with need. He tilted my head, his mouth leaving mine to burn a path up my jaw before brushing over the skin of my earlobe.

"Gabriel." I pushed my hands into his robe, needing to feel his skin beneath my palms. "I need you. *Please*." He groaned against my ear, his hand finding the small of my back and pulling me flush with his hard body.

"Think carefully, Juliet. Once we cross this line, we can't un-cross it. Just say the word, and I'm yours. But you better be damn sure because I want all of you in return—every single piece. Not just your body, but your heart, your mind. I want your trust, your hopes, your fears. I want all that you are, and not just for now, but for good. You will belong to me, and I will belong to you. Do you understand?"

You will belong to me, and I will belong to you.

This wasn't just lovemaking—it was *joining*. Maybe I should have been afraid of the gravity of it, but I wasn't. In so many ways, I belonged to him already. This was just the final step.

"Yes."

Something sparked in his eyes, a flame stoking behind those blue depths. "Yes, what?"

"Yes, I understand. Yes, I'll be yours." My breath sawed in and out as he leaned forward until our noses brushed, his mouth hovering so close, I could feel his next words.

"Thank *God*."

Thirty-Three

Juliet

Yes. One syllable. Three letters. Just a drop in a sea of infinite expressions. And yet, it shook something loose inside me, something powerful that untethered me from all my fears and inhibitions. With one word, the atmosphere became charged, and the moment Gabriel's lips slammed down on mine, heat exploded beneath my skin, scorching my insides with raw desire.

"Open," he growled, and I obeyed, parting my lips to give him the access he demanded. His tongue swept in, hot and slick, his strokes hungry as his mouth moved hard and strong over mine, making my nipples harden. His erection was heavy against my hip bone, and my head rocked back, desire coiling low in my belly as he hitched my thigh up over his hip.

"Please," I begged as his lips dipped to my throat, the scent of his skin surrounding me.

"I've got you. I've always got you." Lifting me, he wrapped my legs around his waist, and the mattress dipped under our weight as he lowered me onto the bed, covering my body with his.

"I've thought of this moment so many times," he said, tugging on the belt of my robe. "Imagining a hundred different ways to please you, to serve you, to leave your body fully satiated."

Oh.

I swallowed hard, my chest rising and falling as I drank in his dark curls framing the contours of his face, the once ocean-blue irises now dark as night. I traced the line of his jaw, and my stomach somersaulted when he groaned into my touch, scraping his stubble against the flat of my palm.

A sharp pulse of need throbbed between my thighs, and I pressed them together, my center already slick and desperate for friction. Before I could find relief, Gabriel forced a knee between my legs, pushing them apart.

"I thought I made myself clear. You belong to *me*, and I will be the one to pleasure you. Just tell me what you want, and I'll give it to you."

My eyes connected with his, letting the fire in them wash over me.

There were a million things I wanted, but I didn't know how to articulate any of them. Before now, Kyle had been my only partner, and sex with him had always been a quiet affair, like scratching an itch in the dark. And though I'd learned how to please *him*, he'd never reciprocated with anything more than the bare minimum.

A blush scalded my cheeks, and I tried to look away, but Gabriel caught my chin. "Don't shy away. I want to earn your trust and make you feel safe, but I need you to be open with me."

"But that's just it. I can't tell you what I want because … I don't know. I've done nothing other than, um, the basics." I hazarded a glance at him, expecting to see astonishment or even amusement in his expression. But what I found instead was a deep tenderness, his gaze full of warmth as he smoothed back the hair at my temple.

"There's no shame in not knowing what you like. Honestly, that you have so much left to discover turns me on." The muscles of his throat worked. "A lot."

"It does?"

He nodded, his forehead dipping to mine. "It makes me want to explore every inch of you until there are no secrets left to uncover. You might not be able to tell me what you want now, but if you'll let me, I promise I'll make you fluent in your body's desires. Will you let me show you?"

I bobbed my head, and he hummed his approval, his fingers tracing over my collarbones before slipping inside my robe to brush his thumb over one sensitive bud. I inhaled sharply as my body arched toward him, my fingers twisting in the sheets.

"*Gabriel.*"

"Patience, beautiful," he murmured, dragging the digit in slow circles over my puckered flesh. "You know I'm going to take care of you, don't you?" His hand moved between the folds of my robe, pushing it open, and I watched as his eyes roamed over my naked body, looking at me in a way no one had ever looked at me.

With raw hunger.

My skin flushed under the intensity of his perusal, and I instinctively flattened a hand over the soft swell of my belly.

"Don't." He took my hand and brought it to his lips. "Every part of you is perfect."

He pressed my palm flat against his chest so I could feel the pounding of his heart. Then he slid my hand down to the belt at his waist, closing my fingers around it as he watched me beneath hooded eyes. I fumbled to unknot it, and he shrugged it off, leaving nothing between us.

"I don't know why I'm nervous." The words burst from my lips before I could stop them. "It's like my first time all over again. Actually, I'm freaking out more now than I did then."

"It is the first time. *Our* first time. And whatever you're feeling, know I'm feeling it too. So, it's okay to be scared. We can be scared together."

Threading his fingers through mine, he dipped his head, claiming my lips in a slow, sensual kiss. His tongue brushed against my bottom lip, and I took him into my mouth with a moan as he teased my nipple, rolling it between his thumb and forefinger.

"Do you like it when I touch you like this?"

"Y-yes," I stuttered. The words had barely passed my lips before the heat of his mouth replaced his hand, his tongue sweeping over my sensitive flesh. My skin caught fire as he grazed his teeth over one taut peak before closing his lips around it and sucking hard.

I was going to *explode*. Any second now, I was going to shatter into a million pieces until there was nothing left but remnants of the girl I used to be.

His hand dipped between my legs, sliding up to the apex of my thighs, and I swallowed a scream when his fingers sank between my soaking folds.

"*Fuck*. You are so wet." He dropped his face into the crook of my neck as he pressed his thumb right against my aching center, dragging the digit in tantalizing circles.

"Gabriel, *please*, just—"

"Just what? You want to come, pretty girl?"

"*Yes*," I hissed.

He chuckled under his breath before withdrawing his hand.

"Not so fast."

I watched, transfixed, as he slid his thumb into his mouth, sweeping his tongue over it and licking the taste of me. I had never seen anything so erotic in my life. Trembling, I reached down and wrapped my fingers around his hard length, his flesh hot and smooth in my palm as I worked my hand up and down his shaft. His eyes widened, then shuttered, a moan ripping from his lips as he rocked in time with my movements.

"You're a goddamn dream, you know that? I never stood a chance when it came to you. Just one look brought me to my knees." Heat bloomed in every corner of my body, and I gripped him tighter as he thrust into my hand, his hips rising and falling in a hypnotic rhythm. "You want to make me come, don't you? Want to make me come with that tight little fist?" He grabbed my wrist, snatching my hand away. "Sorry, but I can't let you do that. The only way I'm finishing tonight is deep inside you."

He pressed a kiss to my palm, then slid down until his face hovered over my belly button. Grabbing my legs, he hooked them over his shoulders, pushing my knees up until I was spread out before him like a buffet table. A flush of heat scalded my cheeks when his eyes fell to the wet juncture of my thighs, and I squirmed beneath him, trying to close them.

"No, beautiful," he said, forcing my legs wider, "let me see your pretty pussy."

I licked my lips. "Gabriel, I don't know if—"

"You are utterly divine, Juliet," he said, dipping his head to brush his lips along the crease of my hip. "And I am going to spend the rest of the night worshiping you."

Without warning, his hot tongue dragged up my center, parting my wet folds before flattening against the apex of my sex, applying pressure right where I needed it.

"*Gabriel,*" I shrieked, nearly blacking out.

My mouth went slack as he buried his face between my thighs, and his tongue raked from my entrance to my clit and back again, each stroke driving me closer to that elusive pinnacle of bliss. His tongue dipped even lower, shamelessly sliding between my cheeks, and my stomach fluttered as a heavy throb pulsed back in a place where I'd never felt it before. Hips bucking, a coil of pleasure tightened inside me as desperate cries spilled past my lips in a rush.

I was so close, dangling on the precipice of that dark abyss, that forbidden place that hovered between heaven and hell, rapture and torture. *I just need him to ...* I sucked in a sharp breath as he pushed two fingers inside me, pumping them into my sex before rotating *hard* and—

I screamed.

My head slammed onto the bed as soul-searing pleasure erupted between my legs, ricocheting through me like lightning and shooting out my limbs. Gabriel held on to my shaking thighs, pressing kisses against my pulsating sex as I rode out the crashing waves of my orgasm, back bowing, spine tingling. Then his arms were around me, grounding me, and I buried my face in his chest as an unexpected rush of tears pricked the back of my eyes.

"I love you," I whispered.

I felt rather than heard his intake of breath, his body tensing as though he was retreating into himself. But I wouldn't let him. Not this time.

Brushing my fingers over the strong angle of his cheekbone, I stared up into those bottomless eyes, a myriad of emotions playing out behind them. "I mean it, Gabriel. I love you. And as much as you want to earn my trust, you should know I want to earn yours too."

His throat bobbed as he pressed my knuckles to his lips. "You don't have to earn a goddamn thing. Just stay by my side and know your existence is all I'll ever need."

He clutched my face in his hands and pulled me into a bruising kiss, our tongues tangling as we traded exhales. Banding an arm around my waist, he dragged me underneath him.

"I need to be inside you. If I don't have this pussy wrapped around my dick soon, I might die. Can I have you? *Please.*" I locked my thighs around his hips in answer, and he hissed, his hard features creasing with pleasure as I accepted the tip of him.

"Wait," he gritted out, his heart pounding so hard I could feel it in my own body. "I need to get something to protect you."

"I'm on the pill," I said, pulse flying. "I don't want anything between us tonight."

"Are you telling me you want me to take you like this?" I moaned into his shoulder as the first few inches of him pushed inside me. "Because if you are ..." He slid a hand up the back of my thighs to open me. "I don't know if I can be gentle. I wanted to take my time with you, but there'll be no chance of that with this bare pussy sliding on my cock. So, tell me what you want. I can put on a condom and give it to you slow and sweet. Or I can stay right here and fuck you hard."

My sex clenched at the second suggestion.

He hummed in my ear. "Yeah, I know what you need. Dammit, I need it too. But I want to hear it from your pretty lips." I whimpered as he pulled out before pushing in again. "Yes, or no, Juliet?

Do you"—his fingers burned a path over my skin—"want me"—his hips pressed down, his ragged breaths falling across my lips—"to fuck you?"

"God, *yes*."

Eyes never leaving mine, he slammed his hips forward, filling me in one thrust, and we both moaned loudly as my sex quivered around his rock-hard flesh.

"It's—*fuck*, it's too good." He swallowed audibly. "Tell me how it feels for you."

"Perfect," I whispered into his neck. "Better than I could have ever imagined."

"Don't tell me that," he pleaded, gripping my backside. "I don't want to lose control, but when you talk like that, it makes me want to fuck you into next week."

"Then do it. Don't hold back with me, Gabriel. I know you want to protect me, but I want—no, I *need* you to let me in. I want to know you. All of you."

"You're sure?" His hips undulated once, and the walls of my sex pulsed deliciously.

"Yes, I need this. I need *you*."

And then I saw it—the moment his restraint snapped. His eyes flooded with a downright primal look, and he gripped my knees, pinning them up by my shoulders. Before my next breath, he plunged into me with a force that made my toes curl.

"You've been torturing me all day," he grunted. "Ever since you sat on my lap this morning. Knew exactly what you were doing, didn't you? Wriggling that sweet bottom around on my cock and pressing your thighs together like you were aching for it." I writhed beneath him, my body already climbing again as he pulled out and slammed back in, his pelvis pressing down against my swollen clit.

"Did you enjoy it, Juliet? Did it make you wet thinking about how hard I was for you sitting on that train? The way you had my cock straining in my jeans, desperate to taste that temptation between your legs."

I cried out as he pistoned his hips, the sound of our flesh slapping together my only anchor as pleasure zipped up my center.

Too quickly my core tightened again, and all my focus zeroed in on Gabriel sinking into me, hard and deep, thrusting against that sweet spot inside me that made me see stars.

Without warning, the trembling in my core turned into a full-on earthquake, and I careened over a cliff, squeezing and pulsing around his hard length as his feverish kisses swallowed my desperate cries.

"Come here, baby." He lifted me, my body still impaled on his, and he locked my legs around his waist as he sank back onto his knees. "Tell me I'm the only man to have you like this," he growled, bucking into me. "That there'll never be anyone else for you. Tell me you're mine, angel. That I *wreck* you the way you wreck me."

"I'm yours," I said as he reached forward to grip the headboard, bouncing me on his lap and driving me up and down his hard shaft.

"I'm yours too. From this moment until my last. You're it for me." His teeth found the curve of my neck just as a guttural sound ripped from his lips. "Oh, fuck yes, Juliet. *Juliet.*"

He dropped his face into the valley of my neck as he came with a tortured groan, his hips jerking as he poured himself into me. I placed a palm on his flushed cheek, and he pressed a kiss against it, his brow damp with sweat. Lowering us to the bed, he drew me into his heaving chest, and I clung to him, sleep clawing at my consciousness as soon as my head hit the pillow.

The last thing I knew as he pulled the sheets over our spent bodies was the sound of rain on the window and Gabriel whispering one word against my ear.

Mine.

Thirty-Four

Juliet

*A*ren't you supposed to be working, Ms. Chandler?

I folded a smile between my teeth as I typed out a response to Gabriel's text under the desk.

Already finished with Benoit's lesson plans for the week, so I've got time to spare. Been doing some shopping ...

I pressed Send on a photo of a sheer light blue lace bodysuit with halter straps, a silk ribbon across the open back, and a sexy high-cut leg that was certain to show off all my assets. Three dots appeared and disappeared twice before he finally responded.

I've never begged for anything in my life, but I'm begging now. Please tell me you'll be wearing that when I see you later tonight.

Hmm, possibly. I might have paid for same-day shipping.

And there goes my focus for the rest of the afternoon ...

My shoulders shook with silent laughter just as a shadow fell across my desk. The sound of Benoit clearing his throat drew my attention up past his tweed jacket to his eyes studying me behind wire frames.

"I hope I'm not interrupting," he said, arching an eyebrow.

"No, not at all." I dropped my phone in my bag before catching sight of the papers in his hand, the red slashes of his handwriting visible on the front page. "What's that?"

"Your short story for *La Nouvelle Revue*."

"Ah," I said lightly, even as my heart drummed in my ears. "So, um ..."

One corner of his mouth lifted. "I've decided to submit it to the editor—*with revisions*," he finished, his voice rising as I blurted out a squeal.

"Sorry, I can't tell you what this means to me."

He nodded, then glanced toward the stack of manila folders sitting on my desk, each labeled with colored tabs and organized by the day of the week. "Are those for me?"

"Yes. Trade you?" I gathered the folders in one hand, taking my story with the other.

"Should I expect any surprises this week?"

I smothered a smile. "I included a few *suggestions*, but feel free to disregard them if you don't agree."

Benoit had been flabbergasted the first time he'd found one of my notes in the margin of his lesson plan. Shortly after becoming his assistant, I'd taken it upon myself to review his sample lesson plans for the entire semester and quickly discovered the curriculum was severely lacking in female representation. So, I wrote him a note, suggesting he consider working in a piece by French author Amantine Lucile Aurore Dupin de Francueil—better known by her pen name George Sand—to round out the course. He'd given me a baleful look, but, to my surprise, had announced to the class the following morning that instead of reading excerpts from *The Three Musketeers* as planned, we would review chapters from *Indiana*.

Since then, we'd fallen into something of a friendship and had taken to calling each other by our first names outside of class. He even encouraged me to be more vocal about my opinions, though he still challenged me in front of the other students to keep them from labeling me a teacher's pet.

"*Veuillez m'excuser.*" Benoit cast a look over his shoulder as I spotted Louise, one of the assistants from the first-floor administration office, standing in the open doorway. "Pardon the interruption, but someone is downstairs looking for you, Ms. Chandler. I told them I would check to see if you were still here. Shall I send them up?"

I dipped my head in a nod, a blush staining my cheeks as I darted a glance at Benoit.

"You seem to have a lot of visitors lately," he said, eyeing me over the rim of his glasses. "Maybe I should just add your name to the door and save people the trouble of looking for you."

"Seriously? *Julien* Benoit and *Juliet* Chandler? It's like some sort of bad pun."

He chuckled, pushing his hands into the pockets of his trousers. "Hmm, you're right. Our names are quite similar."

"Wait," I said, my mouth opening in mock horror, "is that why you picked my admissions essay out of the pile? Because my name is almost identical to yours?"

He gave me a wry grin. "I must confess, that is it exactly. Narcissist that I am, I saw your name and my heart swelled with the hope that I had finally found another soul who shared my literary genius." I snorted a laugh, and he winked at me before returning to his desk.

I had just started flipping through his edits when there was a knock on the door, and I glanced up, my eyes widening when I saw who was standing in the doorway.

Lily.

"Um, hi." She shifted awkwardly, shoving her hands into the back pockets of her ripped denim shorts and digging the toe of one Converse sneaker into the heel of the other. "Gabe said I might find you here. Can I come in?"

I looked over at Benoit only to find him staring at Lily, his mouth tilting into a deep frown.

Right. For all his joking around, his expression made it clear this was not, in fact, my office and visitors were not welcome. Though, now that I thought about it, he hadn't seemed bothered when Cristian stopped by last week.

"Why don't we chat outside?" I said to Lily. "There's a café across the street—"

"You can use the sitting area." Benoit stood abruptly, straightening his tie. "If you'll excuse me, I'm going to get some coffee." He brushed past Lily and disappeared down the hall with hurried footsteps.

Okaaay.

I gestured toward the overstuffed chairs, my eyes briefly landing on the near-full coffee cup sitting on Benoit's desk next to the lesson plans.

Lily lowered herself into one of the armchairs, and I'd barely taken the seat opposite her when she blurted out, "I want to apologize to you for my behavior at the dinner party."

I blinked, my lips parting. "Lily, you don't need to—"

"Yes, I do." She pressed her eyelids closed, a wrinkle forming between her brows. "Just, please, let me get this out. I never meant to humiliate you, Juliet. I was projecting when I said all that stuff about it not being too late to pursue an education." She paused, her hands balling in her lap. "You know how I said my mother is always going on about education being the key to success? Well, I never finished college. In a family full of overachievers, I'm the only one who never saw my education through. So, when I said your pursuit of a degree was an achievement, I genuinely meant it. It never occurred to me you were only attending your program out of interest."

"You couldn't have known, and I stopped Gabriel from telling you because I didn't want to embarrass you."

She nodded. "I gathered as much, especially after I heard you talking to that woman at the gala. When you told her you were a lawyer in America and had published all those articles, I felt like a complete idiot. I mean, how could I not have known the first woman Gabriel brought to meet us would not only be gorgeous but accomplished too?" She stared down at her hands, a deep flush crawling up her cheeks. "I know about you and Gabe."

"He told you?"

She shook her head. "As soon as I saw you two at the dinner party, I knew you weren't just friends, despite what you said. It was the way he looked at you. His eyes always give away everything he's feeling, and when he looks at you, Juliet, they say you have his heart."

"So, you two never ..." I let the end of my sentence fall away. I sounded like a jealous girlfriend, but I had to know the truth. If Gabriel and Lily had history, I would deal with it, but not knowing would only lead to more misunderstandings.

"Gabriel has never looked at me as anything other than a little sister, though, for a long time, I thought I was in love with him." My body tensed and Lily caught the movement. "That's the other reason I came here today. I want to apologize for ..."

Being in love with him?

"... acting like a spoiled brat," she finished. "And hanging all over him when he brought you to meet James and Nora. I was jealous, horribly jealous. And instead of accepting the truth of the situation, I behaved like a child whose favorite toy had been taken away. But you never folded. The whole time you never let your true feelings show. Even after you left, no one suspected you weren't ill, except for me."

"So, when you saw us together at the gala, when you pulled me away from him ..."

She dipped her head. "I'm sorry, Juliet. I was wrong to try to come between you two. Not that it would have worked. He only has eyes for you."

"Do you still love him?" My question was barely more than a whisper.

She blinked slowly. "I'm not sure I ever did. It was more of a childish infatuation, I think. I was always happy to see Gabe when I came to visit, and I even considered moving to Paris one day just to be close to him. But I never missed him when I was home. I had his number and never called. Never texted him to let him know I was thinking about him because I wasn't. I even casually dated other guys from time to time." She tucked a few haphazard strands of hair behind her ear, her eyes settling somewhere over my shoulder.

"You know how people say, out of sight, out of mind? Well, I don't think that's true when it comes to love. When you truly love someone, you're never not thinking about them. They could be across the country, across the world, but a part of them stays with you. It's like a piece of that person becomes embedded in your soul, and no amount of time or distance can break the bond love forges." Her eyes returned to me. "I'm glad Gabe has that with you. He deserves to be happy, deserves to have someone like you in his life."

She reached across the coffee table, placing a hand on my arm. "I know we got off to a bad start, but I would like for us to be friends.

Gabe will always be like family to me, and I couldn't bear it if I spoiled things between me and someone so important to him. Can you forgive me?"

I swallowed before bobbing my head. "Yes, I can—"

Lily sprang out of the chair and flung her arms around me, caging me in with her floral scent and pressing her cheek to mine.

"Thank you, Juliet. You won't regret this." She pulled away, a smile unfurling from the corner of her mouth. "Well, I should get going—" She paused, her eyes widening into saucers. "Is that Tchaikovsky's *Swan Lake*?" She crossed over to a bookshelf near the window, running her fingers over a row of vinyls I'd never noticed.

"Oh, my God, it is." She plucked the album from the stack, staring at it with a look of reverence. "And it looks like a limited first edition too. Your professor must have paid more than a few euros for an original pressing."

"Yes, well, he does seem to have a fondness for collecting old things," I said dryly, but Lily didn't seem to hear. Her eyes scanned over the album cover before flipping it over to read the track list.

"My parents took me to see a performance of Swan Lake at the Birmingham Royal Ballet in Southampton when I was eight. It's what made me fall in love with ballet. The ballerinas, the costumes, the music. It was all so captivating." She ran one finger along the edge of the cover. "Hearing the score performed live by an orchestra was incredible, but I bet it sounds amazing on vinyl too."

I joined her at the window. "Why don't you ask Benoit if you can borrow it?"

"Borrow what?"

Our heads snapped up in unison to find Benoit hovering in the doorway, his hair looking unkempt, as though he had been running his fingers through it. He crossed the room in three purposeful strides, his eyes settling on Lily, who was still clutching the album.

"Sorry," she said. "I was just admiring your album collection."

His eyes raked over her slowly, his jaw tightening, and I could have sworn I heard Lily gulp as she shrank beside me.

I frowned.

What the hell was his problem?

I snatched the album from Lily's rigid fingers and replaced it on the shelf, opening my mouth to tell him no harm had been done to his precious album, but he spoke before I could. "You can borrow it. Take whichever one you want."

Lily shook her head. "Um, thanks, but I don't have a record player." Turning to me, she said, "I'm glad we could talk, Juliet. I'm sure I'll be seeing you soon." She rushed out the door before either of us could say anything else.

I glanced up at Benoit. "Since when are you such a Grinch?"

He ignored me and returned to his desk, flipping through the stack of lesson plans. Seriously? I watched as he uncapped a fountain pen and scratched out a note, his brow furrowing in concentration as though whatever was written on the page held the secrets to the universe.

Why was he acting like this? And why had he looked at Lily like he wanted to take a bite out of her? A thought niggled at the back of my mind, and my lips curved into a slow smile.

"Where's your coffee?" I asked coyly.

"Don't you have a draft to revise, Ms. Chandler?" he snapped, pink tinging the top of his ears.

I huffed a laugh. "Yeah, I'll get right on that, *sir.*"

Thirty-Five

Gabriel

"So, what do you think?" I propped the canvas against the wall, squinting at it from where I knelt on the studio floor. *Still needs something.*

When no response came, I glanced over to where Juliet sat on the couch, her legs tucked beneath her, her skirt riding up just enough to reveal a hint of thigh. My hand twitched, but I forced my eyes up, taking in her frown.

"Everything all right?" I grabbed a rag to wipe a smear of paint from my fingertips, a trickle of concern sliding into my chest. Was her boss bothering her again? Ever since she'd sent him that email, she told me he'd laid off a bit, sending only the occasional "reminder" about something he wanted her to do when she was back in the office.

After she goes back to New York.

"Yeah, it's just my friend Cristian. He's been radio silent for the past week. I know it's probably nothing, but I'm starting to worry a little."

"Friend from school?" I said, gathering the palettes I'd left scattered across the floor.

"Mmm, not exactly, but I did meet him on campus. He's applying for the business program, and we just sort of became friends after that."

"Business program, huh? Sounds like a smart guy." My eyes dragged to hers. "Should I be jealous, Ms. Chandler?"

She tossed her phone down, leaping up to throw her arms around me. "Definitely not. He really *is* just a friend." Her lips curled in a slow smile. "You're the only man I want in my bed."

I dropped the supplies I had just collected, pulling her to me. "Well, good. For a minute there, I thought I might have to challenge him to a duel to stake my claim."

"Ah, pistols at dawn?"

"Nah, I'm more of a slug-it-out kind of guy." She watched me beneath heavy lids, and I smirked. "Do you like that I'm not above throwing hands to protect what's mine?" I leaned in until we were trading breaths. "Does my prim-and-proper good girl like boys who do bad things?"

She sucked in a breath, her pupils dilating. "No, that would be a total cliché." *Uh-huh.* She could deny it all she wanted, but her body was singing a different tune. "What did you want to show me?"

"I forget," I said, nibbling on her lower lip. She giggled, giving me a brief kiss before slipping out of my arms and crossing over to kneel in front of the painting.

"You finished it." She beamed at me over her shoulder. "Your statement piece, right?"

"Yeah." I pushed a hand up the back of my head, looking down at the golden wings arching across the white textural background. "I just feel like it needs something, but I can't figure out what." Capturing the essence of an angel embodied had seemed easy enough when the idea had first come to me. But months later, it still wasn't glowing the way I wanted it to.

Juliet tilted her head to one side, wrinkling her nose in the way she always did whenever she was thinking. By this point, I had learned every one of my girlfriend's quirks and, half of the time, I could tell what she was thinking from her expression alone.

My girlfriend.

God, I loved calling her that.

"What if you made the background darker?" She traced an invisible outline around one gold feather. "These wings make me think of an angel illuminating a place shrouded in deep shadow. Beautiful as they are, if they were surrounded in darkness rather than light, it would better show off their true radiance."

"And what should we call it?" I said, kneeling behind her and threading my arms around her waist, the gears in my mind already turning. "Should we call it *Angel Wings*?"

She hummed, letting her head fall back against my chest. "Let's call it *Angel Eyes*, because it's the angel's light that helps us see."

My heart accelerated, the vision of what the painting should be forming before my eyes. The colors, the brushstrokes—it was all there in my mind, just waiting on the other side of a door that only the woman in my arms held the key to.

"How did I get so lucky?" I whispered against the skin of her throat, breathing her in.

"I could ask you the same question." She brushed her lips over my brow, her warm breaths pelting my forehead. And then we were falling, my back hitting the floor as I pulled her down with me, my hands sliding up the back of her thighs.

She smiled against my lips. "Uh-uh. You promised me you would work if I came over."

"I'm taking a lunch break." I grazed my teeth over the sensitive flesh beneath her ear. "You wouldn't want me to starve, would you?"

She laughed, but her laughter turned into moans as my fingers slipped into her panties, my cock already thickening as I stroked her damp flesh. I captured her mouth in a hard kiss, the heat of her lips rushing through my chest and filling my body with warmth.

This. I want this forever.

Her hands cradled my head as I took the kiss deeper, pushing my tongue past her soft lips and licking the inside of her mouth. She tasted like strawberries and sunshine, and I felt my control slip as her sweet breaths bathed my throat, stoking the hunger in my core.

My thumb climbed her rib cage to one breast, sweeping over the puckered flesh there, and she moaned into my mouth.

"Let me taste you," I groaned, sliding the straps of her top down her shoulders and unfastening her bra. I shoved the material aside and closed my lips around one dusty-rose nipple, rolling my tongue against the distended tip. Her head fell forward, her hair forming a curtain around us as I pressed a hand between her shoulder blades, pulling her deeper into my mouth.

"*Gabriel*." She let go of a harsh breath, her hand moving to stroke me through my jeans. "Take these off." I flipped her over instead, consuming her in another fevered kiss as her fingers fumbled with my zipper, her desperate whimpers turning my dick solid.

"Take. Them. Off," she repeated, biting my lip hard.

"Look who's hungry now?"

"Tease me all you like as long as it ends with you inside me."

I growled, my fingers digging into her hips. "Is that what you want? For me to take you right on this floor?" She moaned her approval, her thighs pressing tighter around my ribs, and I braced myself on top of her, preparing to shove my jeans down and make good on my word.

Without warning, the door swung open, and I swore violently, yanking Juliet against my chest to cover her.

"*Christ*. Save some for the honeymoon." James stood in the doorway, covering his eyes with one hand and gripping a paper bag with the other. He lifted it as if in explanation. "We brought food, but it looks like you guys skipped straight to dessert."

Juliet hurriedly fastened her bra, her face the color of a beetroot.

I scowled at James. "What the hell are you doing here?"

His lips tilted into a cocky grin. "You asked us to come help with the invitations for your opening, remember?"

"That's not until noon."

"Who's us?" Juliet said, getting to her feet just as James said, "It's 12:10, asshole. Maybe if you were looking at a clock instead of Juliet's—"

"You could have at least knocked," I growled.

"You gave me a key."

"For emergencies, dickhead."

"Who's us?" Juliet repeated.

"Hey, guys." Lily bounced through the door carrying another paper bag, followed by Nora hauling an armful of water bottles. She paused, glancing between James, Juliet, and me. "Why's everyone standing around looking at each other?"

James's grin widened. "Oh, Gabe was just telling me how grateful he is to have such a *loyal* best friend, so much so that he wants to buy me VIP tickets to the Tour de France this year."

"Really?" Nora dumped the bottles on the desk. "Those tickets are expensive, aren't they?"

"That's what I told him," James went on, a gleeful look in his eye. "But he insisted, saying only the best for my good buddy James. Isn't that right, Gabe?"

I curled my lip, opening my mouth to tell him to go to hell, but Juliet jumped in. "What have you got there?" She nodded to the package in Lily's arms.

"It's Lebanese food," Lily said. "I hope you guys like falafel."

"Sounds great." Juliet gave me a loaded look before going to help Lily unpack the bags. She wrapped an arm around Lily in an embrace, and Lily smiled, pausing to drop a kiss on Juliet's cheek. I blinked. *Well, that's new.* When had the two of them gotten so close?

"Hey, Gabe, what's this?" Nora peered down at the new photo sitting on the desk between the picture of my mother and the snapshot of James, Nora, and me at the film festival.

"Oh, that?" I crossed the room, sidestepping where Juliet and Lily were busy setting out plates and napkins on top of a clean drop cloth that James had spread out like a picnic blanket. "That's me and Juliet on Bastille Day." My eyes lingered on the image of us sitting on the sprawling lawn of the Champs de Mars. I had my arm draped over Juliet's shoulder as I grinned at the camera. Rather than looking straight ahead at the lens, Juliet's face was tilted toward me, her gaze fixed on my profile, a smile on her lips.

I swallowed the lump in my throat before glancing at Nora. She wasn't looking at the picture anymore, but was staring up at me, a flicker of something passing over her expression. I hesitated, waiting for her to ream me out for not inviting her to watch the fireworks with us. But, to my surprise, she said nothing. She simply squeezed my shoulder, communicating more in that one gesture than she ever had out loud.

That's the thing about true friends—they see things about you that are invisible to the naked eye. The simple act of adding a photo to my workspace would have probably gone unnoticed by a casual observer. But to Nora, who'd spent the last three years peeling me back layer by layer, it wasn't a small thing. She knew what adding the photo meant.

It meant what Juliet and I had was real.

"Should we eat first or work on the invitations?" Lily asked, rolling up her sleeves like she was preparing to perform intensive manual labor rather than stuff envelopes.

"Definitely eat first." I slid into the spot on the floor between Juliet and James just as Nora sat down beside Lily. "If even one invitation arrives with a sauce stain on it, Jean-Claude will have a coronary."

"Not to knock his preference for doing things the old-fashioned way, but wouldn't it be easier to send these out electronically?" James said, spooning moussaka onto his plate.

"Probably," I said, licking a bit of hummus off my thumb and smirking when I caught Juliet watching me. "But Jean-Claude insisted an email could never match the elegance of a hand-delivered invitation. But don't worry. We sent out the save-the-dates electronically, and we'll send a reminder via email before the event so people have the details easily accessible."

"Very wise," Juliet chimed in just as Lily swatted her brother's hand.

"Hands off my pita," she snapped, scooting her plate away from him. "Why can't you get your own? The carton is just over there."

"Because yours is right here," he said matter-of-factly.

Juliet wiped her fingers on a napkin. "Here, James. You can have one of mine."

"Absolutely not," Nora said, waving a fork at Juliet. "You'll only encourage him. It's bad enough he had a mother and two older sisters to spoil him for a quarter of a century. Don't you take up the baton."

"Well, what do you expect?" He reached for Lily's plate again, only to earn an elbow to the ribs. "I was the baby of the family until Lily came along. You can't imagine how difficult it was for seven-year-old me to accept the sudden change in our family dynamic."

"Oh, yes, I can." Nora nudged him with her foot. "You forget, I've seen pictures of you at the hospital when she was born. Your face was redder than hers." She set down her plate, wiping her mouth with a napkin. "And on that note, I'd like to make an announcement."

"Already?" James grinned. "Thought we'd at least get to the baklava before you told them."

"Told us what?" I uncapped a water bottle as Juliet's and Lily's eyes connected across the room, clearly picking up on something I hadn't yet.

"I'm pregnant."

Juliet clasped her hands over her mouth just as Lily overturned a carton of salad. "Oh, my goodness," she squealed, diving onto Nora. "I'm going to be an auntie."

I swiveled to James, the water bottle still suspended halfway to my mouth. "Are you serious? How long have you known?"

"A couple of months now," he said, beaming proudly.

"So, you *can* keep a secret—just not mine." He laughed, and I gave him a wide grin, clapping him on the shoulder. "Congratulations, mate. That's fantastic news."

"Right," Nora said, untangling herself from Lily's arms to accept a hug from Juliet, "and I'm expecting you all to come to our gender reveal party in a few weeks. Make sure to let me know your guesses whether it's a boy or a girl beforehand. The winners will get to take their turns first during the baby names game."

Lily squeaked. "Oh, I hope it's a girl."

"Baby names game?" I said, blinking in confusion.

James's mouth twitched. "Don't try to understand it, mate. Just come for the free beer."

Juliet laughed, shaking her head at James as she nestled into the crook of my arm. I pulled her closer, hooking a hand over her hip and nuzzling her hair.

I looked around at the four of them huddled on the floor of my studio, laughing and talking—and occasionally elbowing, in Lily's case—and realized that, for the first time in a long time, I felt completely at peace, surrounded by people I loved. They might not have been the family I was born into, but they were the family I'd found.

And they were more than enough.

Thirty-Six

Cristian

"So, what do you think of the candidates?"

I blinked, looking up from the computer screen I'd been staring at for however many minutes without seeing a single thing. Caleb sat across from me in my office, leaning back in his chair with his long legs sprawled wide as he waited for me to respond.

"Sorry, what were we discussing?"

He arched a blond eyebrow. "Potential candidates to fill the new event coordinator position. We've gotten a ton of inquiries about hosting events at the restaurant ever since the website went live. Amélie's been doing her best to field them, but it's encroaching on her other responsibilities. And I'd offer to help myself, but I'm shit at party planning."

"No, you've already got enough on your plate with the opening coming up." I frowned down at the screen, scanning the list of names. "Have you prescreened these people?"

"If you're asking whether I weeded out the overqualified, underqualified and past lovers who only applied for the position to have an excuse to stare at your handsome mug all day, then yes, I have."

"If that last bit was an attempt at humor, then I should warn you I'm not in the mood."

"I wish it was," he said, shaking his head, "but unfortunately, I'm telling the truth. Remember Félicité, that go-go dancer from the nightclub we went to back in May? Yeah, you should have *prescreened* her before deciding to take her home for the night."

I cringed. "The one we had to ban from the premises because she kept popping up looking for me?"

"The very same. Guess she thought she'd finally found a back-door entrance. You know, kind of how you found her back-door entr—"

"Finish that statement at your own peril, Martin," I gritted out as he snickered, his lips pulling up in a self-satisfied smirk that reminded me eerily of myself.

Apparently, I had been rubbing off on the kid.

"I'll take another look at these candidates and come back to you." I slammed the laptop shut, more than ready to be done with this meeting. "Anything else we need to discuss?"

Caleb scrubbed a hand over his jaw. "Yeah, there is, actually. I noticed you haven't really been yourself lately. Something bothering you?"

I bit down on my cheek, internally cursing the fact that he was so observant. Ironically, his observation skills were one reason I'd kept him around after his new employee probation period had ended, offering him a full-time position as assistant manager. He had a singular talent for reading people, and he had successfully applied his talents to proposing several additions to staff as well as advancing the restaurant's social media presence from virtually nonexistent to having a following of over 20,000 people. But, as invaluable as his talents were for business, I didn't appreciate when he employed them on me.

"It's nothing."

The truth was, I'd been in some kind of mood ever since the morning I left Juliet's place without saying goodbye. It had been a week and a half since then, and though she'd texted me a few times, I couldn't bring myself to respond. Not after I realized the way I felt about her no longer had anything to do with some scheme involving Gabriel and Marcel.

I was starting to *care* for her—and that was dangerous.

People never chose me. Not my mother, not Marcel. Not even Caleb. As much as he shadowed my every move like a puppy, it was only because I paid him to do so. But when it came down to it, people didn't care about me—they only cared about what I could do for them, and I doubted Juliet would be any different.

If she and lover boy hadn't made up already, they would soon. Gabriel might have botched things the night of the gala, but I could tell Juliet meant something to him, enough for him to put aside his pride and ask me for help with Elise. Pair that with his unrelenting stubbornness, and I was certain he would stop at nothing to make things right with Juliet. And when he did, she wouldn't need me anymore.

So, I bowed out early. Why wait around for the inevitable to happen, right? Right. Only, I hadn't expected walking away from her to suck this much.

"So, who's the girl?"

"What?"

His eyes glinted like a predator closing in on its prey. "Who. Is. The. Girl."

I glowered at him, an uncomfortable heat creeping up my neck. "There is no girl."

"Oh, okay, my mistake," he said with a shrug. "A guy, then?"

"*No.*" I rose from my chair, striding over to the liquor cabinet. "I pay you to be my assistant manager, Caleb, not my therapist. So do us both a favor and cease with your pointless questions." I poured a measure of whiskey, downing it in one go.

"Aww," he whined. "And here I thought we were friends. Remember that time we went out for drinks in Le Marais and you told that one guy who kept following me to piss off or you would break his nose?" He nodded seriously. "Pretty sure you and I have been friends ever since."

"I don't have friends," I said flatly, refilling my glass before returning to my seat.

"You might if you stopped acting like a prickly asshole." He shifted forward, bracing his forearms on his knees. "Seriously, though, you're not going to tell me about whatever girl's got your knickers in a twist?"

"By all the saints. For the last time, there is no girl."

He opened his mouth to say something else, but before he could, there was a knock on the door, followed by Amélie poking her head in. "Sorry to interrupt, but there's someone here to see you, Cristian."

"Who?" I flipped through my calendar. "I don't have any other appointments today."

Amélie shrugged. "She said her name is Juliet, but if you weren't expecting her, I can—"

"*No.*" I shot out of my chair so fast I nearly upended my whiskey. Caleb and Amélie stared at me with twin looks of surprise, and I cleared my throat. "No, I am expecting her. Send her up."

Amélie nodded and disappeared into the hallway, but Caleb's eyes remained glued to me, his eyebrows inching upward.

"No girl, huh?" His lips tilted into a grin so smug my hand itched to slap it off his face.

"*Out.*" I rounded the desk, nodding toward the open door. "Our meeting is over."

Instead of rising to leave, he sank deeper into his chair, resting his chin on steepled fingers. "But you still need to give me the contact information for that editor at *France Today* magazine. You specifically asked me to remind you so I could reach out about running an article on the restaurant in next week's issue."

"Look it up yourself," I hissed, darting a look at the door and listening for footsteps.

"Mmm, I don't think that's a good idea," he said, his eyes glittering with mischief. "I would *hate* to reach out to the wrong person."

Shooting him a look full of dark promises, I snatched a Post-it from the desk drawer and scribbled the information down. "Here, now leave."

He tutted, making no move to take it. "A Post-it? But that could get lost so easily."

I bared my teeth. "Would you prefer I tattoo it on the back of your eyelids?"

He chuckled, slapping the Post-it on his forehead and pushing to stand. "All right, keep your pants on. I'm leaving."

He was almost to the door when Juliet appeared, stepping across the threshold.

"Oh, hello." She frowned up at the flapping piece of paper stuck to Caleb's head. "Um, sorry, but did you know you have a Post-it on your forehead?"

"Yes," he said, switching to English as his eyes perused her in a way that had me grinding my teeth. "It's quite the story. I could tell you about it over drinks sometime—"

Crossing the room in three strides, I planted a firm hand between his shoulder blades and shoved him through the door, kicking it shut behind him as his laughter echoed in the hall.

"Please excuse him," I said, shucking off my jacket and hanging it over the back of the chair Caleb had vacated. "Clearly, he's overworked."

"Well, I can't say I'm surprised. You seem like you'd be a harsh taskmaster."

"Why, darling, you flatter me." My lips quirked when she burst into laughter, her green eyes sparkling with amusement. I watched her for a long moment, letting my eyes trail over a few loose tendrils of hair that had escaped her ponytail to spiral down the sides of her face.

Stop looking at her like that, I commanded myself. *Stop looking at her like you miss her.*

"So, what brings you here today?" I pushed my hands into my pockets, leaning on the desk.

"Hmm, let me see. Maybe it's the fact that you haven't responded to any of my messages? Or that you ghosted me the morning after the gala?" She huffed humorlessly, folding her arms under her chest. "Every time I think I have you figured out, you surprise me."

I smirked. "Well, I should hate to be predictable."

She eyed me for a long beat. "Look, I don't remember much from the night you came over, but if I did something to offend you—"

"No," I said too quickly. "I—I've just been busy, that's all."

Her mouth softened into a sad smile. "You're good at that, you know."

"Good at what?"

"Lying."

I blinked, opening my mouth to say—what? There wasn't a single true thing I could tell her that wouldn't leave me feeling uncomfortably exposed.

Silence gaped between us until her eyes hardened. "I guess coming here was a mistake. I thought—well, I don't know what I thought. I'll just leave you to whatever it is that's been keeping you so busy."

The sight of her retreating form hit me straight in the solar plexus, and I stalked after her, closing a hand around her elbow before she could clear the doorway.

"Don't go. I'm sorry."

She whirled. "Why have you been avoiding me, then?"

I exhaled a tight breath. "What do you want me to say?"

"How about the truth, Cristian? God, why is it always so hard for you to be honest?"

"Because I'm not a good man," I burst out, grabbing her by the shoulders. "Haven't you been listening to me all this time?"

She shook her head. "That's not true. You rescued me when I got into trouble at Galeries, you came over the night of the gala ..."

"Smoke and mirrors, sweetheart. Sooner or later, you'll find out the truth about me." *And when you do, you'll hate me as much as Gabriel does.* I released her, putting as much distance between us as possible without leaving the room. "You should go, Juliet. Go and be happy with Gabriel. I have nothing more to offer you."

Nothing besides more lies.

Turning my back to her, I propped a hand against one wood-paneled wall, taking in slow breaths and listening for the sound of the door closing. But when it didn't come even after several seconds, I glanced over my shoulder to find her still standing there.

"So that's what this is about." She closed the gap between us, blocking any means of escape that wouldn't involve me manhandling her. "Let me guess—you thought as soon as I made up with Gabriel, I would ditch you, right? That I was only using you as a stand-in?" When I didn't answer, she nodded as if confirming the answer to her question.

"For the record, we did make up," she said, her voice softening. "Gabriel's my boyfriend now, but you're still my friend, Cristian—that is, if you want to be. I told you before, you're nobody's replacement. So take up your own space, all right?"

I shook my head, my throat thickening. "I don't deserve you."

"Don't you think I should be the judge of that?" She rested a hand on my biceps, a tiny smile sliding over her features. Then, slowly, she wrapped her arms around me in a gentle embrace, and I cracked completely, folding over her and dragging her against me.

She sucked in a breath. "Cristian—"

"Just for a minute." I said, swallowing. "One minute, and then I'll let you go."

She hesitated a beat, then softened in my arms, sweeping a hand over my shoulder blades in a gesture that soothed an ache so deep, my eyes burned.

To be wanted, to be chosen—my most desperate desire and my secret shame.

I drew back from her, the warmth of her smile shifting something in my chest. Juliet—my friend and the most genuine person I'd ever met. I would never be worthy of her, but I would bask in her light for as long as she would let me.

"So, what's a girl got to do to get a tour around here? I'd love to see the restaurant before we come to opening night in a few weeks."

I froze, a cold shard sliding down my spine.

Shit. I had forgotten all about asking her to come to the opening with Gabriel.

"Um, about that, I don't think you should come to opening night after all."

She frowned. "Why not?"

Goddammit. I didn't want to lie to her again, but what choice did I have?

"It's going to be a frenzy, you know? I won't even have a chance to talk to you. Maybe you could come on a different night? Just let me know when and I'll set it up. VIP table, the works." Her eyes bounced between each of mine, her brows pulling together. "I promise, I'll make it up to you."

She studied me, then rolled her eyes, and I let go of an involuntary breath. "All right, but I want free dessert."

"Anything you want." I grinned. "Now, you said something about a tour?" I offered her my arm, and she laughed, winding her hand around my elbow.

"Lead the way."

Thirty-Seven

Gabriel

Running late—be there as soon as I can.

I fired off the message to James as I climbed the stairs of my apartment building two at a time, digging my keys out of my pocket. As much as I enjoyed living in the seventeenth arrondissement with its wine bars and old-world charm, its location along the northwestern edge of the city made for a long commute. And while I rarely minded the Métro ride, on nights like tonight when I was late to my best friend's baby's gender reveal party, it was less than ideal.

My phone vibrated just as I turned the key in the front door.

No worries, mate. As long as you make it in time for the cake cutting, you're all good. Otherwise, there will be hell to pay (Nora's words, not mine).

I chuckled, tossing my phone down on the kitchen counter as I kicked the door shut behind me. Turning to the living room, my eyes fell across a neat stack of books on the table next to an open notebook full of writing and a rose-gold laptop.

Juliet.

"You here, angel?" I called, hanging my keys on the hook near the door.

"In the bedroom," she answered from down the hall. A grin tipped up the corners of my mouth, her sweet voice vibrating through every inch of my body.

I was so fucking gone for this girl.

The week after our trip to Versailles, I gave Juliet a key to my place. Since she was now spending more nights with me than not, I didn't want her to have to wait around at the bike shop or gallery until I was finished for the day. The decision to give her a key quickly snowballed into us going to her apartment to pack up some of her clothes so she wouldn't have to stop at home before coming over. And when I noticed after the first few nights she was still keeping all of her belongings stacked in the corner of the bedroom as though she wanted to take up as little space as possible, I immediately cleared out a couple of drawers and unpacked her things.

Three weeks later, I still hadn't gotten used to coming home to her. It was like some kind of daydream—the sight of her sweaters in the closet next to my shirts, the smell of her shampoo in my shower, the sound of *Bridgerton* playing in the background while she made dinner, the feeling of waking up with her warm body next to mine. It was almost too good to be true.

What if it could always be like this?

I pushed the thought away and moved down the hall. I already knew it couldn't, so there was no point in letting the idea take root. It was too tempting, too euphoric—too close to the thing I didn't dare hope for.

For her to stay.

I rounded the corner to the bedroom, only to stop dead in my tracks. Juliet was standing in front of the mirror in the red lace dress Simone had given her, the corseted top and sweetheart neckline hugging her curves so perfectly that my heart catapulted into my throat. My greedy eyes roamed over her, dipping to where the dress tapered off beneath her hips, just above a pair of sheer black thigh-high stockings.

Lord have mercy.

On any given day, she looked like an angel, but right now, she was pure sin.

A light blush stained her cheeks when her gaze connected with mine in the mirror. "I wasn't planning on wearing this to the party," she said, turning to face me. "I just thought I'd try it on and see how you liked it for a date night or something."

I prowled toward her, my abdomen stirring. "I like it very much." Hooking a finger under her chin, I tilted her head up. "As long as that date is in this bedroom, then I'm all for it."

She laughed, looping her arms around my neck. "Is it strange that I like how possessive you are?"

"Yeah?" I trailed my lips over the smooth column of her throat, breathing in her warm, familiar scent. "Well, there's plenty more where that came from, beautiful."

She sucked in a sharp breath as I brushed my tongue over her earlobe, dragging it between my teeth. "Gabriel, we can't. We'll be late for James and Nora's, and I still have to shower."

"How convenient," I said, finding the clasp of her dress and unzipping it. "So do I."

She shuddered, her fingers digging into my shoulders as I lowered to my knees, peeling the dress down her body until she was standing in nothing but a lacy thong and stockings.

"Oh, angel," I said darkly, tracing my thumb over the seam of her panties and feeling her wetness through the material, "do you need your man to take care of this?" She let out a throaty moan as I dragged the scrap of fabric down her legs, my cock thickening as I unwrapped her like a goddamn birthday present.

"*Gabriel,*" she gasped as I dragged my nose up her slit.

"I love the way you smell. I love everything about you." Grabbing her hips, I drew her closer. "The way you taste," I said, my tongue disappearing between her folds until her thighs quivered. "The way you feel," I whispered against her sensitive flesh, sweeping my thumbs up the curve of her calves. "Every time I'm in your presence, I am utterly consumed by you."

Rising to my feet, I pulled my shirt over my head before kicking off my jeans and briefs. Then I was diving for her mouth, taking her lips in a sensual kiss that became increasingly desperate as she pressed herself against me. Without breaking the kiss, I hooked my arms under her knees and lifted her, walking us toward the bathroom.

"Wait," she panted as I nipped at her chin, "I'm still wearing my stockings."

"Keep them on. I love the way they look wrapped around my waist."

I pushed the glass door open and flipped on the rain shower, the bathroom already beginning to fill with steam as I adjusted the temperature of the water. Juliet lowered her feet to the tile floor while I painted my fingertips over every familiar swell and valley of her flesh. Folding a hand over her ribs, I grazed a thumb over one taut peak, and she moaned, her eyes going molten as they lifted to mine. She let her gaze linger for a heavy moment, then slowly sank to her knees, stealing all the air from my lungs on the way down.

"Juliet." I traced the soft curve of her lips with the pad of my thumb. "You don't have to do that."

She smiled, bracing herself against my thighs. "I want to, but only for you, Gabriel."

A deep groan rumbled in my chest, and I let my head fall back against the steam-coated wall, desperate to feel her mouth on me again. It had been weeks since the first time she rocked my world with her hot tongue, and there hadn't been a day since when I hadn't replayed it in my mind in vivid detail.

My angel. My tormentor. *Mine.*

She closed a hand around my hard flesh, her thumb sweeping slow circles around the head before she began working her fist up and down my throbbing shaft. After a few pumps that had heat collecting at the base of my spine, she dipped her head to wrap those perfect lips around me. I groaned like some kind of caveman, my vision blurring as she surrounded me in tight, wet heat, fisting the base of my cock while licking and sucking the tip.

"Oh, fuck." My hips rocked in tandem with her movements, my hand cupping the base of her head to guide her. I felt myself swelling in her mouth as she took me to the back of her throat, her tongue painting languid strokes along the underside of my length.

"You have to slow down. I'm going to come if you don't."

Instead of pulling back, she hummed in her throat, sending lightning shooting up my spine. I tangled a hand in her hair, gripping the wet strands as her tongue swirled around my cock. My eyelids fell to half-mast, warm droplets of water sliding over my shoulders as I drove into her mouth again and again, powerless to stop and completely at her mercy.

Gripping my hip with one hand, she slid the other between my splayed legs, palming my backside and trailing one finger up the center of my cheeks before tentatively pressing between them, massaging a spot I never expected her to touch.

My eyes flew wide.

"J-Juliet," I stuttered, my Adam's apple bobbing as a strange ache built in my core. "I don't know if I'm supposed to be enjoying that."

As if in answer, she increased the pressure, teasing and exploring, and my sex became noticeably harder. Cradling my balls in her palm, she squeezed them gently as she tightened her lips, moving her head faster before slipping her finger inside, pushing deeper.

I shouted, my face twisting in shock as I went off like dynamite.

"*Juliet.*" I slammed my fist into the wall, primal moans filling the shower stall. Fire scorched up my spine, rippling down every limb as I pulsed in her mouth repeatedly, the muscles of her throat working as she stared up at me with glassy eyes. She drew back, pressing kisses against my pelvis, and it took everything in me to keep my knees from buckling.

I dragged her to her feet and consumed her mouth in a wild kiss, tasting myself on her tongue as I swept all the shower products off the ledge. With an arm around her waist, I lifted her onto it in one smooth motion, pulling her curves flush with my hard angles.

"I can wait until later," she said, her heart slamming against mine as water raced over us.

"I don't think so." My palms skimmed over her hips as I hauled her to the edge of the ledge. "You think I'm going to let you suck me off like that without taking care of you?" She whimpered as I dropped a hand between her legs, pressing my thumb to the apex of her thighs and moving it in slow circles. "If so, then you have a lot to learn about me. Now, *open*."

I shoved her legs wide, pushing a finger inside her before adding a second, my thumb still circling her clit in meticulous strokes. Her jaw fell slack as she tipped her head back.

"What was that about waiting until later?" I whispered against her ear, cradling the back of her head to keep it from hitting the wall as she rocked and bucked. Her only response was a strangled cry as I deftly rotated my fingers, finding that bundle of nerves against the front wall of her sex. Her thighs pressed in tight around me, and my cock thickened again as she rolled her body urgently, grinding against me and coating my fingers in her wetness.

"Gabriel," she cried as I raked my teeth down the side of her throat. "I need to feel you."

I chuckled, letting my hand fall away as I hitched her legs up around my hips, lining myself up with her entrance. "No need to beg, beautiful. I am more than happy to acquiesce." Slowly, I pushed inside her, pressing my face into the crook of her neck as she quivered around my cock, taking every inch like she was made just for me.

"Dammit," I groaned, retreating an inch or two before sliding in again, relishing the snug feel of her. "I'll never get enough of you, will I? Just going to keep tempting me with this pretty pussy until I lose my goddamn mind."

She choked on a sob as I hooked my elbows beneath her knees, yanking her legs wider and abandoning the slow pace in favor of punching my hips forward in a fast, relentless rhythm.

"Look at us," I growled, the ache behind my ribs building as I watched her eyes drop to where our bodies were joined. "Look how beautiful we are together."

Her body began to tremble, her thighs shaking as I rutted into her with reckless abandon, hitting her deep and driving her back against the wall. Without warning, her sex tightened, clamping down on my dick before pulsing wildly.

"*Gabriel*," she screamed at the ceiling.

"That's right," I grunted, every muscle in my body tensing. "Scream as loud as you want. Let the whole building know who the fuck is making you come."

She moaned through her climax, her fingernails clawing at my back as I fucked her harder, faster, my hips snapping forward as I chased my own release inside her pulsing heat. Jerking forward roughly, I came in an explosion of raw ecstasy, emptying myself inside of her as I roared into the wall beside her head.

"God, I love you. So fucking much. More than I'll ever be able to put into words."

I wrapped her legs around me and staggered back against the wall, sinking to the floor. Pulling her to my chest, I rolled my forehead against hers, letting an unexpected sense of relief wash over me. Because sitting on the floor of my shower with Juliet in my arms, I knew I had found my forever.

Thirty-Eight

Juliet

*S*tay. It was the last word to slip past the barrier of my consciousness before I succumbed to sleep last night and the first
to invade my thoughts when I woke this morning.

I blinked at the sunlight streaming in through the windows before glancing over my shoulder at Gabriel's sleeping form. Carefully,
I extricated myself from his forearm banded around my waist and
pushed into a seated position. My gaze roamed over his features, soft
with sleep, and I pushed back a curtain of dark curls spilling over his
eyes, my heart swelling with affection when he leaned into my touch.

Stay with me.

I'd heard that, right? My brain had been fuzzy last night, especially after all the excitement of Nora and James's party and finding
out they were having a baby boy. Still, I was pretty sure I'd heard

Gabriel whisper those words to me just as I was falling asleep, and I didn't think he meant *stay* as in stay the night. I'd already been crashing at his place for a few weeks, so the only other thing he could have meant was he wanted me to *stay* stay.

As in, here in Paris.

With him.

Ever since Versailles, we'd neglected to talk about the future. Whether that was because we were avoiding the discussion altogether or were too busy enjoying each other's company, I wasn't sure. I wanted to believe it was the latter. Either way, my departure for New York was fast approaching, and eventually, we would have no choice but to talk about what would happen after I left.

Could we really make a long-distance relationship work?

Though I hadn't said anything, I had no intention of holding Gabriel to what he'd said about following me to New York. It wasn't that I didn't believe he would—it's just I would never let him. Why should he have to give up everything just to be with me?

As for me staying in Paris, that seemed so outside the realm of possibility, it was almost laughable. My time here was only ever meant to be for the summer. Was I just supposed to abandon my life in New York, my career that had taken years to build? I could only imagine what my colleagues would say.

And then there was my family and friends to consider. Ember, Grace, my grandmother. Grandma had become my biggest advocate since my grandfather passed, bragging to all her Upper East Side friends that I was on the partner track at my firm and constantly reminding me of how proud my grandfather would be if he were here.

I couldn't let them all down—I just couldn't.

Fingers closed around my wrist, and my eyes fell to Gabriel, his dark lashes fanning over the curve of his cheekbones as he stirred beside me.

"Good morning." I leaned down to plant a kiss on his forehead. In a heartbeat, his arm snaked around me, and I shrieked with laughter as he pulled me beneath him.

"*Bonjour*," he said, burying his face in the crook of my neck, his fingers slipping beneath the hem of my T-shirt.

My breath hitched. "Gabriel, no. I'm still sore from yesterday." I felt the curve of his smile against the base of my throat, and I rolled my eyes, poking him in the ribs. "Where's the off button on this thing?"

He smirked, moving my hand to the waistband of his sweatpants. "Down and a little to the left," he said with a sleepy wink. I snorted as he rolled onto his back, dragging me with him. "All right, I'll behave." He reached up to push a lock of hair behind my ear. "How did you sleep?"

"Good." I dropped my head onto his shoulder, tracing the shape of his lips with a finger. I paused, chewing on whether to mention the *stay* thing. I decided not to. A drowsy confession on the precipice of sleep was one thing, but I didn't want to bring it up in the light of day until we were both ready to have that conversation.

Instead, I asked the question that had been hanging over my head for weeks like a dark cloud.

"Gabriel, who's Elise?"

He stiffened, his grip on my waist tightening. "No one you need to worry about."

I frowned. If she was no one to worry about, why didn't he want to tell me who she was?

A gnawing feeling churned in the pit of my stomach. I thought we were past this. I had forgiven Gabriel for shutting me out the night of the gala, but did he plan to continue keeping things from me? I pulled out of his grasp, moving toward the edge of the bed, but before I could gain my feet, he caught my arm.

"Wait, I'm sorry."

I swiveled toward him. "Don't you trust me?"

A deep line appeared between his brows. "I do. My heart knows I can trust you, but my head ..." He clamped his eyes shut. "It's difficult for me to trust people, Juliet."

My chest tightened. "Gabriel, if you can't trust me then—"

"I'm not saying I don't." He pulled me down until I was seated between his legs, his arms circling my center. "I'm saying my head gets in the way of my heart sometimes."

He dropped a kiss on my shoulder, winding his fingers through mine. "Elise," he began slowly, "is my father's business manager."

"Your father?"

"Yeah. He owns a restaurant in Villefranche-sur-Mer. After my mom passed, he needed help managing the business side of things.

So he brought someone in to oversee the accounts, recommend strategic decisions, things like that. That person was Elise."

"Okay ..." My heart pounded hard and fast in my chest as I braced myself for whatever was coming next.

"We were lovers."

His fingers tightened around mine like he was afraid I would pull away. And part of me wanted to—the part that wished for our relationship to be nothing but cloudless skies and smooth sailing. But real relationships aren't like that. Even the best relationships are made up of two flawed people who choose to love each other anyway and accept everything about the other person. That was the kind of love Gabriel deserved from me, and that was the kind of love I intended to give.

I squeezed his hand. "Okay. When did your, um, relationship start?"

"When I was nineteen."

"And she was ...?"

His chest rose and fell with a breath. "She was thirty-five."

I let go of a stuttering exhale.

Holy crap. She was a predator.

As if he could hear my thoughts, he said, "I was an adult, Juliet. Our relationship was consensual."

"Maybe so, but can you honestly say the power balance was even? The maturity level and experience of a thirty-five-year-old female compared to that of a teenage male ..." I shook my head, biting down on my lip as angry tears pricked my eyes.

"I know." He drew me closer, and I swiped at my cheek as moisture tracked down my face.

"I'm sorry. I'm not trying to sound judgmental." In fact, I couldn't care less about judging her. I only wanted to find the bitch and murder her a little.

"It's okay. It would be a lot for anyone to take in."

I peered at him over my shoulder. "Did your father know?"

"God, no. But maybe if he had, none of what happened would have transpired." Turning me in his lap to face him, he gave me a penetrating look. "You're right. The power dynamic between us *was* highly unbalanced. I was in a vulnerable place in my life when I met Elise. I'd just lost my mom a couple of years earlier and, I don't know, I guess I needed someone. I ..." He swallowed, looking away. "I thought I loved her."

"Did she hurt you in some way?" Bile rose in my throat as I pictured her coercing him into some twisted BDSM relationship.

"No, but she was manipulative. I don't think I saw her behavior for what it was at the time—it was only after our relationship ended that I realized she'd been controlling me all those years." He picked at a loose thread on my T-shirt, shifting his weight beneath me.

"My father was always conservative when it came to business, valuing steady growth over riskier high-return investments. It's what led him to turn our small family-owned restaurant into a business that drew the attention of locals and celebrities alike. But Elise—she liked to play it fast and loose. Whenever she would present an invest-ment opportunity to my father that he didn't agree with, she would come to me and convince me to change his mind. It pretty much always worked."

"Your father trusted you." It wasn't a question, but he nodded anyway.

"He wanted me to manage the restaurant one day, and I think he was just glad I was taking an interest. But the reality couldn't have been further from the truth. I always wanted to pursue my art and open a gallery. The only reason I stuck around as long as I did was to make him happy."

"So, why did things end between you and Elise?"

He dropped his head back against the headboard. "Around when I was twenty-five, she came to me asking for a large sum of money. She was completely out of sorts that night, not at all like her usual self. Elise *never* lost her composure, never let anyone see anything other than the respectable businesswoman she presented to the world. That's how I knew something was off."

"What did she want the money for?"

"I don't know. She was rather vague on the details. She just kept insisting she had this investment opportunity with a closing window and we needed to act fast. But when I asked her whether my father had agreed to it, she deflected, telling me she was sure he would get on board. In the meantime, she wanted me to withdraw the funds from the business account directly."

"Well, that doesn't sound shady at all."

"My thoughts exactly. I never had a reason to question her before then, but this time, I could tell something was wrong. But when I pressed her for information, she became more and more cagey about it until eventually she told me to just forget it."

"I'm afraid to ask, but how much money did she want?"

"Five hundred thousand euros."

My mouth popped open. "She wanted *half a million* euros?"

"Yeah. The only investment strategy my father was routinely comfortable with was real estate, so the amount wasn't totally beyond the pale. Still, we'd never invested that much at one time and with the way she was acting ..."

"So, you didn't give her the money?"

"No," he said, his expression darkening. "But that didn't stop her in the end."

"What do you mean?"

"A week later, my father called me into his office and informed me the bank had called about an unusually large withdrawal. A withdrawal made using my credentials. For five hundred thousand euros."

"She stole your credentials?"

"It wasn't her. It was my cousin, Lucien."

I blinked in confusion. *Lucien.* Where had I heard that name before?

"It wasn't until later that I got the full story, but at the time when my father confronted me, the only thing I knew for sure was Elise had asked me for the same amount of money that had gone missing. My first thought was exactly what you said—that she had gotten a hold of my credentials and made the withdrawal under my name. My second thought was I had been right to assume she didn't have my father's permission. Otherwise, she could have used her own credentials."

"She was on the bank account too?"

"She was my father's business manager—it wasn't uncommon for her to make multiple transactions a day for anything ranging from paying suppliers to wiring earnest money for a new property investment."

I chewed on my lip, turning this information over. "So, if she used your credentials, that must have meant she didn't want the transaction traced back to her. What did you tell your father?"

"The truth. That I didn't take it."

"And he didn't believe you?"

He shook his head, a frustrated sigh pushing past his lips. "There was no proof the account had been hacked or tampered with on the bank's backend. And even if my password had been stolen by a third party, all logins required dual authentication. A code would have been sent directly to my phone. Considering my phone was in my possession while I was speaking with my father, I would have had a hard time convincing him I had no knowledge of the withdrawal."

"But wouldn't Elise have had access to your phone?"

"She would have, but it didn't matter. I already knew she was involved."

I frowned. "So, even after you explained everything to your father about Elise—"

"I didn't tell him about Elise."

"You ... you didn't?"

He sighed, a look of exhaustion coasting over his features. "Even knowing what she had done, I still cared about her. I thought I was protecting her."

I gaped at him. "Gabriel, what she did was embezzlement. It's a criminal offense—"

"You think I don't know that?" he said, his jaw clenching. "Tell me, what would you have done in my place? If you found out I was the one who committed a crime? Would you immediately sell me out? Stand by while I faced prison time?"

"Of course not. I don't know what I would have done."

"Exactly. And I had no time to think it through. I didn't even have time to talk to her and find out the whole story. All I could do was fall on my sword for her. And that's what I did."

"And your father?"

"Disowned me."

I felt all the blood drain from my face as I stared at Gabriel in horror. This entire conversation had already thrown me for a loop, but the revelation that his father had disowned him for something he hadn't even done was enough to break my heart.

"Gabriel, I don't know what to say."

His expression softened. "It's all right. It's all ancient history now."

"Is it?" I asked, searching his eyes. "I know she called the night of the gala. What if—"

"It's taken care of." He brought my fingertips to his lips, pressing a kiss against each one. "She won't bother me—bother *us*—again."

I nodded hesitantly, a hundred questions still flooding my mind.

Why hadn't Gabriel's father believed him when he told him he was innocent? What had Elise actually done with the money? And why was she calling Gabriel after all this time?

"Gabriel, there's still something I don't understand. Why would your cousin take the money? What did he have to gain in all this?"

His expression turned grim. "Funny you should ask—I wanted to know the same thing. As it turns out, they were having an affair."

I swallowed audibly. Could this get any worse? So much about Gabriel made sense to me now—why he was so hesitant about relationships, why he didn't let people into his life easily.

Everyone he loved had betrayed him.

"She was cheating on you?"

His head dipped in a barely perceptible nod. "When I finally confronted her, she confessed that after I wouldn't give her what she wanted, she had gone to Lucien. I didn't believe her at first. I thought she was just lying to lessen her culpability. But then she told me they'd been sleeping together, and suddenly it all made sense. Lucien and I lived in the same house—it would have been easy for him to gain access to my belongings, including my computer and phone."

"Did you confront him about the affair?"

"And say what? *Have you been fucking my girlfriend?* He would have just lied. He always was a snake, no matter how much he tried to hide it. And what did it matter? The damage was already done." He dragged a hand over his face, his shoulders slumping. "So, there you have it—the truth about my past. All my broken pieces laid bare."

I blinked back a surge of hot tears. "You are *not* broken. None of what happened was your fault." His eyes rose to mine, his own rimmed with moisture. Bringing my palms to either side of his face, I brushed my thumbs over the curve of his cheeks. "Tell me what I can do, Gabriel."

He slipped a hand around the base of my neck, pressing my forehead to his. "I just want to forget," he whispered, his breath feathering across my lips.

I nodded, pushing my hands into his hair and swallowing his pain in a slow kiss.

❧ ❧

It was late afternoon by the time I made it back to my apartment. Gabriel had gone to his gallery to take care of a few things in advance of his opening next week, but when I'd offered to go with him, he declined, promising he wouldn't be long. I suspected he needed some time to sort through his feelings, feelings I had caused by forcing him to dredge up his past.

I closed the front door and tossed my keys onto the entryway table just as my phone pulsed.

"Hey, Simone," I said, moving into the kitchen to uncork a bottle of wine. I filled my glass before taking a sip to clear my head. "What's up?"

"Oh, nothing," she said, her voice uncharacteristically sweet. "I was just calling to make sure we were still friends."

I winced. "I'm sorry. I know I've been preoccupied lately. I'll make it up to you."

She huffed. "Even so, how could you not tell me you're a finalist in the *NRF* competition?"

"What?" I said, nearly dropping my wineglass. "How do you know that?"

"They posted the list of finalists on their website this morning."

I set my glass down, my skin humming with adrenaline. It took a few seconds to navigate to the webpage, but eventually I found the list. And sure enough, there was my name, five rows from the top: *Juliet M. Chandler.*

"Oh, my God."

"Wait, you really didn't know? Seems like something Benoit would have told you."

I blinked. *Benoit.* Flipping to my email, I found one unread message from him. "It looks like he did reach out yesterday." I must have missed it between the party and, well, everything that came after. "I ... I think my brain might be short-circuiting."

I could practically hear Simone's smile. "Well, let me help you rewire that bad boy—let's go out tonight. There's a new cabaret bar in Montmartre I've been dying to check out."

"I don't know." I chewed on a thumbnail. "I wouldn't want to celebrate prematurely. I mean, I'm thrilled to have made it to the final round, but I don't want to jinx it."

"Boo, you're no fun," Simone whined. "Fine, we'll put a pin in it for now, but win or lose, we're definitely celebrating. This is a huge accomplishment, babe."

My mouth tilted into a smile. "Thanks. By the way, did you get the invitation to Gabriel's gallery opening?"

"Yes, I did." She gasped, snapping her fingers. "Oh, you know what? Why don't we all go out for drinks after his event? It could be a two-for-one celebration."

I froze on my way to refill my glass. "Crap, I didn't even think about that. I'm his girlfriend, and I haven't planned anything to celebrate his artistic debut."

"So, is that a no on drinks, then? I know it's not exactly glamorous, but we could make a party out of it. Carter and I will be at the opening, and Dean and Karin said they might come too."

"We could do that, but ..." I trailed off, not wanting to shoot down Simone's idea, especially when I didn't have a better one.

Except ... *wait.* Maybe I did.

Placing the phone on speaker, I hurried over to my purse, digging out the flyer for the opening at Marcel's.

It was tomorrow night.

Cristian said he didn't want me to come because he would be too busy to hang out. But that didn't mean Gabriel and I couldn't have a nice time by ourselves.

"Actually, I think I have an idea."

Thirty-Nine

Gabriel

As soon as I stepped out of the cab, I blinked in surprise at the sidewalk filled with people. When Juliet told me we were going out for dinner to celebrate my opening, I'd assumed she would pick a nice place, but I hadn't expected there to be a line spanning the entire length of the block.

"Where did you say we were going?" I extended a hand to help her from the taxi.

"I didn't. It's a surprise." Leaning through the window, she handed the driver twenty euros, swatting my hand away before I could stop her from paying. "It's your night, Gabriel. Let me do something nice for you for once. Please?"

A grin tugged at my lips. "You really didn't need to go through all this trouble." I wound our fingers together and pressed a kiss to her knuckles, my eyes snagging on a sapphire bracelet dangling from her wrist. It looked like the same one she'd worn the night of the gala.

"It's the least I could do. I just hope you like it."

More than a few people glanced our way as we bypassed the line, heading for a set of double doors cordoned off behind a velvet rope. My grin slipped. Even if we had a reservation, I doubted we could just waltz through the front doors.

Before I could say anything, Juliet raised a hand, waving at a man standing by the door.

"Caleb."

He turned his head in our direction, batting a fistful of blond curls away from his forehead a second before his eyes widened in recognition. "Juliet, so good to see you again. If you and your guest will just head to the hostess station, Amélie will get you seated."

"Wow," I said as we cleared the doorway. "I had no idea my girlfriend was so famous."

She blew out a laugh. "Haven't you heard? I'm a finalist for *La Nouvelle Revue Française*. I'm practically literary royalty now."

"Is that so?" I chuckled, tucking her under my arm as we approached the hostess stand.

A petite woman with pink hair looked up, her features lighting with a grin. "Juliet, right?" Her eyes ticked to me before dropping to the screen in front of her. "Let me see, the main dining room is full right now, but ..." She glanced up again, chewing on her lip. "Okay, I'm probably not supposed to do this, but since you're Cristian's guest, I'm sure he won't mind. One of our VIP tables is available until ten o'clock. Think you can finish up by then?"

"I'm pretty sure that won't be a problem," Juliet said.

"You say that now," the woman replied smoothly as she led us to an elevator bank, "but you have yet to see our dessert menu."

The doors slid open to reveal an elevator operator dressed in a vintage double-breasted jacket with gold buttons and a velvet collar.

"*Bonsoir monsieur, mademoiselle.* To the dining room?"

No sooner had we entered the tiny, wood-paneled space than the operator pressed a button for the sixth floor. A few seconds later, the doors opened again onto a spectacular view of the city, a sea of bright lights shining just beyond the dining room's wrap-around windows.

I hovered for a moment, staring at the luminous skyline. I'd never seen such a beautiful view of the city.

Another hostess appeared, directing us to a table on an elevated dais facing Notre-Dame Cathedral.

"So," Juliet said, taking the seat opposite me, "I take it you like this place?"

"Are you kidding? This is incredible. How did you even get a reservation here?" I looked around the crowded space. Not a single table was empty.

Juliet opened her mouth to reply at the same moment our waiter appeared.

"*Bonsoir et bienvenue dans notre restaurant.*" He handed a menu to each of us. "Can I start you off with some cocktails? We also have an excellent wine selection to choose from. I would be happy to provide you with a recommendation." A second waiter appeared beside the first, depositing a leatherbound wine list the size of the King James Bible on our table.

"Um, yes," Juliet said with a nervous laugh. "A recommendation would be great."

The first waiter began listing off his preferred selection of wines, and I watched as Juliet listened intently, her nose wrinkling in concentration. I smiled to myself. She was so damn cute.

Turning to my menu, I flipped it open and—

Every drop of blood drained from my body as I stared at the name at the top of the page.

Marcel's.

My fingers tightened. *No.* It was just a coincidence. There was no way this was my father's restaurant—he wasn't even in Paris. But ... a trickle of unease settled in my stomach. My *father* might not be here, but Lucien was.

And so was—

"Gabriel?" My eyes sliced up to Juliet's, her brows lowering. "Is everything all right?"

"Yeah, sure."

The waiter glanced between us. "I can give you a few minutes to consider the menu if you'd like."

"You order," I rasped to Juliet, pushing back my chair. "I'm going to find the restrooms." I spun away from the table before she could argue, heading for the hall at the far end of the room.

I threw open the door to the men's restroom a minute later, sending up a silent prayer of thanks that it was empty. I crossed over to a row of sinks and flipped on the cold water, dousing my face before grabbing a handful of paper towels and dabbing my collar damp with sweat.

Pull yourself together right the fuck now. The last thing I wanted was to ruin Juliet's big surprise for me by having a panic attack. Leaning against the porcelain countertop, I took a deep breath through my nose.

Even if this *was* my father's restaurant, that didn't mean he had any idea I was here. I could go back out there, order a drink or three, and have a nice evening with my girlfriend. Then we would get the fuck out of here, and I would never come within a kilometer of this place ever again.

The door opened behind me, but I ignored it, pressing my eyelids shut. Then the lock clicked. My eyes snapped open, and I whirled around, coming face-to-face with a pair of amethyst eyes and crimson lips tilting into a wicked smile.

"Hello, Gabriel."

"Elise." I watched her as she moved away from the door, slinking toward me like my worst nightmare come to life. "What the fuck are you doing here?"

She drew up short. "It's opening night at Marcel's. As your father's business manager, it's my job to make sure everything runs smoothly."

"I wasn't aware your duties extended to the men's bathroom."

"I have a wide range of responsibilities," she said, examining her porcelain skin in the mirror. "But this errand is personal."

"Good luck with that." I took a step toward the door, but she blocked my path. "*Move.*"

The tiniest glimmer of anger slipped past her mask of composure. "Why? So you can run back to your little girlfriend with the doe eyes?" She clicked her tongue, sliding her fingers through her shoulder-length hair. "A bit innocent for you, isn't she, Gabriel?" She stepped closer, and my jaw set in a hard line when she placed a hand on my chest. "Is she really enough for you, *mon cher*? I know how rough you like it in bed. Does that *petite fleur* truly satisfy your needs?"

I snatched her wrist away. "Do not touch me."

Her smile widened, as if this whole scenario was some fucked-up version of foreplay. "You used to like it when I touched you. You used to like it a lot." She drew her hand back, but otherwise didn't move, effectively barricading me against the sink. "We could have that again, you know. We could pick up where we left off. It could be like the last three years never happened."

"You're out of your mind. Why don't you just tell me what you really want?"

She looked taken aback at my bluntness, and her eyes sharpened like she was seeing me clearly for the first time. "Very well. I want to offer you a business proposal." She folded her arms, pacing in a semicircle. "I have given a decade of my life to this restaurant. I know it inside and out—every line item, every detail. That is why I know it has the potential to be so much greater than it is at present. With my connections and expertise, we could build it into a global empire."

Her gaze cut to me expectantly, but I simply stared back at her with cold eyes.

"I know Lucien has similar aspirations for the business," she continued, "but he's inexperienced and could never accomplish what I can. I'll admit, he oversaw the opening of the Paris restaurant with reasonable competence, but I'm the one who can turn Marcel's into a multibillion-dollar enterprise across several continents."

"Well, you certainly have the ego for it," I gritted out. "But I fail to see why you're telling me any of this. If you're so confident in your abilities, why don't you just do it?"

"First lesson in business, Gabriel—if you're good at something, never do it for free."

I scoffed. "I'm sure my father pays you well enough, otherwise you wouldn't be here."

She turned to me, her expression serious. "A salary, yes, but I want more than that. I want equity—a share in the profits. Marcel has always been adamant about keeping ownership of the business solely within the family, but he'll have to hand over the reins sooner or later. And when he does, I want my cut." She moved into my personal space again, her sickeningly sweet perfume turning my stomach. "Grant me a portion of the shares, Gabriel, and I promise I'll make you a very rich man. You'll never have to sell another painting again."

Christ. I was going to be sick.

After everything we'd been through, the fact that Elise actually thought she could seduce me, that she could *buy* me, catapulted my rage to new heights.

"Sorry, but you're talking to the wrong cousin. Why don't you go get on your knees for Lucien? If memory serves, you used to be good at that."

She recoiled, giving me a look that I might have mistaken for shame if I didn't know what an expert manipulator she was. After all, she'd strung me along for years, using me as a pawn to control my father. And now here she was again, trying to find a way to get her hands on his legacy. On *my* legacy. Or what used to be mine anyway.

"Marcel will never pass the business to Lucien. You are his true heir, Gabriel."

"Except he disinherited me," I said, eyeing her with disdain. "I'm sure you remember that well enough."

"Anger causes people to say things they don't mean. There aren't many people who can rile up your father, but you are his son, and his love for you is his greatest weakness. He let his emotions get the better of him, and he has regretted it ever since."

No part of me was prepared to hear this, least of all from the person who had betrayed me more than anyone else. "What gives you the right to speak on his behalf? Do you think I've forgotten how you stole from him? Hell, you're trying to steal from him *now*. Cornering me in a bathroom and trying to whore your way into an allocation of the profits. I would rather see my father's restaurant go back to being a seaside shack serving poutine to tourists than to gain global success with you at the helm."

She huffed. "Oh, Gabriel, you always were so dramatic. But once you've had time to think it over, I'm sure you'll see the sense in my proposal."

"Yeah, I seriously doubt that. Now, if you'll excuse me—"

"You're going to have to decide sooner or later, and you may not have as much time as you think. Marcel has been meeting with his lawyers, and I know he's planning to name you as his successor. Do you think it's a coincidence that you're here tonight?"

I stiffened. "What the hell are you talking about? My girlfriend brought me here to celebrate my gallery opening, not that it's any of your business."

She hummed, her eyes glittering in a way that made me uneasy. "Is that so? A naive American who barely knows one end of Paris from the other somehow is able to secure a reservation, and a VIP table no less, on opening night at one of the most exclusive restaurants in the city." She smirked. "I do wonder how she managed it."

"What's that supposed to mean? If you have something to say, spit it out."

She retreated a step, allowing me space to pass, but I hesitated. She knew something, and I wasn't leaving until I found out what it was.

She gave me an almost pitying smile. "While you ruminate on whether to accept my offer, just know I very well may be the lesser of two evils. After all, how much do you trust Lucien? If you're not careful, *mon cher*, he might take more from you than he already has."

My stomach curled in on itself, and it was all I could do not to vomit in the sink.

Juliet.

No, she would *never* betray me like that.

I pushed past Elise and unlocked the door, hurrying back down the hallway as spots danced along the edges of my vision. Elise was a liar, and she was just sowing distrust in my mind to further her own agenda. But ... how *had* Juliet gotten a reservation here tonight? I had been wondering that myself.

I rounded the corner into the dining room, and my eyes found Juliet across the room. She was sitting alone right where I'd left her, still poring over the menu from what I could tell, and some of the tension left my shoulders. Heart hammering in my ears, I wove between the tables, anxious to reach my girl. She would have an explanation for all of this.

I was sure of it.

Halfway across the room, I drew to a halt, nearly knocking into a passing waiter. Lucien had appeared on the other side of the room, casting a look around. After a second, his eyes snagged on whatever he was looking for, and he crossed the room with purposeful strides, heading directly for ...

Juliet spotted him as he approached her, her face splitting into a smile.

Then, my entire world tilted on its axis as I watched the woman I loved wrap her arms around the devil himself.

Forty

Juliet

I glanced up from my menu, scanning the bustling dining room. Gabriel had been gone for a long time, and I was growing anxious. Was he all right? He certainly hadn't looked like it when he stormed away from the table almost fifteen minutes ago. Maybe coming here was a bad idea.

Dropping my gaze back to the menu that was all in French, I tapped the name of the next appetizer into my translation app. I was too embarrassed to ask the waiter for one in English and figured Gabriel could help me order when he returned from the restroom.

Whenever that was.

I had just typed in the words *huîtres chaudes*, which apparently meant broiled oysters, when I sensed eyes on me. I looked up in time to see Cristian heading in my direction, dressed in an impeccable suit. I smiled, shaking my head. The day I caught Cristian Alarie in anything other than designer clothing would be the day the Four Horsemen arrived to herald the apocalypse.

"Hey." I drew him in for a hug and was surprised to find his shoulders rigid.

"Juliet," he said sharply, his face lined with tension as he pulled out of my embrace. "What are you doing here? I thought I told you tonight wasn't a good night for you to come."

My smile faltered as I took in his wild eyes. He looked *panicked*.

"I know, but I couldn't pass up on the opportunity to see Marcel's in all its splendor. You've done a spectacular job, by the way."

Without responding, he darted an anxious look over my shoulder, his eyes scanning the room as though he were looking for someone.

"Um," I tried again, winding my finger around the bracelet he'd given me, "I know how busy tonight is for you, so don't feel pressured to stick around. We'll be fine here by ourselves."

His eyes shot to mine. "*We*? Who is we? Did you bring Gabriel with you?"

I blinked, my brows lowering. "Well, yeah, but ..." He let out a hiss, gripping the back of his neck, and I stared at him, unease creeping up my spine. "Cristian, what's going on?"

"Juliet, listen, I—" He stopped mid-sentence, his eyes connecting with something over my head. Slowly, his gaze fell to mine again, his expression stricken. "Sweetheart, I am so sorry."

I didn't have time to say a single word before a figure shot past me, seizing Cristian by the collar. *Gabriel.* I gaped at him, my mouth falling open as I took in his features coated with rage, his eyes flaming with enough fury to put the fear of God in any mortal.

"You son of a bitch," Gabriel gritted out, his fingers gripping Cristian so tightly, I was certain he was choking him.

"Gabriel, *stop.*" I grabbed him by the elbow and tugged hard. He didn't yield an inch.

He leaned forward, coming nose to nose with a surprisingly silent Cristian. "So, that's how it is, huh? You weren't content to screw me over once, so you slithered your way to Paris to go in for the kill? Answer me, you asshole."

My eyes darted between the two men, Gabriel's expression one of hostility, Cristian's completely shuttered. Why wasn't Cristian *doing* anything?

"Gabriel, would you please stop this?" I pleaded. "You're going to cause a scene."

His eyes scraped to me, and all the warmth drained from my body. Gone were the comforting azure eyes that had become my true north, a violent winter storm now raging in their place. Returning his attention to Cristian, he said, "You are dead to me, Lucien."

I blinked.

Lucien?

The chandeliers flickered as someone dimmed the lights, and a hush fell over the room as a man in a houndstooth blazer came to stand at the center of the room. He was tall and appeared to be in his early sixties with thick salt-and-pepper hair. Beneath the wide bridge of his nose, his mouth stretched into a smile that struck me as oddly familiar.

My eyes cut to Gabriel, my gaze traveling over his features, features that had become so familiar I could see them with my eyes closed. At present, they were arranged in a deep scowl, but usually they were soft with pleasure, his mouth curved in a grin that looked just like—

I sucked in an audible breath, my knees going weak as all the pieces slotted into place.

My father owns a restaurant in Villefranche-sur-Mer.

He and my cousin still live there.

Lucien Alarie, although my intimates call me Cristian.

Go out with Gabriel. If things work out, you can bring him to my restaurant opening.

I'm not a good man, Juliet. Sooner or later, you'll find out the truth about me.

It wasn't her. It was my cousin, Lucien. As it turns out, they were having an affair.

Weeks of conversations came rushing back in rapid-fire succession, and I swayed, planting a hand on the table to keep myself upright. Breathing hard, I looked at Gabriel, who'd finally released Cristian. Or was it Lucien? Tears burned my eyes as my gaze shifted to him.

Oh, Cristian.

What on earth have you done?

"Good evening," a deep voice boomed over a microphone, and my attention shot to the man at the center of the room. "I am Marcel Beaumont, and it is my great honor and pleasure to welcome you to the opening of Marcel's in Paris." There was a polite smattering of applause, though I could barely hear it over the rush of blood thundering in my ears. "When I first envisioned opening a restaurant thirty years ago, I never could have imagined it would grow into what it has become today. At Marcel's, we seek to embody the core values of elegance, commitment and excellence. And in our quest to serve the finest cuisine, our ultimate goal has, and always will be, to cater to the people."

Another round of applause.

"A thousand helping hands came together to bring Marcel's to the great city of Paris," he continued, "but I would like to give a special thanks to my nephew, Lucien, whose vision and hard work has made tonight possible. I would also like to thank my business manager, Elise Lemieux, whose oversight has kept things running smoothly these past several years, my late wife, whose memory serves as a constant source of encouragement and strength, and last but not least, my son, Gabriel, whose presence here tonight makes every-thing I have strived to achieve worthwhile. Please join me in raising a glass to family."

A chorus of "à la famille" detonated around the room like land-mines, followed by a cacophony of clinking glasses. When the lights rose again, my eyes sprang to Gabriel, but he didn't return my gaze, his shoulders rising and falling with heavy breaths.

I placed a tentative hand on his arm. "Gabriel?" He pulled away from me, and I flinched as he stared at me with cold, hard eyes. "Gabriel," I breathed, placing a shaky palm on my chest, "it's me, Juliet."

His Adam's apple bobbed, and a look of sharp pain flickered across his features as his gaze sliced to Cristian before returning to me.

His eyes, those beautiful eyes that lit up my entire world, were lifeless and empty.

"I hope ...," he said in a hoarse whisper, "I hope he was worth it."

I let go of a stuttering exhale, my heart spiraling down into the base of my stomach as he turned and strode in the direction of the exit. My lips formed his name, but the sound got caught in my windpipe, and I took a step on trembling legs to follow him just as a hand caught my elbow.

"Juliet," Cristian said, his voice cracked and broken. "Juliet, please—"

"*No*," I screeched, pulling from his grasp and stumbling back against the table. "I trusted you, and you made a fool out of me."

"Let me help you," he said with pleading eyes.

"Don't," I cried, bordering on hysteria as I fumbled for my purse. "You've done enough."

Without another word, I raced toward the exit, drawing more than a few glances as I weaved between the tables. In the hall, there was a line for the elevator, and I groaned, searching for the emergency exit. I found it beneath a glowing red sign that read *Sortie*, and I dashed for it, throwing open the door and hurrying down the stairwell.

One floor down, I stopped to take off my heels before shooting down the remaining stairs barefoot. By the time I reached the ground floor, I was sweating, but I couldn't care less, so long as I found Gabriel.

Gabriel.

God, the way he had looked at me ... just the memory of it was enough to make my chest cave in. I had to find him—had to figure out a way to explain all this.

The stairwell opened on to a dim hallway, and I peered around in the gloom, taking a second to get my bearings. There were voices coming from the left, and I rushed in that direction. Rounding a corner at top speed, I almost collided with a waiter hoisting a tray over his shoulder, and he spit out a string of less than friendly words as I stumbled to the side before taking off again.

I sped through a maze of identical hallways until I *finally* found the foyer, its dark wood paneling that had felt warm and inviting half an hour ago now cold and tomb-like.

Amélie glanced up from behind the hostess station, her eyebrows furrowing. "Juliet, is everything all right? I just saw your companion—"

I darted past her, not bothering to stop and explain as Caleb threw open the door a second before I dashed through it.

"Where is he?" I swung around to face him as his eyes narrowed with a look of concern.

He pointed in the direction of the river. "He went that way about a minute ago." His eyes traveled down to my bare feet before shooting back up again. "Juliet, do you need help? I can find Cristian if—"

"No," I choked out. "I'm sorry, no, I just—I have to go." I took off toward the river, the hazy glow of the street lamps lighting my way as my feet slapped against the pavement. Cool air whipped at the exposed skin of my arms and legs, and I shook out my limbs as I scurried to the stone retaining wall that lined the river's edge.

Planting both hands on the ledge, I peered down at the dark quay, searching for any signs of movement. My pulse skipped when I caught sight of a lone figure moving beneath the tree line, shrouded in shadows. I couldn't make out any defining features, but I would know that gait anywhere. *Gabriel.* I launched myself down a collection of patchwork steps, nearly rolling an ankle at the bottom before flying down the cobbled path.

"Gabriel," I cried, hissing in pain when my foot caught on a rock. "*Gabriel.*"

He drew up short, spinning around to face me. "Are you kidding me?"

I blinked. Why was he acting this way? He had to know this was just a big misunderstanding, that I would never do anything to hurt him intentionally. Right?

He scoffed, his shoulders bunching with anger. "So, how did he do it? Did he pay you to run into me on that bridge? Drop your notebook just so I would pick it up and come looking for you?"

I tried to regulate my breathing, but it kept spiraling out of my lungs in shallow bursts.

"Gabriel, *please*. You've got this all wrong—"

"You know, you really had me going with the whole innocent act. Helpless American girl, just lying in wait. And I'm the idiot who fell for it, hook, line and sinker."

"*No*," I insisted, desperation leaching into my voice as I reached for him. "Would you please listen—" He jerked out of my hold, and I bit my lip until I tasted blood, my vision blurring with tears.

So that was it? He wasn't even going to hear me out? What about all his declarations of love, his promise that we would always belong to each other? Were those just a bunch of pretty words that crumpled beneath the slightest amount of pressure?

I squeezed a hand around my wrist, and he followed the motion, his attention falling to my forearm. His jaw clenched. "Did *he* give you that?"

"Did who ..." My gaze fell to the chain of sapphires hanging conspicuously from my wrist, and my eyes sprang upward again, a band of steel tightening around my chest.

"Well?" he said coolly. "Did he?"

He wasn't looking for an answer—his eyes told me he already knew.

My tongue skated over dry lips as the silence gaped between us, broken only by the sounds of the river lapping against the quay. I floundered for too many seconds, searching for words that would be less damning than the truth.

I came up empty.

"Yes, but—"

He huffed humorlessly, his eyes drifting closed. "Of course, he did. Just the icing on the whole fucking cake."

I bristled, my temper sparking. "I'm sorry, but what exactly are you accusing me of?"

"It's a little late to play coy. Just tell me one thing—are you sleeping with him?"

I stared at him in horror. "How could you possibly believe I would ever—"

"Answer the question, Juliet."

My head moved back and forth in disbelief. I *wasn't* hearing this. I told him I loved him, had given him my heart, my trust. *Trust.* The thing we kept coming back to. We'd circled it again and again like a winding mountain pass, climbing but never quite reaching the pinnacle. What if we never did? What if he could never give me his trust in return?

I licked the inside of my mouth. "Gabriel, I need you to trust me."

My heart drummed loud and fast in my ears as he stared at me, his expression anguished. He pressed his eyelids shut, his muscles tensing as though he were warring with something within himself. Then slowly, too slowly, he opened his eyes again.

"Then ... this is over."

This is over.

A wave of agony hit me all at once, and I gripped my sides to hold my body together. It felt like a train wreck happening in slow motion, debris flying everywhere, leaving a trail of devastation in its wake. And I was powerless to stop it.

He took a step backward, then another.

"Don't do this, Gabriel," I said, finding my voice. "Don't do something you'll regret later."

Pain slashed across his features. "The only thing I regret is the day I ever laid eyes on you."

Shoving his hands in his pockets, he turned and strode away, leaving me standing alone on the quay as all the feeling drained from my limbs. I fell to my knees.

"Gabriel." I croaked, my mouth dry as ash. I tried again. "*Gabriel.*"

His retreating form grew farther away, his outline becoming fainter as the distance between us stretched. And then I felt it. The cracks in my body as my soul splintered. The wellspring of tears I'd been holding back fell as I watched the man who owned my heart walk out of my life.

Clutching my arms to my chest, I folded over, my hair falling around my face like a shroud, my forehead scraping against the hard ground.

Then I screamed into the night.

Forty-One

Juliet

The first thing I knew was the feeling of hands clutching my arms, tightening around my biceps and pinning me down. And then I heard the screaming. Where was it coming from?

"Juliet. *Juliet*. Babe, wake up."

I jerked awake, blinking in the darkness a second before someone switched on the bedside lamp, and I sucked in a harsh breath, recoiling from the glare. Shivering from head to toe, my eyes connected with Simone's, taking in her face pinched with concern as she slanted over me, palms clutching the sides of my face.

"There you are," she said with a fragile smile. "It's all right. You're all right." My body was still trembling when someone threw open the bedroom door.

"What's happened? Is she okay?"

I peered over Simone's shoulder to find Carter standing at the foot of my bed in a rumpled shirt, running a hand over his face creased with sleep lines.

"She's fine." Simone exchanged a look with him that I couldn't interpret before she returned her gaze to me. "We're fine, aren't we, Juliet?"

I stared up at her, taking in her braids piled up in a messy bun, her slender form draped in one of my oversized T-shirts. And then it hit me all at once, like a nightmare lingering in the shadows, just waiting for me to fall asleep. Flashes of my hysterical phone call to Simone, of Simone and Carter's worried faces as they pushed through a crowd of strangers who had stopped to gawk or do whatever it is people do when they see something horrible happening. The memory of it all came flooding back to me in one crushing torrent, carrying with it the pieces of my shattered heart.

"Did it really happen?" I whispered hoarsely, clinging to her. "Was it real?"

Her lips pressed into a grim line as Carter shifted uncomfortably behind her.

"Yeah, babe. It was real."

⇒⇒⇒ ⇐⇐⇐

The door creaked open, and the sweet aroma of something I couldn't identify wafted into the room. Peeling my eyes open, I found Simone, fully dressed, placing a breakfast tray at the foot of the bed before she parted the silk curtains, letting in a bar of sunlight. I rolled over onto my other side, draping a hand over my eyes and only just resisting the urge to hiss like some sort of vampire.

"Juliet." The bed dipped as she sank down onto it, placing a hand on my shoulder. "You have to eat something, babe."

"I'm tired." I burrowed further into the sheets. Food was the absolute last thing on my mind. Tequila? Maybe. But that would require me to get out of bed, so that was out too.

"I know," she said gently, running her fingers through my tangled hair. "But it's been two days. You have to eat something, even if it's just a few bites."

Two days?

Slowly, I pushed myself into a seated position, ignoring the way my ribs ached in protest. An unexpected side effect of a broken heart? Random injuries due to too much crying.

Simone's mouth curved into a smile as she brought the tray closer, scooping up a spoonful of oatmeal sprinkled with brown sugar and raising it to my lips. I swallowed a mouthful, letting the warm, nutty flavors wash over my tongue.

"You know," she said, scooping up another spoonful, "my grandmother used to quote the philosopher Bernard Paul Heroux, saying *There is no trouble so great or grave that cannot be diminished by a nice bowl of porridge.* Of course, Heroux was actually talking about a cup of tea rather than porridge, but to each his own, right?"

That drew a tiny grin from me, and Simone winked, feeding me another bite.

On Sunday, I finally crawled out of bed. Halting on the way to the door, I caught sight of my reflection in the mirror. If my face muscles weren't out of commission from nonstop cycles of crying and sleeping, I would have laughed. The shirt I was wearing was riddled with sweat stains, and I had on mismatched socks beneath a pair of sleep shorts that were, for whatever reason, on backward. And that was to say nothing of the state of my hair.

Undoubtedly, there were scarecrows who looked better.

Swiping a hand through my bedhead, I pulled open the door and moved down the hall. The minute I entered the living room, Simone looked up from where she sat perched on the sofa, knees tucked beneath her as she pressed a phone to her ear.

"Hey, she's up. I'll have her give you a call." She hung up, watching me carefully as I shuffled toward the kitchen in search of hydration.

"Who was that?" I twisted the cap off a bottle of Evian, drinking half of it in one go.

"Your sister, who is freaking amazing, by the way." She crossed the room, sliding onto one of the kitchen bar stools. "How come you never told me you had a twin?"

"Irish twin," I corrected, sinking down onto the chair beside her.

"Well, your *Irish* twin is a total badass." Her grin slipped. "And she's worried about you."

I stared down at my chipped nail polish. "Does she know?"

"Mm-hmm. She called the morning after ..." She trailed off, letting an awkward stretch of silence fill in the blanks. "I told her what happened. I hope that's okay."

I squeezed Simone's arm gently, trying for a smile that collapsed halfway through. "It's more than okay. Honestly, I can't thank you enough for all you've done these past few days. If it weren't for you, I'm sure Ember would have been on a plane by now."

Simone chuckled. "Yeah, about that ..." I blinked, my eyes going wide. "Don't worry," she rushed on before I had the chance to fly into full-on panic mode. "I talked her out of coming. I promised her you wouldn't be alone for a single minute if you didn't want to be."

I sighed with relief, dropping my head into my hands. The last thing I needed was my sister upending her life to come and rescue me. Ember had always been the muscle in our relationship, and she wasn't above pureeing someone's balls if she thought they'd hurt me.

I lifted my head and glanced around the quiet room. "Where's Carter?"

"Oh, I sent him home. He needed to work on that final assignment due Tuesday."

The final assignment. Right. Apparently, I had forgotten real life was marching on beyond the four walls of my personal tragedy.

"Crap," I muttered, massaging my forehead. "I meant to finish that this weekend."

"Way ahead of you." Simone placed my phone on the counter, pushing it toward me. "I emailed Benoit to let him know you had a virus and were puking your guts out. Not in those exact words, but he got the gist. I'm pretty sure he plans to give you an extension." My eyes shot up, connecting with her amused expression. "Pays to be the teacher's pet, I guess."

I bobbed my head, not bothering to argue.

"Listen," I said, glancing at Simone, "you should probably take off too. I'm sure you have things to do, and you've already done more than I could ever repay you for."

"I don't need repayment for being there for my friend. But ..." She paused, chewing her lip. "Are you sure you want me to go? I'm happy to stay another night."

I shook my head. "No, seriously, I'll be fine." I was going to have to face reality sooner or later. Might as well be sooner.

She gave me a searching look, but didn't argue, and I waited while she collected her things before walking her to the door.

On the threshold, she turned and pulled me into a tight embrace.

"Don't let the bastards keep you down. Your sister may be a total badass, but so are you."

My throat tightened. "Thanks."

As soon as Simone left, I peeled off my soiled clothes and dragged myself into the bathroom to take a shower. Although, *take a shower* was a bit of an overstatement—it was more like me sitting numbly on the tub floor for thirty minutes while hot water pelted down on me from above. But at least I was somewhat cleaner than I had been when I'd gotten in, so I was counting it as a win.

I wrapped my bathrobe around me and crawled back into bed, tucking the blankets beneath my chin. The apartment was too quiet, which only made my thoughts louder. I turned on my side and grabbed the remote from the bedside table, flipping on the small television that sat on top of the dresser.

I regretted it immediately.

Everything reminded me of Gabriel—the documentary on Pierre-Auguste Renoir and the rise of Impressionism, the pop remix of "Can't Take My Eyes Off of You" that played in the background of a commercial. Even the horror slasher film I tried watching for all of ten minutes dragged up memories of him. Because *of course* the male lead had blue eyes. I turned it off, tossing the remote on the floor and burying my head under a pillow.

I thought I knew what heartbreak was before this. When my high school boyfriend Chase Anderson broke up with me weeks before junior prom so he could ask some bubblegum cheerleader who always wore a push-up bra, I could have sworn I had reached the pinnacle of devastation. But that wasn't devastation—it wasn't even close.

Real heartbreak is when the simple act of *existing* becomes difficult, when drawing in a full breath feels like too much effort. It was like being in a constant state of pain, and everything ached—my heart, my chest, my soul. And the worst part was, it felt like the only person who could fix it was the same person who had broken me.

Rolling over, I closed my eyes and did the only thing that ever seemed to give me an ounce of reprieve.

I slept.

Forty-Two

Cristian

I rapped my fist on the door of Juliet's apartment, scraping my palm over the day-old stubble lining my cheeks. It was late on Sunday night, but I had to see her. The past three days had been absolute shit. I'd barely slept, and when I had, I was consumed with so much guilt that I only managed a few hours at a time. Raking a shaky hand through my hair, I paced in front of her door, listening for footsteps that likely weren't coming.

Fuck. What had I done?

You know what you did, my subconscious whispered.

That's right—I selfishly screwed over the only true friend I'd ever had, the only person who chose me as I was, flaws and all. What if she wouldn't forgive me? What if she shut me out of her life completely? No, I couldn't think like that. I just needed to talk to her. Juliet was the best person I knew—she would accept my apology once I explained everything.

She *had* to.

The door swung open so suddenly, I flinched. Standing on the threshold in a sweatshirt that ironically read *All Good Days* was Juliet. Except, she looked nothing like herself. Her usually vibrant hair was dull, hanging listlessly around her ashen face, and her eyes were swollen. They sharpened when they landed on me, some of the familiar spark returning.

"*No.*" She placed a hand on the door, already pushing it closed. "Leave, Cristian. I don't want you here."

I flattened a palm against it, holding it open. "Please, Juliet. I just want to talk to you."

She stormed away, not bothering to force me out, and I followed her inside, supposing that was as much of an invitation as I was likely to get.

"Would you please wait?" I wrapped my fingers around her wrist and wasn't the least bit surprised when she twisted out of my hold. We'd done this dance before, after all.

She whirled on me. "What could you possibly have to say that would make any of this better?"

"Probably nothing, but at least give me a chance to explain. After that, you can throw me out if you want to." I had no intention of letting her do any such thing, but we could cross that bridge when we came to it.

"What is there to explain? How you lied to me?" Her eyes raked over me. "How long had you been planning this?"

My instincts, honed over years of spinning falsehoods, screamed for me to hedge the truth with something more palatable, something that would garner her sympathy. But I pushed those feelings aside. I refused to lie to her again, no matter the consequences.

Blowing out a tired breath, I ran a hand across my mouth. "Since the day I first saw you at Gabriel's gallery. I went there to talk to him and I found you there with him."

Her mouth opened in disbelief. "So, all this time, you were just … using me?"

"No, I mean, at first I was, but—" She took a step away from me, and I clenched my teeth. "Listen, Marcel wanted to make amends with Gabriel, but Gabriel wouldn't accept his phone calls. And when I tried talking to him directly, he all but sucker punched me. He didn't leave me with many options."

She huffed a weak laugh. "I see, so I was just the pawn in all of this."

"Only in the beginning. I needed to get Gabriel to the restaurant, and using someone he cared about seemed like the easiest way." She hugged her elbows, her eyes brightening with tears, and I balled my hands into fists. "I know it was wrong, Juliet, and I am so fucking sorry I did that to you." I rubbed my forehead, letting my eyes drift shut.

"All I've ever wanted since the day Marcel plucked me out of the shitty life I'd been living under my stepfather's roof was to earn his approval and gain his respect. I can admit now I've been going about it the wrong way. You were the one who showed me that." My gaze flicked to her, and some of the tension in my chest eased as her expression softened a fraction.

"Unfortunately, when I hatched this whole plan, I still believed manipulating people was the only way to get what I wanted, and what I wanted was to make Marcel happy. But in doing that, I ended up making the two biggest mistakes of my life."

Juliet went very still. "Which were?"

I swallowed, my voice heavy with regret. "Hurting Gabriel. And hurting you."

She lowered her gaze to her hands. "Well, at least you got what you wanted in the end."

"No, I didn't. Whether or not I have Marcel's approval, I haven't gained it by honest methods. Do you remember when I called you a coward? Well, I was projecting my own insecurities, accusing you of being the thing I was too afraid to admit to my-self—that *I'm* the coward. I've had so many opportunities to tell the truth—to Marcel, to Gabriel, to you. And each time, I failed."

A groove remained between her brows. "Cristian, why didn't you just tell me what was going on when I came to see you? When I asked you why you didn't want me at the opening?"

"Because I was afraid it would cost me your friendship. The truth is, when I first met you, you were just a means to an end. But then I got to know you, and I started to care about you. You challenge me in the best ways while also accepting me for who I am.

And when I told you I wasn't a good man, you didn't cut and run. You stayed and fought for me when I didn't care to fight for myself. So, now I'm here, fighting for you. Just tell me how I can fix this, and I swear, I'll do it."

She clamped her eyes shut. "I'm sorry, Cristian. But it's too late."

"Juliet—"

"Gabriel," she said, her voice fracturing on his name, "broke up with me."

My chest deflated. "He ... he *what*?"

"He ended things when I went after him." She pressed her eyes closed, the delicate muscles of her throat working. "He thought I was in on the plan, and that you and I ..." She trailed off, her breath catching. "Anyway, it's over now. There's nothing you can do."

Silence rang between us as I stared at her. She had to be joking. Gabriel loved Juliet—he would never end things with her, especially not over a family feud she wasn't even a part of.

I darted a tongue over my suddenly parched lips, taking in her appearance with fresh eyes. The look of utter brokenness on her face, her eyes filled with despair. It *couldn't* be true. What in the seven hells was he thinking?

I grimaced as an uncomfortable truth took root in my mind.

If their relationship really was over, then it was entirely *my* fault.

"Juliet," I rasped as a mountain of guilt crashed over me, "I ..."

Without waiting for me to finish, she turned and retreated toward her bedroom, returning a minute later with something clutched in her fist.

"Here." She opened her hand, the sapphire bracelet at the center of her palm. "I don't want this anymore. I thought the person who gave it to me was my friend, but it turns out that was just another lie."

My chest tightened painfully. "I *am* your friend."

She shook her head. "You *were* my friend, Cristian."

"No," I gritted out through clenched teeth, my breath coming in sharp, short pants. "I'm not letting you give up."

I'm not letting you give up on me.

I closed the distance between us and placed my hand over hers, folding the bracelet into her palm. Wrapping my arms around her, I pulled her into my chest, squeezing her shoulders as they shook with a soft sob. I had never felt more wretched in my life as I stood there, holding her while she cried because of what *I* had done.

"I am going to fix this, Juliet," I murmured against her hair, my eyes burning. "So, do me a favor and hold on to the bracelet for me, okay? It's my promise to you that I'm going to make this right, no matter what it takes."

I dropped a kiss on her forehead, then spun away from her, striding toward the door.

This wasn't the first time I'd screwed up, and heaven knows it wouldn't be the last. But if spending time with Juliet had taught me anything, it was that to get what I wanted in life, I couldn't keep deceiving people. I would have to be honest.

And honest I would be, beginning with the man at the eye of the storm.

Forty-Three

Gabriel

I woke from a restless sleep to the sound of my phone vibrating somewhere on the floor.

Opening one bleary eye, I peeled myself off the couch in my studio where I'd passed out last night—and the night before that and the one before that too. Rolling into a seated position, I groaned and dropped my head into my hands as a dull pain throbbed in my temples.

Why on earth was the phone so loud?

I shoved aside a near-empty whiskey bottle and reached for the device, wincing as the screen lit up with Nora's name. I hit Ignore and chucked it aside, pushing to my feet and staggering toward the bathroom. I flipped on the faucet and splashed my face with water, willing myself not to vomit. After another round of binge drinking yesterday, it was a miracle I could even stand upright.

Swaying, I returned to my studio and shuffled over to my gym bag in search of clean clothes. I hadn't been home in three days. After the disaster at the restaurant, I had gone back to the apartment long enough to pack a bag and grab a bottle of whiskey before coming here. I couldn't bear to be there with Juliet's things, though, doubtless she'd gone to collect them by now.

My eyes drifted down to the photo of us on Bastille Day. It was like taking a bullet, seeing her face bright with laughter, her eyes fixed on me like I was the center of her universe. *Right.* What a joke that turned out to be. I turned the photo over and braced my hands on the desk, dropping my head between my shoulders.

I still couldn't believe it. The idea that Juliet—the girl who loved sweaters and art and French DJs, who laughed and danced and was always so full of joy, who smelled like lavender and tasted like sunshine—the idea that *she* would betray me was unfathomable. I'd woken up more than once over the past few nights wondering whether it had just been a bad dream. But no—I had seen it with my own eyes. She *brought* me to my father's restaurant; she *knew* Lucien. And the bracelet. That had been the nail in the coffin. No, I'd had every right to end things with her.

So why did I feel like absolute shit?

My phone vibrated again, and I growled irritably, snatching it off the floor. Did no one have respect for a man's privacy? Blinking at the screen, I saw a new voicemail from Jean-Claude and pressed play.

"Gabriel, *mon cher*," his voice boomed, setting off a fresh wave of pounding in my head, "*comment ça va*? I was just calling to see what time you wanted to do the final walkthrough at the gallery. I know you probably have it all under control, but you'll forgive me for wanting to confirm in person that everything is set for Wednesday. Give me a call. *Bonne journée.*"

Right—the gallery opening was this week. The culmination of all my hard work, my dream finally coming true. Except, for some reason, it didn't seem as important as it used to.

I jolted as someone pounded on the front door, hard enough to rattle the glass.

"Gabriel, are you in there?" called a muffled voice. "Open up, asshole."

I flung open the door of my studio, hissing as a bar of sunlight hit me directly in the face. Shading my eyes, I stumbled across the room, pausing to brace myself against a wall as a wave of nausea rolled through me. Once I was certain I wouldn't vomit all over the newly waxed floors, I proceeded to the entrance with the caution of a man approaching the gallows, squinting at a silhouetted figure standing in the doorway.

When I saw who it was, I stiffened.

"I know you see me, Gabriel," Lucien growled, pacing like a caged predator. "Let me in. I need to talk to you."

I bristled, opening the door. "What part of *you're dead to me* did you not understand?"

He stopped pacing, casting a resentful look in my direction. "I don't give a fuck about that. You can hate me until we're both cold in our graves. I'm here because of Juliet."

My eyes flew wide before narrowing into slits. "How dare you come here and say her name to me after what you've done? You ruined *everything*."

"Yes, I screwed up," he said, his gray eyes burning with a cold intensity. "But so did you." He took a step toward me, evidently in the mood to be reckless with his life. "Tell me you didn't break up with Juliet."

"She told you, did she?" A rush of jealousy seized me. "I suppose you've been to see her?"

"I have," he said curtly. "The question is, why haven't you? Seriously, you can't be this stupid. But on the off chance you are, let me spell it out for you—letting go of her was a huge mistake, the biggest one you'll ever make. You want to hate me? Fine. But for her sake, give me fifteen minutes of your time. I'll even throw in a free punch to the face as a bonus."

I blinked at him in bewilderment.

There were many things I didn't understand about my cousin, but of one thing I was certain—Lucien was the poster child of vanity. I had no reason to hear him out, no reason to trust a single word he said. But the fact that he was willing to risk damage to his *face* spoke volumes.

Lucien would rather sell his soul than damage his good looks.

I regarded him skeptically. "I'll give you ten minutes and not a second longer."

He followed me inside, trailing behind me as I reentered my studio. Leaning against the desk, I watched him cross the threshold, his eyes sweeping from one end of the room to the other.

"This is a nice space, Gabriel," he said, making a slow circuit before stopping to examine one of my newly finished paintings. "It has an intimate but rustic feel. It's very you."

"Sorry, but did you come here to talk about the furnishings? Because if so, you can leave."

He turned to me, giving me a severe look. "No, I came to apprise you of the truth—the whole truth. But before I get to that, I'll skip to the punch line and tell you that Juliet is innocent."

My pulse accelerated against my will. "Her association with you would suggest otherwise."

"Yes, well, I tend to have that effect," he said dryly. "But it doesn't change the fact that she's not the guilty party. I am. She was just the sacrificial lamb. The price for atonement."

I exhaled through clenched teeth. "Explain."

"Six months ago, we put a plan in motion to open a restaurant in Paris. It was my idea and was something I had been hoping to do for years. Marcel saw it as a chance to reconcile with you. I suspect he's wanted to bring you back into the family for a while, and what better way to do that than to build a kingdom and hand you the keys?" He snorted humorlessly. "Anyway, it took some time, but eventually, he tracked down your new number and attempted to initiate contact. And when that failed, he sent me. He trusted me to find you, to convince you to come to the restaurant opening."

"And Juliet?"

"After you all but slammed the door in my face the day I came here to see you, I returned later that afternoon to drop off a note for you in the hope that you would contact me at some point. And that's when I saw you with Juliet."

With Juliet at the gallery.

Wait. Was he referring to that day when we …

My lip curled in outrage. "You were spying on us?" If I found out he'd been watching us through the window or some shit, he was a dead man.

He sighed, rolling his eyes dramatically. "No, I was *not* spying on you. Believe it or not, voyeurism isn't my style. But I saw enough to deduce she was important to you, and if anyone could convince you to come to the restaurant, it would be her."

I shook my head in disbelief. "Why am I not surprised? When you couldn't get what you wanted through honest means, you resorted to deceit. Classic Lucien."

His eyes flashed with anger. "Yes, I did. You can look down on me from the moral high ground all you want, but there is little I wouldn't do for Marcel. He plucked me out of the gutter and gave me a chance at a future. I owe him everything." I opened and closed my mouth, but no sound came out. "So yes," he barreled on, "I sought Juliet out and persuaded her to bring you to the restaurant.

She had no idea who I was to you. She didn't make that connection until you tried to throttle me in the middle of the dining room."

"She didn't know who you were?"

"No. When I introduced myself to her, I told her I went by the name Cristian."

My brows slammed down. Where had I heard that name? Pressing my eyes shut, I searched my memory for something, some conversation dangling just out of reach. Slowly but surely, it came back to me. *It's my friend Cristian. He's been radio silent for the past week. I'm starting to worry.* That's right—Juliet *had* mentioned him. Of course, I had no idea who she was talking about at the time. And how could I?

"So, you gave her a false name?" I scoffed. "Someone ought to give you a medal for the number of lies you tell."

He sliced a hand through the air. "It wasn't a lie. Cristian *is* my name. My middle name. I told you before, I've always hated the name Lucien, and everyone outside of the family calls me Cristian. I even tried to tell you as much—"

"Do you think I give a shit?" I launched to my feet, closing the distance between us in two strides. "Do you think I care about *any* of this? There is nothing—and I mean *nothing*—you could say to justify you seducing Juliet."

He jerked away from me, his eyes going comically round, and I had to admit his shocked expression was almost convincing.

"She told me about the bracelet," I continued. "She admitted *you* bought it for her."

"Yes, I did," he said, a frown pulling at his brow. "There was a misunderstanding at Galeries, and I bought the bracelet to get her out of trouble. But I don't see what that has to do with anything." He gave me a confused look. "Gabriel, why would I seduce your girlfriend?"

"Because you've done it before—when you had an affair with Elise."

A palpable silence descended over the room as Lucien stared at me with a blank expression.

"I'm sorry, what?"

"Three years ago, when you withdrew five hundred thousand euros from our business account using *my* credentials—thanks for that, by the way—Elise told me you did it at her request because the two of you were having an affair."

He blinked slowly, his eyes growing distant as they settled on a point over my shoulder.

"So that's what it was," he said quietly. He moved to the couch before dropping onto it, his gaze still holding a faraway look. When his eyes finally returned to mine, they were filled with sadness. "I always wondered why you left without saying goodbye. Now I know." Tilting forward, he swiped the whiskey from the floor, popping the cork.

"To Elise," he said, raising the bottle before taking a long swig. "The bitch is more cunning than I gave her credit for."

"What are you talking about?"

"I'm talking about the fact that she played you like a fucking piano—just like she played me." He gave me a hard look. "There was never any affair, Gabriel. I never touched Elise."

All the air evacuated my lungs in an instant, my knees giving way as I slumped into a chair.

No. That couldn't be right. For years, I'd been living in the shadow of a betrayal that never even happened? Lucien watched me, nodding as though coming to the same conclusion himself.

"Then, why?" I croaked. "Why did you take the money? Or did she lie about that too?"

His Adam's apple rose and fell as he held my gaze. "No, that part was true. I took the money." A hint of color rose in his cheeks as he lowered his eyes to his hands. "Elise came to me with a proposal for an investment opportunity—a new seaside property in Monaco that was in the early stages of development. The company in charge of the project was still looking for investors, and based on returns for similar ventures in the area, I knew we stood to gain a fortune. I researched the company, reviewed the investment documents, even went to check out the stretch of land where they planned to break ground. Everything was legitimate."

"So, what happened?"

"Elise happened," he growled. "The property was just the carrot she used to lure me into withdrawing the money. And like a fool, I trusted her when she asked me to deposit the funds in a separate offshore account rather than wiring it directly to the developer's investment fund."

"And you did all of this without saying a word to my father?"

"I planned to tell him." He rested his forehead on a fist. "I was going to present everything to him as soon as the contracts came through. But they never came, and that's when I realized Elise never planned to make the investment. It was all just an elaborate ruse to get her hands on the money without leaving an incriminating paper trail."

"But why? What did she need that kind of money for?"

"I asked myself the same question. As soon as I realized her intentions were less than honorable, I stopped looking into the property and started looking into *her*. As it turned out, Elise had gotten in over her head with some unsavory people down in Monte Carlo, and she owed them a huge gambling debt. These guys were involved in all sorts of illegal activity—arms dealing, drugs, trafficking. You name it, they've done it. She always had an appetite for risk, so I wasn't surprised to find out she had a taste for high-stakes gambling as well. But her luck finally ran out, and she had to come up with the money to pay off her debt. Fast."

"And if she couldn't come up with the money?"

He cast me a dry look. "These weren't the type of guys to accept an IOU, Gabriel."

"Mother of God." I scrubbed a hand over my mouth. "Do you have proof of all this?"

He nodded seriously. "I do. I've been amassing a file since the day I discovered her scheme. In addition to the original confirmation of the electronic funds transfer, I have documentation proving the offshore account was owned by a shell company, of which she was the sole owner. I also have records on the men she gambled with as well as incriminating photographs, audio recordings, security footage ..."

I gaped at him. "How the hell do you have all of that?"

"I have a private investigator on retainer."

An unexpected laugh caught in my throat. "You're insane."

His lips twitched. "Why, thank you."

And then I did laugh. We both did, and to my surprise, the ache that had been living in my chest for the past three days—the past three *years*—finally eased a bit.

"Gabriel," he said after our laughter finally died down. "I need you to know I am truly sorry, especially about Juliet. It's my fault your relationship ended."

"No, it's mine." I ran a hand over my forehead and through my hair, my throat tightening as the full weight of what I had done descended on me. "I'm the one who jumped to conclusions and assumed the worst of her. She told me I had it all wrong, but I wouldn't listen. I'd just come from talking to Elise, which had my head all kinds of fucked up. Then I saw you with her, and I just—" I shook my head, pressing my eyelids shut.

"It doesn't matter. I'm the one who messed up. I'm the one who's responsible for all of this. If I had just confronted my trust issues sooner, worked through them rather than trying to outrun them, none of this would have happened. All these years, I've kept my pain about the past locked inside, letting it damage me to the point that I hurt someone who didn't deserve it."

I glanced at him. "That's what you were trying to tell me before, wasn't it? That afternoon we met at the café—you told me I needed to deal with my issues before I ended up hurting someone who was innocent in all this. I should have listened to you."

"Well, it's hard to trust the word of a man who you thought betrayed you. And in a way, I did. I never should have taken the money behind your back. I should have told you the truth."

"Why didn't you?"

He expelled a sigh. "When Elise presented the investment idea, she told me you had already turned it down. In hindsight, I believe she told me that on purpose. Just like she told you we were having an affair to sow mistrust between us, she told me you passed on the opportunity because she knew I wouldn't be able to resist the chance to come out on top for once."

I frowned. "What do you mean?"

His eyes drifted down to the whiskey bottle in his hands. "All I've ever wanted to do is make Marcel proud, to have the one thing that you always seemed to take for granted. A father. I worked three times as hard, all in the hope that one day I might gain his favor. But no matter what I did, he reserved all his attention for you, his son."

I swallowed hard, my eyes raking over him. Suddenly, a completely different person was sitting in front of me. How had I not seen it before? The clothes, the image, the relentless pursuit of perfection—it was all to prove himself worthy. Worthy of love.

"I never knew you felt like that. All this time, I thought you just saw me as competition."

He chuckled. "Well, you weren't wrong. But part of me admired you too. You've always been true to yourself, Gabriel. No matter what anyone else wants, you never let it get in the way of following your own dreams. And look, you've built all of this." His gaze bounced around the room before he rose to his feet. "Well, anyway, I believe my ten minutes is up."

"You're leaving already?" I asked, surprising us both.

He blinked. "Yes. Touching though this has been, I have another stop to make on my apology tour." His lips settled into a grim line. "It's time I told Marcel the truth. About everything."

"Lucien—" I paused, clearing my throat. "*Cristian*, are you sure you want to do that?"

His mouth curved in a faint smile. "I am. It's time that Elise paid for all the wreckage she's caused. All these years, she's been holding the role I played in her treachery over my head, but I won't let her do it anymore. And if that means I go down with her, then so be it. At least my conscience will be clear." His smile widened. "For once."

He extended a hand to me, and I hesitated for a beat before taking it.

"Good luck, Cristian."

He nodded, holding my gaze as he gripped my hand. "And to you, cousin."

Forty-Four

Juliet

"I'm sorry, Juliet."

I glanced up from the polished wood of Benoit's desk to look at him, his mouth set in a firm line as he studied me with a solemn expression.

I swallowed, shaking my head. "You have nothing to be sorry for. You kept your word and submitted my piece to the competition. You gave me a shot at something most new writers could only dream of. You have my gratitude, Julien."

And I meant it—I was grateful.

Benoit had tactfully waited until Tuesday morning when I was due to come in to his office to deliver the news that my piece hadn't won the magazine competition. And while it had been a devastating blow considering everything else going on, I was resolved to accept the outcome with my head held high. I had tried my best, and that's all that mattered.

He leaned back in his chair as the sun directed a shaft of light through the window. "You should know that making it to the final round is a huge accomplishment. I told you, *La Nouvelle Revue Française* receives thousands of submissions each year, and only a small percentage of those make it past the initial round." He steepled his fingers beneath his chin. "Don't let this stop you, Juliet. You are incredibly talented, and more importantly, you are disciplined and thorough. With your level of dedication, you are certain to go far as long as you don't give up."

"Thank you, I appreciate that." I laughed weakly. "And don't worry, I'm not one to stay down for long. If anything, I'm disappointed to miss out on the magazine's annual event this weekend. Any chance you can sneak me in the back door?"

He gave me a half-smile. "I wish I could. I would have asked you to come as my plus one, but I hadn't planned on attending this year, and now the RSVP deadline has passed. If I had known ..." His voice petered out, but his meaning was clear.

If he had known I wouldn't be invited myself as one of the competition winners.

"It's not a big deal." I glanced over at the desk that used to be mine. "So, any word on your assistant's return?" His lengthy exhale was all the answer I needed. "I see. Well, I hope you find someone to replace him soon."

"Are you sure I can't entice you to stay?" He gestured around the space. "It's no corner office on Park Avenue, but you would be most welcome."

"You want me to stay on as your assistant?" I said, suppressing a smile. "Goodness, maybe you didn't resent my notes quite as much as you let on."

He let out a low chuckle, though his eyes held a look of sincerity. "Not just as my assistant, but as my *teaching* assistant. Your knowledge of the material, together with your education and experience, would more than qualify you for the position."

I blinked. "You're serious?" It was a pointless question. Julien Benoit was many things—a collector of antiques, a lover of classical literature, a connoisseur of tweed jackets—but a jokester, he was not. Shifting my weight, I toyed with the cuff of my sleeve. "I don't know what to say. I truly appreciate the offer. It's only ..."

"Say no more," he said, cutting me off with a wave of his hand. "I didn't expect you to accept, but I would have been remiss if I didn't at least ask. Now, before you go, I wanted to give you a list of publications you might consider submitting to when you return to New York. Despite the outcome of this competition, I think your piece was very solid, and I'm sure another magazine or journal would be happy to pick it up." He reached inside his jacket pocket and extracted a white envelope, handing it to me. "It's not often I say this, but it has been a pleasure working with you, Juliet. I wish you the best of luck in your future endeavors."

"Thank you, sir." My throat tightened. "Likewise."

I turned and hurried from the room before he could see the tears stinging my eyes.

⇒⇒⇒ ⇐⇐⇐

I pushed through the door of my apartment building, stopping by the mailboxes to check for any last packages and making a mental note to leave a forwarding address with the landlord. Cresting the stairs, I rooted around in my purse in search of my keys just as my phone vibrated. I fished it out, propping it between my chin and shoulder as I unlocked the door and stepped inside.

"Hello?"

"Juliet, it's Tom."

I halted, a trickle of unease settling in my stomach. "Oh, hi, Tom. How's it—"

"Hey, listen," he cut across me, the sound of his keyboard filling the background. "I know you've got a few days left in Berlin, but I want to loop you in on a new deal I've got lined up. One of our private equity clients is looking to acquire a major tech company out in Silicon Valley, and I want you to be the lead associate on the transaction." Another phone rang somewhere, and he paused to pick it up, rattling off a hurried *Yes, okay, that's fine* before hanging up again.

"As I was saying," he continued, "I'd love to get you on this matter. Now, I won't hide the ball—the timing on this is gonna be a shitstorm. You know how these PE guys like to have their deals tied up in a neat little bow by Christmas, so it'll be all hands on deck as soon as the target company launches their virtual data room. Can I loop you in on this email thread with the investment banker?"

I drew in a breath, feeling suddenly winded. "Well, Tom, I'm not sure if—"

"Look, this is the big leagues, kid. I'm talking about a two-billion-dollar acquisition. You nail this, and you'll be sitting pretty when it comes time for you to be considered for partnership. Not to mention it will guarantee you a sizable year-end bonus."

I plucked at my lip, leaning my hip against the kitchen counter.

Blunt manner aside, I knew Tom was telling the truth. These were the kinds of deals associates were desperate for, the ones that proved to the firm's leadership you could cut it. The old me would have given Tom a yes on the spot, then cleared my calendar for the foreseeable future. I would have reminded myself nothing was more important than the job and my friends and family would understand when I canceled plans with them for the third time in a row. I would've made sure my desk drawers were stocked with energy supplements and double-checked that my office closet had a change of clothes. But more than any of that, the old me wouldn't have been standing in a Paris apartment, wondering at what point I'd handed over my one precious life in exchange for a bonus check and a shiny new deal toy.

"Can I have a few days to think about it?"

A long pause.

"All right, but I need your answer by end of day tomorrow. This isn't the kind of deal you want to pass up on, Juliet. You've worked hard since joining the firm, and an opportunity like this could distinguish your career."

"Yeah, I got it." I cleared my throat. "You'll have my answer tomorrow."

I disconnected the call, staring down at the dark screen. I hadn't even touched down in New York yet, and already I could feel the walls of the firm closing in on me.

Of course, I would have to say yes. No doubt Tom had only agreed to give me an extra day just to humor me, but I wouldn't be the least bit surprised to find he had already added me to the client-matter file.

I shoved aside an empty box I'd set out to pack the kitchen supplies in and padded toward the living room in search of my laptop. *I'm just going to check.* If he had added me to the matter without my consent, what then? It wasn't like I was going to turn the deal down, anyway.

I had just powered on my laptop when there was a knock on the door, and I left my computer on the coffee table, heading for the entryway. Swinging the door open, my eyes fell wide when they collided with the figure standing on the other side. He stared back at me, running a hand down the front of his starched white button-down before tucking it into the pocket of his jeans, his throat bobbing beneath a clean-shaven jaw.

Kyle.

"Hey, Jules." His eyes ticked between each of mine, before darting over my shoulder. "Did I catch you at a bad time?"

I shook my head. "No, I—I just wasn't expecting you." I glanced behind me into the apartment before returning my attention to him. "Um, do you want to come in?"

"Yeah," he said with a relieved sigh. "That would be great."

I stepped aside to let him pass, moving toward the kitchen as soon as the door closed.

"Tea?" I offered, already moving to put the kettle on without waiting for a reply. I was keenly aware of his eyes on me as he lowered himself onto a bar stool while I busied myself with retrieving a couple of mugs from the cabinet.

After a minute that felt like an eternity, he said, "I know this must be a shock, me showing up here out of the blue." I hummed, keeping my eyes firmly on the tea preparations. "But after I found out you were coming home early, I thought I might fly over and help you pack up. Maybe talk things over."

My gaze flew to his, and he gave me a sheepish grin. "Our calendars are still synced, so I got the notification when you made the flight change." He watched me for a beat longer than was comfortable, possibly waiting for an explanation. When none came, he continued, "Anyway, I was hoping to talk to you in person, and I didn't want to leave it until you got back to New York." His eyes dropped to the tea I placed in front of him. "I thought I might meet you halfway instead."

I swallowed thickly, unsure of how to respond to that.

He fiddled with the mug in his hands. Then, as if coming to a decision, he rose from his chair and rounded the counter with a look of determination.

"Listen, I've had a lot of time to think in your absence, and I've concluded that you were right. About everything." His chest expanded on an inhale as his eyes wandered around the kitchen. When they returned to mine, they were too soft, too familiar.

"I'll admit, my pride was wounded when you ended things, and for a while, I told myself it didn't matter. That *you* didn't matter. But then, I was sitting alone in our apartment one night, and it finally hit me that you were right—that somewhere along the way, I *had* become more engrossed with the idea of you rather than the reality of you. I was so caught up in the pursuit of success that I stopped seeing you altogether. And it took me having to face a future without you to realize that."

"Kyle," I said, shaking my head, "just because you see that now doesn't mean things would be any different in the future."

"It would be different, Jules, because *I'm* different. I was a pretentious dick, okay? You didn't deserve the way I treated you, and for that, I apologize." He absently rearranged the salt and pepper shakers as though measuring his next words.

"While you were gone, I realized all this shit isn't half as important as we make it seem. The promotions, the prestigious awards, the flashy cases—it's all just a song and dance to keep the corporate machine running, to distract us from the things that really matter, like actually *living* instead of just existing. When I die, I don't want my obituary to read like a résumé or for there to be a bunch of guys in suits standing around at my funeral applauding how I dedicated my life to the job instead of to the people I cared about."

He took a weighted step toward me, crowding me against the counter. "I want to have a family, and I want one with you. I'll make an effort to be more present, for you and for our future kids should we choose to have them. And whether or not you want to continue practicing law I'll support whatever decision you make."

I brought the tea to my lips, taking a shaky sip before setting it down. It was strange hearing Kyle say all the things I'd once hoped to hear, words that might have saved our relationship if only they had come sooner.

He folded a hand over my arm. "I know I missed the mark, but I want another shot. And I'm prepared to make whatever concessions you deem necessary in order for that to happen."

I pulled out of his grasp, grabbing the mugs and placing them in the sink. Bracing my hands on the counter, I let my eyes drift shut for a moment before turning to face him.

"Listen, Kyle, I appreciate you saying all this, but there's something you need to know."

He paused, his brows drawing together. Then his lips flattened into a hard line as a flicker of realization passed behind his eyes. "Is this about that guy? The one who threatened to—let me see, how did he phrase it—put me in the fucking ground?" He scoffed, and I lifted my chin in defiance. Yes, Gabriel had threatened him—because he *deserved* it. And even though Gabriel and I were over, I wasn't going to apologize for his behavior when he had been acting in my defense.

Kyle dragged a hand over his mouth, propping the other on his hip as he regarded me.

"Okay," he said finally, "if you had a summer fling, then so be it. Maybe you've been on the straight and narrow too long and needed a chance to rebel a little. Or, I don't know, maybe you did it out of resentment toward me. Either way, I'm prepared to look past it."

"It wasn't just a fling, Kyle." I swallowed around a knot in my throat. "I fell in love with him. It was ... what we had was real."

His eyes hardened, and a muscle in his jaw twitched, giving away his irritation. "Is that so? Well, if it was so real, where is he?" His words hit me directly in the chest, winding me, and I released a shuddering exhale.

"You should go."

He straightened, drawing himself up to his full height as we stared at each other on opposite sides of an invisible line. His expression oscillated between frustration and regret before he nodded curtly, and I followed him to the door.

"My offer still stands," he said, turning to me again. Lifting a hand, he brushed my cheek lightly with his knuckles. "Whatever happened with that guy, it doesn't matter. He's gone, and I'm here. And we can still have it all." He stared at me for another moment, then dipped his head to place a kiss where his hand had been. "Come home, sweetheart."

I stepped out of his reach, retreating toward the kitchen as an ache expanded in my chest.

Come home.

The trouble was, I wasn't sure where home was anymore.

Forty-Five

Gabriel

Blowing out an anxious breath, I curled my hand into a fist and raised it to Juliet's door. But before I could knock, I dropped it again, dragging it up over my forehead.

I had really fucking blown it.

After talking to Cristian yesterday, I'd come straight here intending to beg Juliet for forgiveness. But whether out of fear or self-loathing, I couldn't bring myself to knock and ended up sitting outside her door for hours, head in my hands, heart breaking all over again. Like a bad dream, the memory of the night I ruined everything kept playing on a loop in my head until I was sick from it, my stomach churning with so much shame and regret that I couldn't bear to face her. All she wanted was for me to trust her, and I failed.

I'd come back this morning, but she either hadn't been home or hadn't answered. And now, here I was again, except this time, I wasn't leaving. I would wait all day for her if that's what it took. Because the truth was, there was no me without her, no future I wanted any part of if she wasn't in it. And even though I couldn't take back what I'd done, I was prepared to spend the rest of my life showing her I was worthy of her love, her trust, *her*.

Bracing myself, I lifted my hand to the door again just as it swung open, revealing a man standing on the other side of it. A flicker of surprise lit his features, and he blinked, taking me in with a calculating look.

He took a step forward, filling the doorway. "And who might you be?"

There was an edge to his tone that suggested he knew *exactly* who I was, just like I knew who he was. If the American accent and general air of privilege hadn't given him away, the way he was glaring at me now certainly would have done the job.

Kyle.

I gave him an unimpressed look. "I'm here to see Juliet."

His expression darkened. "She's not receiving visitors right now." He stepped into the hallway, pulling the door behind him as though he meant to keep me from entering. "Whatever you have to say to her, you can say to me."

"I doubt that," I said, making an effort to sound calm despite the tension in my shoulders. "And you don't speak for her, or did you miss the part where she told you she's not your property?"

His eyes flashed with anger. "Just who do you think you are? What—you think just because she had a little fun with you for the summer that you have some sort of claim on her?" He scoffed. "Well, I'm sorry to inform you, but your acquaintance has come to an end. I'm here to take Juliet home. Where she belongs."

Cold fingers of dread climbed the length of my spine, closing around my throat until it was suddenly hard to breathe. *No.* Juliet wasn't going anywhere with this asshole. Was she?

My hands tightened into fists. "I don't care what you're here to do. I'm not leaving until I speak to her. Now, are you going to step aside, or shall I assist you?"

"You arrogant son of—"

"Kyle?" Juliet's voice floated through the open doorway a second before she appeared. Her eyes widened when they landed on me. "Gabriel."

Kyle made a rude noise in his throat at the familiarity in her tone, and he moved to her side, placing a possessive hand on her arm. "I've already told him you don't want company."

She stiffened. "Don't you think that should have been my decision?"

Annoyance flickered across his face before he covered it up with an indulgent smile. "Of course, sweetheart. I was only looking out for you." He dropped a kiss on her forehead, and it was all I could do not to throw him down the stairs.

"Do you want me to stay?" he said to her, tucking a loose tendril of hair behind her ear before sliding his gaze to me. I bared my teeth at him in a grin that said *Keep fucking with me and find out.*

She shook her head, moving out of his hold. "No, I'll be fine. You should go."

He deposited his hand back in his pocket as if he wasn't at all bothered by her rebuff, but the tense set of his jaw indicated otherwise. "Okay, I'm staying at the Ritz if you need anything."

Giving her one last smile, he tossed a menacing glare in my direction before disappearing down the stairs. I waited until I heard the scrape of the building door before turning to face her again. My eyes trailed over her, an army of emotions warring for dominance in my chest. Fear, regret, shame. But one feeling rose above them all.

Love.

"Juliet," I rasped, my throat full of knives. "Can we please talk?" She huffed bitterly and looked away, folding her arms protectively across her chest. "I know I'm the last person you want to see, but I'm begging you. Please, just give me a few minutes of your time."

She gave me a wary look, and my heart fractured at the hurt in her eyes. "I'm not sure that's a good idea, Gabriel."

I winced. *She doesn't trust me.* And why would she? She had placed her heart in my hands, only for me to crush it like diamond dust at the first sign of trouble.

"At least tell me you aren't considering going back with that guy."

Her eyes narrowed. "I really don't see how that's any of your concern."

Not my concern? Like hell it wasn't.

"No," I said, my voice laced with panic as I sliced a hand through the air. "I won't let you do that." As soon as the words left my mouth, I knew I'd said the wrong thing.

She bristled, a look of indignation coating her features as she squared her shoulders. "You won't *let* me?" She jabbed a finger toward my chest. "After you left me standing on a dark quay like I meant nothing, like everything we had meant nothing."

"*Have*," I said, my stomach pitching violently. "Everything we *have*. And I know I messed up, but if you'll just—"

She cut me off with a dismissive shake of her head. "No. You don't get to show up here with some half-baked apology and think everything is going to be all right. And for the record, I've had enough of men telling me what to do for one day, so if you'll excuse me."

Her words rang with finality, and I surged forward on instinct, blocking her escape. "I'm sorry I overstepped. I didn't come here to pile on and be yet another person trying to pull you in a direction. I came because I have something to say to you, and afterward, if you want me to go ..." I swallowed hard. "If you tell me you don't want to see me again, I swear, I'll respect that."

She raised her eyes to me, and for a second, I could have sworn something shifted in her expression, her gaze swirling with the tiniest sliver of emotion.

"Please," I said, holding my breath like my entire life was hanging in the balance. Just as I thought I would implode from the silence, she nodded once and gestured inside.

Juliet

The door slammed shut behind us, closing us in with a silence I could almost feel.

When Gabriel showed up at my apartment, my traitorous heart had leapt at the sight of him, my chest filling with a relief I didn't ask for. If Kyle hadn't been standing there, I might have lost my head entirely and thrown myself into his arms. As it was, Kyle's presence had been the restraining force I needed, that extra sixty seconds to lock down my feelings and remind myself why we were in this situation. Why I had lost four pounds in the past week, and Gabriel was sporting more stubble on his jaw than usual, dark splotches under his eyes.

We had broken up for a reason, and I couldn't afford to forget that.

"Juliet." My eyes snapped up, finding his across the three feet of space that separated us, and he stared at me so intently I was forced to look away. He took a hesitant step forward, the floorboards creaking under his weight. "Juliet ... if I thought there were words sufficient to express how deeply I regret my actions, how truly sorry I am for not trusting you, I would say them to you until my voice gave out."

He took another step, and I glanced up without meaning to.

Bad idea.

The second I clocked the look on his face, some small measure of my resistance crumbled.

He looked so vulnerable.

"As it stands, I know there's nothing I could ever say to make up for what I've done. You deserved so much better from me. You ..." His Adam's apple rose and fell, his expression pained. "You deserve so much better *than* me. You deserve someone who will give you all their trust without holding back. And God knows I want to be that for you."

Another inch of space disappeared as he moved closer, and my hands brushed against the entryway table as I drew in a slow breath, trying not to be utterly consumed by him. His scent was all around me now, his warmth, his dark lashes and eyes the color of the sea. It was too much, much more than I bargained for when I agreed he could stay. I thought I would rage at him a bit, or at least maintain a cold indifference before telling him to kick rocks. Instead, here I was, trembling in my own foyer, my heart quickening at the deep rasp of his voice.

Really impressive, Juliet.

"I know I don't deserve your forgiveness," he said, his breath catching. "But I'm going to ask for it anyway because I can't bear to walk the earth without you by my side. And I know I've got issues to work through, and I promise you I will. Only ..." His forehead dropped to mine, and my hand moved of its own accord, reaching up to touch his face. "If you choose to forgive me, know that what happened last week—my utter failure to believe in you, to believe in us—will never happen again." He shuddered as my fingers grazed his cheek, his eyes closing in surrender, and he leaned in, the magnetic force of him drawing me despite the steady ache in my chest.

"Please give me another chance," he whispered. "I swear on my life, I won't let you down."

His hands were on my waist now, sliding up my ribs in a familiar caress that had my knees swaying. It would be so easy to give in and let him kiss away the pain. To move ten feet to the sofa and lose ourselves in each other, soothing each other's sorrow in a way only we could. But ...

"No." I took a step back, sounding sturdier than I felt. "You hurt me." My hands shook as he dropped to his knees in front of me.

"And I have never been sorrier in my life." He pressed his head against my stomach, and when he looked up again, his eyes were ringed with moisture. "But I swear, I'll never hurt you again, baby. Please give me a chance to show you."

I clamped a hand over my mouth to stop a sob from slipping past my lips. "I can't just forgive you because you want me to, Gabriel. All my life, I've allowed other people to decide for me, letting their voices crowd out my own until my wants became buried beneath their needs. But I finally understand I have to make choices based on what's right for *me*. And maybe that means I'll have to let other people down, but at least I won't be letting myself down."

I lowered myself to the floor, cupping his face between my palms. "You were the one who helped me see that. You encouraged me to move beyond the shadow of my grandfather's dreams and figure out what I wanted for myself. You challenged me to stand up to Tom when he overstepped my boundaries." His throat moved on a hard swallow as I ran my thumb beneath his lower lip. "Being with you has made me stronger in so many ways, and I'll always be grateful for that. But whatever decision I make next needs to be the one I make for myself."

And then, whether because I needed to or because it might be the last time, I brushed my lips over his, cherishing the feel of them, the taste as his mouth moved reverently over mine like he could feel it too, the finality of it all. After too few seconds, I pulled back, and he stared down at me like he was memorizing every curve and line of my face.

"I need you to go now," I said quietly, my heart ripping right down the middle. "Please."

I waited for him to argue, and part of me, the old Juliet who still lived somewhere inside, wished he would. But he didn't. Instead, he took both my hands and pressed a hard kiss against them, his damp eyes holding mine. Then he pushed to his feet and disappeared through the door.

Forty-Six

Gabriel

Soft chords of jazz guitar drifted from in-ceiling speakers, mingling with the hum of voices and the clink of champagne glasses as dozens of people, mostly strangers, milled about the gallery. Hands in my pockets, I watched from the corner, taking in the scene as though peering through a looking glass. All I had ever wanted was right in front of me, and yet, I was apart from it, a stranger in a world of my own design.

Shouldn't I feel excitement or at least some sense of satisfaction? Where was the joy I thought would accompany this moment? This was the endgame after all—the thing I wanted most.

The thing I want most.

What if this *wasn't* what I wanted most anymore? What if the thing I wanted most wasn't even a thing at all, but a person?

One person in particular.

Sinking back against the wall, I pressed a fist to my chest to loosen the tension that had lived there since Juliet asked me to leave her apartment yesterday. It had nearly killed me to do it, but she needed space, and I respected that. Never mind the fact that I'd wanted to call her about a dozen times since and had written and deleted twice as many texts. In the end, I'd settled for sending her one message—*I will love you forever.*

She hadn't responded.

I blew out a shaky breath, shifting my weight.

What if she wouldn't forgive me? Was I just supposed to live my life without her? Impossible. The thought alone was enough to gut me.

"Gabriel."

Jean-Claude headed in my direction, maneuvering around a journalist who was examining one of my paintings. Or at least I thought he was a journalist, given the way he kept pulling out a notepad every so often to jot something down.

"What are you doing hiding in the corner, *mon cher*?" Jean-Claude said when he reached me. "This is your big night. Several people are waiting to meet you."

"Just taking a breather." I waved away the offered glass of champagne.

He frowned. "Not drinking either?"

"No. I want to keep a clear head tonight." That, and I refused to numb my emotions. If I couldn't have Juliet close to me tonight, then I would settle for the pain of her absence.

"Hmm," he said, eyeing me critically. "You shouldn't take yourself so seriously, Gabriel. You deserve a chance to relax and celebrate all you've accomplished."

"Right." I feigned a smile. "So, how's it going out there? Any interested patrons?"

"Any interested patrons?" he repeated, giving me an incredulous look. "My dear man, over half your paintings have sold already, and I imagine a fair few will go over the coming days as well. Good thing we decided to keep a reserve in storage—at this rate, you won't have anything left to display." He rubbed his jaw thoughtfully. "I should mention, there's one painting in particular that's garnering a great deal of interest. It's called *Angel Eyes*."

I swiveled toward him. "My statement piece?"

"Yes, that's the one."

"It's not for sale," I said, my jaw tightening. "I'm serious—no one is to buy that painting."

His brows knitted together. "Are you sure? If your concern is the price, I can assure you the offers have been most generous. You would be pleased with the amount—"

"I'm not selling it," I barked, and he blinked, startled. I released a long breath, rubbing the back of my neck. "I'm sorry. I think I need to get some air. Excuse me."

I pushed toward the exit and had almost made my escape when a voice rang out from behind me. "And just where do you think you're going?"

I turned in time to see a flash of red before Lily launched herself at me, James and Nora coming up behind her. Nora gave her sister-in-law an amused look. "Lily, you really must learn how to hug people without tackling them." Nora stepped around her, drawing me into a gentler embrace. "The gallery is a smashing success, Gabe. We're so proud of you."

"It's bloody brilliant, is what it is," James said, throwing an arm around me. "Congratulations, mate. Well done."

"Thanks, guys." A genuine smile tugged at my lips. "I appreciate it."

Nora arched an eyebrow. "Yes, well, just don't go getting too big for your britches. We still need you at the cycling shop, you know. At least until this little one arrives." She swept a hand over the barely visible swell of her stomach.

I squeezed her arm. "No worries. I'll be around for a while yet."

"Oh good," James said with an exaggerated sigh. "And here I thought I'd have to persuade you to stay with a raise or something. Thanks for saving me the trouble, buddy."

I eyed him coolly as Lily laughed behind her hand and Nora rolled her eyes.

"Pardon me." The journalist I'd seen earlier approached, stepping into our circle. "You're the artist, Gabriel Beaumont?" I nodded. "I thought so. Alain Moreau. I'm a journalist for *Le Monde*

Artistique magazine. I was wondering if I could ask you a few questions."

"Yeah, sure."

"We'll just be near the refreshment table," Nora said, looping her arm through Lily's. James clapped me on the shoulder before following them.

"Friends of yours, Monsieur Beaumont?" He reached into his jacket pocket to retrieve a small audio recorder. "Sorry, is it all right if I record this?"

"Yes, and yes. And Gabriel is fine."

"Right, Gabriel." He turned on the recorder. "So, as you know, Paris has long been considered the art capital of the world, but recent years have seen an uptick in galleries across the city. Between the influx of international artists due to Brexit and the arrival of a new generation of talent, there's no question the art scene is awash with competition right now. Tell me, how do you plan to distinguish yourself as a debut artist?"

"By telling the truth. My goal has always been to be as honest as I can, and every painting is just an expression of what lives inside me—in my heart and mind. I have no ambition aside from that."

He regarded me with interest. "But surely you must take your cues from other contemporary artists?"

"I take my cues from my creator, though I'll admit to holding an admiration for my fellow artists. There is much we can learn from one another as we all strive to improve in our craft."

"Spoken like a man of confidence, and little wonder—I hear you've sold several paintings already. That's more than what most new artists achieve in a month's time. How does it feel to be such an instant success? More than one critic is already calling you the debut artist of the year."

I folded my arms, looking over his shoulder. "Whether I'm a true success has yet to be seen, but I'm honored people enjoy my work."

"So modest, though I imagine that will change over time. There's no room for humility at the top. By the way, how's the view from up there?" He chuckled at his own lame joke, but something uncomfortable shifted in my stomach at hearing it.

Just make sure when you make it to the top, you aren't all alone up there. Success is nothing without someone to share it with.

James's comment from weeks ago came back to me with startling clarity, and I swallowed hard.

"Lonely," I murmured.

The journalist's smile faltered. "I'm sorry. What did you say?" I opened my mouth to ask him to move on to the next question when my gaze snagged on a woman studying a painting across the room, her long braids hanging down her back as she peered up at it.

Simone.

"I'm sorry," I said to the journalist. "If you'll excuse me for a moment."

I didn't wait for his response as I moved toward Simone as quickly as I could. Pushing past a cluster of people gathered around a high-top table, I finally got a clear view of her, Carter moving sedately at her side. She glanced over her shoulder as though she'd sensed me approaching.

"Hey," I said breathlessly, my eyes flicking between her and Carter before darting around the immediate area. I didn't bother hiding who I was looking for.

"She's not here," Simone said, her tone frosty.

Disappointment slammed into my chest. "Oh."

"But she wanted us to support your debut," Carter chimed in. "You've done a fine job, by the way."

"Yes, very nice job," Simone said stiffly, pressing her lips into a tight line as though it was taking her a great deal of effort not to ream me out for what I'd done to her friend.

Part of me wished she would.

She sniffed. "Now, if you'll excuse us, I suddenly find myself in need of a glass of wine." She strode in the direction of the refreshments table as if she couldn't get away from me fast enough. Carter turned to follow her, but I caught his arm.

"Please," I said, fighting to keep my voice steady, "tell me how she is."

He gave me a sympathetic look. "Listen, it's not my place to get involved in whatever's going on between you and Juliet. If you want to know how she is, you'll have to ask her yourself." He stepped past me before slowing to a halt. He turned to me again, indecision warring on his face. "And you'd better do it quickly before you miss your chance."

"What do you mean?"

"I mean, Juliet's leaving."

My pulse jumped. "Leaving? I thought your program didn't end for another week, at least."

He shrugged. "She got permission from Benoit to take off early. Final assignments are done, and since she lost that magazine competition—"

"Wait, *what*?" The floor swayed beneath my feet, and I braced a hand on the wall to steady myself. "She lost the *NRF* competition?" Carter nodded, looking uncomfortable.

"When?" I choked out. "When is she leaving?"

"Sunday." He looked behind him toward Simone's retreating figure. "Look, that's all I know. I probably shouldn't have said anything, but I did, so do what you want with the information." He tucked his hands in his pockets and walked away, leaving me shaken to the core.

Sunday. I pushed both hands into my hair, dragging in a ragged breath to slow my galloping heart.

Juliet Chandler, the love of my life, was leaving in three days.

Fuck.

⇝⇛ ⇚⇜

I was still standing against the wall an hour later when the final guests departed. Thankfully, no one else had tried to talk to me after my conversation with Carter, not even that journalist. It was just as well—I was in no mood to finish the interview anyway.

"Well, *mon cher*," Jean-Claude slurred, his cheeks flushed with wine, "all in all, a good night, wouldn't you say?"

"Sure." I gave him a rigid smile. "Why don't you head home? We can debrief in the morning." He nodded, blinking one eye closed, and I snorted. "Or perhaps in the afternoon."

He grinned. "*Bonne idée.* Good night, my dear Gabriel."

I escorted him to the door, making sure he was safely deposited in a taxi before locking up. Facing the empty gallery again, I drew up short when I spotted a lone figure standing at the far end of the room, his hands tucked neatly behind his back as he stared up at my statement piece.

I straightened, striding toward him. "I'm sorry, sir, but the gallery is closed."

Slowly, he turned to me, the sharp lines of his profile coming into view, the accent lights catching on his salt-and-pepper hair. His lips curved, the corners of his dark eyes crinkling, and I stopped abruptly, the entire world coming to a standstill as I locked eyes with my father.

"*Bonsoir, mon fils.*"

"*Papa,*" I said in a cracked whisper. "What are you doing here?"

His eyes drifted back to the painting. "I came to see your gallery, of course. It's impressive, though I can't say I'm surprised. You always had your mother's talent." He took a tentative step toward me, his hands disappearing into his pockets. "It's good to see you, son."

My gaze lingered on him, my throat suddenly too thick to even swallow.

"I had hoped to speak with you at the restaurant the other night," he continued, watching me carefully, "but I understood from Lucien there was a bit of an incident."

"Yeah, you could say that," I said, unable to keep the bitterness out of my tone. I had only ruined the best thing that had ever happened to me, but sure, let's call it an *incident*.

"Well, I was sorry to hear it. If there's anything I can do—"

"There isn't."

There was nothing anyone could do now.

He gave me a lingering look. "Jumping to conclusions, letting our emotions get the better of us—it seems to be something we Beaumont men have in common." My eyes darted upward, landing on his sad smile. "Like father, like son."

"I'm ... I'm not sure I follow."

"I've never been one to mince words, so I'll just come out and say it—I made a terrible mistake when I wrongly accused you. I allowed my emotions to override my judgment, and I have paid for it dearly." He drew in a breath before letting it go. "The things I said, I said in anger, but I didn't mean a word of it. You are my son, and everything I have is and always has been yours."

He took a step closer, his eyes softening around the edges. "Perhaps this may be too little, too late, but I owe you an apology,

Gabriel. You cannot imagine how sorry I have been all these years, how much I have regretted letting my insecurities drive you away."

"Insecurities?"

He nodded, his eyes drifting over my shoulder. "Since you were born, I always felt you belonged more to your mother than to me. I never begrudged the bond you shared, but I always hoped you and I would have something similar one day. After she died, I confess I hoped you would take a greater interest in the restaurant, that you might learn to love it as much as I did. But your heart always belonged to your art, and I should have never tried to change you."

His eyes returned to mine. "When that money went missing, I knew you weren't telling the whole truth, and in a moment of weakness, I wondered if you might have taken it to open a gallery."

"I never—"

"I know," he said, raising a hand. "I know it wasn't you. But you see, it was my own fear that led me to that conclusion. I tried so hard to hold on to you, Gabriel, and the idea of losing you for good—it was more than I was prepared to handle at the time. If I could go back, I would have just given you the money myself. I would have given you whatever you needed to further your ambitions. You are my son, but your life is your own."

My throat bobbed as he placed a hand on my shoulder.

"I know everything won't be fixed between us overnight, but I hope in time you will forgive me. I am sorry for doubting you, *mon fils*, and I love you. So very much." He clutched my arm tightly, his eyes damp, and the sight of it loosened something in my chest.

For years, I'd imagined how it would be coming face-to-face with my father again, about how angry I would be, how hard it would be for me to forgive him. And yet, now that the moment had arrived, I found I wasn't reaching for a list of past wrongs or shoring up reasons not to give him a second chance. He was right—things wouldn't be fixed overnight, but the fact that he was here, acknowledging his mistakes, meant everything to me. And that was enough for now.

I wrapped an arm around him, warmth stinging my own eyes, and he hugged me back before clearing his throat and searching his jacket for a handkerchief.

"Listen," I said, "there's something I need to tell you about that money."

"If you're referring to the fact that Elise manipulated Lucien into stealing it to cover her disgraceful gambling debts, then I know all about it. Lucien had a great deal to say on the matter, and my lawyers are no doubt still sorting through all the evidence he's collected. If there's any justice in the world, Elise will be behind bars before the year is out."

"And what about Luc—Cristian?"

The corners of his mouth tightened. "I have yet to decide what to do about him."

I tucked my arms against my chest, feeling oddly protective. "Papa, you should know what Cristian did, he did for you. Everything he's ever done has only been to earn your approval."

"My approval?" His lips tilted down. "That's ridiculous. He knows how much I value him."

I shook my head. "He doesn't. You should tell him."

He stared at me for several long seconds, then exhaled slowly, running a hand over his mouth. "It would seem I have more than one mistake to make amends for." Sighing, he turned to my statement piece again. "This painting is lovely, by the way. Lucien tells me we are looking for artwork to display in the restaurant dining room, and I was hoping to purchase it, but your agent told me it's not for sale?"

"No, it's not." I wet my parched lips. "It's all I have left of her."

"Ah, yes. Juliet, right?"

"Yes." My chest squeezed. "She's the best thing that ever happened to me, and I ruined it."

He shook his head. "No failure is final. So long as you draw breath, there is time to fix it."

"But she's leaving," I said, my voice hitching. "She's going back to New York."

"So, stop her." He regarded me seriously. "Learn from my mistakes, Gabriel, and don't let three years go by before you make things right."

With a nod, he retreated toward the exit, pausing at the door.

"If you change your mind about the painting, do let me know." His mouth softened in a smile. "Nothing would make me prouder than to share my son's creation with everyone who visits Marcel's. I am sure they would marvel at what you have made, just as I have."

Forty-Seven

Cristian

I stared at the glass tumbler in my hand, rotating it slowly and watching as shards of refracted light floated around the dim space. Taking a sip of the amber liquid, I let my head fall back just as my office door swung open, an overexcited Caleb bounding through it.

"Hey boss, I—" He froze, his eyes sweeping over me. "Are you all right?"

"Did you need something?" I said, ignoring his question as my eyes drifted over his shoulder to a blank stretch of wall. I gazed at it ruefully. I'd intended to fill that space with framed critic reviews from the restaurant opening.

Now, I would probably never get the chance.

"Um, I just thought I'd let you know we're expecting another full house tonight." He opened a folder, flipping through a stack of papers half-heartedly. "Reservations are completely booked for the next month, and I expect we'll maintain this level of foot traffic through the fall at least." He tapered off, regarding me. "You know what, I should just come back later. It seems I've caught you at a bad time."

"Whatever gave you that impression?" I said, pouring myself another measure of whiskey.

"Uh, you're drinking alone in the dark at two o'clock in the afternoon." He gave me a searching look. "Has something happened?"

I glanced at him, pushing down the strange, irrational urge to laugh.

Yes, quite a few things had happened.

I had single-handedly wrecked Gabriel's life—*again*—and had hurt someone I cared about in the process, someone who was kind and far too innocent for this world. I had come clean about Elise's unlawful behavior, including my own involvement, and as a result, had put all of my future plans for the restaurant in jeopardy. And above all, I'd all but certainly lost the respect of the man I admired most in the world, a man who had put so much faith in me.

"No, nothing's happened. I've simply exceeded my daily capacity for human interaction and am now recharging in my lair."

Caleb blinked, then huffed. "Very funny. Have you ever considered taking the stage?"

"What? And leave you here to run this place into the ground?"

"I could make it at least a week without you."

"Two days tops."

He chuckled. "Yeah, you're probably right." His laughter faded as he scrubbed a hand over his jaw, thoughtful ridges forming between his brows. "You know, you don't always have to mask your feelings. You're allowed to have a bad day sometimes." I stilled, my eyes springing to his as he lifted one shoulder in a shrug. "You're only human, after all."

Tucking the folder under his arm, he turned and disappeared through the doorway, leaving me to stare after him. After a moment, a grin tugged at the corner of my mouth.

Maybe the kid was finally growing up.

I was still lost in thought when my phone pulsed, and I answered it without looking down.

"Lucien, you *fucking* bastard." Elise's frantic voice careened through the phone, her tone pitching dangerously. "What the hell have you done?"

"What I should have done a long time ago." I paused, picking up on the sound of a car engine followed by an ear-piercing screech of tires on pavement. "Based on your background music, am I correct in assuming you're fleeing the police?" I tsked, adjusting my cufflinks. "Well, I hope you took the BMW. I hear it's one of the best vehicles for long-distance driving."

"Fuck *you*," she seethed, and I relaxed back in my chair, crossing an ankle over my knee as my mind conjured a delightful image of her foaming at the mouth. "You had better watch your back, Lucien. You have no idea what I'm capable of."

"Empty threats will get you nowhere, Elise," I said, throwing her words back in her face.

"Go to hell."

"Ladies first."

I disconnected the call, letting my head fall back as a deep laugh broke free of my chest.

⋙ ⋘

An hour later, the sound of footsteps drew my attention away from a pile of invoices I'd neglected to review, and I glanced up just as Marcel appeared in the doorway. I straightened, my eyes trailing over him. He looked tired, more tired than I had ever seen him. His suit was wrinkled and his jaw unshaven, but there was still a sharpness in his gaze. I rose as he closed the door, buttoning my jacket as though suiting up for battle. And in a way I was, except I already knew how it would end.

With my defeat.

"No need to stand." He lifted a hand as he lowered himself into the chair opposite mine. "I can't stay long anyway. I have to meet with the attorneys to discuss the next steps."

I nodded, the weight of his words settling in my gut like an anvil. "Can I get you anything to drink? Water, or perhaps something stronger?" I gestured to the whiskey bottle still open on the desk, but he waved me off, his gaze lingering on the pile of papers.

"Hard at work, as always, I see."

"Just finishing up a few things." Whatever happened, I didn't want to leave my successor with a mountain of paperwork.

Marcel lifted his eyes again, resting them on me, and I drew in a slow inhale.

This was it. The moment I would finally pay for all I had done.

I should have been resentful as I waited for judgment, but in a twist of irony, all I felt was relief. Relief that all of this—the lies and the secrecy, the guilt I'd been harboring for years—would be behind me at last. And even if I ended up behind bars, I would finally be free.

"I have just one request," I said, clearing my throat. "I would ask that you keep Caleb and Amélie on at the restaurant. They've both contributed a great deal to the success of this operation."

Marcel arched an eyebrow. "And why would I dismiss your staff?"

"Because ..." *I'm about to be fired, arrested, or some combination of the two.*

Marcel studied me before speaking again. "I have spoken with Gabriel, and he is due to meet with the attorneys next week to prepare a sworn statement to submit to the authorities." I bobbed my head numbly but said nothing. "We have discussed what he plans to disclose. Perhaps you would like to hear it?"

And what would be the point in that? I already knew what Gabriel would say—after all, I'd been in possession of all the facts much longer than he had.

"He will attest," Marcel went on without waiting for a reply, "to the fact that Elise Lemieux, with whom he was in a romantic relationship, asked him to withdraw half a million euros from our business account. But when she refused to disclose the purpose for such funds, he denied her request. A week later, that exact amount of money was transferred using his credentials to an offshore account of a shell company owned solely by Elise."

I worked to keep my face impassive. Why was he making me listen to all this?

"In addition to confirming he did not initiate nor authorize the transaction, he will attest that at the time of the transfer, he was attending a seminar on brushwork technique. As it happens, the professor hosting the seminar has a no-technology policy, and thus, Gabriel left his phone at home that day. We have already contacted the professor who will affirm both Gabriel's presence at the seminar and that he was not in possession of any electronic devices."

I shifted uncomfortably. I was already well aware of this—it was how I had been able to access his phone and complete the transfer myself.

"When Gabriel learned what had happened, he suspected Elise used his device without his consent to make the transfer in his name. However, because he had no proof, he refused to implicate her when I questioned him, thus leading me to make an erroneous conclusion.

However, thanks to the evidence you provided, we now know Elise was involved in an illegal gambling ring and used the money to pay off her debts."

"I know," I said, unable to keep silent anymore. "I already know all of this because I—"

"*You* were with me," Marcel interrupted, his expression smooth. "That day I was scheduled to meet with a wine seller in Provence, and I brought you along with me. You always had good taste in wine, and with your keen negotiating skills, I insisted you join me. Unfortunately, due to inclement weather, we had to cancel our appointment halfway through our journey, but it wasn't a complete waste of a trip. We stopped by a lovely restaurant near Saint-André-les-Alpes and shared a dinner of *filet de turbot rôti au beurre*. I remember it well. As soon as I tasted their white wine sauce, I insisted we had to have it on our menu."

I stared at him, surprise hitting me square in the chest. What was he talking about? Marcel had gone on that trip alone, and we both knew it.

"But why?" I croaked, unable to draw a full breath. "Why would you—"

"There is a time for everything, Lucien, a season for every activity under the heavens. A time to tear and a time to mend, a time to be silent and a time to speak, a time to love and a time to hate, a time for war and a time for peace." His lips tipped up. "The words of King Solomon, the wisest man to ever live."

A time to tear and a time to mend.

Was this why he and Gabriel had decided to cover for me?

He pushed to his feet, folding his hands behind him as he crossed the room. He paused in front of a framed picture of the restaurant from thirty years prior, its bright red awning swaying in a sea breeze, the name Marcel's painted in gold letters across the front window.

"You know, you've always been so dedicated to the restaurant, ever since you were a teenager. Always eager, always reliable. I never had to worry about whether you would show up for work on time or whether I could trust you to handle your responsibilities. Perhaps it was for this reason I was less vocal in my appreciation and even took you for granted."

I dropped my gaze as a rush of blood pressed beneath the surface of my skin.

"A common flaw in human nature, I think," he went on. "Ignoring all the abundance we have in favor of seeking the thing we lack." He turned to me. "I owe you an apology, Lucien, for not telling you how much I have valued you all these years. I realize I paid more attention to Gabriel, but it wasn't because he was my son. It was because he was the one that I was most at risk of losing. Still, I should have expressed my appreciation to you. If I had, maybe you wouldn't have felt you needed to work to gain my approval."

He moved back to the desk, coming to stand in front of me.

"This family has seen enough division, wouldn't you say? Now that the dust has finally settled, I hope we can put a bookend on this chapter and move forward together."

Together.

"That sounds—" *Like more than I deserve.* "That sounds good, sir. And what of Gabriel?"

"I've learned my lesson about exerting my will over him. Ultimately, it will be his decision as to how much he wants to be involved in the restaurant's management."

A trickle of discomfort slid down my spine. "When you say management, do you mean as ..." My throat bobbed. "As the owner?"

Marcel blinked at me, and I immediately wished I could pull back the words. Gabriel was his son, and Marcel had every right to pass his business on to him.

"Yes," Marcel said slowly, his eyes searching mine. "As *co*-owner. With you."

"Co-owner?" I rasped.

Marcel nodded, the ghost of a smile passing over his features. "Much as I'd like to, I can't go on forever. Perhaps I have another ten years in me, but eventually I will have to slow down. And when I do, it will be with the knowledge that my legacy is in the capable hands of my sons."

My throat thickened as he placed his hands on my arms. "You *are* my son, too, Lucien, in every way that matters. You never needed to earn my love. You have it, now and always."

I cleared my throat to push away the emotion clogging it. "Thank you, Mar—*Uncle.*"

"Well, don't thank me just yet. With mercy comes responsibility. From here on out, I expect you to conduct yourself with integrity, understand?"

I nodded as a rush of energy pulsed in my veins. *A second chance. A fresh start.* It seemed too good to be true, and I might have suspected the entire thing was a fever dream if not for the steady weight of Marcel's hands on my shoulders.

"Good," he said with a note of finality. "And I expect you to be a team player from now on. No more solo missions. You and Gabriel will have to learn to work together."

"What is it I'll have to do?"

I jolted, swiveling to find Gabriel in the doorway, looking rather worse for wear.

"Gabriel," Marcel said, a deep valley forming between his brows as he too took in his appearance. "Is everything all right?"

Gabriel shook his head, his eyes flying to mine. "I need to speak with Cristian."

Marcel's eyes ticked from him to me and back again. "Very well."

Clapping me on the shoulder, he nodded to Gabriel on the way out before leaving us alone. An awkward silence descended as we stared at each other from opposite ends of the room, and I licked my lips, unsure of what to say. I doubted our heart-to-heart the other day was enough to fix everything between us, but perhaps the fact that he was here meant there was hope for us yet.

"Did you mean it?" he said finally, approaching me with a hard look. "Before, when you told me you were sorry about what happened with Juliet—did you mean it?"

I blinked at him in surprise before giving him a sharp nod. "Yes, of course I meant it."

"Good." He blew out a breath. "Because I'm going to need your help to win her back."

Forty-Eight

Juliet

"You're kidding. He did *not* say that."

"He did," I countered, glancing down at Ember's wide-eyed gaze filling the screen. Propping my phone up on the bathroom counter, I examined my reflection, fingering the blunt ends of my freshly trimmed hair. "He said he was sorry for being a pretentious dick."

She scoffed. "Well, screw me sideways. I never thought I'd see the day when Kyle Alexander Worthington the Third would apologize for anything."

I shrugged. "People change, I guess."

She hummed, giving me a thoughtful look. "Speaking of change, I'm loving this blowout on you. It's *très chic.*" She plucked at her lip, tilting her head to one side. "Seriously, I'm tempted to book a flight to Paris."

"You know they have blowout bars in New York, right?" I abandoned my post in front of the mirror and returned to the bedroom. "There's practically one on every street corner."

Ember groaned dramatically, collapsing on her sofa a second before Bailey followed suit, hopping up onto her lap and rolling onto his back. "I hate getting blowouts in New York. I swear, every time I get one, I end up looking like Farrah Fawcett circa 1975."

I snort-laughed and opened a window, the early evening breeze carrying with it the now familiar scent of the river. Turning in place, I looked around the room that had been mine for the past few months before my eyes snagged on the suitcase lying open on the floor. I stared at it.

Ember's voice cut through the silence. "Are you sure about this, Jules?"

I nodded, releasing a slow breath. "Yeah, about as sure as I'll ever be."

As much as I wanted to be certain my decision was the right one, the truth was, I still had my doubts. What if I woke up in ten years asking myself, *What if I had made a different choice*? I guessed that was a possibility I would have to live with.

"I should message Kyle. He's planning to send a car tomorrow."

"Wow, he's really laying on the charm, isn't he?" Ember shooed Bailey away, climbing to her feet. "Well, I'd better let you get to it then. Call me tomorrow?"

"Yep." I gave her a weak smile. "Talk soon." I ended the call, but before I could set the phone down, it rang again. *Simone.*

"Hello?"

"Hey, babe," she said cheerfully, and I immediately narrowed my eyes in suspicion. *Please, God, don't let this be about a last-minute shopping trip.* "What are you doing right now?"

"Oh, um," I hedged, "I'm on campus. I had to handle a few things for Benoit."

She snorted in amusement. "No, you're not. I can see your kitchen light on beneath the front door. Open up, you little liar."

I winced, my cheeks warming as I shuffled down the hallway.

In true Simone fashion, the second I threw open the door, she glided across the threshold like she was on a runway, wearing an emerald-green cocktail dress and carrying a garment bag. She held it out to me. "Get dressed, we're going out."

I frowned. "What?"

"I'm taking you out to celebrate being a finalist in the *NRF* competition. I told you, win or lose, we're celebrating, remember?"

I eyed the bag, then her again. "Are you serious?"

"Yes," she said, ushering me in the direction of the bathroom. "And we don't have a lot of time either. So put that on and meet me downstairs when you're ready."

Fifteen minutes later, I stood outside on the sidewalk in a strapless, red satin cocktail dress with a sweetheart neckline and an asymmetrical skirt, accented with a pair of drop pearl earrings and champagne-gold kitten heels. A driver stepped out of a black Mercedes and rounded the car to open the door.

He dipped his head in a nod, a scar stretching across his right cheek. "*Bonsoir, mademoiselle.*"

"*Bonsoir.*" I paused to study him. He looked familiar, but I couldn't place where I'd seen him before. Giving him a nod, I slid into the back seat next to Simone as she applied bronzer to her cheeks. "Where did you say we were going again?" No way we were going to a bar or a nightclub dressed like this. Maybe the Opéra Garnier?

"I didn't." She closed her compact powder with a click. "Guess you'll have to trust me."

Okay, the opera it is, then.

I turned to stare out the window, bouncing a knee nervously as the car maneuvered through a maze of streets. After about a minute, I gave up on trying to figure out the direction in which we were headed. With its medieval lanes and angled boulevards, the roads in Paris were a complete nightmare for someone used to New York's grid system. Three turns and a roundabout later, we were pulling up in front of a building I would have recognized in my sleep.

Marcel's.

I shifted uneasily as the driver opened my door again, helping me out of the car.

"Simone," I said, darting a confused look around at the mass of people congregated on the sidewalk. "What are we doing here?"

Without responding, she waved at a figure headed in our direction.

"Carter?" I said, surprise coloring my tone as he pulled me in for a side hug.

"Juliet." He bobbed his head toward me. "You sure do clean up nice." Simone cleared her throat, throwing him a wide-eyed look, and he chuckled before dropping a kiss on her cheek. "As do you, baby doll." She clicked her tongue in feigned annoyance, but I didn't miss the affectionate look in her eyes when he draped an arm around her. He peered around at the crowd, all dressed in sleek evening attire. "So, should we head inside?"

"Not yet." Simone pulled out her phone, her fingers flying across the keyboard as she typed out a message. "We're just waiting for—"

"I'm here," called a familiar voice, and I turned in time to see Benoit sans glasses striding toward us. "Sorry I'm a few minutes late. *La circulation était horrible.*" His eyes dropped to mine as he straightened his navy suit jacket before smoothing a hand over his elegantly styled hair. A slow smile spread across his lips. "Ms. Chandler."

"Julien?" I said, forgetting that Simone and Carter were within earshot. "I almost didn't recognize you without the tweed." I eyed him carefully, taking in his polished leather loafers and his white linen pocket square. "Are you sure you're our professor?"

He arched an amused eyebrow. "I can produce my engraved Victorian pocket watch if you wish to verify my identity."

Carter snorted under his breath. "Oh yeah, that's definitely our professor."

Benoit glanced at him sidelong. "That will do, Mr. Andrews." He extended an arm to me and I took it, clamping my lips together to smother a laugh.

A warm breeze ruffled my dress as Benoit steered us toward the entrance, and some of the unease I'd felt earlier returned as we approached its wrought iron doors.

"Um, is this some sort of university event?" But even as I said it, I doubted the plausibility of my statement. I didn't recognize a single person here apart from our small party.

"Not quite." Benoit held the door open, allowing Simone, Carter and me to pass through it before following. Inside, I slowed to a halt, and a rush of emotion filled my chest as my eyes swept over the familiar wood-paneled walls. As if I could come here and *not* think of Gabriel.

It had only been a week ago that the two of us had been in this very room together, happy and carefree. And all it took was five seconds of being here again for the memory to rush back in vivid color. I pressed my eyelids shut, my heart squeezing.

Despite everything, I was still in love with him. Hopelessly and madly.

It had taken all my resolve to turn Gabriel away after he showed up at my apartment, full of regret, heart in his hands. I believed him when he said he was sorry and that he would work on his trust issues. Still, I knew I had made the right decision. I had needed space to decide my future on my *own* terms, and no matter what happened next, I would always be proud of myself for that. After a lifetime of letting others dictate my life, I'd finally taken a stand.

For me.

The press of Benoit's hand on my arm brought me back to the present as we neared the elevators, and I grinned when I spotted two more familiar faces.

"You're delusional," Caleb said, scowling. "If it came down to a fight to the death between John Wick and Jason Bourne, John Wick would win hands down. The man is a walking massacre."

Amélie tossed her rose-gold hair over one shoulder. "Of course, you would say that. Only a Neanderthal would value blunt force over the tactical sophistication of a true assassin."

"Tactical sophisti—woman, John Wick killed a man with a *pencil*. His creative genius is unparalleled."

"Oh, please. I suppose you would be equally impressed if he started throwing rocks too."

Caleb's cheeks reddened. "Check the body count, princess. No *way* can—"

"Excuse me," Benoit interjected. "I hate to interrupt this riveting discussion, but might we be permitted to use the elevator?"

Caleb's and Amélie's startled gazes snapped to us, and Amélie straightened, flushing slightly. "Of course, *monsieur*. Please excuse us, we did not see you and your party waiting."

I folded my lips between my teeth. Something told me when the two of them got into it, they didn't see a lot of things.

"Juliet." Caleb cast me a wide grin. "You actually came."

Confusion pulled down the corners of mouth. "What do you mean *actually*?" I glanced around at the assembled group. "Is there something I should know?"

Caleb opened his mouth again, but Amélie clapped a hand over it. "Right this way," she said, rushing to open the elevator doors. She gave me a lingering smile before pressing the button for the seventh floor. "Have fun."

The doors glided shut, closing us in with a deafening silence. Tossing a look over my shoulder, my eyes bounced between Simone and Carter's blank expressions before shifting to Benoit. His gaze was fixed straight ahead, but I didn't miss the muscle twitching in his cheek.

"Okay, seriously, is no one going to tell me what's going on?"

My accusatory tone was met with another wave of silence, and I was sorely tempted to stomp my foot in frustration. But before I could give in to the childish impulse, the doors swung open again to reveal a rooftop terrace buzzing with voices and clinking champagne glasses. I clamped my mouth shut as I stepped out of the elevator, my eyes drifting over the scene.

The open-air terrace glowed with beautiful string lights that swayed in the breeze above pedestal tables decorated with candles and white linen tablecloths. Wide cedar pergolas surrounded by lush greenery divided the space, and lavender from the rooftop garden scented the air. I blinked in astonishment as elegantly dressed men and women roamed between dove-gray benches and the stone railing overlooking the city before my eyes finally landed on my reflection in a gold arched mirror, its glossy finish covered in thick scroll writing.

La Nouvelle Revue Française welcomes you to its 2024 Paris Writers Networking Event.

I sucked in a breath, my hand flying to the base of my throat as Benoit drew up beside me, his warm eyes sparkling. He gently took my elbow, leading me out onto the terrace.

"But how?" I croaked. "I thought—"

"Julien, my dear friend." A man with a hairstyle worthy of Patrick Dempsey sauntered toward us, lifting a tumbler of amber liquid in greeting.

"Ah, the man of the hour. An impressive event, as always, André."

André clicked his tongue, his expression turning severe. "Well, it almost didn't happen if you can believe it."

"Oh, why is that?" Benoit asked, his lips twitching in an almost imperceptible grin.

"Our original venue met with the most unexpected accident two days ago. One of the main water pipes burst, causing damage to the flooring, and the owners were forced to cancel all events for the next several weeks." He shook his head. "They put us in an impossible position. With the event only thirty-six hours away, we were sure we would have to cancel. But then, out of the blue, our program coordinator received an offer from this place. Quite fortunate, actually." He peered around, his expression brightening. "I think we might host the event here next year as well. Our guests were tired of stuffy ballrooms anyway," he finished with a conspiratorial grin. His eyes ticked to me. "And who is this *petite fleur*?"

"This is my student, Juliet Chandler," Benoit said, a flicker of pride lighting his features. "Juliet, may I introduce André Laurent, the editor-in-chief of the *NRF*."

André's eyes widened. "Mademoiselle Chandler." He swirled his drink, giving me a regretful look. "I read your submission, and I must say I was disappointed I couldn't feature it in our latest issue. If only it were up to me, I would have, but there is a panel of judges that oversees the competition, and some of them are rather prickly traditionalists."

"I hope you are not referring to me," Benoit said in a dry tone, eyeing his friend.

My eyes widened. "You were a judge for the competition?"

"Not this year," he said with a soft smile. "But in years past, yes."

"Yes," André agreed ruefully, "that is until he abandoned me to focus on academia full time. Incredibly selfish of him, wouldn't you say, Juliet?" A laugh bubbled out of my throat as Benoit released an exasperated breath. "But in all seriousness, I would love to have you submit your piece again. We have a smaller competition in the spring if you're interested. That is, if another publication hasn't snapped you up by then."

"In that case, you very well may be disappointed, André."

Our eyes swiveled in unison to a woman gliding toward us, batting a hand through her chin-length hair before smoothing it over her black lace gown.

"Ah," André grunted. "Another traitor."

"Traitor?" Her eyes glinted with amusement. "Is that what you call your favorite protégée?

"*Former* favorite," he said stiffly. "And now, my greatest competition."

She laughed, waving a hand at André before turning to me. "Hello again, Juliet."

"Celine." I let out a surprised exhale as she air-kissed my cheeks. "So lovely to see you."

"You two are acquainted?" Benoit asked.

She nodded. "I had the pleasure of meeting Juliet a few weeks ago at a charity gala, and I admit, I've been hoping to hear from her ever since." Her eyes returned to mine. "When I saw you made the list of finalists for the *NRF* competition, I was afraid you'd slipped through my fingers, but maybe there is hope for me yet. Tell me, have you given any more thought to becoming a contributor for *La Femme*?"

André regarded her coolly. "You know it's in poor taste to come to my event and poach my talent, right?"

Celine gave him a sweet smile. "From what I heard, she's not your talent yet." She looped an arm through mine. "Now, if you gentlemen don't mind, I would like to borrow Juliet for a bit. There are some people I want to introduce her to."

I've never met a celebrity, but after spending an evening in Celine's company, I had a pretty good idea of what it must be like. Celine knew *everyone*. And I didn't just mean her colleagues from *La Femme*, who were also in attendance at tonight's event.

Within an hour, she had introduced me to at least three published authors, a literary agent, another magazine editor and a publisher, all of whom had peppered me with questions about my writing. I was under no illusion as to why. Though none of them had seen my work, it was clear my association with Celine spoke volumes, and by the time she excused herself to go to the powder room, I'd received several business cards and even a request to submit a writing sample.

It wasn't much, but it was definitely a start.

Hovering at the back of the terrace, I stopped to take a breather beneath one of the illuminated pergolas, flipping through the small treasure trove of cards.

Just this morning, after much soul-searching, I had finally come to a decision about my future. I was *staying* in Paris. The realization that I no longer belonged in New York, but here pursuing my writing had been both terrifying and exhilarating. But once I had made up my mind, the rest had been easier.

I called Tom to not only turn down the deal, but also to tender my notice of resignation. Shortly after that, I had emailed Benoit to accept the teaching assistant position. I'd then spent the rest of the afternoon unpacking, requesting an extension on my lease, and drafting a lengthy message to Kyle reiterating our relationship was over.

The scariest part of it all had been acknowledging there was no guarantee my decision would work out in my favor. Writing, like any act of creation, is something of a gamble. People might love your work and you might rise to the heights of international acclaim, or your efforts might collect dust in a bottom drawer while you keep searching for your big break. But either way, having the courage to try is what makes all the difference in my book.

And try, I would.

I caught sight of a figure moving in the shadows, and my pulse skipped when our eyes connected across the terrace. Slowly, I approached him, and he watched me carefully, eyes searching. After a long beat, my lips twitched with a smile.

"A burst water pipe?"

Cristian grinned, sinking his hands into his pockets. "A most unfortunate event. Doubtless, the owners will be more careful with their maintenance in the future."

"Uh-huh." I folded my arms, arching an eyebrow at him. "And you just so happened to find out about it in time to host the event here tonight?"

He shrugged, his silver eyes gleaming. "What can I say? Good news travels fast."

I huffed, chewing on my smile. "So, I guess I have you to thank for all of this." I gestured to the bustling space behind me, the party now in full swing as a live band struck up a song.

He shook his head. "As much as I love to take credit for a plan well executed, I wasn't the mastermind behind tonight. I might have pulled some strings, but the rest ..." He trailed off, and my heart beat out of rhythm when he nodded toward the elevator. "He's waiting downstairs for you, sweetheart."

Taking my hand, he placed a soft kiss on the back of it, and I hesitated only a second before throwing my arms around him. "Thank you, Cristian."

He chuckled, squeezing me gently. "Just promise to name one of your children after me and we'll call it even."

I laughed, swiping at a lone tear trailing over my cheek as he released me. Giving his hand a final squeeze, I back away slowly, then turned and bolted for the elevator.

Forty-Nine

Gabriel

Standing beside the window overlooking the Seine, I watched as the last rays of light faded from the evening sky. The silvery zinc rooftops turned midnight blue as the sun dipped toward the horizon, and the pink-gold air glowed behind the Eiffel Tower, casting it in silhouette.

I would always remember the first time I saw it. Looking down on the luminous city from the hilltop in Montmartre, I had watched as the tower came to life, sparkling with hundreds of white lights and illuminating the night. Since then, I'd fallen in love with Paris, with its people, its culture, and I promised long ago to never leave it.

But that was before I found the one person I couldn't live without.

The air shifted behind me, and I could feel her presence without even looking.

"Gabriel."

Her voice wrapped around every muscle in my body, the sweet texture of it seeping into my skin and imprinting on my soul. I turned, taking in the shimmering red of her dress, the sunset burnishing the brown-gold of her hair. She was as beautiful as the day I first saw her, and I knew with a bone-deep certainty I would have found this woman in any place, in any lifetime.

"Juliet."

Her sparkling green gaze roamed over me as I approached her slowly. There were so many things I wanted to tell her, but if this moment was all we had, there was only one thing I needed her to know.

"I love you so much more."

She swallowed, her slender throat bobbing. "More than what?"

"Anything. Everything." Her breath caught as I lifted a hand to stroke her cheek. "And if you'll let me, I promise to show you every day for the rest of our lives." I reached into my jacket pocket, and my mouth twitched in amusement when her eyes fell wide.

"Don't worry. It's not a ring."

Yet.

I extracted a piece of paper, handing it to her, and she unfolded it with trembling fingers. A strangled noise slipped past her lips as she scanned it, and when she looked up again, her eyes were bright with tears. "Are you serious?"

I nodded. I had never been more serious about anything in my life.

"I told you I would do whatever it takes to keep you, and I meant it." I glanced down at the ticket to New York with my name on it. "If that means following you across the ocean, across the world, then I will. Because I do trust you, Juliet. And I'll do whatever it takes to prove it."

"But everything is here." She released a shaky exhale, clutching the paper tighter. "Your friends and family, your gallery, your whole life—"

"*You* are my life," I said, cupping her face between my palms. "And I'm done running from it. I'm not holding anything back this time, I swear. Please believe in me again."

She pressed her eyelids shut before wrapping her fingers around my wrists. "No. You're not coming with me to New York."

All the air seeped from my lungs. "What?"

She didn't want me to come with her?

"You're not coming with me," she repeated, her smile a thing of beauty as her eyes swam with moisture. "Because I'm staying here in Paris. With you." As soon as the words left her lips, I swore the earth shifted beneath my feet, my entire world igniting with color.

"Are ..." I swallowed against a rush of emotion rising in my throat. "Are you sure?"

She nodded as tears slipped from the corners of her eyes, trailing down her cheeks. "I am. I may not know what the future holds, but I believe in you—in us." Her hands left my wrists to trace my jaw, and a hard shudder moved through me. "I forgive you, Gabriel. And I love you too."

In a heartbeat, I captured her lips in an earth-shattering kiss, moving over her mouth hard and strong. Our tongues brushed in wild, desperate strokes as I pulled her body flush with mine, swallowing her tiny whimpers and kissing her like the world was ending.

And in a way, it almost had.

Walking away from Juliet was the biggest mistake of my life, and when I thought I'd lost her for good, it was like the stars had fallen straight out of the sky, plunging my world into total darkness. But now that I had her in my arms again, I was never letting go.

Juliet Chandler, my salvation, was mine forever.

Epilogue

Juliet

"You know this is reckless, right?"

I shaded my eyes against the sunlight glinting off the river and squinted up at Gabriel before giving his scarf a playful tug. "Oh, come on, don't be such a spoilsport. It'll be fun."

"And dangerous." He propped his bike against the bridge parapet, sliding his arms around me and pulling me close as the autumn breeze ruffled his hair. "Remind me why you want a picture of us riding across this bridge together?"

"Because, it's where we met, and I want to capture the memory to show our—" A blush scalded my ears when I realized what I'd just been about to say.

A slow smile stretched across his features. "To show who?"

"James and Nora," I blurted out.

"Yeah, sure." He nuzzled my temple. "To show James and Nora." Pressing a kiss to my forehead, he reached for the bike before seating himself on it. "All right, hop on, Chandler."

He leaned back to make room for me, and I hopped up onto the handlebars, facing him.

"Okay, ready."

"All right, hang on." He pushed off, pedaling up the slope of the bridge. "The sooner you take the picture, the better. I want to deliver you to your first day of work in one piece."

I laughed, opening my camera app. "Good point. I'm sure Benoit won't appreciate it if I show up tomorrow with unexplained bruises."

Ever since I'd accepted the teaching assistant position with Benoit, the weeks had sped by in a blur. In addition to applying for a work visa and reviewing the course material for the fall semester, I'd also started working on a new story for *La Femme*. Celine loved the piece I wrote for the *NRF* and insisted it was exactly the sort of thing *La Femme*'s readership would enjoy. We agreed on three paid submissions to start, but she was already dropping hints about publishing my romance novella as a serial. As soon as I mentioned it to Grace, she immediately purchased a subscription.

Simone had returned to Los Angeles, and although I missed her, we caught up at least once a week. Things between her and Carter were still going strong despite her declarations about not being a love-at-first-sight kind of girl. The last time we spoke, she'd been visiting him in his hometown in Montana. She claimed she would never move so far away from Rodeo Drive, but Carter seemed determined to make a country girl out of her yet.

James and Nora were, well, James and Nora, and business at Le Peloton Café was busy as usual. Lily had decided to stay in Paris until her little nephew arrived, and despite James's grumblings, I suspected he and Nora were grateful for the extra help.

As for Gabriel, it was a miracle I was able to see him as much as I did. Between giving bike tours, working on his next collection of paintings and meeting with his father and Cristian regularly to discuss the future of Marcel's, his schedule had gotten hectic. But somehow, he still made our relationship a priority. Aside from spending every night together, we'd also kept up our tradition of exploring the city on the weekends. At the rate we were going, I was pretty sure we'd have every museum, monument, and art gallery conquered by Christmas.

Speaking of Christmas ...

"I was thinking about inviting Ember to come for the holidays. What do you think?"

"You want to talk about this now?" Gabriel said, swerving around a flock of birds. "Aren't you supposed to be taking a picture?" When I huffed, he shook his head, a smile playing on his lips. "Okay, fine. Yes, I would love to host your sister at our place for the holidays."

Our place.

We hadn't had a formal discussion about me moving in yet, but it was evident from the way Gabriel kept carting my things to his apartment that he wanted me to. And what did I want? Honestly, I couldn't be happier at the prospect of living together, but I also wasn't ready to give up my Île Saint-Louis apartment just yet. But the beauty of it was, whenever we did finally discuss our living arrangements, I knew Gabriel would support whatever I was most comfortable with.

"Should we invite Cristian too?"

Over the past few weeks, I had been on a not-so-subtle campaign to help Gabriel and Cristian mend fences. After the *NRF* party, the two of them seemed to be on decent terms, but their relationship was still on the road to recovery. After all, a three-year misunderstanding wouldn't just go away overnight. So, to bridge the gap between them, I'd been coming up with every excuse in the book for them to spend time together.

So far, they were being good sports about it.

"How about this?" Gabriel slowed to a halt, pulling over a few feet from the spot where we'd first crashed into each other. "Let's take the picture, and then we can go home and talk about the holidays to your heart's content."

"Fine." I smiled up at the camera. "Ready? One, two—"

Just as I clicked the shutter, Gabriel's mouth found mine in a tender kiss, his warm breath bathing my throat. Our lips moved gently at first, but what started as a soft tease quickly descended into something else entirely, and my phone slipped from my fingertips as I wrapped my arms around him.

"Home," he rasped.

"Home," I agreed.

Nipping my bottom lip, he swiped my phone from the ground before setting off again, pedaling the rest of the way across the bridge. As he weaved around traffic and pedestrians, he didn't specify whether we were going to my place or his, but he didn't need to.

To me, home would always be wherever he was.

Acknowledgements

First and foremost, thank you to my Heavenly Father for making my dream a reality, and for giving me the courage to write my first book.

Thank you to my husband, Steven, for being my biggest supporter, for reading my early drafts and for cheering me on throughout this journey to becoming a published author. None of this would be possible without your unwavering support, love, and endless stream of jokes.

Thank you to my bestie, Colleen, for reading every word I've ever written, for spending countless hours brainstorming with me, and for being one of the kindest, most genuine people I know. I couldn't have finished this book without your wisdom, encouragement, and friendship.

Thank you to Elena, my mentor and founder of the Women Interested in Leaving Law (WILL) program. You were the first person to ever tell me I could follow my dream of becoming an author, and this book would not exist without you. To all the women in the WILL Creator's Circle, thank you for helping me be brave on this journey from lawyering to publishing.

Thank you to Danika, Ashley, Sarah and all the wonderful women in the Author Ever After community. I've learned so much from each of you, and I couldn't have asked for a better group of writer gal pals.

Thank you to my editors, Jennifer Sommersby and Paula Dawn, for helping me turn this book into something I'm truly proud of.

Thank you to my sister, Nikki, for always having my back, no matter how crazy my dreams are.

And a special thank you to YOU, beautiful reader! It means everything to me that you took a chance on my debut novel, and I want you to know I truly appreciate you! Thank you for spending time with Juliet and Gabriel—I hope you loved experiencing their story as much as I loved writing it.

About the Author

Ellie Jennings is a lawyer-turned-romance author who lives in the Windy City with her wisecracking husband and high-school sweetheart. She's been reading romance since before she probably should have and can usually be found somewhere swooning over a fictional character's happily ever after. When she's not writing steamy, witty love stories with dirty-talking, passionate heroes and strong, lovable heroines, she's either baking something sweet, jamming out to a good country song, or planning her next adventure. If you love steamy romance, heartfelt characters, and the City of Love, you're in the right place.

Follow Ellie on Instagram (@authorelliejennings) or sign up for her newsletter at elliejennings.com/newsletter for updates, bonus content and more!

www.elliejennings.com